MOMENT OF TRUTH

He had to stop thi... thinking about lov... it. He closed his e... like to bring their l... so close they beca...

"Cole?" An all ... his reverie. "Are you here?"

Cole cleared his throat and started to rise.

"There you are!" The door to his room stood wide open and his vision stepped right in. "Don't get up. It's so warm this evening. You look very comfortable, and I'm certain you need your rest after the difficult few days you've passed."

He swallowed hard. "Difficult. Yes."

Cole watched her float into his room with a rustle of full-skirted blue taffeta. Her torso was perfectly encased in a fitted jacket of the same blue as the skirt. It was fastened with a row of tiny buttons that reached from her waist up to her cleavage. Mentally he calculated how long it would take him to release each of those buttons.

"Are you all right? You seem distracted this evening." Maudie said as she sat, then looked up at him with her big blue eyes. "Cole, I think it's time I told you the real reason why I'm so interested in Carew's death."

Cole noticed she looked more serious, more troubled than he'd ever seen her. He took out the chair at the other end of the table and sat down, leaning toward her.

"I think it's possible she was my mother," Maudie said.

PASSION BLAZES IN A ZEBRA HEARTFIRE!

COLORADO MOONFIRE (3730, $4.25/$5.50)
by Charlotte Hubbard

Lila O'Riley left Ireland, determined to make her own way in America. Finding work and saving pennies presented no problem for the independent lass; locating love was another story. Then one hot night, Lila meets Marshal Barry Thompson. Sparks fly between the fiery beauty and the lawman. Lila learns that America is the promised land, indeed!

MIDNIGHT LOVESTORM (3705, $4.25/$5.50)
by Linda Windsor

Dr. Catalina McCulloch was eager to begin her practice in Los Reyes, California. On her trip from East Texas, the train is robbed by the notorious, masked bandit known as Archangel. Before making his escape, the thief grabs Cat, kisses her fervently, and steals her heart. Even at the risk of losing her standing in the community, Cat must find her mysterious lover once again. No matter what the future might bring . . .

MOUNTAIN ECSTASY (3729, $4.25/$5.50)
by Linda Sandifer

As a divorced woman, Hattie Longmore knew that she faced prejudice. Hoping to escape wagging tongues, she traveled to her brother's Idaho ranch, only to learn of his murder from long, lean Jim Rider. Hattie seeks comfort in Rider's powerful arms, but she soon discovers that this strong cowboy has one weakness . . . marriage. Trying to lasso this wandering man's heart is a challenge that Hattie enthusiastically undertakes.

RENEGADE BRIDE (3813, $4.25/$5.50)
by Barbara Ankrum

In her heart, Mariah Parsons always believed that she would marry the man who had given her her first kiss at age sixteen. Four years later, she is actually on her way West to begin her life with him . . . and she meets Creed Deveraux. Creed is a rough-and-tumble bounty hunter with a masculine swagger and a powerful magnetism. Mariah finds herself drawn to this bold wilderness man, and their passion is as unbridled as the Montana landscape.

ROYAL ECSTASY (3861, $4.25/$5.50)
by Robin Gideon

The name Princess Jade Crosse has become hated throughout the kingdom. After her husband's death, her "advisors" have punished and taxed the commoners with relentless glee. Sir Lyon Beauchane has sworn to stop this evil tyrant and her cruel ways. Scaling the castle wall, he meets this "wicked" woman face to face . . . and is overpowered by love. Beauchane learns the truth behind Jade's imprisonment. Together they struggle to free Jade from her jailors and from her inhibitions.

Available wherever paperbacks are sold, or order direct from the Publisher. Send cover price plus 50¢ per copy for mailing and handling to Zebra Books, Dept. 4416, 475 Park Avenue South, New York, N.Y. 10016. Residents of New York and Tennessee must include sales tax. DO NOT SEND CASH. For a free Zebra/ Pinnacle catalog please write to the above address.

GARDA PARKER

SCARLET LADY

ZEBRA BOOKS
KENSINGTON PUBLISHING CORP.

ZEBRA BOOKS are published by

Kensington Publishing Corp.
475 Park Avenue South
New York, NY 10016

Zebra, the Z logo, Heartfire Romance, and the
Heartfire Romance logo are trademarks of Kensington
Publishing Corp.

First Printing: December, 1993

Printed in the United States of America

Chapter 1

Trapped by a dratted bustle!

Maudie Boone Dearden straddled the splintering wooden sill, the voluminous scarlet skirts of her taffeta costume billowing around her like a deflating hot air balloon. Escaping through the window of a second story bedroom over the Republican Theater seemed like the best idea, the only idea, at the moment, but she hadn't bargained for this—being thwarted by her own undergarments!

Her hands clad in black lace fingerless gloves, Maudie held the window up with one, and with the other she swatted at the offending bustle strapped behind her waist. She managed to shift it one way and then the other, but the bustle, advertised as "indestructible with normal wear," pressed into the small of her back, immobilizing her. She wondered if the bustle maker would consider her present predicament "normal wear."

Maudie cursed under her breath. "Stupid invention," she muttered. "No doubt devised by a man. My backside feels like it's been caught and caged like a canary."

Now, through maneuvering, she was wedged between the window casing and the bustle. A springy curl that had come loose from her brilliant blond wig dangled crazily in front of her eyes, while the top coil was snagged in the window latch. With even the slightest movement it tugged at the pins holding it to her head, causing stinging moisture to fill her eyes with every snap of a strand of her own hair.

Across the dusty street, standing ready to depart, was the pair of oxen-drawn wagons owned by a Mr. Seth Weston, who hauled goods, and people if need be, to the Black Hills in Dakota Territory. A couple of prospectors climbed aboard, and a family of four was already in line with their own wagon. Maudie saw Weston check his pocket watch, then glance impatiently up and down the freight platform. He was looking for her and she knew it.

Piled along the side of the rear wagon she could see all her cases, bandboxes, and hatboxes that held everything she owned in the world, and some things she hadn't owned until she decided she wanted to and had simply acquired them from fawning theater patrons. Inside of one was the cursed lace fan that a rotund Mrs. Van der Something, hostess at a dinner for the traveling theatrical troupe of which Maudie was a leading actress, had persisted waving in her face. Maudie had grown so weary of the thing fluttering under her nose

8

she'd simply purloined it at the odd moment Mrs. Van Whatever-her-name-was had let loose of it.

The Republican's theater manager had warned Maudie just as she was going on stage that the woman had called the sheriff on her and he'd be waiting at curtain close to arrest her. Arrest Maudie Boone Dearden, for the alleged theft of a cheap lace fan! Maudie could understand if they were after her for the silver champagne flute she'd slipped into her velvet pouch that evening. But a fan? She vowed she wouldn't spend one more night in jail for anything—certainly not for so trivial a thing as a stolen fan.

She had to get out of this blasted window trap and onto that freight wagon before the sheriff could find her. Then she'd be safely off to Deadwood Gulch, where no one could touch her. Everybody knew the only things that had gone to Deadwood were gold seekers and soiled doves. And actors, of course. Actors were, after all, the very reason she was going to Deadwood. Not law and order. That noble combination had yet to find a place in the Black Hills. If it had, perhaps the questionable death of a famous actress wouldn't be left unsolved.

A high-pitched caterwauling coming from below suddenly captured Maudie's attention. She jerked her head around and out the window so fast the wig ripped off and hung like a lamp shade above her head. A fiery red curtain of her own hair fell over her eyes.

"Ow!" She swept her hair away and glanced back into the room to see if her outburst had given her away. It was empty. Her exclamation had been drowned out by the escalating disturbance below in the street.

She craned her neck around and looked back out the window, blowing a stray lock of disheveled hair out of her eye with a cocked tip of her bottom lip. Below, a freight wagon had pulled to a halt in front of the theater. A huge wooden crate sat on the back of it, inside of which were more house cats than Maudie'd ever seen in one town, even in the borough of Brooklyn in New York.

A pounding followed by shouting came to the bedroom door. Maudie twisted her head around to see if the pile of chairs atop the bureau she'd shoved against the door still held. She could see the door's hinges vibrating loose and knew it was only a matter of moments before the law burst through and collared her.

Bracing her arms against the window casing in front of her, Maudie gave a wrench to her backside that caused the pernicious bustle to spring out the window. She almost lost her balance, but was able to steady herself, precariously straddling the sill as if she were atop a skinny mule. She eased her inside leg out, not an easy task given the layers of petticoats twisted around her, and dangled it next to the other.

She looked down over her white stockinged legs, past her intricately embroidered high heeled red boots, to the rooftop of the overhang that graced the theater's main door. She closed her eyes and clutched her stomach, willing away her quick calculation of how many feet down it was.

Behind her she heard the door give, heard the unmistakable scraping of the bureau across the bare wood floor. Summoning the courage she'd used in past theatrical roles when she'd played boys swinging from rooftops or jumping from balconies, she pushed hard and propelled herself off the window, hoping the dratted bustle wouldn't catapult her back up into the waiting arms of the sheriff and his deputy.

She landed on the rooftop with a thud cushioned by rustling taffeta, layers of muslin underskirts, and the bustle, which this time acted as protection to her backside. She righted herself in time to see the wagons to Deadwood pull away from the freight platform and rumble out of town.

Now what? Maudie ignored her racing pulse and flattened her body against the wall, as much as was possible given the weighty ill-shaped costume, and with a deft sidestep inched to the end of the railed overhang. A portly man with a battered wide-brimmed hat was laboriously climbing up onto the driver's box of the cat-filled freight wagon. Maudie's eyes swept over the wooden crate of screeching, clawing felines, then settled on a pile of lumpy burlap sacks resting in a bed of straw at the end.

She saw the driver lift his long-handled whip, saw his beefy arm raise over his head and start down, and saw the end of the whip begin a long curl over his eight-ox team just as the sheriff and his deputy leaned out the bedroom window and shouted her a command to stop where she was. As the freighter lurched away from the theater, Maudie climbed over the rail and, clutching a heart-shaped locket that dangled on a chain around her neck, jumped. Her many skirts puffed up around her, and she landed like a sack of beans in a pile of straw and lumpy burlap bags.

It was a pretty spectacular exit, she thought, and

11

wished she could have seen it. For Maudie Boone Dearden, glittering star of the stage, spectacular entrances and exits were her signature. Yes, by glory, she certainly wished she could have seen this one.

The straw and sacks jerked under her, and she heard spluttering coming from beneath.

"What the blue-assed mule . . . ?" a man's voice yelled over the din of screeching cats.

Maudie pushed at the skirts that had flown up over her face. She tried to sit up, but the rolling of the freight wagon gathering speed over the rutted road kept her off balance. She managed to turn over and brace herself against one of the burlap sacks, until she realized her hands and elbows were wet. A lurch of the wagon and she lost her balance again, dropping face first into the wet bag.

The wetness wasn't as bad as the smell. That was god-awful and like none she'd ever experienced before. And being in the theater and in jail had given her a lot of experience where smells were concerned.

The man behind her grabbed her arms and pulled her up to a sitting position. "Just what the hell do you think you're doing?"

Maudie pulled her skirts down over her legs and wiped her wet hands in the straw. She lifted her eyes and stared straight into the face of a bedraggled, dirty man with buck teeth and one crossed eye who instantly reminded her of a giant rat with a broken nose.

"I'll thank you to keep a civil tongue in your head, sir." Maudie attempted to straighten her hair, but the smell on her hands stopped her.

"Well, well now," the rat man said, rising to his

12

knees and leaning close to her face, "lookee what we got here."

Maudie watched his slithering tongue and his twitching lips and imagined long rodent whiskers protruding from each side of his equally protruding front teeth, and suddenly felt like a chunk of cheese anchored to a big wooden rat trap.

"I seen you on the stage in the Republican," the man said. "You musta seen me, too, didn't you? Had to foller me, didn't you, girlie?" He reached out a grimy hand toward her bosom.

Outraged by his ludicrous assumption, Maudie grabbed his hand and wrenched his thumb toward the back of it until he shrieked as loud as the cats. She was strong, and that move was one of the few useful tricks her no-good father, a New York policeman, had taught her. The rat man begged mercy, and she let go of him. He shoved his thumb into his mouth and sucked it like a hurt boy. Maudie grimaced at the sight. Then he lifted a doubled fist and aimed it in the direction of her face. She screamed, hauled her knee back and let fly with her booted foot, kicking him in the groin.

The wagon hauled to a stop. The cats' screeching had increased in volume and, doubled over in pain, the rat man reached through the crate bars and pulled the tail of one. It let out a piercing scream of pain.

Maudie slapped his hand. "What'd you do a nasty thing like that for?"

"They was humpin'. I hate when they do that. Cats hump all the time anywhere they want, any other cats they want."

"Well, that's their privilege."

13

"It ain't fair. I don't get no humpin' when I want with who I want. It ain't fair."

Maudie was about to mention that cats were also known to bathe on a regular basis, but didn't want to provoke him further.

"McCall!" The wagon driver's voice boomed along the side of the freighter. "What'd I tell you about no passengers?"

"I didn't bring her," the rat man whined.

The driver stepped around the end of the wagon, stopped at the sight of Maudie, pushed his battered hat to the back of his large head and propped his hands on his wide hips. He stared at her over his bulbous pock-marked nose.

"What'd I tell you about draggin' whores along with us?" he growled at the other man.

"I didn't," McCall whined again.

"Excuse me, sir, I am not a whore, I'm an actress, and this . . . Mr. McCall is telling the truth. He did not bring me." Maudie straightened her skirts and noticed a widening wet stain over one side of them.

"Look, madam," the driver shouted over the hissing cats, "if you're tryin' to rescue your cat or something, I can tell you I don't have him. He's one I missed. Now, get offen my wagon and get yourself back to town."

"I'm not looking for my cat. I merely was detained at the theater, and missed my ride to Deadwood. Your wagon appeared to be heading in the same direction, and I thought if I rode with you a bit we might possibly catch up with the others. I truly thought you'd want to come to the aid of a lady in distress."

14

"Lady?" Convulsed with laughter, the portly driver bent over his girth.

"Yes, *lady*," Maudie asserted, "and you'd be wise to remove your hat in my presence, Mr. . . . ?"

McCall giggled like a schoolgirl as he watched the exchange. The way he snorted between giggles and twitched his thick wet lips, Maudie thought it a wonder the cats hadn't found a way to claw him through the bars of their prison crate and make a meal out of him.

"Well, excuse me, your ladyship. Pleased to make your acquaintance. Thompson's the name. My friends call me Phatty. That's with a pee aitch," he added hastily.

"Yes, well," Maudie eyed the straining waist of his filthy striped trousers, "how do you do Mr. Pee Aitch Phatty Thompson? And how long before we catch up with those other wagons?"

"Won't."

"Won't? What do you mean 'won't'?"

"I mean we won't catch up with those other wagons. They're goin' to Fort Laramie first. I got us a shortcut."

"Shortcut to where?" Maudie eyed him suspiciously.

"Deadwood. That's where we're headin' too." Phatty Thompson spat into the mud. "We'll be there afore them."

Only slightly relieved, Maudie let out a short sigh. "In that case, I'll just ride along with you then."

"Oh, you will, will you?"

"I shall pay you for the passage, of course, as soon as we get to Deadwood. All of my belongings are on one of those wagons, including my money." Maudie thought that little lie was a stroke of genius on her part.

15

All her belongings were on one of those wagons, that was true. But not her money. She didn't have any money. There would be some waiting for her in Dead-wood, or so she'd been told. In any case, it simply wouldn't do to let them think she had money on her person.

"Let her stay, Phatty, let her stay," McCall pleaded.

Phatty Thompson settled his hat squarely back on his head. "It'll be fifty dollars dust, your ladyship. Think you can afford me?"

Maudie swallowed, holding her composure. "That's a bit steep. The transport was only thirty-five. Perhaps you can make an adjustment in the fare, Mr. Thomp-son. As I said, I'll pay you upon arrival."

"Fifty dollars dust, I said." Thompson's eyes bore into her. "Take it or get offen my wagon right now."

"I'll take it," Maudie said, exasperated. Then she added, almost as an afterthought, "Dust?"

"Gold dust, your ladyship. You got that much gold dust? That's the currency used in Deadwood, and that's the currency used on this wagon."

"Gold . . . ?" Maudie thought fast. "I'll simply make an exchange at a bank. Will that do?"

The oxen got skittish about something and jerked the wagon forward. Maudie fell back against the cat crate, but righted herself quickly.

"Hey! Whoa there, whoa!" Thompson shouted.

"Seems like they're anxious to get moving, as am I, Mr. Thompson." Maudie felt her backside becoming damp through her skirts. She pushed herself up and climbed to the top of the pile of burlap sacks, and

16

leaned on the cat crate. "What is it you're carrying in these sacks? They seem to be leaking."

"Chicken heads," the rat man said, nodding.

"What?" Maudie held both hands straight out from her shoulders.

"Chicken heads," McCall said again. "For the cats."

"For the cats. Of course. Can't they wait to be fed in Deadwood?"

"Takes short of two weeks to Deadwood. They'd be pretty hungry by then," McCall said.

"Or dead," Thompson said.

Maudie felt her insides drop toward her knees. "I should be that lucky," she muttered toward the cats.

Outside the newly constructed Deadwood Gulch sheriff's office, Cole Branch leaned back against the raw-planked wall, a cheroot poised between his lips. He stifled a cough. The smoke burned sharply at the back of his throat. He never liked these things, but he was of a mind that a cheroot dangling from the lips was just the right bit of business in the creation of a certain persona.

Cole's current persona was as temporary sheriff of Deadwood City. What a concept, he thought, Deadwood a city and Cole Branch a sheriff. What a concept. He surveyed the remnants of yesterday's July Fourth Centennial celebration. Ragged flag banners flapped in the morning breeze. Broken brew kegs lay among various other debris in the street. Drunks were sleeping it off propped up against their hitched mules. Cole had been more a participant in the freewheeling festivities than he had been a controller of order in the wild city. Deadwood a city, he mused again. That appellation was as incongruous as Cole Branch a sheriff.

"Good morning, Sheriff Branch," Cora Pettigrew confirmed the concept.

Cole snatched the cheroot from his lips. "Miz Pettigrew," he drawled, lifting his wide-brimmed hat and pushing his shoulders away from the wall. "And young Miz Pettigrew." He nodded toward her daughter, Penelope, a well-developed young woman of almost seventeen.

Penelope made it quite obvious that she was aware of her own emerging feminine wiles. From beneath a cascade of golden curls she gave Cole a slow sweep with snapping green eyes that held more than a hint of suggestion.

"Mornin', Sheriff Branch," she said softly. "It's a beautiful one, isn't it? Promises a lovers' moon for the evenin'."

Cole shifted nervously in his new boots as the long-faced Cora Pettigrew sent a disapproving glance to Penelope and an accusing one to him. The rush of guilt he felt annoyed him. In the less than two weeks since the Pettigrew women had arrived in Deadwood City to join their husband and father, Cole had done nothing to encourage the girl. In his opinion she was a nubile little snip who was trying on her flowering womanhood much like he was trying on this damned sheriff's outfit. Her signals were clearly meant to provoke his deflowering of her, and those signals carried an unspoken scheme of maneuvering him into marriage. He'd seen firsthand the kind of weight on a man's spirit that was.

18

He had no intentions of even considering such a thing, with Penelope or with any other female. He wouldn't be in Deadwood long enough for attachments to form anyway, whether by his or someone else's finagling, and that's the way he liked it.

Mrs. Pettigrew abruptly drew her daughter around and pointed her down the crude plank path toward a grocer's establishment. Penelope turned and sent a come-hither smile to Cole, who made a great show of ignoring her by fixing his attention on her mother. She waited for Mrs. Pettigrew several paces away; out the corner of his eye Cole watched her bend provocatively at the waist and make a show of brushing her skirts.

"Such a shame about Madame Carew, isn't it, Sheriff?" Cora Pettigrew said in a respectfully hushed voice. She drew her crocheted black shawl tightly around her narrow shoulders.

"A shame," Cole concurred.

"Such a wonderful actress."

"Yes."

"So believable."

"Very believable."

"Why, her death scene in the second act of *Scarlet Lady* brought tears to my eyes. Who could have known?" Mrs. Pettigrew drew a white handkerchief from her bag and dabbed at the corners of her eyes. "Who could have known that would be her real-life death scene? Did you see it? It was such a horrifying accident, just horrifying."

"No, I didn't see it. The night I attended the play the walls came tumbling down, but not the rest of the scenery. She lived to play another night."

"Oh, it was a wonderful play. I do hope they find someone to take over for Madame Carew. Shame to let the play die along with her. Well, good day, Sheriff."

Cole tipped his hat and watched their departure, watched Mrs. Pettigrew's bustle twitching in choppy rhythm to Penelope's bustle which swayed beguilingly. When Penelope Pettigrew had presented her swelling breasts to him, it had taken every ounce of determination he possessed to keep his eyes off her. An alarm inside his head sounded: *form no attachments*.

Attachments anchored a man. Caused complications.

Especially sexual attachments. Sexual involvement combined with love sounded a death knell for a man's freedom. The only way to avoid that, he'd learned, was to stay detached and uninvolved. Sex for sex's sake with a woman who felt the same way was the only kind for him.

"Sheriff, I need to talk to you."

A raspy voice and tug at his arm drew Cole's attention away from Penelope Pettigrew and her bobbing bustle. The cheroot burned the tips of his fingers and he dropped it. He turned and peered down into the bespectacled face of Theodore Bartles, a milliner who'd recently arrived in Deadwood. The only milliners Cole had ever known had been female. He'd looked with suspicion on Theodore Bartles and his chosen profession.

Not so the women in town. From the few respectable ladies to the countless whores and dance hall girls, Theodore Bartles was a popular, sensitive man who understood their desires. He possessed a sixth sense when it came to which bit of froufrou went where on milady's chapeau, setting her apart from everyone else and making a statement about her personality or position in Deadwood's increasingly evolving social scene. Cole had to marvel at that kind of intuition in a man.

"Mr. Bartles . . ."

"Call me Theo. Sheriff, I've spoken to you about this repeatedly, and you've managed each time to elude my request. Now the incident has happened again. I insist you investigate."

"Mr. Bartles, I—"

"Call me Theo."

Cole thumbed his hat to the back of his head. The little man possessed an imposing presence that Cole had noticed on occasion could catch and hold an audience, whether of one or a half dozen, enthralled. That was talent.

"I think that investigation is best left to the Pinkerton agent," Cole said. "I'm expecting him any day now."

"Pinkerton agent! Sheriff Branch, really. This is not a Wells Fargo robbery we're talking about. This is the theft of a few pieces of fabric used in the creation of ladies' hats. These fabrics were difficult to come by and hard to match. Their theft is indeed a crime. I feel"— Bartles sent a darting glance around them and, satisfied no ladies were in hearing vicinity, leaned toward Cole and whispered one word, heavy with meaning— ". . . violated." He straightened and peered up, fastening a sharp gaze on Cole. "You've done nothing about this. You haven't even been by to look for clues. I demand you come to my shop by tomorrow or I shall

21

report you to the presently–forming town board. I trust I make myself clear. Pinkerton agent, indeed."

Theodore Bartles turned to leave, then turned back. "If you insist on wearing a John B. Stetson, then please do it correctly." He stood on tiptoes, grabbed Cole's hat with both hands, yanked it forward and tilted it at an angle over his forehead, then strutted down the walk.

"Mr. Bartles, I promise I'll be by," Cole called to the little man's retreating form.

"Call me Theo!" Bartles shouted over his shoulder.

Cole had to admire Theo's monologue which was bigger than he was. The firm set of his narrow shoulders declared to the world that he meant business. He was slight, but watching him scurry toward his shop, Cole thought he could mix it up with the town toughs and even beat the best of them if he'd been of a mind to.

The noise of a Deadwood day escalated. Deadwood nights were much longer than its days since most of the saloons and whore houses were open twenty-four hours. Cole loved the early morning, when the saloons cleared out and the revellers were sleeping it off, and before respectable citizens, outnumbered by the former at least three to one, felt at ease enough to walk the streets without threat to life and limb. But once the day began, there was no stopping the cacophony of people, wagons, children, horses, oxen, mules, and . . .

A new sound assaulted Cole's hearing—screeching and howling like a whore fight in the lower end of town called the badlands. Except it was coming from the upper end of Main Street, and growing closer and louder.

Cole hated to do it, but he stepped out into the street and watched a moment as mud and manure closed over the toes of his black boots. He peered toward the disturbance, then became one more in a crowd of onlookers as a scene such as he'd never before witnessed unfolded in front of him.

Phatty Thompson sat atop his freight wagon box as usual, but this time he was accompanied by a flame-haired woman clad in a brilliant scarlet dress. Towering behind them was a two-story wooden crate filled with . . . what? As they drew nearer, Cole confirmed what he imagined.

Cats! Brown cats. Gray cats. Black cats. Yellow cats. Calico cats. Tortoise shell cats. Cats howling, screeching, clawing, meowing pitifully.

As the startling contraption passed before him, more mud and manure splashed over Cole's boots and pants. He saw Phatty's scowl, the red-haired woman's state of dishevelment, a derelict of a human being sitting at the back on a pile of stained empty burlap bags. A stench of something akin to rotting flesh blew at him in their wake.

Phatty reined in the freight wagon several storefronts down from where Cole stood. A group of whores descended like a flock of colorful hens clucking and cheeping over Phatty's cats. He lumbered down from the box and fended them off, calling out, "Let me see your dust! Dust first!"

The whores waved bulging pokes and paper money

from the States at him. He took the money while the derelict doled out the cats.

Cole watched the flame-haired woman on top of the wagon box, wondering if he should help her down. A moment later he realized she didn't need help. She alit from the tall wagon to the muddy street as if she'd simply sprouted wings and flown down. Two raucous cowboys scooped her up in crossed arms and bore her along as if on a sedan chair. As she was carried in his direction, her expression broke into a brilliant warm smile, and her eyes glittered like sapphires. She was clearly enjoying the reception. Cole could feel the heat even from his fair distance away.

He stepped back at the spectacle of the two men, hats drooping over their eyes, laughing and shouting as the woman bounced along on their arms, a thick lock of her flame hair flopping over one eye, a misshapen cage-like contraption whacking the back of one of her bearers.

Suddenly her smile turned to anger. For reasons Cole couldn't read from where he stood, she'd begun to protest the ride, but the rowdies ignored her. As they neared him, he heard her protests loud and clear.

"Put me down this instant! I am not one of your mail-order whores! How dare you!"

When they were abreast of Cole, one of her boots shot out and connected with his gut just above his belt. He doubled over and stepped quickly back.

"Don't just stand there like a dumbstruck galoot, Sheriff!" She smacked one of the men on the back of his head. "Get me out of this!"

Cole pulled into his six-foot-and-then-some height

and quickly assessed the woman perched on the arms of the two laughing cowboys. His response summed up his assessment. "I thought you were enjoying the ride, ma'am."

He instantly regretted the remark. In a flash she turned into a red whirlwind. Kicking, swinging her arms, and using her cage contraption as a weapon, she connected with various body parts on all three of them. At first, the two cowboys reacted as if her outburst were a lark, and they joined wholeheartedly in the tussle. But when the menace in red landed a fisted blow on one of them that sent him sprawling in the mud, they and the crowd they'd drawn knew hers was no game.

Cole thought of summoning a law officer to break up the fight. Then he remembered—*he* was the law!

"All right, all right, that's it! Stop it right now!" Cole dodged the flying cage and grabbed the woman from behind with his arms around her waist, lifting her up and away from the two men she was pummeling.

She kicked and flailed as he spun around with her, until finally he was able to set her firmly on her feet. He held her tight with one arm. She was still fuming, but set to neatening her clothes as best she could. Cole spread his other arm to the crowd.

"All right now, break it up. Show's over."

The crowd dispersed and the two cowboys meekly pulled their hats from the mud and limped away, scraping street matter from their shirts and pants. Cole held the woman steady until his olfactory sense could no longer stand the assault.

"Whew! What've you been using for perfume? You should think about getting your money back."

The woman whirled on him, and he threw up his hands in defense. She was tall enough that her snapping cornflower blue eyes were almost on a level with his.

"Perfume? Listen, Mr. . . ."

"Sheriff," he corrected her and reminded himself, "Sheriff Cole Branch."

Maudie stepped back and took a good look at him, starting from his muddy black intricately hand-tooled boots, up over his indigo denim pants that had yet to lose their sturdy nap, past his black leather vest with the brilliant tin star pinned to it. Her gaze tarried just below his jaw at the open neck of his natural homespun shirt, where the ties of a blue neckerchief moved almost imperceptibly in the barely stirring air, then lingered a moment on his black mustache, then traveled up to his collar-length black hair and the lock that rustled over his forehead, the black Stetson shoved to the back of his head, then back down to his deep dark eyes, which she caught and held.

"Sheriff, you say?" She didn't hide in her voice the skepticism she felt and knew was evident in her gaze.

He nodded.

"Well . . . Sheriff, I'll have you know this perfume, as you so eloquently named it, is residue from bags of chicken heads. Yes, you heard right, chicken heads. I've spent the last twelve days living on a rutted trail with two escapees from humanity and eighty-three house cats, any one of which was better company than those two. I've been bumped, rained on, stepped on, pawed—by the one who resembles a rat, *not* by the cats. I've been tipped out of the wagon and watched

26

the lucky cats escape, only to be rounded up by well-meaning prospectors who thought it a lark to round me up along with them. I've been unable to bathe, nor to wash these clothes, and even found taking care of the necessary an exercise in agility, deception, and stamina. I believe I may have caught fleas, again from the rat man, probably not from the cats. What's more, I've been forced to carry around bits and pieces of me in a . . ." Breathless, she held up the contraption.

". . . a bustle," he finished.

"The dratted thing!" Maudie threw it down. "It's what got me into this disgusting predicament in the first place."

He looked closely at it. "I'm not sure I want to know how a French wire bustle could have anything to do with : . . you mean you didn't choose to take up with . . . ?" He motioned toward the freighter of cats with the battling crowd of whores and children around it.

"Of course I didn't choose to! Are you daft?"

"I'm not certain I can, at the moment, answer that question in a way that would satisfy either one of us."

Maudie eyed him for a moment, suddenly feeling exhausted. All the fire sputtered out of her.

His mood seemed to soften. "Do you have any trunks?"

"I did. Or I will have when the Weston freight party from Cheyenne arrives. When is it due?"

"Day after tomorrow."

"Oh, for the love of . . ." Maudie felt irritation escalate inside her.

"Is that a problem?"

"Of course it is!" She picked up the bustle and shook it at him. "Does any of *this* look wearable? My real clothes are traveling, very comfortably no doubt, with the Weston Freight Company."

"Mmm-hmm." He twisted the ends of his waxed mustache up into beguiling curls.

"You don't believe me, do you?" The heat of anger flooded Maudie's face.

"Now ma'am, far be it for me to . . ." He stepped back as she took a step toward him.

"It doesn't matter one whit to me whether you believe me or not. Which way's the theater?"

"Which one?"

"This place has more than one theater?" She didn't conceal her surprise.

"Depends on how you define the word 'theater'."

Maudie nodded. She understood what the word sometimes meant in western towns. She thought a minute, and recalled the exact name she'd been given. "The Deadwood Variety Theater."

"That way." He pointed beyond a row of makeshift stores and saloons.

Maudie gathered up her stained and odoriferous skirts, wrapped the strings of the bustle around her wrist, pushed a lock of hair off her face and hooked it behind a loosening comb, then stomped down the boardwalk in the direction of the sheriff's outstretched finger.

She passed several women and more than several men who cut a wide path for her as she neared them. She didn't blame them. She could barely stand herself.

So law and order had come to Deadwood after all,

despite the reports, she fumed as she stomped along. Law and order such as it was.

Just what role was Cole Branch playing? He was as new to the role of sheriff as the recently acquired western costume he wore.

Interesting that a frontier sheriff would identify her bustle as of the French wire variety.

Even more interesting was that after so many years in and around theaters and actors, Maudie Boone Dearden knew a fake mustache when she saw one.

Chapter 2

Just inside the lobby of the Deadwood Variety Theater, Maudie came upon a three-legged easel, on which was propped a painted lobby card, a long swath of black ribbon draped over it. The sign below the picture read, *Madame Clara Carew, author and leading actress of Scarlet Lady, owner of the current company playing the Deadwood Variety Theater.*

"The late Clara Carew," Maudie whispered.

Clutching the heart-shaped locket around her neck, Maudie stared long and hard. The woman painted with soft brush strokes stared back with unseeing eyes. Maudie could feel her heart thudding inside her chest.

Every time she entered a new theater, a shiver would course along her spine and chill her blood. Now the pulse under her jaw escalated. She rubbed her locket as she studied Clara Carew's visage, paying close attention to her response, straining to determine if this time the chills felt different, meant something profound. She'd reversed the course of her travels from San Francisco to Deadwood. It had been a miserable journey. She wondered if she had done the right thing.

She leaned toward the painting. "Mama?" she whispered. She waited. No answer came to her.

Every time the shivers came, chilling her to the bone, they brought an icy-sharp flash to her mind that illuminated the past events of her life like scenes from a play, events that had brought her to the very spot on which she stood. This time it was a scene in a jail cell, a filthy place in some one-horse town west of Cheyenne. She'd shared it with a woman who called herself Melody Sweet, an actress who'd outlived her costumes, and her teeth, by the look of her. Maudie clenched her jaw just thinking about the state she'd been reduced to. All things being relative, some low points in her life had been lower than others.

Taking a part in a shyster theater manager's company hadn't been her most brilliant move, but she'd needed money, as always. Being on the run since she'd turned fourteen hadn't provided her with the opportunity to acquire a little nest egg. Sometimes she had to obtain food and money by dubious means, money becoming a priority over food at times. Money would get her to San Francisco. San Francisco held more hope than ever that she would find her mother.

"You stole something, didn't you? What'd they get you for, honey?" the whiskey-voiced Melody had asked Maudie. She'd plopped her lumpy body down on the wood pallet that was supposed to serve as their shared bed.

Maudie shrugged and leaned against the bars of the cell door.

"Thought so. I'm good at recognizin'." Melody was obviously proud of what she thought was one of her greatest attributes.

It made no difference to Maudie what the crime of the moment had been. A night in jail was just another aggravation, just another stumbling block on her trail to find a treasure that was seemingly ever-elusive. Yet Maudie was one addicted to the quest.

"A loaf of bread," she told the older woman.

"You pinched a loaf of bread and they pinched you!" she cackled. Maudie didn't laugh with her. "It's gettin' tougher and tougher to make a livin', ain't it, sweetie? Pretty bad when they pinch a girl for takin' a little something to eat."

"I rather think it was the ham that got them all worked up."

"You took some ham?"

"Not a big piece."

"Still, how can they fault you for takin' food? People ought to be more generous."

"They were more generous than they meant to be," Maudie said. "I took some money, too."

"Very much?"

"A handful."

"That much."

"I wouldn't have taken any of it if I hadn't needed it. I would have paid it back . . . someday. I never thought I'd get caught."

"You wouldn't get caught if you were any good at it. Who taught you to steal in the first place?"

Maudie let out a wry laugh. "Dear old daddy."

"Banks or what?"

32

"Or what. My father was a policeman in New York. It didn't pay enough to suit him so he went on the take. He said people were so stupid, it was easy to sell them something he convinced them they needed. Protection from undesirable elements, he said. Only he became the undesirable element and the protection all in one tidy blue package."

"You following in his footsteps?"

"I hope not. He got shot. An honest shopkeeper was forced to protect himself from the protection. That poor innocent man went to jail for killing a law officer. I blew the whistle on my old man but not in time to save the shopkeeper from committing suicide over the shock and shame."

Melody let out a long, low whistle. "There's other teachers and other ways of learnin' how to fend for yourself."

Maudie nodded knowingly. "What are you in for?"

Melody rolled over on her side, crooked her elbow and propped her head on her hand. "Some uppity church woman said I degraded her preacher. *Her* preacher. As if he belonged to her in the first place."

"Did you?"

"No more'n he degraded me. Said he felt the passion of the Lord, and if he diddled me then I'd be cleansed."

"And you fell for that old trick?"

"Well, I didn't actually fall for it. I'm an actress, and sometimes it's difficult to get suitable roles. Suitable meanin' somebody can pay. I take 'em where I can get 'em. So I took one in this theater I knew had something more going on upstairs than it did on the stage, but I figured it couldn't hurt. At least the men were there spendin' their hard-earned cash. How was I to know the preacher had been more tempted by the devil than inspired by the Lord? Next thing I know I'm upstairs, and he's . . ."

Maudie's interest had been piqued by something she'd said. "You're an actress?"

"Yes, honey, can't you tell?"

"As much as you could tell that I'm one," Maudie replied.

The woman fluttered her eyelashes, not wanting to let on that her talent for "recognizin' " had let her down this time. "You look like an orphan. Where you been workin'?"

"Here and there. Wherever there's work, and the place is livable. I'm older than you think, and younger than I feel."

"Ain't we all. Where you headin' next?"

"Out of this tin can as soon as I can."

The woman laughed, showing yellowed teeth. "Then where?"

That was the problem. Maudie didn't know where she was heading next. She'd run out of leads. And she'd run out of decent traveling theater companies, too. She'd taken up playing some of the railroad camps she'd come upon traveling from the east, and even mining towns that didn't look as if they'd be around very long. All a part of her quest. But there were some things she simply wouldn't do, and that was be an actress "upstairs," the polite way of referring to whores. She'd long ago run out of youth, she knew

34

that, and she was running out of her twenties just as fast.

"San Francisco."

"That's a long ways from here."

"I know. I'm looking for someone."

"A man?"

Maudie curled her lip and shook her head. "That's the last thing I'd be looking for. You can't trust anybody these days, least of all a man."

"Who said anything about trustin' em? I just wish there was three or four good ones a body could get next to now and then. So I got me an idea where I can be a great actress and pick out a man as well."

"And where is that?" Maudie asked languidly.

"There's a rip-roarin' town back in Dakota Territory. They call it Deadwood Gulch. I hope that name don't mean what kind of men are there!"

"It just might. That's where General Custer discovered gold. Every sort imaginable is flocking to that place. Life isn't worth a plugged nickel, so I hear."

"Custer," the woman sighed, "now there is a man worth following."

"Where've you been? The entire Seventh Cavalry followed him, and they're all dead now, him, too, wiped out by the Indians. Shows you what stealing from other people can get you."

The woman flipped onto her back and stretched out. "Well, there's plenty of other men in Deadwood, and a theater. The owner just died, leading lady in all the plays, too. Heard tell she came to a nasty end. Tough luck. But"—she swept her gnarled hand through her

35

matted hair—"I'm just right for all the parts she played."

The hair on the back of Maudie's neck had prickled, she remembered, as she stared at the painted face in the Deadwood Variety Theater lobby. She'd pumped Melody Sweet for information about the dead actress and learned that her name was Clara Carew. Maudie'd heard of her.

"How'd she die?" Maudie knew she was being morbid, but she'd always been curious, and she felt this information was very important somehow.

"Scenery fell down on her. Heard tell it might not have been an accident at all."

"Why?"

"Who knows? Somebody must have had it in for her. Tough luck, but good for me. Soon as I get out of here, I'm headin' right for the place." Melody stretched out on the pallet and yawned.

"How old was she?" Maudie pressed.

"Headin' for the half century, so they said. Been acting a long time. Too long for some people, probably."

"Where was she from?"

"Someplace in the east. Heard tell she was on the run from something. Probably some man. Heard she was a beauty once upon a time. Probably just got used up. Amazing she got to be that old."

Maudie's heart pounded in her chest. Something told her she should get to Deadwood, too. Maybe the cold trail she'd been following had heated up behind her. She clutched her locket. She had to get out, get some money from someplace, and hightail it to Dakota Territory.

It had almost been too easy to break out of that jail. Melody had the baby-faced deputy all hot and bothered stroking him through the cell bars, and Maudie had simply lifted the keys from his pocket, unlocked the door, led him in like a slavering young bull, then slammed the door on the both of them and bolted.

Just outside of Cheyenne she was caught by a well-dressed man in a well-cut suit.

"I've been watching you rather closely," he'd said, holding her at arm's length.

Maudie didn't blame him for that. She was dirty, and she smelled like month-old laundry, which was just about the last time she'd had a bath. But she was mad as hell at him for stopping her.

"I didn't do anything," she sputtered and kicked him.

"You did too," the man said, screwing up his face in pain, "that's why we want you so bad."

"For a chunk of stale bread and a piece of ham that's seen better days? What's this country coming to?"

She threw dirt on his clothes and started off on a run. He sacked her by a tree and plastered her down on the ground. She gave him a knee in the groin. He flipped her over on her stomach and put his knee in the middle of her back. Gasping for breath, he'd told her a wild story and proposed a wild scheme.

"Name's Cutherbert T. Golden. Pinkerton." She struggled while he fidgeted inside his coat pocket, retrieved his credentials, and shoved a piece of paper under her nose.

"Pinkerton!" Maudie spluttered into the grass. "Stars and garters, I didn't do anything to warrant being arrested by the Pinkertons!"

"I'm not here to arrest you. I'm here to offer you employment!"

Maudie stopped struggling. "What'd you say?"

Golden stood up and helped her to her feet. "I want to hire you. You'd be a Pinkerton agent, or at least act like one. You're a pretty good actress. I've seen you."

Maudie couldn't believe what she was hearing. "I hate policeman. Why would I want to even consider playing one, let alone being one?"

"Money. I understand you need money."

Maudie cocked her head. "How'd you know that?"

"It's my business to know. You need money to get to San Francisco. You're looking for an actress named Gwen-Ada Boone. You took her name for your middle name. You've heard she might be there using a different name. And you think she's your mother."

Maudie's eyes narrowed. "How do you know any of this?"

"Like I said, it's my business."

"What do you know about Gwen-Ada Boone? Is she there? In San Francisco?"

He passed over her questions. "The way I look at it, you need me and I need you. Remember, you're a thief and now you've broke jail. I can take you in, claim my own reward. Or you can work for me, and I can drop the charges. The money will be good if you do the job right and don't cause me any problems."

"I've got business someplace."

38

"It better be Deadwood Gulch in Dakota Territory."

Maudie's eyes widened. "Wh-why?"

"Some big actress died there recently."

"Clara Carew?"

"One in the same. We have reason to believe she was murdered. You've heard of her."

Maudie blanched. If Carew was her mother, the thought of her being murdered sickened her. She steadied herself with great effort.

"Only recently. Why are the Pinkertons interested in her? And what's that got to do with me?"

Golden grinned. "You're just like her now, aren't you? You're an actress and you're a thief. So was she. Allegedly she lifted a valuable set of jewelry back in St. Louis. Ruby necklace and earbob things. Poor rich little bride-to-be wants to wear them in her wedding on New Year's Eve. They were her beloved aunt's bequest to her. So her wealthy daddy has offered a reward."

"What's all this got to do with me?" Maudie's mind was racing. Was Carew her mother? If she had been, she certainly wouldn't have stolen any jewelry. Gwen-Ada didn't have that in her, she was positive of that. "If Madame Carew is dead, just go pick up the rubies and get your reward and that's the end of it."

"Not that simple. The jewelry's missing. Somebody filched the rubies, and my guess is it's the same one who killed Carew, assuming that it wasn't an accident, of course. And I do. Assume that it wasn't an accident, that is."

"How do you know about all this? Isn't there a sheriff or something in this place who can take care of things for you? I'm no detective and as I told you, I hate—"

"Policemen, I know. Having a father like Patrick Dearden could do that to you, I guess."

Maudie'd heard the Pinkertons had secret ways of finding things out, but this one astounded her with his knowledge.

"They haven't settled on a permanent sheriff. I've been working with a federal marshal on this. The town doesn't even have a government yet, so no one's got real jurisdiction there."

"Gold towns only last as long as the ore. By the time I got there the place might be long gone." Maudie wanted to get rid of Cutherbert T. Golden and get on with her own business. She was growing impatient with their conversation.

"Not this time. I figure you can get into the acting company and ask a lot of questions without raising anyone's suspicions. Soon as the perpetrator found out who I was they'd cover their tracks."

"Why don't you cover your own tracks and get into the theater company yourself?"

"I can't do that acting stuff. I'm too obviously suave for that sort of thing. And besides, Deadwood is not my kind of town. I'm much more cosmopolitan than . . ." He eyed her with disdain.

"Me?" Maudie spat.

"Very discerning." Golden picked out a nub of ear-wax and flicked it into the air past Maudie.

She grimaced and thought for a moment while she studied his smug face. "How much does it pay?"

"You'll get some up-front money. I can up the reward from the bride's daddy half again as much and cut you in on half of that." A crooked sneer hovered over his lips. "Sounding better all the time, isn't it? It'll be enough to set me up for the rest of my life if the rubies come back in time. And enough to get you back and forth across this country twice. So, what's it going to be? Back to the hoosegow or take an honest paying job for once in your life?"

Maudie stared at him. "There's nothing honest about this and you know it. Let me see the money." She stuck out her hand.

"Now, listen here, you don't think I'm that stupid, do you? You'll get your money when you get to Deadwood, and the rest when you finish the job. *If* you finish the job."

"And just how do you think I'm going to get myself to this Deadwood to do the job in the first place? That is, if I decide I'm going to do it."

"You'll decide you will."

"Well, I can't go looking like this. I haven't got any money for clothes or transportation. And a meal now and then might persuade me to be more cooperative, you know."

"Yes, I do know. That's why there's work waiting for you in Cheyenne."

Maudie looked askance. "What kind of work?"

"Why, acting, of course. I'll escort you to the Republican Theater in Cheyenne, where you'll be a part of an acting company. You'll make a little money there, enough to legitimize you as a real actress."

"I *am* a real actress!"

"Of course you are. Enough money," he continued,

41

"for some clothes and food and transportation to Deadwood."

"What will I do for money once I'm there?"

"In Deadwood you will find Wells Fargo certificates deposited in your name at the Miners and Mechanics Bank."

Maudie's thoughts swirled. If she determined early that Madame Carew was not her mother, she'd just take that money and . . .

"Don't even think about taking the money and hightailing it out of town either." Golden scrutinized her knowingly.

Much as she hated policemen, Maudie had to marvel at the man's acuity. "I wouldn't think of such a thing." She set her facial muscles to effect the mask she'd used often while playing out a few weak hands of poker. "What'll I do if I find the rubies, turn them over to the law?"

"*When* you find the rubies you don't tell anybody. You hang onto them until you hear from me."

"How will I hear from you. By letter?"

"Ha! There's no mail service to Deadwood Gulch yet. No telegraph either."

"Then how can I contact you?"

"I'll contact you, never fear. And you'd better be there when I do. Any slipup and your sweet little fanny'll be occupying a jail cell for a long time. And don't go telling anybody you're working for me either."

Maudie frowned. "Why not? I'd probably learn more sooner if people knew I was working with the Pinkertons."

Golden clucked and shook his head. "Get savvy. If

42

anyone knows you're a Pinkerton they'll shut up and you'll never get the rubies. And I'll never get the reward. And you'll never get your money. So keep still about that." Golden eyed her from toe to head. "Play your cards right little lady, and me and you will be going so far away nobody will ever find us."

"Thank you, but I prefer the money unattached. I've got my own destination in mind."

Golden's lascivious assessment of her turned to scorn. "Then keep your nose clean and do as I say."

"How long would I have to stay in Cheyenne?" Maudie was feeling the bit in her teeth now. She wanted to get to Deadwood as soon as possible. If Melody Sweet and this Pinkerton agent were right, it was possible Carew was her mother. The sooner she knew whether she was or not, the better for Maudie. Years of searching had left her dispirited and weary.

"A few weeks," Golden told her. "Long enough for you to make a name for yourself. We want you to arrive in Deadwood expected, and well-known enough to make somebody jealous enough to strike again."

"A few weeks!" Maudie flared, completely ignoring his reference to setting her up like a rabbit in a pen full of dogs. "By that time the thief could be long gone!"

"I can see you don't know how the devious mind of a criminal works," Golden said smugly.

Oh yes, Maudie Boone Dearden did indeed know how the devious mind of a criminal worked. To wit, following Golden's delivery of her to Cheyenne and her short run at the Republican in a dreadful play, she had purloined trinkets to sell to book her passage to Deadwood and had subsequently performed her daring escape onto Phatty Thompson's wagon full of cats.

Money was still an object, yet she was in Deadwood long before she ever would have hoped to be. And she was in the Deadwood Variety Theater staring at a painting of Clara Carew, who may or may not have been her mother. Stage makeup and wigs could do wonders in transforming a person.

I don't know her. At least I don't think I know her.

Maudie did not determine at that moment whether she was grateful or disappointed that the woman in the painting was not who she'd been searching for almost half her life, had been alternately hoping or dreading she'd find alive or dead. Every time something like this happened, a new theater, another acting troupe, a different leading actress, her emotions were battered about, her vulnerability surfaced once again. And after each of these times she was finding that it took much longer for her to regain strength and courage to start over. Then she'd set her sights on San Francisco. San Francisco held all the answers, she was certain of it, and she was anxious to get moving again.

This time she had to stay in one place for a while, even if Clara Carew was not the actress she'd been searching for. This time she couldn't move on so suddenly. This time she was being paid to stay.

Slowly she took her first look around the opera house. Dark, empty theaters always gave Maudie a feeling of foreboding, and this time was no exception. Hadn't she had enough experience with theaters by now to be immune to such feelings? Maybe it was because she'd never found what she'd been looking for, and her hopeful search had always turned to disappointment. Maybe it was just the usual superstition that plagued every theater person she'd ever met.

She peered up into the overhead rigging, but couldn't see much in the dim light that was coming from an open back stage door. If she wanted to examine those hemp lines closely, she knew she'd have to climb up to the flyloft to do it, and she hadn't the energy nor the inclination to do so at the moment.

"Looking for something?" a woman's voice spoke behind her.

Maudie jumped and spun around, pressing a hand to the locket that lay over her heart. "Ye gods, you scared me!"

"As you did me." A petite young woman with long brown hair pulled back in a switch stood at the stage prow. "Are you looking for something?" she repeated.

Maudie swallowed as if to push her thudding heart back down where it belonged. "Someone, actually. Is the theater owner about?"

"No one's here except me. No one's ever here these days except me." The woman eyed Maudie up and down with an openly appraising expression. "I think you're in the wrong place. You want the Green Front, or the Gem, or maybe Mrs. Mundy's House of Mystic Pleasures on Lower Main."

Maudie pulled herself together as best she could. She was unpresentable in looks and odor, and explaining how she had been reduced to such a state was beyond her at the moment. "I know what you must be thinking, but I am an actress, newly arrived." When the woman's face registered stark skepticism, Maudie continued. "I've been on the Lyceum circuit. Had a marvelous run in *Mrs. Burnham's Persuasion* at the Republican Theater in Cheyenne. Perhaps you saw the write-up in *Leslie's Illustrated*. Then we went into *Scarlet Lady*, a wonderful play. But I decided it was time to strike out on my own since the big roles were always going to the same leading actress. I was getting nowhere, I thought.

"Anyway, I heard that Madame Clara Carew's company was here in Deadwood, and I struck out immediately. I mean, who wouldn't want to work with the great Carew? Had no idea how far away this place was, and on the way I met with several life-threatening misfortunes, and . . ."

Maudie took a much-needed breath when she saw the changes of understanding spreading over the woman's face. "Oh my, you *are* an actress, aren't you? I can tell by the way you carry yourself." Maudie reached out with her right hand. "I'm Maudie Boone Dearden. And you're . . . ?"

The woman held out her hand. "Taryn Edwards. I'm sorry I mistook you for . . ."

"I know. I look a sight. A bath would be divine. Are you part of Madame Carew's company?"

"I was. You've heard about Carew, haven't you? Everyone has. We've all been shaken by it. Well, I mean, wouldn't you be shaken, too?" Taryn lifted a lock of her long chestnut hair and secured it behind her ear with a trembling hand.

"Heard?" Maudie cocked her head.

"Yes. The accident and all. Can't believe you haven't heard about it. Where'd you say you've been appearing?"

"Oh yes, now that you mention it, I believe I did

hear something about an accident in a theater. You don't mean it was Madame Carew?" When Taryn nodded, Maudie feigned shock. "Such a tragedy. How did it happen?"

"Some scenery came down on her. Oh, it was quite dramatic. If the Madame had lived, she'd have been proud of her final scene. She was emoting into the rafters. Maybe that was it."

"What?"

"The rafters couldn't take it. They let loose of the backdrop and the flats, and, well . . ." Taryn made a sweeping downward stroke with both hands.

Maudie frowned. "Must have been awful."

"Yes, we were all sick just looking at her lying there with this awful expression on her face, like she'd just eaten some bad food from a restaurant in China Town. Kind of green."

Maudie held up one hand. "Don't tell me any more."

"Faint, are you?"

"No. But I haven't eaten in a long while, and when I did it wasn't fit for human consumption. And I'm weary from my journey. I just don't feel terribly strong enough right now to hear the details of the tragedy."

Taryn looked around surreptitiously, then leaned toward Maudie conspiratorially. "Tragedy to no one but Carew. She won't be missed, I can tell you."

Maudie lowered her voice. "You mean, people didn't like her?"

"Like her? They loathed her. She was a shrew, a nasty, lying, conniving shrew who thought only of herself."

"I always thought she was a big star of the stage. She had her own company, gave people work, wrote her own plays."

"And performed all the good roles. Never gave anybody else a chance. Paid them nothing. Treated them like dirt. Serves her right."

Maudie looked at Taryn carefully. "I know how hard it must have been for you as an ingenue not to be considered for lead roles."

Taryn's big brown eyes lifted to Maudie's. "Yes, it was." The relief in her voice was evident. Here was someone who understood, someone to commiserate with. "Madame Carew made me play little girls, sometimes even little boys. She taped me down flat with muslin strips so I wouldn't look too . . . you know." She gestured out in front of her bosom with both hands.

"I know," Maudie said sympathetically.

"Lady Fan would never let that happen to me. She told me so."

"Who's Lady Fan?"

"An actress. Arrived about two weeks before the accident. She's wonderful. Not at all like old Carew."

"And is she an ingenue, too?"

"Oh, no. But I wouldn't mind her playing Madame Carew's roles."

"It wouldn't bother you?"

"No. She's so nice, so generous. Let me have the light during my scenes with her. And I won't have to tape my breasts if she takes over the company." Taryn's eyes shone admiringly.

Maudie was suddenly more than curious. "So Lady

Fan will take over the company now that Carew is gone?"

"I don't know. There's our director to consider. Would you like to audition?"

"Yes, but not in this sorry state. Doubt I'd even be cast as a scullery maid looking like I do right now. Would you know of a hotel or boardinghouse that might be sympathetic to an actress who is . . . waiting for her belongings and money to arrive?"

"Yes, I do. Miss Parrott's, where I stay. I'll take you there, if you like."

"Would I ever like!" Maudie smiled.

Taryn walked Maudie the short distance to Pauline Parrott's establishment. Indeed she was right about the woman's measure of sympathy.

"I understand, dearie," Miss Parrott said, nodding. "It's hard work being in the theater, in the *serious* theater, that is. I know. Tried it myself when I was a girl. Not that kind with the curtained boxes where an actress cadges drinks . . . and more."

Maudie nodded. She knew how young girls could be led astray by unscrupulous theater owners.

"I run a clean house exclusively for respectable theatrical women," Miss Parrott continued. "Only those working in Mr. and Mrs. Langrishe's new shows, or at the Deadwood Variety Theater—shame about Madame Carew, isn't it?—are allowed into Pauline Parrott's Boarding House for Ladies. None are welcome from the Gem or Green Front."

Fortunately, the robust and painfully neat Miss Parrott had discerning sharp gray eyes and prided herself on being a shrewd judge of character. "You can rest assured here, my dear. I can tell you are serious about your work in the theater. You're a real actress. You're welcome here. Nine dollars a week room and board. Adjustments made for any meals not taken. Fair enough?"

"More than fair, Miss Parrott. I, uh, am without funds at the moment. . . ."

Miss Parrott held up her hand. "Bother. You won't be for long. And please call me Polly. Everyone does."

Maudie wondered briefly whatever possessed a family named Parrott to name their daughter something that could be shortened to Polly, and why the grown woman would agree to suffer such an indignity.

"I'm expecting a deposit to be made for me at the local bank. I'll get it tomorrow and pay you in advance." This was one time Maudie wanted to make an honest business arrangement. Miss Pauline "Polly" Parrott was opening her heart and her home, and Maudie recognized her genuine warmth.

For no additional charge Miss Parrott herself had given Maudie a carbolic acid de-licing treatment while searching for fleas because, as she stated as fact, "you just never know where some people have been, do you, dearie?" Somehow her voice had carried not a trace of insinuation. Maudie thought she was either the sweetest, most understanding woman in the world, or the best damned actress in the States or on the frontier.

Miss Parrott introduced her to Carolyn, an orphan she'd met on her journey to the Black Hills. The girl was about fifteen or sixteen with thick-braided dark hair and coarse olive skin. She gave Maudie a thorough hair washing, poured a bath, and brought fluffy white towels and a comfortable deep blue wrapper. Maudie had accepted it all gratefully, and enjoyed Carolyn's hovering about her.

"More hot water, Miss Dearden?" Carolyn poised a spouted copper pail over Maudie's feet.

Maudie uttered a languid affirmative. In the elaborate folding tin tub that Miss Parrott had brought all the way to Deadwood from San Antonio, she lounged amid lather so rich it foamed over the rim. Miss Parrott had set up the tub in a cozy room in her boardinghouse on the terraced Williams Street at the base of Deadwood's Forest Hill, euphemistically known as the residential district.

Carefully Carolyn poured hot water into the tub, and Maudie felt its flush of heat around the backs of her legs.

"Does the mud ever leave this place?" Maudie asked, but wasn't sure if she cared or not at the moment if Deadwood were submerged in chicken heads.

"Don't know, ma'am. Never seen it without it."

"Never?" Suddenly Maudie did care.

"Miss Parrott says it'll get beastly hot, then the mud should go away." Carolyn brought a low pine stand closer to the tub.

"Beastly hot," Maudie reiterated.

"Miss Parrott says then it'll be nothin' but dust 'round here owin' to the hills not havin' any trees and such."

"Lovely," Maudie muttered.

"Yes, ma'am." Carolyn scurried out into the hall, and returned with a tray of tea things, biscuits, and a pot of jam.

"Well, Carolyn, aside from your climate predictions, you and this bathtub and this boardinghouse are the best things that have happened to me in an age. Thank you for your hospitality."

Carolyn blushed and offered an awkward curtsy. "You're welcome, Miss Dearden." She backed toward the bath room door. "You . . . you're the most beautiful lady I've ever seen, even better than the whores," she said in a rush before scurrying out.

Maudie smiled and sighed at the well-intended compliment. Perhaps a relaxing evening and good hot meal would make up for one of the most awful days of her life, one of the most awful fortnights of her life.

Maudie spread some jam on a biscuit and poured a cup of tea, then settled against the back of the tub amid the fragrant bubbles sipping and nibbling. Ever since she'd started working with traveling theatrical troupes, she'd trained herself to rest in the odd moment she could catch between scenes or while moving from one troupe or one town to another.

Or when her exploits landed her in a cramped jail cell. She shuddered.

Relaxing, she gave her aching body over to the warm water and special softening soap. The tea and jam-smeared biscuit were welcome respites from hardtack and greasy pork, and coffee it took two hands to push a spoon through. One of the less offensive things that could be said about Phatty Thompson and the rat man McCall was that they were lousy cooks. She closed her eyes and enjoyed her bath.

When she'd toweled off and smoothed on a cream Carolyn had left for her, Maudie sought out Polly

Parrott to see if there was a dress she might borrow for the evening. Carolyn had somehow managed to make her embroidered boots look almost new, but everything else she'd been wearing had to be destroyed, and the offending bustle discarded, much to Maudie's delight.

"Yes, indeed, dearie," Polly said, opening a clothes press and passing a palm over a line of garments. "Always keep things from our ladies who've moved on. Never know when someone just like yourself might be in need. Take what you need, but if you leave permanently, do the courtesy of returning what you can."

Maudie thanked the woman and selected a forest green skirt with matching fitted jacket, and a cream lace blouse. A dark green brocade pouch completed the ensemble.

Polly motioned to a bureau that contained stockings and undergarments, and Maudie found a few things available and a few things missing. The missing items did not concern her. Women were forced into too many underpinnings as it was, especially corsets that twisted the body into unnatural contortions. She had a naturally curvaceous form. Who but herself would know if she omitted the occasional undergarment?

She swept her freshly washed and brushed hair into soft swirls around her head and anchored it with her own combs she'd salvaged and washed. A little powder, cheek and lip stain from Miss Parrott's collection, a quick check in a beveled-glass mirror, and she was beginning to feel like the woman she was before her wretched journey from Cheyenne.

Chapter 3

"Supper hour's been and gone, but I'd be happy to fix something for you, dearie," Polly offered, yawning.

Maudie caught the added "but I'd rather not" in the unspoken end of the sentence. "Oh, I couldn't ask you to do that, but I would appreciate a recommendation for a good restaurant, if there is such a thing in Deadwood."

"I think the new Grand Central Hotel would suit you, dearie. Just tell Aunt Lou Marchbanks I sent you, and she'll make an arrangement on the bill."

"Thank you, Miss . . . Polly. I'm certain you understand that as an actress I've learned to work a few miracles where a restaurant bill is concerned, so perhaps I won't need to resort to that."

Maudie thought of several games of ladylike yet skillful poker in which she'd settled more than a few outstanding bills for food, rent, and clothing. She was a bit anxious to test her touch again.

Though past what in the east would be the usual supper hour, the Grand Central Hotel's attractively appointed dining room was filled with diners and quick-footed servers. Maudie paused just inside the double front doors, still holding her skirts above her ankles as she'd done while walking overtown. All the women of Deadwood walked with lifted skirts because of the mud, and the practice was adopted by Maudie immediately.

She watched trays of food pass by, and noted with great surprise that the meals appeared to be prepared with care, and were of a variety she'd found in eastern restaurants. What she didn't see readily was an empty table.

She started into the crowd of white-clothed tables. Toward the far back she thought she could see the end of a vacant one and headed toward it.

"For heaven's sake!" a female voice whispered loudly as she passed a pair of diners. "That's that woman."

"What woman?" her male companion replied in what Maudie detected was an extremely bored tone.

"The one on the wagon full of cats that pulled into town today. She has some nerve coming into a respectable public establishment."

Maudie stopped just out of earshot of the woman. She licked her lips, then lifted a tray from a surprised young waiter who was just about to set it on a stand. She turned slowly around, retraced her steps, and stopped at the table where the offending woman sat.

She remembered a stage direction in a script she'd read recently. *Agatha looks aghast.* Indeed the woman looked aghast when Maudie approached their table.

"Excuse me," she said sweetly. "My sister, Lou

Marchbanks, is in charge of this dining room, and she's so very busy, I myself will attend to your needs this evening." She flashed a dazzling smile as the woman's companion, no doubt her husband, gave Maudie an unmistakable look of male appreciation.

"Horace, get up," the woman demanded. "We're leaving."

"But, Margaret, dearest—"

"Don't dearest me. I saw how you looked at that . . ."

The man rose quickly, and Maudie smiled with satisfaction as she watched him scurry after the bobbing square shoulders of his insulted wife.

"I wouldn't go around bragging about your *sister* if I were you," a vaguely familiar voice drawled behind her. Maudie twisted around just as Cole Branch was folding his long, lean body into a chair at the table she'd just cleared of diners. "Aunt Lou Marchbanks is a mahogany-colored daughter of a former slave, and she's pretty picky about who she lets claim kin to her."

Maudie felt her face flush with embarrassment. Then she became piqued. "What do you think you're doing? Get up from there. This is my table."

Cole glanced from the table to her. "Really? Since no one was sitting at it, I naturally thought it was free. Sorry. Squatter's rights, you know."

"It was cleared for me," she said firmly. His satisfied smile had Maudie wanting to rearrange it for him one moment, charmed by it the next.

"I don't see how you can prove that," he baited.

"Prove it! Why you . . ."

"Now, now. Don't raise your voice. People are beginning to stare. It wouldn't behoove a lady to behave with less than perfect decorum in public, you know."

"Just get up," she sputtered in a stage whisper.

"Just find another table," he whispered in kind.

Maudie pulled into her full height and scanned the room. Not an empty table in sight. The sight and aroma of freshly prepared food filled her senses. She was starving. Her stomach rumbled loudly. Cole Branch lowered his eyes to the middle of her body, and an amused grin played at the corners of his mustache.

"There isn't another table," she whispered back through clenched teeth.

"And you're much too refined to join a man who hasn't escorted you into a public room, so I'll spare you the affront of inviting you to join me for supper."

Cole picked up the single-page menu a waiter had dropped on the table as he scurried by. He made a big show of studying it.

"Mmm, the beefsteak looks good. Love roasted onions." He smacked his lips. "Or perhaps the chicken. It's always so juicy. Don't know how Aunt Lou crisps the outside like that. And those biscuits, lightest thing this side of a cloud's own fleece."

Maudie ripped the opposite chair away from the table and sat down hard. Fleecing the hide of Cole Branch came suddenly into her mind as a pleasant diversion.

Cole swept the menu around and placed it in front of her. She snatched it up and was studying it closely when a prim young woman with tightly wound hair, wearing a long starched white apron came to take their order.

"Sir?" the young woman asked timidly.

"Beefsteak, rare," Cole announced.

"Yes sir. Sixteen or twenty-four ounce?"

"Twenty-four. Double on the potatoes. And the biggest mug of Parkhurst's brew you can carry."

The girl's small gray eyes widened as she fixed them on Maudie in shock. Maudie stirred uncomfortably in her chair. Then the girl shifted her gaze back to Cole.

"And what will *you* have, sir?"

Both Cole and Maudie looked up at her, puzzled.

"I just told you. Beefsteak, potatoes, and beer," Cole said.

"That was for you? Oh, sir, I'm sorry. I thought you were ordering for your wife. So many of the new professional gentlemen . . ."

"Wife! Listen here, young woman," Maudie exclaimed, fairly bursting with indignation, "I'm not this . . . person's wife, and furthermore I can order a meal for myself. I'll have the chicken and biscuits."

"And to drink, miss?" the girl asked quickly, swallowing hard.

"Parkhurst's brew. But put it in a teapot and bring me a cup and saucer. I don't suppose you have a lime. If you do, please bring that, too. Thank you."

The girl stood rooted, it seemed, to the edge of their table. Her jaw slackened, and once again her wide eyes were pinned on Maudie.

Maudie looked up and stared back. "Did you get that?" No response. Maudie tugged on her long white apron. "I said, did you get my order?"

The girl blinked as if coming out of a trance. "Yes, ma'am, yes, of course."

She took off on a run toward the kitchen, and Maudie knew she'd be the talk around the steel cooking pots this evening. Even in a raw town like Deadwood, certain kinds of ladies were expected to do only certain kinds of things, and clearly Maudie had just overstepped some boundaries. So be it. Maudie had been overstepping boundaries for years, and she wasn't about to change for residents of a place like Deadwood Gulch.

"So . . . Branch, isn't it? Did you say *Sheriff* Branch?"

Cole Branch's reasoning left him for a fleeting moment. He was caught in the cornflower blue of her direct gaze, and had to summon the strength to drag his eyes down to an imaginary crumb on the tablecloth which he studiously wiped away.

"That's right. And while I feel I've known you for half my life, what with your auspicious arrival earlier today, with whom will I have the pleasure of sharing dinner this evening?"

"I have no idea who you'll take pleasure in this evening, but at the moment you are seated at my table, and I am Maudie Boone Dearden."

"Maudie Boone . . ."

"Dearden."

"Interesting name."

"I thought so when I chose it."

"You mean it isn't real?" he asked.

"Parts of it are." She narrowed her eyes.

"Which parts?"

"I'm sure my telling you would shock your sense of propriety and interfere with your digestive processes, so we'll just let the subject rest."

59

He raised an eyebrow, and a half-smile tilted one corner of his mouth. Cole Branch was becoming very intrigued with Maudie Boone Dearden, real name or not.

The waiter girl brought his tall glass of beer, and a teapot and cup and saucer for Maudie. No lime, but a lemon slice was perched along the rim. The girl stepped back and waited.

Maudie looked up once, then again, staring long enough to scare the girl away. She poured the brew through the narrow spout. It foamed up and threatened to pour over the top like the bubbles from her bath earlier. Maudie slapped her palm over the teacup and held back the rush.

Cole watched her, entranced. This woman did not pretend anything. Except maybe in the service of her beverage, but he wondered if she did that to keep from drawing attention to the fact that she was drinking brew in a respectable public place, something that ladies simply did not do. That notion seemed somehow . . . nice. He cocked his head at this thought. He knew from the start what profession she was in.

"Maudie Boone Dearden is a perfect name for an actress," he said, watching her. "I've heard it before, or something like it."

"I doubt you've heard of me. Perhaps you know of another actress with a similar name?"

"Perhaps." He had the feeling she wasn't just making conversation. "You made quite an entrance today."

"Spectacular entrances and grand exits are my stage signature," Maudie responded.

"Must take precise timing." Cole gauged her expression carefully.

"It does. However, my particular entrance into Deadwood is one I'd rather forget."

"Why, whatever do you mean?" Cole teased. "The sight of a freight wagon loaded with house cats, a crazy derelict waving from the top of the crate, a filthy fat bullwhacker, and a wild-looking woman in a stained scarlet dress was the most exciting thing to happen in Deadwood in days! I have to hand it to you. You looked confident, as if that was your usual traveling attire and customary mode of transportation."

"I'm glad I was so convincing."

"You were. To all but the, pardon me, respectable ladies."

Maudie busied herself unfolding a napkin and placing it over her lap. "I saw them. I read their faces. They stared at me as I passed, curiosity, hope, then disappointment on their faces. I know those looks well. They were curious about the female riding with the driver, hopeful she might possibly be a woman like themselves, then disappointed when they discovered she wasn't."

"You should know that in Deadwood no respectable woman wears red in public. That's strictly reserved for upstairs girls or . . . theatrical persons . . ."

". . . usually lumped together as one kind," Maudie finished for him. "It's a marvel how fast moral convention rivals the rush for gold to a raw frontier, isn't it?"

Cole silently concurred.

"So what are you doing about Carew's death?"

"What?" The directness with which she suddenly changed the subject unsettled him.

"Madame Carew, the actress. Her death. I'm sure you don't think it was an accident."

"Why shouldn't I think that? I've no reason to think otherwise. And besides, what business is it of yours how she died?"

Cole watched her face. She didn't waver in her calm demeanor. She was an actress all right. Her expression spoke only of strength and control, and he admired her for it. But her eyes gave her away. There was more emotion going on behind those blue depths than glittered outwardly. And Cole Branch wanted to know what could be of such monumental importance to a woman like Maudie Boone Dearden. He also wondered what he meant by *a woman like* her.

Maudie lifted her palm and squeezed a few drops of lemon into her teacup, then carried the rim to her lips. She sipped in a most ladylike manner, but Cole noted that she didn't grimace when the biting brew touched her tongue. In fact, she appeared to savor its taste. And he enjoyed the sight.

"The world of the theater is a very small one," she said, "regardless of where or in what remote place the circuit takes a company. Carew was famous among patrons and performers alike. As an actress, I find suspicious the notion of scenery simply falling on a performer. It's well-known in the theater that riggers have an unspoken creed about protecting actors."

"Yes, I know there is. But that doesn't mean it can't or won't happen on occasion."

"Rarely. Is that what you think happened?"

Cole considered keeping silent on the matter. He knew why he hadn't investigated Carew's death as thoroughly as he should have. He reconsidered. "It was Carew's fiftieth performance in a play called *Scarlet Lady*."

"Her most successful original work."

"So I've heard. In the finale of the second act . . ."

"The walls of the city fall in on her character."

"Right. Well, they fell in on cue, but instead of rising from the ashes and rubble, Carew was crushed under the weight and killed instantly."

Maudie pondered a moment. "I admit some pieces of scenery are heavy enough to severely hurt, but not, in most cases, heavy enough to kill a person."

"Not even flat frames or backdrop counterweights?"

Maudie leveled a direct gaze at him, her eyes lingering on his mustache. He seemed to know rather easily enough theatrical terms to make her think he'd been around theaters more than just since Carew's accident. She withheld vocalizing her observation for the moment.

"That depends on how they were constructed. Did you examine the overhead rigging?"

"No. I believe it's better to leave everything as is until the Pinkerton man arrives. Last time the federal marshal came through he informed me the agent should be here any day."

Maudie took a larger swallow from her teacup. "You mean you haven't looked at them already, secured them against the possibility of someone tampering with the evidence?"

The waiter girl arrived then, struggling under a heavy-laden tray. She set the chicken down in front of Maudie. Cole's beefsteak dripped off the plate, the roasted onions piled like stage sandbags in the middle of it.

Maudie watched as he attacked the steak with relish. She'd always enjoyed watching a man who loved food consume a meal. There was something sensual about it, basic. She dropped her eyes, feeling heat rising to her face.

"I don't think anyone will tamper with the evidence, as you call it. The Pinkerton man can make a much more precise assessment than I can," Cole said between bites. "I'm a temporary lawman here, anyway. Everybody's waiting for Bill Hickok to make up his mind if he wants the job or not."

"Wild Bill Hickok is in Deadwood?" Even though she'd broached the topic, Maudie felt relieved to move away from the subject of Carew's death for the moment. Excitedly, she scanned the dining room.

"Yes, but he doesn't take meals here. Hangs out at the Number Ten saloon. Came to Deadwood in April with a pal of his named Colorado Charlie, and Calamity Jane, and a couple of others. Folks say it was quite a spectacle. They rode in like a circus parade."

"Calamity Jane. I've heard a lot about her."

"All of it and none of it true," Cole laughed. "How's the chicken?"

"Mmm," Maudie smacked her lips. "Delicious. Just like my mother used to . . ." Her voice trailed away.

"Nothing like the smell and taste of good cooking to bring back the memory of home," Cole said, his own voice distant.

"Wild Bill Hickok," Maudie mused, moving away from both their memories. "I saw him perform in Ned

Buntline's dreadful play, *Scouts of the Prairie,* in New York about three years ago."

"You've been to New York?" Cole eyed her with what Maudie believed was more than just idle curiosity.

"I'm an actress, remember? We get around." She took another swallow from her teacup. "Anyway, he was traveling with Buffalo Bill Cody's troupe. The critics sliced the play to ribbons, along with Buffalo Bill's performance. But Wild Bill could do no wrong no matter how bad he was. Everybody had heard of his exploits across the west, thanks to dime novels. He was a genuine hero."

"Pretty hard to imagine Wild Bill Hickok as an actor, isn't it?" Cole took a long drink of his brew, never once taking his eyes off Maudie.

"Oh, he was no actor. The audiences adored him on stage simply in the act of being himself. You could tell he loved it. Dressed like a peacock and all puffed up like one." She laughed. "I remember the wildest incident about that performance. There was an actress playing an Indian maiden named Dove Eye who'd been captured. Wild Bill was supposed to shoot his way into a pack of Indians and, single-handedly, of course, rescue her. He rushed in and spouted this awful line, something like, 'Fear not, fair maid! By heavens, you are safe at last with Wild Bill, who is ever ready to risk his life and die, if need be, in defense of weak and defenseless womanhood!' " Maudie burst out laughing.

Cole was quite suddenly aware of how much he was enjoying her company. And he felt an unexpected loneliness, as if her presence made it clear just how devoid of female companionship he'd lived his adult life. He smiled warmly.

"Must have been awful. A man like Wild Bill probably believes his own reputation, even if a lot of it is pure fairy tale. He must have been mortified."

"Can't say as I blame him, with lines like that. And to make things worse, there was an operator in the gallery who persisted in training the spotlight right on Wild Bill. He kept jerking across the stage trying to get away from that light, hiding behind bits of scenery and props. But the beam kept finding him. Finally, he just stepped out center stage, hauled out his pistol and shot out the light. Scored a bull's eye, not to mention a hit with the audience! Even the ones showered with flying glass!" She laughed again, pouring out the last of the contents of the teapot.

Cole leaned in, fascinated by Maudie's story and the wonderful way she had of telling it. Her eyes sparkled with merriment, reflecting flickering gaslight from around the room. He suddenly thought she should always be center stage in a soft wash of light.

"I saw him score a similar hit one night in a theater in Binghamton," he recalled, running a finger around the rim of his mug.

"Binghamton?" Maudie's eyes narrowed. "That's in New York."

He nodded.

"You've been to New York?"

"Actresses aren't the only ones who get around, you know."

"I wasn't aware sheriffs played a circuit. I supposed

they stayed in one place doing what they do. What do sheriffs do, anyway?"

"Whatever they're supposed to, wherever they are."

Maudie raised her teacup in a silent toast to his manner, matching her own, of saying just as much as he wanted to about himself and nothing more. She relaxed. This was the most fun she'd had with a man in a long time. No one had ever met the challenge of her quick wit and quicker tongue. She sensed Cole Branch would make a great sparring partner.

"What happened in Binghamton?"

"Wild Bill was about out of money at the faro tables in New York City, so you can bet his mood was edging toward the foul side. Then he got wind of a cheapjack theatrical company in Binghamton presenting *Scouts of the Prairie* starring 'the one and only Wild Bill Hickok.' Well, since he was the one and the absolutely only Wild Bill, and had got fed up with that play and dropped out in a fit of pique, his famous temper was not improved by this bit of news."

Maudie grinned appreciatively. "What did he do?"

"Well, he was smokin' by the time he arrived. He bought a front row seat. His eyesight was failing, and he wanted the clearest view possible of the counterfeiter. Soon this so-called Wild Bill makes his grand entrance slashing and shooting through a band of less-than-wild Comanches. You know the scene, it's played down on the apron in hot lights."

Maudie nodded, but a questioning smile played over the corners of her mouth.

"The scene was even more ridiculous than he thought with someone else playing the role. So that famous temper boiled over like a pot of unwatched potatoes. He jumped up on the stage and grabbed the imposter and flung him through the raised tomahawks of some highly amused Comanches, and right on through the painted flats into the scrim!"

Maudie threw her head back, emitting a rich and lusty laugh that caused the other diners in the room to stare. She didn't seem embarrassed by the attention. Cole relished her enjoyment of his story, and he was caught up in his own embellishment of the already elaborate legend that was Wild Bill Hickok, wishing in the briefest of moments he was telling her about himself.

"I heard he had stage fright. Imagine that. The great Indian scout and gunman, Wild Bill Hickok, with stage fright."

"It happens to the best." When Maudie's eyes lifted questioningly to Cole's, he added, "So I've been told."

"Just goes to show that looks can be deceiving," she said, her gaze direct and level.

"Could be," Cole responded, running a fork-speared chunk of roasted potato through the meat juice on his plate.

Maudie watched him a moment. She had been riveted by his tale, but also by his obvious familiarity with theatrical terms; they didn't exactly trip over the tongue of those who hadn't been regulars backstage or out front trodding the boards. If Cole Branch was starring as Sheriff of Deadwood, his opening night had been fairly recent. She decided that she would withhold the many questions about him that filled her mind until the reviews were in.

"In a way, it's kind of sad, isn't it?" Cole said finally. "Wild Bill was my hero. I wanted to be just like him."

"A bad actor?"

He grimaced. "No. I mean, I believed he was fearless, brave, strong, invincible. Nothing bothered him."

Maudie regarded him a long, uncomfortable moment. He shifted his weight. They reached for the salt cellar at the same moment. Her fingers were around it first. His cupped over hers, instantly warming her hand.

"Oh, go ahead." She started to withdraw it, but he held her hand fast. After a seemingly long moment, he released her, his fingers sliding away. Reluctantly, she thought. And she surprised herself by sharing his reluctance.

"Ladies first."

Maudie dipped a small spoon into the salt and sprinkled it lightly over what was left of her meal. "I fear all the clues to Madame Carew's death will be cold since you've waited all this time to follow them."

"Perhaps. I didn't think it would take the Pinkertons so long to get a man here. They have a reputation for quick response and accurate judgment. The marshal assured me he'd be here within two weeks. That was two weeks ago."

"Maybe the agent was . . . held up by unforeseen events."

Cole's eyes met her gaze dead on, and Maudie concentrated on her biscuits.

"Like what?" Cole asked.

"How should I know? I'm just saying anything is

possible. I'm concerned that the killer has had plenty of time to cover his tracks."

"What makes you so sure there is a killer, and that it's a man?"

Maudie lowered her fork. "Just an assumption. Just the way you're assuming your Pinkerton agent is a man."

"It's a dangerous job. The Pinkertons are highly trained."

She looked at him scornfully, dabbing the corners of her mouth with a napkin. "Regardless of the danger and the fact that I'm a woman, *I'm* going to find out what happened to Madame Carew."

Cole searched her face. "Why do you care so much? Did you know her?"

Maudie drained her teacup. "Everybody knows everybody in the theater."

"I suppose. Privacy is at a minimum for actors. There's no place to be alone. Everybody seems to know everybody and everything about everybody. It's like a prison in a way." His voice took on a faraway quality.

Maudie's list of suspicions about Cole Branch lengthened. "Some prisons we make for ourselves out of necessity, Sheriff. Others are unfairly made for us. No spirit should be caged. Freedom is the only thing worth having in life."

Cole's eyes bored into hers. She tore her gaze away and busied herself with the contents of her brocade bag.

"Oh no."

"What?"

"It seems I've left my money back at the boardinghouse. Well, I'll just speak to Lou Marchbanks. I'm sure she'll allow me to come by tomorrow and pay her."

"Being as she's your sister, and all." Cole's dark eyes glittered devilishly.

Maudie flushed. "One does what one is forced to do in certain circumstances."

"One should be prudent in one's choice of action, however. I'll take care of the bill."

"Oh no—no. Thank you anyway." Maudie stood up. "I can take care of it myself. I wouldn't want to be indebted to you."

"I think I'd like you to be indebted to me," Cole drawled in a suggestive way that made Maudie's chest contract.

"Very well then. I shall repay you," she said, rising. "Good evening, Sheriff. Regardless of your generosity, I still intend to get to the truth of this murder where you have failed to do so." She started away from the table.

"Be careful of the truth," he said to her retreating back. "Sometimes it's better not to know."

Maudie pretended she didn't hear his last words. She didn't want to wonder what he meant by them, or why they disturbed her so.

She left the restaurant, grateful for a breath of different air, no matter how foul it was.

Cole Branch the man—not just his words—disturbed her, and she didn't like it one bit.

For Maudie Boone Dearden to admit that a man had gotten to her was an admission of some proportion. She'd certainly been around handsome men before. Some actors were so handsome they bordered on being called beautiful. Some actors were so ugly their acting abilities were the only positive things they possessed, and they'd honed their skills so sharply that they could mesmerize women to the point where their physical shortcomings went unnoticed.

In either case, Maudie had remained immune to them. She'd come close once or twice at particularly lonely times, but she kept her emotions out of any relationship, always brief, she'd allowed herself to have.

She had to admit Cole Branch was handsome, very handsome, lean, rugged but not weathered. And she liked that. There was a smoothness about him, yet a rugged leanness she found very appealing. Even with his exasperating way of calmly but, she surmised, deliberately misunderstanding her, he exuded a sensual masculinity that Maudie, who prided herself on withstanding the snake-charming ways in which certain men pursued actresses, would have to be sculpted in granite not to succumb to. How was it that in all her vast experience she'd never before met a man quite like him?

She cautioned herself to dispense with such thoughts. She'd vowed that her wings would never be clipped. Least of all by a policeman—a cop, as they called them in Brooklyn where her father had walked the beat. Cops were supposed to be heroes. Fathers were supposed to be heroes.

If there was one thing Maudie knew for certain, there were no heroes anywhere.

And being involved with a man or, God forbid,

married to one, was a prison of its own kind. She'd learned that just watching her mother and father, and every now and then she needed to remind herself of it. Especially when she was feeling lonely.

And now she'd met Cole Branch, a man who called himself sheriff. Sheriff was just another word for cop.

On her way back to the boardinghouse Maudie spotted Phatty Thompson's freighter. There were still a couple of dozen cats inside the crate. They stirred out of their huddled sleep when she touched the bars.

"Poor things," she whispered, "all locked up in jail." One yellowish cat rubbed its nose against her hand, then licked her fingers.

"You're hungry, aren't you?" She thought they were probably as hungry for freedom as they were for food.

Maudie sent a furtive glance up and down the street. Convinced no one was watching her, she unlatched the crate door. She felt a connection to them as she watched the cats run free, disappearing into the dark night. They were searching for their own place just like she'd been doing for so long.

The only difference between them was that cats were adept at finding and making their own niche. For Maudie Boone Dearden, that was hard, hard work.

Chapter 4

Maudie slept in the feathertick bed like a kitten against its mother's stomach. When she awoke Monday morning it was with a surprising sense that her life was about to set a course. Where had that feeling come from? And why in Deadwood City, or Gulch, as it seemed to be interchangeably referred to, in Dakota Territory, of all places on God's green earth? She'd been certain, had believed with all her heart, that her life would be on course once she got to San Francisco.

She stretched and rose, donned the blue wrapper, then went to the dressing table to brush out her hair. She looked at herself in the mirror. No one had ever told her so, but she knew her hair was just like her mother's, long, thick, lustrous. She watched the brush slide through it, and remembered how, so very long ago, she used to brush her mother's hair for her. Those were times when Maudie's mother was bone tired, weary more from a husband's brutality than from long hours on a stage. On stage, Gwen-Ada Boone sparkled with life. At home, she was drained and defeated.

Maudie fingered the heart-shaped locket she was never without, the only memento she had of her mother. Inside was a tiny likeness of the two of them together, Gwen-Ada as a lovely young mother, and Maudie as an infant. Gwen-Ada had purchased a locket for each of them, and they'd made a pact between them that they would wear them always. They'd sealed their vow with a kiss and by hooking the third fingers of their left hands. Gwen-Ada had told her that finger had a direct line to the heart. Maudie was barely five at the time, but the memory was as vivid as if the incident had happened yesterday.

"Oh, Mama," Maudie sighed. "Will I ever find you? Can you be found? Do you want to be found? Don't leave San Francisco before I get there. If you're there." She set the brush down. One tear escaped the corner of her eye and traveled slowly down her cheek. She brushed it away and willed back any others. "Are you still alive, Mama?"

The thought had crept into her mind more and more lately. Had Patrick Dearden told her the truth for once? Had her mother died in an insane asylum as a result of the guilt she bore over taking up with an actor and leaving him to take care of Maudie alone? If it were so, it was the only time he'd ever told the truth, and Maudie'd carried his words in the back of her mind for over twenty years.

Living with her father had been like being in a prison. When she turned fourteen she'd run away with a traveling theater company. But she'd found that her freedom was just another prison of sorts.

Carolyn called through the door that breakfast was being served, interrupting her thoughts.

Maudie dressed in a brown print skirt she'd found in the clothes press, and a man's cream-colored shirt she'd found in the back of a bureau drawer in her room. She used lacy black stocking garters to hold the sleeves up from the cuffs, and they puffed out in a becoming manner. She tied a pale yellow scarf at a jaunty angle around her neck, then went down to breakfast.

"If the Weston freight party were to arrive today, Polly, what time would that be?" Maudie took a chair at the end of the long pine dining table around which were already seated the other five tenants of the boardinghouse.

"Could be anytime," Polly told her. "If they don't get in before sundown, then most likely it'll be tomorrow."

"If it makes it at all," Taryn whispered dramatically.

"If the Indians don't get it," another woman muttered. She was dour-faced, not much older than herself, Maudie discerned, with a matronly bosom which she rested on the dining table.

"Arletta," Polly said sternly, "don't blame every freight delay on the poor Indians."

"Well, they're the reason no stage coach comes here. It was awful riding in those wagons." Arletta pouted. "We're actresses, not mining hardware, after all."

"Coach lines have been trying to get here, but something always stops them," Polly explained to Maudie. "Deadwood and the other towns in the gulch have barely settled, so there are no real roads. Those that do exist more often than not are flooded over."

"Or mudded over," Maudie added. "What is it about the mud in this place?"

"The Whitewood and Deadwood Creeks overflow periodically. Then there's the people's garbage, and of course there's the manure from every four-legged animal that walks into town," an actress named Nancy Springer explained with a haughty sniff. Nancy, while still rather youthful, clearly would be cast in character roles like the heroine's maiden aunt, Maudie thought. She had gray-streaked coarse dark hair pulled back into a doughnut at the nape of her neck, and a pinched face with a pinched nose upon which perched a pair of tiny gold-rimmed spectacles pinched together over small brown eyes.

"And some two-legged ones, I suspect." Maudie wrinkled her nose. "The stench is abominable."

"Not as bad as it will be late in summer," a woman named Lula Gale said with disdain. "With any luck I'll be out of here by then."

"Lula doesn't like it here," Taryn told Maudie. "She's our wardrobe mistress. The back rooms of the theater are dark and dingy, and it's difficult for her to see back there."

Lula loudly slurped her coffee. "And I can't keep the doors open because of the mud and all the drunks. Place is a sewer if you ask me."

"Why don't they build more boardwalks along the storefronts and street crossings, and of course the stage doors?" Maudie asked.

"They did once," Arletta answered.

"Why'd they take them up?"

"They didn't. The boardwalks dammed the drainage holes in the streets and just broke up. The rest are under the mud someplace."

"Lord," Maudie muttered. She downed a breakfast of hot cakes and ham fit for a wrangler, aware that the women were watching her with fascination.

"You don't care how much food you put away, do you?" Arletta asked directly.

"I've always had a big appetite," Maudie said.

"Don't you worry about getting fat?" Taryn asked. "I mean, I eat like a bird so I'll get good ladies' parts in the plays. Mr. LaFountain says no female who lets herself go stays in the theater very long."

"Who's he?" Maudie sipped her coffee.

"Our esteemed director," Arletta answered breathlessly.

"Madame Carew said a woman who eats like a man will never get a husband," Nancy sniffed.

"Why would any woman want a husband?" Maudie sniffed back. "What's she need with one? A woman can do anything for herself a man can do for her."

"Not everything," Taryn giggled, blushing.

"Well, I wouldn't starve myself for any man. He'd only turn me into an out-of-shape, overworked servant with a bunch of children he ignores, while he's out looking at women who are starving themselves or stuffing themselves into ungodly contraptions."

The three actresses stared at her. She knew what they were thinking. They wished they could enjoy food the way she did and still maintain a trim shape. They suggested through eyebrow communication, that per-

78

haps she wore one of those new French corsets that all the women were talking about.

"Phatty Thompson stopped by this morning," Polly broke the tension in the room. "Seems anxious for the money he says you owe him, Maudie."

Maudie lowered her fork, sighing. "I know. While that was the worst ordeal in travelling I've ever experienced, I supposed a debt is a debt. Paying Mr. Thompson will just about put me where I am at this moment. Penniless. Except I'll have some clothes, if my things arrive in one piece."

"Will you come to the opera house today, Maudie?" An actress of dubious age who called herself Jewel Diamond spoke for the first time. Jewel appeared to have a sweet disposition, the kind of woman who would never argue with a director no matter how wrong his direction might be. "I heard we're starting rehearsals again."

"Yes, soon as I get to the bank and then do a little shopping. I do hope there'll be a part for me in the company."

The women suddenly froze in concert and stared at her.

"Did I say something wrong?" Maudie scanned their faces.

"No respectable woman goes shopping on Monday afternoons in Deadwood," Polly said. "That's when the upstairs girls do their shopping."

"Then perhaps it will be less crowded," Maudie said, pushing her chair back and rising. "Or not, judging on how few women I saw when I arrived yesterday.

In any case, their presence won't bother me. I hope mine doesn't bother them."

"She won't last long here," Maudie heard Jewel say as she carried her dishes to the kitchen.

"With any luck," Maudie responded under her breath, and headed out the door.

At the base of the Williams Street stairs the famed gold camp of Deadwood stretched in front of her. She likened the speed with which the town had sprung up to the way mushrooms grew overnight if the temperature and fertilizer were exactly right. At first, the way it looked like a wild clump springing out of a pile of debris, Maudie wondered what had made her think that Deadwood was the place she'd get her life on course. Must have been the homey tasting chicken and biscuits she'd eaten before going to bed. Or perhaps it was the company she'd kept over dinner. She tried to force the thought of Cole Branch away and was disturbed at how much effort it took to do so.

Her walk took her into the heart of town, and she grew fascinated with it. Everywhere were tents and canvas-sided buildings with false wood fronts, signs of every size and shape proclaiming saloons, shops, restaurants, hotels, and more saloons. Tattered red and white banners from the Fourth of July Centennial celebration still fluttered in the wind. A dirty bathhouse with a cluttered front stood at the end of one street.

Deadwood was supposed to be the biggest of the gold settlements that had sprung up in the Black Hills. She'd expected a real city. Though there were many people about, even at this hour of the morning, Deadwood's Main Street was nothing more than a meandering muddy gash about fifty feet wide, with a placer mine occupying the center.

So this was the new El Dorado everybody had been talking about. In the papers she'd read accounts of "gold sprouting from every peak in the Black Hills," and that nearly ten thousand people had moved to the Gulch before the cry of "gold!" was barely out of the first prospector's mouth. It was clear to her that the prospect of getting rich, no matter the odds or the dangers involved, was a magnet for all kinds. The crowd along the street was a mix of dirt-covered miners, buckskin-clad hunters, slick gamblers and dandies, New England puritans, Chinese in loose gray cotton pants and shirts, drunks, children, prostitutes. And Indians who'd been here all along. Maudie scanned their faces as she ambled along a partially reconstructed boardwalk.

The air buzzed with industriousness. Saws in musical rhythm sliced into fragrant new wood and hammers rang out in syncopated rhythm. How many times had she heard and smelled the construction of theatrical sets?

Gamblers called those who were feeling lucky to their green-clothed tables; a preacher's impassioned cry called for men to consider their spiritual health; a freighter called for cargo to be picked up and distributed. They could be stage managers, roustabouts, or riggers. Everywhere wheels turned in thick mud churned loudly in the clear damp air like the sound of excited theater patrons arriving in their rigs and carriages on opening night.

The wood-tossed hillside beyond was a towering

backdrop to the town. A mass of fallen trees was a chilling reminder of the tornado, then turned into burnt timber and blown into mass of landlocked flotsam and jetsam, was the devastation of nature that had given Deadwood its name.

And here she was looking for . . . what? More dead wood with which to clutter her life? Or hope, like the shoots of new grass that were peeking through the debris?

It struck Maudie that the signs and false fronts of the buildings were like playbills and stage sets—it was behind their names, behind their flimsy walls and alleys where the real story was played out. Deadwood could be the biggest production in which Maudie'd ever appeared, and this one of her most demanding roles.

She passed the Big Horn Store, merely a giant tent set up practically in the middle of the street. She'd have to go to the Miners & Mechanics Bank before she could begin shopping for the necessities she needed.

Just down the boardwalk at its door she met Cole Branch striding toward her. She decided that his sheriff costume, which she noticed was a bit wrinkled, seemed somehow to fit him better in the morning light. She studied his mustache. It was a good one, she decided. Well-constructed.

"Starting your investigation into Madame Carew's death bright and early, aren't you, Sheriff?" she baited him.

"And a gracious good morning to you, too, Miss . . . Dearden, wasn't it?"

"Still is. Good morning." She dipped her head and continued on to the bank.

"Wait a minute, Miss Dearden. Could I have a word with you?"

"I think I have time to spare at least one."

"Why do I get the feeling you don't like me?"

Maudie tipped her head, scrutinizing his face. "Let's see, that's . . ." she counted on her fingers, "ten words for you. So I guess I have to answer in ten. I don't know why you get a feeling like that."

"I think you do."

Maudie's gaze passed his shoulders. Perhaps today she'd begin to learn something about Cole Branch. On the way to learning everything else she needed to learn, that is. She mustn't forget why she came to Deadwood Gulch in the first place.

She collected her thoughts, then returned his direct gaze. "I've been wondering about you, Sheriff," she said at last.

"I'm flattered."

"Don't be. There's something about you that doesn't quite ring true to me. I don't know what it is yet, but I plan to find out."

"You'll be disappointed. There's nothing at all complicated about me."

"We'll see. Further, I don't think you've been doing your job as sheriff."

"Madame Carew again, right? Why are you so determined to prove her death was a murder?"

"I'm not. That is, I'd simply like to know the truth."

"Why? Was she a relative of yours? Nobody gets so interested in a death out here unless they've got a stake in it somehow. Like an inheritance or something.

Money's the only thing anybody puts a value on out here. Certainly not human life."

"I'm not from 'out here'," she retorted. "A suspicious death in any theater is of concern to me. I mean, if it can happen to one actress, it can happen to us all. Since I plan to work in that company, I'd like to be certain it's absolutely legitimate. Safe. Surely you can understand that."

"Maybe."

"Well, if *you* can't, I'm certain Wild Bill Hickok can. He knew Carew. I'll just ask him what he thinks about her death."

"Just like that, you think you're going to get help from Wild Bill Hickok." Cole chuckled.

"Yes."

"You'll find him in the saloon. If you don't place any importance on respectability, feel free to fight your way through a room full of gamblers and degenerates to get to his table. *If* you get there in one piece, and then *if* he's sober, maybe, if you're lucky, he'll acknowledge your presence."

"He'll talk to me. I've heard he's partial to women. And . . . he's an actor."

"We've established that's debatable."

Cole tipped his hat as several prostitutes pushed by them on the sidewalk. The way they looked at Cole suggested to Maudie that he knew them well, if not intimately. A couple of the women ran their hands daringly over his body which he seemed not to mind, practically welcomed it. She lifted an eyebrow and controlled the involuntary pruning of her lips. It shouldn't matter to her who he was intimate with.

"Mornin', Candy. Mornin' Brandy." Maudie watched as two white-blondes, who looked like twin sisters passed him with suggestive smiles.

"Nice to see you, Beauty." She wasn't. She had a long horse face and unnaturally black, stringy hair.

"Dorine, you're looking fine this morning," he greeted a woman with the largest breasts and tiniest waist Maudie had ever seen. Her dyed red hair rivaled Maudie's naturally dark flame mane.

"Well, Miss Dolly," he said to a girl who appeared young enough to play with dolls. With her fat yellow braids and pink frock, she looked like she should be propped up in a toy store window in St. Louis.

"What've you got in that basket?" Cole asked Dolly. The girl proudly lifted the wicker top. Cole exclaimed, "Ah, what a lovely cat. Seems to have a nice disposition. I've seen at least one that came in yesterday who doesn't." He looked playfully at Maudie.

"When you and your friends have finished visiting," Maudie said as she spun around and opened the door to the bank, "why don't you meander down to the theater? You might learn something." She disappeared inside the building to a chorus of muffled comments from the girls and an amused laugh from Cole.

Maudie paused just inside the doorway. The bank was as shiny as a brand new penny. She scanned its small public area, and noted beyond the teller window an enormous brass-fronted safe, which was set in a decorative framework as if it were a piece of art on display. The atmosphere was bright as newly washed gold from the sun streaming through the front window bathing walls of new wood.

Only one teller was working, a short, square-bodied man with a flushed face and heavily pomaded hair. A wood-and-brass nameplate perched above his polished cubicle identified him as Mr. Buford. He was busy with a woman customer.

The transaction was being discussed by the two in hushed yet urgent tones. As far as Maudie could determine, Buford seemed unable to comprehend the woman's request.

"I'll be with you in a moment," he addressed Maudie over the woman's shoulder.

The woman turned slightly toward Maudie, then back quickly to Mr. Buford. She pushed an envelope at him, insisting quietly yet firmly that he take it and follow the instructions inside. Then she turned and hurried toward the door without once acknowledging Maudie's presence. Maudie did not catch more than a glimpse of her face hidden behind a wide-brimmed ecru straw hat, but she admired her statuesque carriage and the manner in which her pale green linen skirt and jacket hugged the back of her softly rounded shape. The slight limp in the woman's gait seemed only to enhance her grace and dignity.

Maudie stepped forward.

"How do you do," she said, leaning back to read the man's nameplate again, "Mr. Buford."

Buford shoved the previous client's envelope aside. "Good morning, good morning, and welcome, Miss . . . ?" Buford's already flushed face deepened in color as he peered through his barred window up past her face and fastened his awestruck gaze on Maudie's hair.

"Dearden. A deposit has been made in my name, and I'm here to make a partial withdrawal."

Buford simply stared at her.

"Mr. Buford? Would you check my account please?"

Buford took out a handkerchief and mopped his brow. "Yes, yes of course. What was the name again?"

"Dearden."

"Just one moment."

Maudie watched as the man waddled to a small back room. She heard him open and close several drawers, heard papers shuffle. Then he waddled back to the teller's window and removed his spectacles.

"Sorry, miss, there is no account in your name."

Maudie's stomach clutched anxiously. "Are you certain?"

"Of course I am certain." Buford sniffed and raised his double-jowled chin until the folds settled over his stiff shirt collar.

"Perhaps you misunderstood the name. Dearden. D-e-a-r-d-e-n. Would you mind checking again?"

Buford glared into her face, no longer fascinated by her hair. Maudie knew her urgent second request had insulted him. He obviously took great pride in the organization of his accounts. Her gaze insisted he look into them once again, silently announcing she would not leave until he did so.

Buford sighed through his nostrils. "Very well." He turned and retraced his steps to the back room. This time she heard only one drawer open and close loudly before he returned, his way of telling her he knew his business.

"As I told you, there is no account in your name."

"But I was led to believe . . ."

"No doubt you were," he said smugly.

Maudie lifted her own strong chin. "Mr. Buford, I've been assured that a number of Wells Fargo certificates would be delivered to this bank last week and placed in an account with my name on it."

Buford looked askance at her and narrowed his pink-rimmed pale eyes. "Mm-hmm."

Maudie's ire threatened to erupt. "Are you suggesting that the Wells Fargo Company is not to be trusted?"

"Not if it is the same company who paid for your luxurious travel arrangements to Deadwood, Miss . . . Dearden, did you say?"

Was there no one who'd missed her arrival yesterday?

"I'd like to see the manager, please."

"I *am* the manager."

Maudie was determined not to let this irritating man see her fuming. "Perhaps the messenger was delayed," she returned with studied calm.

"Yes, perhaps," Buford said with exaggerated doubt. His eyes lingered over her bosom. "Perhaps a loan could be arranged. With the proper collateral, that is," he whispered hoarsely, licking his thick lips.

Maudie narrowed her eyes. "I'm afraid my need would never be great enough, nor your meager holdings attractive enough to warrant such a distasteful business venture." She curled the corner of her mouth in a satisfied smile when the color drained from Buford's face. "I'll check again tomorrow to see if the messenger has arrived."

And every day after that until you wipe that smirk off your fat lips, Maudie thought. She'd never demanded respect for herself just because she was a woman, but she did expect common courtesy. She never ceased to be amazed at how preconceived notions of convention remained unaltered, walked hand-in-hand with age-old expectations, man and woman.

Maudie turned and, without another word to the man, walked quickly out of the bank and onto the busy boardwalk. The warm sun washed over her in a soothing wave.

Buford could be right, she reasoned. Perhaps there would be no deposit made in her name. But how could that happen? Golden was a real Pinkerton agent, she'd seen proof of it. And he needed her as much as she needed him. They had a business deal. He'd said the money would be waiting for her. Where was it? She'd have to think of something on her own now.

As she walked resolutely along the intermittent boardwalk, she idly noted that men outnumbered women in Deadwood as much as the quest for gold outweighed all basic human need. It was just as well, she decided. These men took from women the same greedy way they took gold from the earth.

As she pondered over this thought, Maudie came upon a shop with a display window artfully arranged with ladies' hats and accessories. It was the first suggestion of gentility outside of Miss Parrott's boardinghouse she'd seen in Deadwood. She could use some softness right now, she thought, use some nearness to a lighter part of life. She peered through the display window just in time to see Cole Branch passing through a curtained door at the back of the shop. Maudie squinted through the glass. Cole Branch shopping in a ladies' millinery shop? This she had to see!

Inside the shop Maudie took in a deep breath of a lovely perfume that reminded her of the flower vendors setting up their carts on a Brooklyn morning. She smiled to herself, pausing to admire a particularly elegant hat of unique design.

Cole Branch, his Stetson pushed to the back of his head, was studying several pieces of fabric. What in the world? Was he hiring the milliner to fashion a new hat for him? Hardly. Perhaps he was ordering something for a lady. Maudie turned slightly and gave him a sidelong glance. What kind of lady would Cold Branch have in his life? she wondered. She turned back to the hat. Why in the world should she care about that?

She heard voices murmuring beyond a tall open-backed étagère upon which several colorful fabric flowers, feathers, hand-painted scarves, and swatches of sheer fabrics were displayed. A man and a woman were speaking in hushed tones. As she wandered past the display Maudie saw the pale green linen suit and straw hat of the woman who'd been in the bank.

Maudie was entranced by the woman's hands, noting their fine-boned elegance as they turned over a square of woven fabric in muted blues and lavenders. She admired the woman's fluid grace, no movement wasted, no nervous fluttering. Who was she?

Suddenly the woman glanced her way as if sensing Maudie's presence. She pressed the fabric into the man's hands, turned away from Maudie, and hurried out of the shop. This time her limp seemed more pronounced. The man she had been speaking with, who was of slight build and had an impeccable elegance about himself, watched her leave. He sighed when the door closed behind her. Maudie knew that look. The man was smitten by the woman in the straw hat. She warmed inside, all traces of the anger and disappointment she had carried with her from the bank vanishing in an instant.

"Well, well, it's still Miss Dearden, no doubt," Cole Branch said behind her. "And what brings you into Bartles Millinery this fine day?"

As she turned to face him, he slipped off his hat. "I might ask the same of you," she responded sweetly. "Shopping for a gift for one of your lady friends? Oh, of course not. You wouldn't want to show partiality. You're buying something for each of them." Maudie checked her sarcasm. What had come over her to say such a thing?

"May I show you something of my latest creation, mademoiselle?" a male voice said behind her before he could respond.

Maudie turned. A slight man in a trim gray morning coat, with silver streaks at the temples of his head of full, dark hair, smiled up at her. The man who had been talking to the woman in the straw hat.

Cole Branch stepped forward. "What's this? Speechless?" he asked Maudie. When Maudie glared at him, he looked properly mollified, then offered a proper introduction. "Miss Maudie Boone Dearden, actress"—he gestured to his right—"Mr. Theodore Bartles, milliner"—he gestured to his left.

"A male milliner. I've never known one before," Maudie smiled, holding out her right hand. "How perfectly delightful."

"How do you do Miss Dearden?" Bartles's smile was as warm and engulfing as the hand he closed over hers. His gray eyes sparkled in appreciation. "I'm honored to make your acquaintance. I adore the theater. What play will I see you in?"

"Thank you, Mr. Bartles. How refreshing to meet a gentleman in Deadwood . . . at last." She sent a cursory glance toward Cole, then tilted her head down to smile genuinely into Bartles's sincere dark eyes. "I don't know what play they'll be doing, but I hope to become a member of the Variety Theater company."

"Splendid!" Bartles clapped his long-fingered hands. "Call me Theo. I've heard they'll be opening Madame Carew's *Scarlet Lady* again. It's a wonderful play, but of course it will have to be recast." His voice lowered to a respectful timbre. "You heard about Madame's unfortunate accident."

"Yes, I did. Just awful." Something lit in Maudie's mind. "I take it you know something about her death, since the sheriff is here."

"Oh no . . ." Theo started.

"Mr. Bartles has suffered his own loss," Cole broke in. "Someone has been coming into his shop and pilfering cloth and thread and . . . things."

Maudie stared at him with raised eyebrows.

"I know it doesn't seem like much," Theo said as if reading her mind, "but these things are important to me. As I've explained to the sheriff, these pieces of fabric, fasteners, thread, and the like are difficult to obtain and necessary to my work."

"I understand, Mr. Bartles. And has the sheriff uncovered any clues as to the identity of the perpetrator?" Maudie kept her gaze on Theo's face.

"I don't know. Have you, Sheriff?"

"I'm afraid not," Cole answered, keeping his gaze fixed on the milliner. "I can't even tell how she got in here."

"Assuming it's a female, of course," Maudie said sharply.

"Of course it's a female. What would a man want with ladies' hat fabric?" Cole responded.

"What indeed," Theo put in mildly.

Both Maudie and Cole stared at him, then at each other, then burst out laughing.

"Since you're the only milliner in Deadwood," Maudie said, "I think it's safe to assume you are not stealing from yourself."

"Very safe," Theo concurred with good-nature officiousness.

"Well, don't you worry, Theo, with Sheriff Branch on the scene, you can be assured this case will be solved before the next centennial celebration!"

"I appreciate your confidence," Cole said sarcastically, taking out a cheroot from the shirt pocket beneath his black leather vest. "And here I was about to inform you of the arrival of Weston's freighters. I believe you have an interest in the goods they bear? But then I'm sure you've all the news about their whereabouts already." He licked the end of the cheroot, placed it between his front teeth, and bobbed it up and down.

"The freighters! Where are they?" Maudie said excitedly.

"Pardon?" Cole drawled.

Maudie knew what he was up to. "All right. I'm sorry if I offended you. I've no doubt you'll do a stellar job on this investigation . . . or any other, for that matter. Now, where are Weston's freighters?"

"Thank you, I think. Gaston's Freight Office beyond the Big Horn Store."

"Thank you. Theo, it was a pleasure to meet you. I'm sure we'll see each other again," Maudie called as she opened the shop door to leave.

"I know we will, Miss Dearden. At the theater. I'm particularly fond of the theater."

Maudie watched him, remembering how he had looked at the woman in the straw hat. Theo Bartles's fondness for the theater had something to do with that woman, she was certain.

"If you need any help with your things, let me know," Cole said as she closed the door.

Out on the boardwalk, Maudie was surprised to discover that her hands were trembling. Was it the excitement of learning Weston's freighters had arrived? Or was it being near Cole Branch again? She wondered about his offer to help her with her belongings.

She wondered a lot of things about Cole Branch. What had she learned about him so far? His clothes were definitely a costume of sorts. He hadn't been a sheriff for long, she was certain of that, and perhaps had never been one before. She sensed a theatrical comportment about him, oddly enough.

And she knew all kinds of women were attracted to him. That wasn't the kind of thing she'd particularly cared to learn. Something told her she'd have to watch herself as carefully as she planned to watch him.

Chapter 5

"Lovely woman, Miss Dearden." Theo watched out his shop window as Maudie walked away. "Don't you agree, Sheriff?"

Cole paced the length of the millinery shop, lifting fabric bolts, looking under shelves. He didn't know exactly what he should be looking for, but he wanted to make a good show of it for Bartles.

"Sheriff?" Theo turned from the window. "Mr. Branch?"

Cole stood up quickly and spun around. "I'm sorry, did you say something?"

"I did indeed. I was remarking on feminine charms. One woman's in particular."

"I guess I had my mind on other things."

Theo nodded knowingly. "You're not finding this particularly easy, are you, Sheriff Branch?"

Cole dropped his gaze momentarily, then addressed the milliner directly. "Well, I am pretty new at it. Never been a sheriff before."

"Yes, but everyone knows you're the right man for the job."

"Maybe not everyone." Cole had to admit that he himself had doubts about his effectiveness as the town's lawman.

"Don't be modest. I'm not the only one who will never forget how you saved Mr. Pettigrew from getting shot in the back that day."

Cole returned to his search knowing he was going to be embarrassed by Theo's speech.

"I tell you, Sheriff, we were all stunned when Mr. Pettigrew refused to defend his daughter's honor to that young prospector. Never thought he'd turn and walk away like that. When the young whelp pulled his gun and took aim at Mr. Pettigrew's back, everyone froze. Except you."

"Now, Mr. Bartles, it was just a . . . a reflex. I didn't think about it. Besides, Mr. Pettigrew's religion prevents him from defending himself. I was obliged to do it for him."

"That's exactly what I'm saying. Nobody moved except you. The way you grabbed that gun out of the holster of a passing citizen and shot that weapon right out of the prospector's hand before he could even crook his finger over the trigger, I tell you, it was thrilling! You're an amazing shootist, Sheriff."

"Well, I don't know about that. I'm just glad nobody got hurt." Cole shifted uncomfortably under Theo's praise.

"Yes, sir, the federal marshal knew a good man when he saw one. And just in time, too. The ruffians hereabouts would have done the city in before it even got started if it hadn't been for you."

Cole touched his Stetson and headed for the door. "Thanks, Mr. Bartles. Let me know if you see or hear anything more about your lost items. I'll be back again."

"Thank you, Sheriff. I appreciate your interest. Good day."

Out on the street, Cole decided to take a turn around the town. Bartles was right. He was having difficulty being a sheriff. But maybe it was growing on him.

He stepped into muddy Main Street and crossed to his office. His office. He went in and stood near the desk. His desk. He ran his fingers over the new wood.

He'd arrived in Deadwood in the heat of the gold rush barely three months before on his way to California. The place was an El Dorado to countless men and women, and he figured it would be a haven to him. He could blend in with the countless misfits from elsewhere who were thronging to Deadwood by the wagonload. It had seemed like a perfect place to take his time passing through.

The shooting incident Theo had recounted for him had occurred in the presence of a federal marshal who'd come to set up an office for Wild Bill Hickok. Hickok hadn't arrived by the time the marshal had to leave. He pressed Cole into taking the job and Cole had reluctantly accepted. At least he was earning some money and had a room free of charge.

"Some job for an actor," Cole muttered, and dropped down onto the wooden chair. He propped his feet up on the desktop, then lowered them quickly when he saw street matter dropping off his heels.

Actually it *wasn't* that bad a job for an actor, when he thought about it. He had no problem acting the role, and most of the time he even enjoyed it. Nobody truly expected him to arrest anyone on serious charges. Deadwood was a town without a government, a place where law and order had little influence and no one seemed to care. People generally did what they wanted to do here whenever they wanted to do it. The job of sheriff was all show, just like the town, and he liked being a member of such a diverse cast of characters. But, as usual in every brand-new town, theaters opened and acting troupes arrived.

Cole's mind vaguely ambled backward over his life. He had literally been born in a trunk in a cheap hotel somewhere in a western gold town his parents were appearing in at the time. Mary and Jared Braddock were actors in a traveling theater company. From the moment Cole was born he traveled right along with them, and before he was four years old he'd made his own debut. He became known as "Braddock's Bad Boy," appearing in skits as the quintessential rotten kid.

He smiled now, remembering what a great life it was for a child. He loved being around all those people. No schools, no teachers, none, that is, except for his parents and a cast of other talented actors. And they did a damned good job of it, he allowed now. Taught him every trick of the trade, from juggling to trick shooting.

But thinking about his parents led to other, darker memories. Was it the nomadic life, the lack of a real home, the almost suffocating closeness of a theater company that alienated actors from the simple pleasures other people enjoyed? Cole remembered how his parents fought, remembered how his father drank himself into oblivion almost every night and sometimes couldn't go on stage because of his inebriation. And he remembered how he watched it all as if he were a member of the audience rather than a principal player. When he was sixteen he left them in some nameless town and started a journey west, deciding then and there that an actor's life was no life for him.

Not long after that, his mother had died of a lung disease. He never got over blaming himself for not being there to take care of her. When he'd figured he was man enough, he set out to make peace with his father. He found him in a town in Missouri, working in a play. Cole meant to surprise him at curtain close, but a terrible accident had occurred, and before the play was over, Jared Braddock lay dead on the stage floor.

"You were damned good, Daddy. The best." Cole brushed the corner of one eye.

He'd vowed never to go near a theater again after that. And he'd managed to keep that vow, too, until recently. As sheriff of Deadwood he'd been forced to enter the Deadwood Variety Theater to make an initial investigation into the actress Clara Carew's unfortunate demise.

He swallowed hard, then rose. He needed another walk around town, needed people around him. He needed to talk to someone.

* * *

Maurice Gaston's Freight Office was nothing more than a log-and-canvas shelter that served as a repository for all manner of incoming goods. By the looks of it, Maudie decided, nothing was ever outgoing. Crates and boxes and bales tumbled one upon the other with no attempt at organization, much less concern for anything fragile. Teams of oxen stood beyond the building, so covered with mud it was impossible to know what color they had been before their journey.

Men crowded inside the canvas walls, shouted and waved at a barrel-chested hulk of a man behind a counter at a side entrance. "Hey Moose," one let loose directly behind Maudie, causing her to jump, "you got a lady on the premises!"

Maurice Gaston grunted something unintelligible in a loud voice, all the while shifting a fat cigar around his thick lips, letting it rest occasionally in the space where one front tooth was missing. When Maudie approached the counter, he spat the cigar to the floor and grinned a yellow-toothed greeting.

"What can I do fer you, mademoiselle?" His French accent was as thick as the hairy arm that tore a battered straw hat from his greasy hair.

Maudie had to shout above the voices of the crowd. "Some things of mine were to be delivered by Mr. Weston. I understand his wagons arrived this morning."

"Oui, they did," Gaston said sadly. "So sorry."

"Sorry? Why?" Maudie felt moistness form just under her bosom, her personal sign that panic was about to set in.

"Accident. Holdup. Who knows?" Gaston said,

101

waving his arms. "Much goods lost. What's left . . ." He motioned indeterminately behind him.

Maudie rushed to a pile of battered trunks and debris, and spied her bandbox near the bottom, nearly folded in half by a heavy crate. She tried to pry it loose with an iron bar laying nearby, but to no avail. Frustration mounted inside her. Even with the strength she knew she possessed, she couldn't lift the load. She sank down on her knees and clamped her eyes closed. She was in a rat hole of a town, had no money, had none of her own things, and wasn't even wearing her own clothes. What on earth was she going to do now?

"I didn't hear your answer clearly," a voice addressed her from above.

She snapped her head up. Cole Branch was standing over her.

"What?"

"I said I would help you with your things if you needed me, but I don't think I quite heard your answer." He scanned the battered pile of trunks and boxes. "Are all these yours? Whew! Maybe I should have thought twice about offering my services. Ah well, I never go back on my word."

"I don't need you to help me," she sputtered. "I can do everything myself." She tried to stand, but her skirt caught under her boots and she dropped back down.

"I've no doubt about that," Cole came back, a teasing glint in his eyes. "Just as soon as you're able to stand up. Here, let me help you." Before she could protest, he'd slipped his hands under her arms and lifted her to her feet. "Is this what you're trying to get at?" He pointed to her crushed bandbox at the bottom of the pile.

She nodded woodenly.

Cole used the crowbar and lifted the offending crate as if it were a feather pillow. It dropped with a thud accompanied by the sound of tinkling glass. Maudie winced. Gathering renewed strength, she thanked him with tight lips, then reached down and pulled her flattened bandbox away from the pile.

"Is that it, then? Looks like you're going to have a lot of shopping to do." Cole settled his hat down over his forehead the way Theo had instructed.

"No, it isn't. There were trunks . . ." She turned one way and then the other.

"Let's keep looking," Cole said with sympathy, "I'm sure you'll find everything."

Together they conducted a thorough search of the rest of the building, observing anyone who made a claim for goods and hauled anything away. It was all over in an hour, and she was left with only the bandbox.

Sadly she looked inside the case, knowing what she'd find. A few pieces of glass jewelry smashed to bits, several lace handkerchiefs covered with grime, a watersoaked playbill from a Cheyenne theater, and a container of hardened face powder. In perfect shape, untouched by devastation, lay the stolen fan and silver champagne flute. She held one up in each hand and stared dumbstruck at the pieces.

She dropped down on what was left of some broken crates. "Nothing's left. I have nothing," she said matter-of-factly. She wasn't despairing, simply stating a fact.

Cole dropped down beside her and placed an arm around her shoulders. Maudie knew she should have pulled away from such a public display, but she didn't. Propriety hadn't meant much to her before, why should it now? His arm felt comforting, sincere.

"Pardone, mademoiselle, monsieur," Gaston addressed them.

"Yes?" Maudie looked up wanly.

"Gaston's store 'round back. We sell, we buy. Makes no nevermind. You sell?" He pointed at the objects now laying limply in her hands.

"No, Gaston, I don't think Miss Dearden wants to sell family heirlooms." Cole got to his feet.

"Heirlooms worth even more," Gaston assured.

"They're all she has left. She'd never part with them."

Maudie listened to the exchange glumly, and looked down at the only two items she possessed, items that hadn't belonged to her in the first place.

"They're not heirlooms," she said, standing. "Not my heirlooms, anyway."

Cole gave her a quizzical look.

"You sell?" Gaston asked hopefully.

"I sell."

Five minutes later Cole and Maudie left Gaston's New and Secondhand Store and Freight Office, she with a little pouch of gold dust tied in a doubled handkerchief. Gaston had taken pity on her and offered her thirty dollars for the two items. She'd managed to get him up to forty, but at twenty dollars an ounce for gold dust, the pouch offered little comfort where Maudie's finances were concerned. Hardly enough to live on, and nothing to put toward passage to San Francisco. She was glad she'd thus far eluded Phatty Thompson; she would have to continue to until he left town. But she knew it was only a matter of time until he tracked her down to demand payment. She'd just have to dazzle him with footwork.

"Anything else I can help you with this morning?" Cole stopped outside the freight office door and shaded his eyes in the warming sun. "As you know, we sheriffs are here to serve."

Maudie looked up into his dark gaze. For once she didn't have the heart to come back with a cutting remark. He had made her difficult situation easier to bear with his presence. "Thank you, no. You've been very kind. I have to get over to the Variety. I suspect I'm already late for rehearsal."

"From what I hear, that's a criminal offense. I hope I won't have to investigate yet another case in that theater."

This time Maudie couldn't help herself. "What do you mean 'another?' You haven't begun investigating the first." She smiled teasingly. "Thank you again . . . Sheriff." Then she turned and set out for the Deadwood Variety Theater.

Banker Buford caught up with her just as she was about to go inside the theater. "Miss Dearden," he puffed, "I'm so glad I found you. I fear an apology is in order."

"Really," Maudie said stiffly.

"Yes, there was indeed a deposit left in your name.

It came in just before you did, and I hadn't time to record it before you requested funds. Please come by any time and I'll arrange a withdrawal." Flustered, Buford hurried away.

Maudie stepped into the theater lobby, relief flooding over her. She hesitated then, puzzling over Buford's words. The deposit was made just before she'd gone in. She'd seen only one other person in the bank that morning—the woman in the green suit and straw hat.

Maudie's mind filled with questions, but before she could think on them, Taryn rushed through a curtained door and gestured to her.

"Maudie," she whispered, "I'm so glad you're here. I told Mr. LaFountain about you and I think he has a part you'd be interested in. Come on!"

Maudie followed her into the theater and up to the stage.

"Mr. LaFountain?" Taryn called to a portly, bald man who stood center stage under a single work light. "Here's the one we were telling you about." She urged Maudie to the stage.

"You're late!" LaFountain boomed with an English accent that made it sound as if she were "light."

"I'm afraid I wasn't certain of an exact time I was to be here," Maudie said evenly.

"Don't make the same mistake twice." He handed her a script for *Scarlet Lady*. "Learn the lines marked. Rehearsals begin tomorrow at nine sharp. That's all."

Maudie watched LaFountain's rounded back in a black frock coat and felt the floorboards give when he descended the four stairs from the stage to the orchestra-level floor. She peered behind her. Arletta, Jewel, and Nancy stared glumly at their scripts. Taryn eagerly flipped through hers, her smile widening with each page.

A slight young man with brown hair and a pretty face stood beside them watching with disinterested eyes. He strutted toward Maudie and extended a hand.

"I'm Sterling Hale, your leading man."

Maudie accepted the proffered hand. It was limp as wilted cabbage. "I'm Maudie Boone Dearden." She offered a warm smile.

"I know. You didn't get Carew's role, so you're not above me." He strutted away.

Taryn fluttered over to her. "Isn't he wonderful?" she gushed.

"I have no idea," Maudie said. "What's he talking about?"

"Did you look at your script? You have the second lead. Sterling's the only male in the play."

"So he thinks of himself as the second lead below Madame Carew. Since I'm the new member of the company, he wants to make sure I know what my place is."

Taryn looked down and scraped her toe along the stage floor.

"Don't worry, I don't mind. Why's everybody so glum?" She scanned the faces of the other women.

"Because nothing's changed. Nancy got the part of the old woman who dies in the first act. She always gets that kind of part. Arletta's got two lines at the opening of the second act, and Jewel plays the villainess just like she always did."

"What about you?"

"I got the beautiful young woman's part. Mr. La-Fountain says he'll find a little boy or girl in town to play the part I used to play."

Maudie knew the play well. With Madame Carew gone, Jewel was right for her part. Why hadn't she been cast? And who would play that role?

Taryn read her mind. "I'm so thrilled! Lady Fan's playing Madame's part. That means you and I will play her daughters. Sisters! Isn't that exciting?" She looked in the direction of the stage door.

Maudie followed her gaze and saw the woman in the green suit and straw hat she'd been seeing practically every place she'd been today. The woman turned and headed toward backstage.

"Was that your Lady Fan?" she asked Taryn.

"Yes. Isn't she beautiful?"

"I don't know. I couldn't see her face." Her eyes still on the door, Maudie asked, "Does she have another name?"

"If she does, I've never heard it." Taryn picked up a shawl and flung it around her shoulders. "Are you coming, Maudie? We can start learning our lines tonight after supper."

"I'll be along. You go on without me. I have some business to take care of. Oh, Taryn?"

Taryn turned back to her. "Yes?"

"Would you show me exactly where Madame Carew was standing when the scenery fell on her?"

Taryn looked at her, puzzled. "All right." She walked upstage center. "Why?"

"I just thought I'd say a little prayer for her."

Taryn shrugged, pointed to a spot on the floor, then hurried down the stage stairs and up the center aisle, disappearing behind the entrance draperies.

When she was certain everyone had left the theater, Maudie set her bag down and wandered around the perimeter of the stage. She peered up into the overhead rigging. In the dim light she saw the hemp lengths hanging like a row of gallows, and she shivered. She walked upstage and looked at the wood-framed painted muslin flats. They were as flexible as any she'd ever worked in front of, but with correct mounting on the stage she reasoned they would stay secure no matter what chaotic actions a scene called for. There seemed to be no reason why, under usual theatrical circumstances, any of the scenery pieces, backdrop, or rigging should come crashing down. A closer investigation would have to be conducted, and Maudie didn't feel ready yet to attempt such a thing.

She stood center stage for a long moment, pondering the life of the actress who called herself Madame Clara Carew. She knew she would have to dig very deep to find out more about the woman. Was she using her real name? If so, Maudie was wasting valuable time she could be using to travel toward San Francisco by lingering in Deadwood? Remember the money, she told herself. Remember the agreement you made. Regardless of anything else she might be or pretend to be, Maudie always honored promises. Especially those she made to herself.

Maudie took one last look around, then picked up her script and bag and left by the front entrance.

Maudie was elated. And exhausted. She felt wonderful being in a production rehearsal again, even if it was a play she'd done before, even if the other actors were superstitious about the fact that Madame Carew had died while appearing in it. She had a good meaty role, knew her lines well, and was excited about her work. But the constant reblocking of the scenes by Lawrence LaFountain was draining. She'd never worked with a director who changed his mind so often and in so short a period of time.

The week's rehearsals were almost as exhausting as Maudie's surreptitious investigation into Clara Carew's death. All she'd managed to discover was that everyone in the theater company had disliked Carew.

The other odd thing about the rehearsals was that she'd never played a scene with the mysterious Lady Fan. Cast as one of the character's daughters, Maudie knew they'd appear in scenes together, but LaFountain's erratic direction and scheduling of odd rehearsals never presented the opportunity for her to get close to the woman. And no matter how energetically she tried to arrange what she hoped would look like a chance meeting, Lady Fan seemed always a moment or two out of reach.

Maudie felt she was getting nowhere.

Recently she'd started to observe Cole Branch in the theater. Oddly, she was always aware of his presence before she caught sight of him. Then suddenly their eyes would find each other, lock for a moment, before one of them looked away. What was it that prevented them from acknowledging they'd sought each other out?

One afternoon, she left the theater late, dog tired and hungry. She supposed she'd missed Polly's supper once again, since the other actresses had scurried back to the boardinghouse immediately after rehearsal, and she'd lingered on the pretense of walking through her scene again. She'd wanted to look around some more. As she'd started on another search she saw Lula Gale coming out of the wardrobe, a heavy-skirted costume draped over one arm, a needle held between her lips with a long thread hanging down. Maudie was forced to abandon her idea lest Lula became suspicious. Maybe if she hurried home now, Polly would have saved a little food for her.

She moved resolutely through the jostling, quipping miners and gamblers in the street, avoiding eye contact and watching carefully where she was stepping. She didn't see the immovable object that stopped her until she'd walked right into it, dropping her bag. It was a man.

She looked up past well-built shoulders into a weathered face atop a tall body, into puffy steel blue eyes. Stunned, she stepped back. A slight smile curled the corners of his mouth, slightly obscured by a long brown stallion's tails mustache. Grazing the shoulders of a fringed buckskin shirt, his brown hair was swept back under a wide-brimmed tan hat.

"Ma'am," he said softly, removing his hat. With the other hand he leaned on what appeared to be an oversize shillelagh.

"Excuse me," Maudie said breathlessly. "Wasn't looking where I was going, I guess."

"Bad practice," the tall man answered, bending to pick up her bag. He took a white handkerchief from his shirt pocket and brushed the dirt from it. A dull stain remained. "A little sodium carbonate will take that out fine."

Suddenly the man's expression changed and Maudie felt herself being thrust back against a pair of swinging doors belonging to a building behind her, and pushed to the floor. She froze as she heard the crack of a gunshot and felt a cold whir of air buzzing past her ear. A shattering of glass echoed in her head.

When just as suddenly all was silent, the tall man stepped through the doors. "I apologize for pushing you like that, ma'am." With a groan she defined as one of pain, he bent down to retrieve his cane and hat, then held out a hand to help her to her feet. "If ever I can be of service to you in the future, I will be honored."

He escorted her back outside the swinging doors, donned his hat, then used his cane to push the doors apart and went back inside. Maudie realized then that the building was a saloon.

A young man in an ink-stained white shirt hurried over to her. He held a pencil and paper in his blackened fingers. "Care to make a statement for the *Black Hills Pioneer?* How did it feel when the great Wild Bill Hickok saved your life?"

Maudie's breath caught in her throat. "Wild . . . was that Wild Bill Hickok?" To think she hadn't recognized him! He was much thinner than she'd remembered.

"Yes ma'am, you'd been a goner if he hadn't pushed you into the saloon and winged that crazy galoot."

"He saved my life? Someone was trying to . . . to shoot me?" Maudie was flabbergasted. Did someone want to kill her, too? She didn't think she'd been in Deadwood long enough to annoy anyone that much. And the play hadn't even opened.

"No, not you. Someone was trying to kill *him*. Someone's always going after Wild Bill Hickok."

Maudie was dumbstruck. "That . . . gentleman . . . was Wild Bill? Doesn't seem to be anything very wild about him now."

She turned away from the reporter and peered over the saloon's batwings. Wild Bill sat drinking at a table at the end of the bar facing the door. His hat was still on, his shillelagh leaned against the table, and he'd donned blue-tinted spectacles.

"We heard he just wants to settle down, do some prospectin' and make a strike," the reporter told her.

"I heard he came to Deadwood to be sheriff," Maudie said. "What's the cane for?"

"Got a touch of rheumatism. Fashioned that cane himself from the butt end of a billiard cue. Made of rosewood and heavy as a Sioux war club."

"It looks mean."

The reporter laughed. "It does the job. Eases the pain of walking, and doubles as a weapon."

Maudie smiled. "Like right out of a dime novel." It seemed that life in the west in general, and in Deadwood in particular, was just like theater—nothing was ever truly what it seemed.

"Yep, sure was. Those days of Wild Bill giving a

good story are over," the reporter sighed. "Now Bill just wants to go prospectin'."

Maudie peered over the batwing doors again. "Looks like he's doing most of his prospecting on a green cloth. Is he particular who he cracks a deck with?"

"Nope. Sometimes I think he oughta be. Leads a charmed life, I swear."

"I'll say. I saw him on the stage once . . ."

"Oh, his actin' days are over too, ma'am," the reporter assured her.

"Good thing."

"Yes, ma'am."

The doors to Nuttall and Mann's Number Ten Saloon swung in the air behind Maudie as she pushed purposefully through them. The piano player escalated an arpeggio to the topmost key, then dropped his hands in his lap and grinned wide-eyed at her. Maudie strode up to the table where arguably the west's greatest hero sat alone.

"Mr. Hickok?"

"Ma'am?" He stood up.

Maudie noticed his fancy brocaded waistcoat and the brace of pearl-handled pistols tucked butt-end-first into gray pinstriped trousers. She held out her right hand. He took it tentatively.

"I'm Maudie Boone Dearden. I want to thank you for saving my life, and . . ."

"Boone . . . ?"

Maudie watched as he considered her, looking her over as if seeing her for the first time. "I'd like to ask you a few questions, if you don't mind."

"About what?"

"About Clara Carew."

"She's dead."

"I know. That's why I need to talk to you."

"I don't see why. You an actress?"

Maudie nodded.

Bill let out a long breath through his nostrils. "Have a seat. I suppose you play cards, too."

"I've been known to." Maudie pulled out a chair opposite him, her back to the doors.

Wild Bill opened a new deck of cards, spread them across the table, slipped out the two jokers, flipped one end and watched the remaining fifty-two flip up and over like a row of dominoes.

"A little five card, then, while we talk?" His voice was so quiet Maudie had difficulty hearing it. He seemed tired, very tired.

A crowd gathered in the room. The place was growing raucous. Maudie shifted in her chair uncomfortably. She scanned the room, glimpsing the young reporter. In a corner sat the rat man, McCall, watching her with his rodent eyes. She shifted her gaze as Cole Branch entered the saloon. The place hushed as drinks were ordered.

He seemed to be showing up everywhere she was. She was aware of her pulse quickening as their eyes locked for several hot moments.

McCall walked to the table. "Anybody get into this game?" He kept his eyes on Maudie and licked his lips.

" 'Fraid not," Bill told him. "This is two-hand only. Maybe later."

McCall glowered at Wild Bill Hickok, then shot a

lascivious glance at Maudie. As Maudie scanned the room to find Cole Branch again, she noticed she was indeed the only woman in the saloon.

Shifting and lowering his eyes from the door repeatedly, Wild Bill dealt the cards. She picked them up absently and arranged them while deciding just what she planned to ask Wild Bill Hickok. She wanted to make the most of the opportunity.

Wild Bill dropped three cards face down in front of him. "How many?"

"I'll play these."

Wild Bill fixed her with steely amusement. "No cards, eh? I'll take three." He slipped the cards in among the two in his hand, then switched them around. "Two." He pushed a pile of chips to the middle of the table.

Maudie studied her hand. "I'll raise you two," she said, then loosened her bag strings and rummaged inside it until she found the pouch of gold dust. She didn't feel comfortable bringing it out in front of the saloon full of men. Her gaze came up sharply to Wild Bill's.

"Hank," he said to the bartender, holding up his glass, "bring me another of these." As if reading her mind, he added, "And a chip stake for the lady." He turned back to Maudie. "Pardon me. Will you have something to drink?"

"No, thank you," she said quietly.

The bartender rushed over with Bill's drink and a handful of chips. Bill took a long swallow and Maudie counted out some chips and pushed them toward the pot.

Wild Bill's wiry eyebrows arched. He pushed more chips into the middle. "And two more."

Maudie folded, then opened, her cards. "Mr. Hickok, have you thought much about Madame Carew's death? I don't think it was an accident. You were in a play with her once. You knew her. Do you think someone might have wanted her dead?" She studied her cards, slowly counted out more chips and pushed them into the pot. "Call. Mr. Hickok, I truly need your help."

Wild Bill dropped his cards face up on the table, queens showing. "Three lovely ladies," he smiled at her.

Maudie dropped and fanned her cards deftly. "Full house, treys up." She avoided his gaze and pulled in the chips. "So, will you, Mr. Hickok? Help me, I mean?"

Wild Bill put two chips in the middle of the green cloth. "Deal . . . and maybe I'll think about it."

Before an hour had passed, Maudie knew that Wild Bill Hickok was a sick man. When he took off his glasses, she saw the irritation in his eyes, saw his hands shake. She recognized the symptoms of the blood disease. It looked to her as if Cole Branch could be in for a longer run as sheriff than he'd bargained for.

Maudie could tell Wild Bill enjoyed being famous, and that he would talk more of the past than the present if given the chance. He drank a lot of some kind of pink liquor, but she observed that he never appeared drunk.

Some hero, she thought. Sick and drinking the day away and being bested in a card game by a woman.

And the people of Deadwood have asked him to be their town marshal. They can't see the real person, only the legend.

"Mr. Hickok, what *do* you think about Madame Carew's accident?"

"Nothing."

"Nothing?" She didn't believe him.

"Nothing."

"But surely you have an opinion about it. You've been on the stage. You understand about theater, about actors."

Wild Bill flicked his cards. "You gonna play some more or keep talkin' into the night?" He shook his head. "Just like a woman."

Maudie refused to be rankled by his last statement, and raised his latest bet. "Do you know Cole Branch?"

Wild Bill covered the bet. "I've heard of him." He let his eyes shift and his gaze land for the merest moment on Cole where he stood amid the crowd at the bar.

"I'd say you're made from the same mold."

"How fortuitous for him. Straight beats your flush." He dragged in the pot. "Why'd you come to Deadwood?" he asked her abruptly.

"No reason."

"Nobody comes to Deadwood without a reason. You don't look like a gold-digger. You selling something?"

"Of course not."

"Ah." Wild Bill nodded knowingly. "It's a rich husband you're after, then."

"From these pickings? Hardly," she sniffed.

"Another hand?"

"No thanks. I'm looking for someone who may know something about Carew's death. And maybe a little about someone else."

"People can get lost here."

"Or dead?"

"That, too." A dark look passed over his face. "Who else do you want to know about?" Wild Bill dealt another hand. His pile was diminishing, regardless of his last win. Maudie's pile had grown considerably.

Maudie picked up her cards, realizing Hickok had issued a silent order and she'd just as silently obeyed. She looked around the room and saw dozens of pairs of eyes on them.

"I'll take three," she said, dropping her cards on the table. "May I tell you the name privately?"

Bill sent three cards sliding toward her. He picked up and fanned his own cards. "I'll play these." He shoved his remaining chips into the center of the table, then reached into his pants pocket and extracted a folded paper. Signaling the saloon keeper with a finger in the air, he managed to get a stub of a pencil from the bar. He shoved the paper and pencil toward Maudie.

Maudie took them. She started to write on the paper, then noticed it was a worn playbill from a theater in New York. Its creases were dirty and frayed, looking as if he'd carried it around with him for a long time. She opened it. Printed at the top were the words, *Scouts of the Prairie, Ned Buntline's Masterpiece Featuring Buffalo Bill Cody and Wild Bill Hickok.*

Maudie smiled. "I saw you in this play."

Wild Bill frowned and didn't take his eyes off his

cards. Maudie opened the playbill. Her eyes scanned the cast list.

She froze, her eyes fastened to one line. *The Indian Maiden . . . Gwen-Ada Boone.*

Maudie's gaze flashed to Wild Bill. He didn't look at her. She searched for Cole, and couldn't find him. She lowered her head back to the playbill. Again she looked up at Wild Bill; again he didn't raise his eyes.

Slowly Maudie folded the playbill and slid it back to him. The revelation came over her in a wave of heat. She'd seen her mother and hadn't even known it! How many other missed opportunities had there been?

Stunned, Maudie picked up her cards, methodically rearranged them, shoved all of her chips into the center, then dropped the cards on the table. "Flush, queen high," she said dully, trying to map out her exit from the saloon.

Bill folded the playbill, put it back in his pocket, then spread his own cards. "Flush. King high." He drew in the hefty pot of chips.

Maudie, stunned, was out of chips to play, literally and figuratively. The smoke in the room and the smell of unwashed men began to nauseate her. She scanned the crowd and caught a glimpse of Cole Branch in a group at the end of the bar. She was comforted by his presence for the second time that day, she noted.

Shakily, she rose, preparing to leave.

"Watch yourself going out, miss," Wild Bill said. "Someone might mistake you for an upstairs girl, and it'd be awhile before you could ask more questions."

Maudie wondered if she'd just been insulted by Wild Bill Hickok. She doubted it. The man possessed a rather kindly face. Kindly? Hadn't he shot and killed countless men? Maybe all that was a myth, too.

Maudie sensed some of the other men starting to close in around her, and knew a moment of fear.

"Say now . . ." A dirty man with a ragged scruff of beard took her arm. "If you're all through at this table, I know of another one with a lot more action."

Maudie jerked her arm free. Her composure returned. "Don't touch me." Her voice was gritty.

"I'm more what you lookin' fer, ain't I, beautiful?" another man said, shoving the bearded one out of his way and pushing his own portly middle against her arm.

"I got to her before you," the first man grunted, and shoved him back.

A free-for-all ensued, and Cole jumped into the center of it before Maudie even realized what was happening. He lifted her up as easily as he had the crate at Gaston's Freight, and deposited her firmly in Wild Bill Hickok's lap. Then he charged into the thrashing crowd, arms slicing through the air, fists connecting squarely on jaws or stomachs.

Maudie tried to get into the fray, but Wild Bill kept one arm around her waist. With the other he wielded his shillelagh, cracking it over the head or back of any of the bodies Cole threw his way. The piano player came out of his trance and pounded a frantic tune in rhythm to the boot scuffle, fist percussion and bottle tinkling.

Maudie settled back and watched with calm fascination as Cole emerged from the rollicking sea of bodies, shirt torn, one hand bleeding. Miraculously, the Stetson was still firmly in place on his head.

"No need to get up, sir," he shouted over the melee to Wild Bill. "I'll escort the lady outside." He took Maudie's arm and pulled her off Hickok's lap, turned her around and steered her toward the door.

Maudie tried to wrestle out of Cole's grip, but his fingers only tightened around her arm. "I've told you I can take care of myself," she said through clenched teeth.

"I've heard you," he replied in kind, "but in case you hadn't noticed, I've been forced to rescue you again." When she started to issue a cutting remark, he pushed her through the batwing doors out onto the boardwalk. "No need to thank me. As I told you earlier, we sheriffs exist only to serve fair damsels in distress. It's my duty, ma'am." He doffed his hat.

Maudie spun around. Both barrels would be blazing if she had any guns. "Don't you ma'am me in that tone of voice! I've been ma'amed enough for one day, thank you very much."

"Well, if you keep doing fool things like walking into saloons as if you own the place, you'll be ma'amed right out of town. It's time you—"

Cole abruptly halted his speech as the sound of sobbing interrupted their argument. He stepped past her and Maudie turned to follow him. A little girl she guessed to be about seven or eight in ragged pants and patched shirt huddled in the mud holding a cat with a bleeding leg. She sobbed, and tears streaked down her dirty face.

"Here now, little one, what's all this?" Cole patted her head.

The child fell silent and lifted the hurt cat. Cole hunched down and looked at the quivering animal. He examined the leg carefully. He took out his white handkerchief and wiped away her tears. Then he dipped the cloth in a nearby watering trough, wiped away the blood, and fashioned a bandage from it, wrapping it securely around the cat's leg.

"There. It's not broken, just cut. He'll be good as new."

Maudie saw the little girl's grateful smile. "Thank you, Mr. Sheriff. I found him. He's all I've got. Him and my best friend, Wild Bill Hickok. He's my hero." She said the last rather proudly.

Cole stood and reached into his pocket. He extracted a coin which he gave to the girl. "You go to the kitchen door of the Grand Central and tell Aunt Lou I said to give you some food. Pay her, now. Maybe she's got something for him, too." He pointed at the cat.

Maudie watched the girl scamper off, noting with interest the artistic patterns and interesting fabrics that made up the patches of her shirt.

Cole turned to her, picking up where he'd left off. ". . . Time you paid attention to how things work around here. Stop putting both of us in awkward positions." His eyes bored into hers, but there was no real admonishment in them.

"Both of us!" she countered. "I thought I was very clear in stating that I don't need you and don't want you to get me out of anything. I can take care of myself.

I've done it all my life, and I see no reason to become helpless now."

"Is that right?" Cole drawled. "Let's see, no money, no worldly goods, at least not visible ones." He added the last with a look that traveled the length of her dress.

"Oh-h, you are the most exasperating—"

"You bring it out in me. When I'm around you I feel like Wild Bill in that ridiculous play." He lunged exageratedly, one hand stretched in front in one of the classic poses of a bad actor. "Fear not, fair maid!" he emoted in a preposterous falsetto. "By heavens, you are safe at last with Wild Cole Branch, who is ever ready to risk life and limb on behalf of the weak and defenseless example of womanhood that stands before me!"

"Did you ever play Binghamton?"

Cole turned to face an amused Wild Bill Hickok. Maudie enjoyed the embarrassed flush that spread up over Cole's face.

Wild Bill tipped his wide-brimmed hat toward Maudie, and started back toward the Number Ten Saloon.

"Mr. Hickok?" Maudie called to him.

He turned slowly. "Ma'am?"

"You've got a great mustache."

Wild Bill smiled enigmatically as he stroked one of the stallion tails. Another tip of his hat and he pressed open the batwing doors and slipped inside the saloon.

Maudie watched after him as the doors came to a standstill. She tipped her own hat to the great Wild Bill Hickok. He was a hero after all, at least to the little girl in the patched clothes. And, it appeared, to Cole Branch. She herself knew a hero when she saw one.

The way she knew a real mustache when she saw one.

She gave Cole a sidelong glance that had him stroking his own mustache.

Chapter 6

"Everybody's a critic, sir," Cole said to Wild Bill without looking up from the newspaper article he was reading.

At the long, narrow lunch counter of a long, narrow restaurant wedged in a long, narrow alley next to the Bella Union Theater, aptly called The Crumbs of Comfort Along the Crack in the Wall, he bent over a heaping plate of pickled pigs' feet and sauerkraut. He held a pair of ill-fitting wire-rimmed spectacles in place with his right hand, which had been bandaged after his fight in the Number Ten Saloon the day before. With his left hand he raised the pinkish-tan pieces of swine underpinnings in a high arc over his tipped-back head and dropped the delectable bites into his open mouth.

"So they are," Hickok responded with a weary sigh, swirling a biscuit through some gravy then popping it into his mouth. He sat at the end of the counter, his back to the wall, bending over a plate of rabbit stew. Cole hoped it was rabbit. The sudden increase in the cat population in a place where little value was placed on human life, let alone animal life, could cause a man to pause and reflect on the contents of several dishes served in Deadwood's more accessible eateries.

Cole read every line in the Saturday edition of the *Black Hills Pioneer*. He'd propped it against his Stetson, which rested over a pearl-handled Colt he'd placed a strategic palm's width away from his plate. He'd read somewhere that real western lawmen always set their hats and guns on tables and bar tops to display their jurisdiction over the space around them. Cole had perfected, and rather smoothly he figured, that bit of lawman protocol even better than he had cheroot-dangling.

Not that anyone could miss his Colt. A single-action revolver, custom-made with a twelve-inch barrel, it was a gift from the famed (or infamous depending on one's point of view) Ned Buntline, dime-novelist and author of some of the worst plays in which Cole had ever had the displeasure of being cast. Buntline had bragged how the Colt was exactly like the Specials he'd peddled in Dodge City to the likes of Bat Masterson and Wyatt Earp. In a rare act of generosity he'd presented the gun to Cole after he'd seen the young actor showing off with it after the close of a play.

Cole stopped chewing on a particularly gristly piece of pig's foot and concentrated on the *Pioneer's* rather nasty review of a variety entertainment at the Melodeon Theater earlier in the week. He let out a harsh breath through his nostrils that anyone within hearing distance might have defined as a snort.

"I feel terrible about what they said about the Queen of Song. She traveled a long distance to bring

127

her act to Deadwood. Nobody understands how much an actor puts into a performance, no matter who it's for or how they're feeling at the time." He shook his head. "Everybody's a critic, no matter how little they know about anything."

"Having once been the object of a less than glowing review, I share your sentiments," Hickok said evenly.

Cole leveled a sympathetic gaze on Hickok. "I apologize, sir, if I stirred up any unpleasant memories."

The last thing Cole wanted to do was to upset Wild Bill Hickok. He liked the man. Here was a living western hero of legends and dime novels sitting right next to him slurping his stew. Cole hoped some of the man's heroic stature would rub off on him.

"I witnessed that lady's performance," Hickok returned. "That critic knows whereof he speaks."

Cole stopped reading long enough to remove a sliver of pig's foot from between two lower side teeth with the aid of a wooden pick. He was grateful for the kind of diners The Crumbs catered to, and relaxed and allowed himself the privilege of engaging in an act natural to all chewing creatures. He slid the pick back and forth between his teeth at the corner of his mouth.

As Cole read the contents of the printed advertising boxes that were neatly arranged in rows on both sides of the feature stories, he scratched his head. "People always have to acquire," he said over the pick and newspaper. "Why do you suppose that is?"

Deadwood City was little more than three months old, but its fame had already spread far and wide. Daily it swelled by the hundreds as wagon train after wagon train pulled in unloading gold-seeking prospectors and the usual tent-town lowlifes. He marvelled at how, even in a town of lumber and canvas that had sprung up out of mud and debris from the tumble-down hillsides, people were still in need of life's fineries, all the trappings of civilization.

Stores selling mining supplies had been followed by grocers, tobacconists, druggists. Then came apparel and millinery shops, and finally, when the smoke from the fat cigars in the crowded saloons and the roar of the stamp mills cleared, a newspaper office.

"Never tried to figure that," Hickok said, scraping his plate. "I figure there aren't any more frontiers left to conquer, in a country or in a man."

Cole figured a man should know his own frontiers had been conquered when he caught a glimpse of a brand-new newspaper, or felt the tickle under his nose of a red ostrich feather from a woman's fashionable hat. Just like he was feeling now. What the . . . ?

"I daresay you won't find any clues in there," a low female voice stated.

Cole looked up, then lowered the wooden pick slowly away from his teeth. Maudie Boone Dearden. He hadn't seen her in almost twenty-four hours. That's why he must feel so rested, he opined. She seemed to possess an uncanny knack of knowing exactly where he was at almost any given moment, and then making certain she shared that moment with him. Yes sir, the west's rapidly dwindling frontier and Deadwood's escalating civilization were infringing on even a man's most private moments.

"Miss Dearden, isn't it?" Wild Bill squinted toward her.

"Unfortunately, yes," Cole muttered. "Hang onto your hat and anything else you deem valuable."

Maudie ignored Cole. "Good afternoon, Mr. Hickok."

"Good afternoon. You look lovely today. The blue in your waistcoat matches perfectly the color of your exquisite eyes."

"Thank you, Mr. Hickok. Please, you may call me Maudie. You certainly know how to flatter a lady." She noted with amusement that Wild Bill's blue-tinted glasses made everything he saw look blue.

"Not flattery, Miss Maudie, merely the truth as I see it," Hickok rejoined.

"And what mayhem are you devising at high noon that will no doubt put us both in total danger?" Cole asked. "In other words, what brings you here at this particular moment?"

"Ignoring your barbs, as usual," Maudie said with an air of indifference. "Other than that, I'm taking a brief moment out of my busy schedule to have a bite to eat, before rushing off in pursuit of business."

Maudie removed her hat with its bobbing red ostrich feather and placed it several inches beyond her right hand on the counter. Cole noticed the bulging canvas bag she set down next to her hat. He wondered whether women in general were in the habit of displaying their jurisdiction over the space around them, or if this trait were peculiar to Maudie Boone Dearden.

"I'd think you'd want to take lunch with your dear sister, Aunt Lou Marchbanks, where you could get it for free," Cole said slyly.

"You're Lou's sister?" Wild Bill exclaimed, peering more closely at Maudie.

She glared at Cole and gritted her teeth. "That's how rumors get started." Leaning around Cole's shoulders, she smiled sweetly at Hickok. "Not by blood, but in the truest sense of womanhood, we are sisters."

"I see," Hickok replied, but it was obvious from the way his brows formed a pleat between his eyes and the manner in which his magnificent mustache twitched, that he did not.

Maudie brought her eyes back to Cole's mustache. It seemed a bit fuller this afternoon, a little darker. She wasn't sure whether she liked the one he was wearing when she first laid eyes on him better.

"I've been looking for you," she said to Cole.

"Now it's my turn to be flattered." He gave her a dazzling smile.

"Don't be. I'm disappointed I found you."

"I'd ask why, but that would only precipitate further conversation, and I'm sure you want to move on."

"If I hadn't found you," Maudie opened the huge pouch and pushed her hand inside, "I might have held out hope you were out investigating Madame Carew's death."

"That again?" Cole let out a weary sigh.

"Yes, that again. But since I have found you I shall repay my debt to you for the dinner you bought for me. Dust, paper, or coin?"

Cole stared at the bulging pouch. "What have you got in there, a bank exchange?" He found it rather curious that a seemingly down-on-her-luck actress, penniless only a short time ago, now had funds in three forms and carried them around in a pouch the size of a respectable saddlebag.

"I believe this will cover it, and whatever it is you seem to be devouring right now." Maudie shuddered as she examined the remnant on his plate, then placed several coins from the States next to his hat. Cole stared at the money. "It's customary to say thank you when such a transaction has been made," she said dourly.

"Thank you," he replied. "I don't usually allow a woman to . . ."

"Pay for your dinner? It wouldn't be proper, I suppose?" Maudie baited.

"Well, as a matter of fact, I was brought up to always pay for a lady's—"

Maudie's hand shot up. "Please, I'd rather not talk about your personal life, if you don't mind."

Cole's mouth twitched. What an exasperating woman!

Wild Bill leaned around Cole's shoulder. "Long as you two are talking business, mind if I have a looksee at the *Pioneer?*"

Cole folded the newspaper and handed it to him. "We are not talking business, sir, at least not the kind you're referring to." Wild Bill shrugged, and Cole turned back to Maudie. "I would appreciate it, Miss Dearden, if you would stop badgering me about food, money, and the death of that actress."

Maudie flared. "Why? Is it so beneath you to involve yourself with such riffraff as actors?" She hoped to provoke him into divulging information about himself.

Cole flared right back. "I associate with a lot of

riffraff, as I'm sure you've noticed. Present company included."

Wild Bill cleared his throat.

"I mean excluded!"

"Well, thank you for that lovely compliment." Maudie's dark blue eyes flashed, and she grabbed the small slate that the menu had been scrawled upon.

"You're welcome, I'm sure." Cole meant to refix his concentration on the newspaper, but Wild Bill seemed deeply engrossed behind it.

He turned back to Maudie and watched her facial muscles move under her fine skin as she perused the menu. He hadn't noticed before how finely sculpted her profile was. She was beautiful, carried herself regally, turned heads wherever she walked.

Damn, this woman was already like a burr in his trousers. He had thought he would be able to carry this sheriff thing off without much of a hitch until the Pinkerton got to town. He didn't know jack-squat about investigations and clue-finding. All he had wanted to do was coast along until the Pinkerton agent arrived and did what Pinkerton agents do best, solve the alleged crime. Then he'd make his report to the federal marshal, get his money, and get back on the road to California. But Miss Maudie Boone Dearden had come along and landed like a fly in the syrup.

He thought a minute.

What if when the Pinkerton arrived, she told him that he hadn't been doing his job? What if the Pinkerton then discovered he was an imposter? What if he reported him to the federal marshal? What if . . . ?

Maybe a little honey would be much more effective

than the vinegar he'd been pouring on Maudie since she'd arrived.

"Miss Dearden . . . Maudie, if I may. I understand your frustration."

"You may *not* call me Maudie. And I doubt you do understand my frustration. You're quite typical, you know."

"Typical of what?"

"You're just another cop with selective vision."

"Just what is that supposed to mean?"

"It means, Sheriff, that you are like a lot of cops. When it suits you, you turn your eyes away from the problem. If it's too much trouble on one side of town, you're busy on the other side getting what you can for yourself." Her eyes glittered accusingly.

Cole flared. "Now just a minute, lady. You don't know anything about me. I do my best to avoid trouble, yes. Seems the best way to stay alive these days. But when there's a job to be done . . ." He leaned back slightly and toyed with the remains of his sauerkraut. "Even though it might not be apparent to you, Miss Dearden, I have been investigating Madame Carew's death"—he swallowed a mouthful of coffee—"to the best of my ability. Perhaps I'm just too close to the incident now. Perhaps I'm overlooking something. That's why, in my best judgment and experience, I've decided to wait for the Pinkerton agent's arrival so that we can attack the situation together. A fresh look, a new pair of eyes. You understand."

"Oh, I understand, all right." Maudie pretended to be engrossed in the menu selections, even though only three items were listed, two having a line running through them indicating, she guessed, that the restaurant had run out of them. "You've let the trail get cold, and now you have no idea in the world how to start the search over."

"Now just a minute . . ." Cole's frustration boiled over.

"For example, have you inquired as to whether Madame Carew had enemies? Anyone who might have had a reason for wanting her dead?"

Cole glared at her in silence.

"I thought not. That would be the most obvious place to start. Obvious, that is, once you examined the scene of the mishap and inspected the rigging. You've done that, of course." She looked up as the woman behind the counter stopped to take her order. "Is it truly rabbit in the rabbit stew?" When the woman smiled wanly at her, Maudie said, "I'll just have coffee and a couple of biscuits, please."

"I conducted my initial investigation to the best of my ability and as I saw fit," Cole told her. Why did he feel the need to justify himself to her?

"I have a feeling that's part of the reason why nothing has been accomplished." Maudie cut into a biscuit.

"Says here," Wild Bill said, pointing at an article in the *Pioneer*, "that there's some question about Madame Carew's integrity. Seems there's a stolen ruby necklace and eardrops that disappeared from some wealthy easterner's home after a supper given for the Madame. Seems they lay the theft to her."

Maudie's attention switched from her biscuit toward Hickok a hair faster than did Cole's from his pickled pigs' feet.

135

"Says here," Hickok went on without looking up, "that the editor got this information from an anonymous source." He lowered the newspaper and looked over at the two whose gazes were fixed upon him. "Do you suppose they made that up for what they call 'dramatic effect'?"

Cole said nothing. He thought no one in Deadwood knew about the stolen rubies except himself and the absent federal marshal. Who could have told the *Times* editor?

Maudie concentrated on spreading jam over a biscuit as she spoke. "Made up or not, one would think that a juicy tidbit like that would have reached the ears of a sheriff who'd supposedly been asking a lot of questions about a possible murder. Wouldn't one?"

Wild Bill folded the newspaper and handed it to Cole as he rose, leaning on his shillelagh. "Always thought the worst thing that could happen to a man was to be wounded by the ammunition of logic aimed by the hair-trigger finger of a woman." He dropped his hat onto his head. "Don't worry, it's not fatal . . . usually." He grinned, stroked his mustache, gave his customary glance around the room and, seemingly satisfied he could walk through the crowd without incident, strode out of the restaurant.

Cole watched Hickok's retreating back and pondered the wisdom of his parting words. He drained his coffee cup, then leveled his gaze on Maudie. "What kind of business are you pursuing?"

Maudie took a dainty bite of her biscuit. "Personal," she answered, lifting her chin to chew the biscuit with what he distinctly detected was a look of enjoyment.

"I suppose you're off to the theater to snoop around, aren't you? Why can't you just leave this alone until the Pinkerton arrives? Look, I promise to let you in on his investigation, *if* he wants to let you in. How would that be, Maudie?"

"Miss Dearden to you. The fact is, what business I have here in this lunch room or anywhere else for that matter isn't any business of yours. But as a matter of fact, I *am* going to the theater. Rehearsals have begun for *Scarlet Lady*. I've been given a role in it."

Cole snapped his head around and looked at her full-on. "Not the one Carew was playing when she . . . died."

"Of course not! Do I look old enough to play Carew's roles? Never mind. I really don't want to hear your opinion on that. An actress who calls herself Lady Fan has been cast in that role."

"Ah, yes. I've seen her. She'd be right for it."

Maudie looked at Cole carefully. "What does she look like? How old is she? Has she been here long?"

Cole listened to the rapid-fire delivery of her questions with curiosity. At least she hadn't said anything about the rubies. That was just as well. But she certainly wasn't masking her intense interest in this new actress. He wondered why. He thought a moment, and then a surprising realization came to him. "I don't really know what she looks like."

"But you said you've seen her," Maudie pressed.

"I have, but only from a distance. Mostly from the back. And she wears hats so big her face is always in shadow."

Maudie frowned. "Then you couldn't tell her age for certain."

"Not for certain. But she's, well, older, I'd say."

"As old as Carew?"

"I have no idea. I never saw Carew up close when she was alive. Only in performance, and I was at the back of the theater. People sometimes look a lot older in death. Fan carries herself so that she appears younger, but I couldn't honestly say."

"How long did you say she's been in Deadwood?"

Maudie pushed the plate containing the remaining biscuit away from her, and sipped the coffee that Cole knew must be cold by now.

"I didn't say."

"Can you estimate the time of her arrival, then?"

He heard the edge in her voice. "Well, let's see now. It was right around the time Carew . . . no, it was maybe two or three weeks before Carew died. I remember now, because she arrived with Jack Langrishe's company and appeared in their production of *The Streets of New York*. She didn't have a big part. It didn't matter though, because on opening night there was a torrential downpour and the canvas roof of the new theater collapsed and they had to close down for a few days to rebuild. Lady Fan ended up in Madame Carew's company, and she had a bit part in *Scarlet Lady*. I thought that was odd."

"What was odd? The fact that she left a theater that had blown down?"

"No. I thought it was odd that she didn't have a larger part. She possessed a presence on the stage that was rather commanding. She reminded me of an actress I'd seen some years ago."

"Well, there's a lot of jealousy among actors. If she's as good as you say, it's possible Carew felt threatened by her, isn't it?"

"It's possible, yes. Anything is possible."

Maudie picked up her hat and set it jauntily over her carefully coiled hair. She gathered up her canvas bag and slid away from the counter. "I'm certain that your ongoing investigation, *Sheriff*, will uncover many possibilities." She turned and walked out of the restaurant, causing every head, both male and female, to turn. And leaving Cole Branch to pay her meal fare once again.

Maudie let herself into the back of the dimly lit theater through an ill-fitting rear door. Some of the newest theaters in Deadwood were erected as quickly as a few boards could be nailed together and some cloth hung, making entrance and egress convenient to anyone who could lift the weight of a blanket.

She'd marvelled at the differences between the ornate and sumptuous theaters in the east and those plainly constructed buildings she'd encountered as she had travelled west. It seemed frontier theater was being born right in front of her path toward California, as if theaters were springing up for her and her alone. To witness the birth of a new stage in each new mining camp or town was for Maudie to feel the ghostly presence of her mother. She always felt a rush of anticipation and trepidation upon stepping into a new theater.

And each time she was in an empty theater, she sensed the same desolation and foreboding, as if something were about to materialize out of nothing. She sensed those feelings again as she stood inside the Deadwood Variety Theater. It smelled of new wood, yet it felt somehow older, more solid than some of the other theaters she had been in. And now, as she did always, she called out with a strong voice, "Is anyone here?" No answer.

She set her canvas pouch just inside the opening, and left the door ajar to let in a bit of the late afternoon light. The shaft of sun comforted her slightly as her eyes adjusted to the dusky, dark interior. She never minded being alone, except in empty theaters. She knew she expected something from a theater, something most any theater could not give her. Her mother. This theater was no exception. She felt a fluttering anticipation more profound than any she had ever experienced.

Maudie stepped up onto the boards from stage right, past the stage manager's desk. She looked along the apron at the row of crudely hooded footlights. She stepped back and felt the ropes that were anchored with sandbags, and followed them up toward pulleys in the flyloft used to raise and lower scrims and other set pieces. She pulled. The ropes felt secure on each side. She moved her hat's ostrich feather out of the way and peered up into the darkness above. She could make out nothing more than shadows of hemp rigging that resembled a heavy-stranded cobweb.

At breakfast she'd heard the other actresses at the boardinghouse exclaiming about how quickly the scrim containing the city wall scenery for *Scarlet Lady* had been rehung. She walked upstage and brushed her hand over it, feeling the layers of paint. She walked toward one edge and tugged gently on it when she reached the end. She tugged harder. It felt secure. Why shouldn't it? Wouldn't the stage crew want to be doubly certain the scenery did not cause another tragedy?

She walked back to the other side, and gripped the edge of the scrim. She tugged. It, too, felt secure. She tugged again, harder. This time she felt something give. She pulled again, this time hearing a faint ripping sound. Was it possible the stage crew hadn't done as good a job in securing the scrim as they should have following Carew's accident? That seemed unlikely to Maudie.

Peering harder through the semidarkness she spotted a rope ladder leading up to the rigging loft. There was no doubt about it. She'd have to climb up and feel along the scrim to find out what had made it rip like that. It wasn't old enough to be frayed, but perhaps it hadn't been mended properly after the accident. She wondered how any stage crew member could have been anything less than diligent in seeing that the problem was corrected.

She tested the ladder and checked where it was anchored to the floor. Satisfied it would hold her weight, she took off her hat, then picked up her skirt and petticoat hems and tucked them securely in the waistband. As she started her ascent she could feel cool air on her thinly clad posterior and bare thighs.

She was almost to the top when her pulse started to pound erratically in her ears. This was just the way she had felt outside the Republican Theater in Cheyenne right before she jumped into the wagonload of cats and came face to face with the rat man, McCall. Her palms started to sweat and slip around the rope rungs. Just a little bit farther, that's all she needed to go. She needed to get high enough so that she could reach along the pipe that held the scrim. She needed to find the spot where the tear had begun.

The rope ladder swayed to her right as she reached out with her left hand. Her breath caught in her throat and she swallowed hard. She caught the pipe and steadied the ladder. Carefully she inched her fingers along the eyelets that guided the rope ties through the scrim and around the pipe. The first was secure, the second, the third . . . there! The fourth, fifth, and sixth eyelets felt frayed under her fingertips. She could not extend her reach any farther to tell if others were in the same condition, but the holes she'd touched were sufficiently torn to allow the weight of the scrim to pull them apart under the right conditions. She'd have to think about just what the right conditions would be.

Gripping the rail along the edge she inched her way toward the rear rigging. She reached out toward the hemp lines and pulled each one toward her, examined it and let it fall back. The light was too dim to make an accurate assessment.

Then something caught her eye. She reached for one of the lines and brought it back, adjusting her hand to get it out of her own shadow. There. She discovered frayed strand ends sewn together. She turned the line and saw that the repair was done with a strong red thread. She braced herself against the rail, took the line in both hands and tried to pull it apart. It gave only a tiny bit.

Maudie frowned and moved along the rail until she'd examined all the rigging lines. She found several with weakened strands reinforced with red thread. What experienced roustabout or stage constructor would repair hemp lines with anything other than re-placement hemp? Had the lines been purposely cut and then repaired so no one would know?

She wondered if Cole had made a similar discovery. If he had, wouldn't he have said something about it? Perhaps not. He was still waiting for his precious Pink-erton man. She wondered if maybe she was onto some-thing.

Her right hand was getting tired and her palm sore from gripping the rope ladder rung so tightly. And she'd reached out so far at an angle that she could not push her way back to grab the ladder with her other hand in order to facilitate her climb back down.

Don't panic! Relax, breathe deeply, think carefully. She tried to inch her hand back along the scrim pipe, but her perspiring fingers caught the hemp lines through the eyelets, and she could not smoothly work her way along. Her arms were growing tired. She felt the rope rung through the soles of her boots and her feet started to tremble. Then her left arm started to vi-brate from its angle and her weight on it. Somehow her hand was wedged through the hemp lines and she couldn't free it.

Now she knew the deepening chill of real panic. She pulled, trying to dislodge her hand, and heard the ripping sound again. If she could just lean against the ladder with her torso, perhaps she could get her right hand over far enough to move the hemp that entwined her left hand. Slowly, she attempted to put her plan into action.

But she lost her balance. Her boot heels caught the ladder rung. Her back arched. She gripped her right hand onto the scrim pipe just as the ladder slipped away from her feet.

And then she learned exactly what the right conditions were for bringing down the scenery.

Strained by her weight, with a sickening rip the scrim's eyelets gave way and, as Maudie hung suspended in the air, her two hands gripping the ropes, the pipe dislodged at one end and the canvas gave way and came down at an angle, bringing her down with it. For a split second she anticipated the thud her body would make as it hit the stage floor, the clang the pipe would make as it fell over her, and the crunch her bones would make as they crumbled. And possibly the last sigh she would sigh before she died without finding her mother. What she actually heard was something else.

"Oooph!"

Maudie landed face down on something both soft and hard at the same time. The canvas scrim fell down over her like a shroud. She waited a moment. She was certain she was still alive. Imagine that! All that panic for nothing! She was still alive!

Underneath her something moved, letting out a whoosh of air like a depressed bellows. It moved again. Summoning her courage, she looked down and saw a blue shirt and a heaving chest. A man!

144

She pushed against the man's shoulders and managed only to scramble them both more deeply among the folds of the canvas. His head rolled from side to side and he coughed hard and gagged.

"Cole Branch! What are you doing under here?"

"Investigating, of course," he said between breaths, biting off the words through tightened lips.

Suddenly Maudie was aware that Cole's hands were cupped over her posterior. His wide palms and long fingers radiated a half-sphere of warmth through her thin cotton lawn drawers, and that heat was languidly flowing into other parts of her body. His fingers barely moved, but under them Maudie felt her skin swell with arousal.

"Just what is it you think you're doing?" she sputtered, attempting to appear unmoved by the location of his hands. It was one of her better moments on the stage.

"Searching for clues, of course. That's what you've been begging me to do since the moment you arrived in Deadwood, isn't it?"

In the darkness of their canvas shroud she knew he was grinning smugly, but she was determined to remain calm, not play the hysterical, properly outraged young maiden.

"And what exactly do you expect to discover in the location in which you've focused your, ah, investigation?"

"I believe I may have found it."

"Found what?"

"The most perfect female backside in the contiguous United States and the frontier."

His hands continued to lightly trace the shape of her hips and rounded bottom, an unnerving sensation. But she would rather die than let him know how much his touch was unsettling her.

"I was unaware the investigation had taken such a peculiar turn," she said.

He gazed at her for a long moment. "So was I," he said thickly.

Maudie sucked in her breath, then attempted to push her body away from his and disentangle herself from the pile of canvas and Cole's legs and arms. He didn't move, she noticed, and he seemed to be enjoying her struggle as her body pressed against his.

"You could help to get us out from under here, you know."

Cole heard the exasperated tremor in her voice. He was afraid if he moved he'd shatter his control, such as it was at the moment, and he'd do something he'd regret for certain once he was outside in the harsh light of a Deadwood day. But the longer he lay beneath Maudie's voluptuous curves, with the wonderful soft rounded parts of her body sweeping over him, pressing into him, the more he knew his resolve to form no attachments was seriously threatened by her presence. His body was aching to form an attachment to Maudie's, and he was seriously questioning whether or not his mind would have the strength to prevent it from happening.

He didn't move for a long time, then somehow managed to give her the help she was demanding. He grasped her behind tighter in his hands, pushed with his pelvis and chest, and flipped her onto her back. He drew up onto his knees, straddling her, slipped his hands out from under her, and flung the canvas off of them.

Maudie breathed heavily. "Air! I thought I was going to suffocate under there!"

Cole lowered his hands and rested them on either side of her shoulders. A heavy lock of her dark flame hair had flopped over her forehead and covered one eye. It was beguiling, provocative, entrancing. As she breathed, her chest rose and fell in deep rhythm, lifting and dropping the bodice of her blouse, which had opened during her fall.

Maudie's one visible eye glittered at him. "You can help me up now," she said, obviously working at steadying her voice.

Cole held his gaze on that lock of hair hiding her eye. "I . . . I'm not through with my investigation."

"What . . . do you mean?" Maudie's breathing became more ragged.

Bending his arms, he slowly lowered his torso. Smoothly his chest pressed down against hers. His lips skimmed over hers, then over her cheek and up to the lock of her hair. He buried his face in it for a moment, feeling her body go rigid under his. With his lips he lifted and pushed the lock of hair away from her face. He closed his eyes and lowered his lips to kiss her eyelids. He heard her catch and hold her breath. He trailed his mouth over her cheek, then brought it to rest on her parted lips.

For a moment neither of them breathed or moved, frozen it seemed in a curtain-call pose. Then he felt the slight quiver of her lips against his. That was his cue.

Some other part of Cole Branch possessed him as he possessed Maudie's lips. He lost his sense of being in her kiss, her tongue, her soft receiving and giving mouth. He was swept away over a sea of waving prairie grass, above gold-veined mountains, into an open blue sky where a soul could soar unencumbered by the weight of flesh and blood reality.

When he felt he might expire from the sheer gripping emotion he'd let take over his mind and body, he extricated his lips from hers. Above her his chest heaved for air, for steadying clear-headed air.

"Miss Dearden . . ." he managed.

Maudie inhaled and held her breath, then let it out in a long column. "Under the circumstances I think you may . . . call me Maudie." She moved one shoulder and winced in the effort. "I owe you an apology."

Cole worked to gain mental control over his raging physical desire. "For what?" he asked breathlessly.

Maudie smiled. "You *do* know how to conduct a thorough investigation."

Cole held her gaze, then laughed deep in his throat. He felt his groin stir and sensed the unmistakable burgeoning ache there gather momentum. He felt where his thighs straddled her hips. If he didn't get his demanding body away from her inviting one this instant, he knew he'd be lost, knew he'd be devastated by his own emotions. With a great deal of groaning, he pushed himself to his feet.

He moved with the agility of a mountain cat, and stood up. A dizziness swept over him as his blood rushed to his lower reaches. Or was it from the burning desire to throw his body back down over hers and absorb every inch of her inside his barren shell?

Maudie stirred as if coming out of a dream-filled sleep. What had she given in to? Worse, what might she have given in to? Without looking at him she rolled to her side and pushed herself away from the stage floor and the canvas scrim. He helped her to her feet, and she worked at ignoring the strength and warmth in his hands as they brushed against her skin. She hurried to put distance between them, bending to retrieve her bag.

She busied herself in the bag, attempting to regain her composure before she had to face Cole again, see his eyes, see her lips' own moistness on his mouth. She had to remember why she was there, what she was looking for. She couldn't allow this kind of thing to happen again. Especially not with a cop! But he wasn't just a cop and she knew it. It was worse. He was a man she had willingly responded to. A threat to her very existence. A man Maudie could give herself away to, lose everything for.

She cleared her throat, took a deep breath, and turned around, becoming the Maudie Boone Dearden she was when she arrived in Deadwood.

"Why . . . why are you here, what were you doing here before . . . ?" she started to ask him.

"This is where we came in, isn't it? I believe I mentioned to you that I was investigating," he replied.

Maudie pulled into her full height. "Investigating, my Aunt Fanny's fanny! You followed me! That's what you did, you followed me, didn't you?" Maudie planted her fists on her hips.

Cole pressed his lips into a hard line, letting out a long breath through his nostrils. "All right, so I followed you."

"Why?"

"You are not above suspicion, you know, lady. And you're a stranger in this town."

"Everybody is a stranger in this town! Why single me out?"

"A crime has been committed in this theater, and no one is exempt from scrutiny by the law. That's why."

"Oh, really! Up to this point you haven't spent one minute of your time on this crime, as you now so conveniently call it. And the moment I start looking into it, you're right on my tail." Her cheeks burned at her last comment, and she spun around and limped to where her hat lay at the foot of the rope ladder. "So to speak," she muttered as she bent down, picked up the hat with two hands, and plopped it on her head.

"And a nice one it is, too," Cole said, leveling his gaze on her posterior.

Maudie gasped as she planted both hands over her buttocks, which were covered only by her short white cotton lawn drawers. She had forgotten that before her climb she had tucked the hem of her skirts into her waistband, and her backside was now delineated by long white garters attached to white stockings.

Quickly Maudie snapped at her skirts and petticoats until they settled down around her legs. Then she spun around, the ostrich feather bobbing in an arc over her face, tapping the end of her nose. She blew it away with a column of air sent up from a corner of her mouth.

"Well, Inspector, what did you find up there before

you made your death-defying exit?" Cole asked with exaggerated gravity. "Not a very graceful one, I might add."

She looked up into the darkened flyloft and saw the rigging pipe dangling over her, swaying crazily, rope rigging ties hanging in the air. Another spectacular entrance, or exit, depending on how one looked at it, for Maudie Boone Dearden, who lived to tell about it! Damn! She hated missing that one, too!

Maudie lowered her gaze. She could see his goading grin in the semidarkness. "If you think I'm going to tell you anything, you can think again. You'll just have to figure it out for yourself."

"*If* there's anything to figure."

"You just admitted that a crime had been committed here." Maudie's frustration mounted. "Or was that just a way for you to torment me?"

"Did I?" Cole inclined his head in her direction.

"Yes, you did! You know you said it!"

"I meant, did I torment you? Oh, I really hope I tormented you."

"Oh!" Maudie expended the word on a disgusted breath. "You are the most exasperating man I've ever met!"

"Really? The most, you say? Well, now, lady, I am flattered." He searched around for his hat, found it, and planted it at the back of his head.

"Believe me, I would not flatter you, ever. And stop calling me lady!"

Cole placed one hand over his heart; the other he held out, palm cocked in a halting gesture. "Forgive

151

me. I mistook you for one. It won't happen again, I assure you."

Maudie started for the back door.

"Where are you going?"

His voice held a tinge of disappointment, but Maudie was not about to be derailed by an amateur cop in some bastard town. She took a deep breath, settled her resolve around her like a boned corset, and lifted her chin at an impervious angle.

"The rest of the company will be straggling in at any moment to begin rehearsal. I don't want to be seen here . . . and in this condition. Unless you wish to be discovered, I suggest you make as hasty a retreat yourself. Although I almost wish you would get caught. I'd love to hear how you slick talk your way out of this one." She turned on her heel and sashayed out of the theater.

Cole watched Maudie's departure, all the while working hard to control a bewildered grin that played at the corners of his mouth. He couldn't help himself. She was one fascinating creature. The flags that were being sent up inside him were as red as the dress she wore the day she arrived in Deadwood, but he was intrigued by her, Maudie Boone Dearden, an actress of the stage. An actress in life, he suspected.

Shaking his head, he turned to inspect the partially dangling scrim. Carefully he stepped over the canvas to get to the pipe on which it was fastened. He leaned down and tried to discover exactly where it had ripped away from the rigging. Unable to see very well in the dim light, he felt along the swaying pipe with both hands, touched the eyelets, the canvas, the hemp rigging lines.

Then something caught his attention.

He felt again. The ropes weren't frayed. The eyelets weren't frayed. There were clean edges to both. A chill coursed through him. They'd been cut!

Suddenly he heard voices coming from the front of the theater. Quickly, and as quietly as possible, he slipped out the back and shut the door.

In the light of the waning afternoon, he frowned and contemplated his fate. He knew he would have to put more realism into his act as Sheriff of Deadwood now.

Damn, if he hadn't been so taken with Maudie Boone Dearden, he wouldn't be in the mess he knew he was about to be in.

There went yet another of his frontiers. There went his resolve about involvements.

And where the hell was that Pinkerton agent?

Chapter 7

Once outside the theater, Cole took a deep breath, trying to calm his nerves. He'd experienced an eerie feeling as he'd stood on the Deadwood Variety Theater stage. He knew the age-old stories that were told about theater ghosts, and this theater seemed to have more than its share of them. Did ghosts move into new theaters when they tired of the old ones they'd been trapped in? He couldn't answer that one. But he wished he'd never violated his own vow and stepped back into a theater. Echoes of the past resounded in his mind.

Right now he needed to take a long walk to clear his head. After that, he'd decide what he should do.

The threat of rain darkened the sky overhead as he walked. He shook his head. Just what Deadwood needed, more water. He stepped over a drunk sleeping it off outside one of the saloons, then turned a corner. Near the Big Horn Store his path crossed with that of Penelope Pettigrew.

"Hello, Sheriff Branch," she said flirtatiously.

"Miz Pettigrew." He tipped his hat.

"My it's warm today, isn't it? Makes a body want to shed all her clothes and slip into a cool lake." She cocked her head slyly and eyed him up and down.

"I don't think that will be necessary," he said, scanning the sky. "If you wait a while longer, nature will give you a drenching."

Penelope giggled. "I've heard of a lovely spot to watch the rain sweep down Whitewood Creek. It's very private. I'd dearly love to see it, but I couldn't possibly go there alone, unprotected."

"That's probably very wise."

"Yes. Well, then, my only opportunity of seeing it would be in . . . your company. May I count on you, Sheriff?"

Cole stepped back. She had a quick mind, he'd give her that. "Miz Pettigrew, you may count on me to take care of business, but you may not count on me to take you to Whitewood Creek or anywhere else."

Penelope sniffed and lifted her pointed chin, showing she did not take his rebuff lightly. "I'll wager you wouldn't say that to Miss Dearden, would you? She has all the men drooling over her."

"Miss Dearden seems very capable of staying out of their way. In any case, drooling doesn't sound to me like anything a lovely girl like you would want to attract."

"I bet she's had lots of experience with men," Penelope countered snippily.

Cole squared his shoulders. "I don't think you're in a position to know anything about Miss Dearden's life."

155

Neither did he, he realized. Suddenly he wanted to know more about Maudie, a lot more. Bartles was right. She was a striking woman, beautiful. He thought about past female companionship, and his present lack of it. Penelope reminded him of some of the girls he'd met in the theater, but he supposed she wouldn't want to know that. He'd discovered them early, but not before they'd discovered him. He always wanted to stay with one, but the actresses he knew were more interested in sampling many men. He'd had his heart broken more than once. He could take it. It was watching his mother and father hurt themselves and hurt each other that he couldn't take, and he wanted none of it in his own life.

"Perhaps not. But I'll have you know that several of them have ignored her to seek my favors." Penelope rearranged a pair of long nape curls over her shoulder, letting her fingertips brush lightly over her breast.

"And I'm sure you've been happily engaged in obliging them." When her eyes blazed, Cole amended his statement. "By giving them the pleasure of your charming company, of course. Just be careful, Miz Pettigrew. Remember what happened the last time you toyed with the affections of one of those young prospectors."

Penelope softened. "I know. But it was so exciting watching you save my father from certain death. Surely you can understand I have to have suitors. There's nothing else to do in Deadwood for a woman of my background." She dropped her gaze, then lifted it to flutter rather awkwardly her dark eyelashes.

"Though I would certainly make time for you, Sheriff, if you'd be of a mind to . . ."

Anxious to take his leave of Penelope Pettigrew, Cole tipped his hat. "That's mighty sweet of you, Miz Pettigrew." He searched for a way to reject her without making her feel rejected. "Unfortunately my work in Deadwood prevents me from shall we say, more pleasant diversion. Why, I'd never be able to concentrate on my work if I had such a lovely lady as yourself on my mind all the time. You understand. You could help me retain my concentration by simply ignoring me. The safety of Deadwood is at stake."

Penelope smiled with satisfaction. "Why, of course, Sheriff. I shall try my best not to distract you. It's my civic duty. Leave it to me."

Cole tipped his hat again. "I'm grateful to you. I suggest you get on home now before the skies open up and ruin your lovely attire."

Penelope scanned the heavens with trepidation, nodded at him, then turned and walked quickly away. He noticed she no longer used a bustle to enhance her suggestive gait.

Cole resumed his walk, reflecting on recent events. The marshal had told him a Pinkerton agent would eventually arrive to investigate the stolen rubies. He had been extremely relieved knowing that an experienced lawman would handle something so important. Relieved, that was, until Maudie Boone Dearden had stepped off a wagon load of cats and demanded to know what he was doing to solve the alleged murder of Clara Carew. He'd been fearless about so many things in his life. But not this time. She had a lot of nerve, that woman. And more.

Well, he'd done it. He'd made an investigation. But his palms were sweating, and his stomach was all tied up in knots. He knew that that had less to do with being in a theater again than with holding Maudie Boone Dearden in his arms.

"Maudie!"

Taryn's face was flushed and her dark hair bounced as she ran in breathless excitement up the center aisle of the theater to the audience door just as Maudie entered. On the stage the rest of the theatrical company huddled in a tight group, their hushed voices revealing amazement and alarm.

"You won't believe this!" Taryn breathed, one hand over her heart and the other on Maudie's forearm.

"What?"

Maudie reached out a hand and placed it over Taryn's, as much to steady herself as to steady the girl, and hoped her response sounded as surprised and puzzled as it might have been had she known nothing of what she was about to hear. Following her discovery of the faulty overhead stage rigging, and her subsequent fall into the arms of Cole Branch, Maudie had been involved in a self-battle to regain her bearings. She'd allowed herself only a slight few minutes to pull herself together before reentering the theater. She couldn't abide actors who were so arrogant as to arrive late for rehearsal, thereby keeping everyone else waiting for what they supposed was their auspicious entrance. And she prided herself in her own self-discipline where punctuality was concerned. Now she was having difficulty even remembering where she was.

Taryn shifted her eyes and lowered her voice. "Something very eerie has happened."

"What?"

"Something so strange, I might begin to believe in the theater ghosts I've heard tales about."

"What is it?"

"Something so incredible—"

With mounting impatience, Maudie shook the girl. "Taryn, say it, for heaven's sake! What is so eerie, strange, and incredible? And believe me, theater ghosts do exist, though I daresay this theater isn't old enough to have any yet."

Taryn leaned close to her and whispered, "Well, it's old enough to have at least one, isn't it?"

Maudie leaned toward Taryn. "Oh, of course. Madame Carew. How silly of me."

Taryn nodded. "When we all arrived, Mr. LaFountain was standing center stage looking as if he'd seen her."

"Why?" *Good acting, Maudie, old girl. That delivery sounded almost as if you have no idea what she is about to tell you.*

Taryn brought her lips close to Maudie's ear. "The backdrop. It was hanging grotesquely by its pipe and strings. And . . ." she paused, no doubt for dramatic effect, "it had fallen down exactly, I mean *exactly* the way it had come down on Madame the night she . . . met with her unfortunate accident."

Maudie leaned back. "No-o-o."

"Yes. It's true. We were all afraid to look, afraid we might find Madame crumpled beneath it as she was that night."

"And was she?" Maudie whispered.

Taryn's jaw dropped. "Of course not! At least . . . I don't think so."

Maudie shook her head, feigning disbelief. "How do you think it happened?"

"We don't know. We're all agog over it. Nancy fainted, and Arletta set to wailing as if she'd lost her best friend or something. Sterling is furious. He hasn't stopped talking about how his art is being compromised by cheap tricks. And Jewel, well, she's so kind about everything, she's been comforting Mr. LaFountain ever since."

Maudie felt something of a twinge of intuition. "Was Mr. LaFountain very close to Madame Carew?"

"He liked us to think so. But I heard them arguing more than once. If you ask me, there was no love lost between those two."

"Why do you suppose that was? Could you tell what they were arguing about?"

"The others thought it was because he was a foreigner. I had a feeling they knew each other from before they came to Deadwood, but I can't say for certain. They were both very strong-minded, is my guess."

"So they butted heads over how the theater should be run, and you think maybe that had something to do with a past association. Is that right?"

"I guess it's possible." Taryn frowned. "Why do you ask?"

Maudie busied herself in her canvas pouch. "Oh, no reason. I've met lots of people like that. The eastern theater is full of them. So, now what? Do we fix the backdrop and raise it back up?"

"Oh, no. Mr. LaFountain has asked me to fetch Sheriff Branch. That's where I was going when you arrived."

"The Sheriff? Cole Branch?" The name caught in Maudie's throat.

"Yes. If anybody can get to the bottom of what happened, he can. Don't you think?"

Maudie watched Taryn's saucerlike eyes, innocent eyes. She wondered if she'd ever been that trusting.

"I'm afraid I haven't been in Deadwood long enough to know what the sheriff is capable of."

It probably wouldn't bother Cole Branch in the least, Maudie was certain, to blab it to the company that he'd found her dangling from the top of the scrim and she'd fallen right on him, bringing the backdrop down with her. More insistently came the stark realization that Cole might tell what had transpired between them immediately after her fall. He wouldn't do that, would he? Dishonor a lady's reputation? Wait a minute. Hadn't they had a discussion on more than one occasion about her status as a lady? Now she was worried. If the others in the theater knew what had happened between her and Cole, Maudie would find it impossible to suppress the memory of it. Every time she was among them she'd know what they were thinking. She couldn't have that. She had to forget it ever happened or it would interfere with her quest. She couldn't let that happen.

161

She tried to focus her attention back to the scrim. So it had fallen in precisely the same manner as it had that fateful night when Madame Carew was killed. A curious thought gripped her mind. *Precisely*.

Her concentration wavered. It wasn't difficult to picture Cole Branch starring in the present scenario, surrounded by a supporting bevy of ingenues with questioning eyes leveled right on her. How would she make one of her spectacular exits given that material?

"I've got to hurry." Taryn peered anxiously over her shoulder at the impatient director. "We can't touch anything until Sheriff Branch has made a thorough investigation."

"And he certainly knows how to make a thorough investigation," Maudie muttered.

"What?"

"Nothing." Maudie closed her bag. "It sounds as if rehearsal will be delayed. I think I'll go out for a bite to eat. I've been too busy all day to stop long enough for—"

"I don't think that's a very good idea," a male voice said from behind her.

Maudie spun around and came face to face with Cole. She took a deep breath and squared her shoulders, a brief exercise she always did just before stepping out on stage in whatever role she was playing at the time.

"Why, if it isn't *Sheriff* Branch," she said as if her tongue had been dipped in honey.

"Sheriff Branch! How fortuitous!" Taryn gushed.

"Absolutely fortuitous," Maudie gushed. "One

162

might think you'd been waiting in the wings for your cue."

Cole tipped his hat in gentlemanly fashion. "Yes ma'am. We law officers pride ourselves on our quick responses."

"I can see that."

"I was just rushing out to find you," Taryn finished.

"Then it's lucky I just happened to stop by to see how the play was progressing." He smiled warmly down on the girl.

Taryn was obviously pleased by Cole's admission, and by his attention. "I have seen you here on occasion. I supposed you were just making your usual rounds. Was that the case," she smiled up at him rather coyly, Maudie observed, "or is there something about the theater that you truly are interested in?"

"Well, now, I don't know that much about the theater, you understand, but I know what I like when I see it," Cole rejoined with a smile so dazzling it lifted his mustache. He leveled his gaze on Maudie.

Maudie felt a rush of heat rise over her throat and face. If she didn't get control of herself soon, she admonished, this kind of thing could get way out of hand.

Taryn turned and ran down the aisle toward the stage. "Mr. LaFountain! Sheriff Branch is here. Isn't it amazing? I didn't have to fetch him. He was coming by anyway."

"Amazing, simply amazing," Maudie chided, though in the next moment she wished she had curbed her sharp tongue. She didn't know what to expect from Cole Branch's sudden appearance in the theater.

"That's me, lady, that's me, utterly amazing," Cole

chided back. "What say we both go up and investigate? I'm sure you won't be able to withhold your astute observations or conjecture on just how this recent mishap occurred." He took her firmly by the elbow and propelled her toward the stage.

"I'm quite certain I can withhold my observations better than you can," Maudie gritted over her shoulder.

Every encounter with Cole Branch was more exasperating than the last. One minute she was accusing him of not seriously investigating the death of Clara Carew, and the next she was wishing he wasn't so quick to arrive on the scene. And sometimes at night she wished she could let the entire scenario fade away and see what would happen if she concentrated on just the two of them.

It seemed to Maudie as she watched him in action that Cole was milking his role as the investigating law officer for all it was worth. He ordered the lights turned up full. He slowly paced the length of the still-dangling pipe, pausing at the pile of crumpled scrim. In Maudie's vivid imagination, she was certain everyone could see the indentation of where only a short time ago her body had been pressing against his. All the while, Cole tapped his chin with the pad of his thumb and the knuckle of his forefinger. Every now and then he touched a loose hemp line and breathed a cryptic "Hmm." Finally he went under the pulley rope and around behind the pipe and canvas, before abruptly stopping to face the assembly and reversed his striding.

"Is everyone in the company present?" Cole asked.

"Yes, all of us except Lula," Arletta answered.

"Who's Lula?"

"Wardrobe," Taryn told him. "Lula takes care of making and mending costumes.

"Where might she be found?"

"Right now?" Sterling sniffed. "I'd venture a guess she's at the Green Front. Likes to bend an elbow with the lowest—"

"She lives at Miss Parrott's like the rest of us," Taryn interrupted defensively.

Cole appeared to be taking a mental note. He walked close to where they stood, and questioned them in a group about the time of their arrival, what condition the canvas was in the day before, if the pipe had been secure above them during their last rehearsal, their whereabouts in the last twenty-four hours. The acting company responded to his queries with unbridled forthrightness. Their answers were so direct and ordinary, they had to be telling the truth. Cole nodded pensively as they spoke. When they had finished he paced slowly back and forth in front of the scrim. He strode toward stage left, paused a moment, then spun around and asked sharply, "Do any of you know if Madame Carew had any enemies?"

Maudie's eyes went heavenward. Talk about dramatic effect. This was overacting of the worst kind.

Glances both meaningless and meaningful passed among the acting company and the director. They murmured low that they knew of no enemies in quite the way the sheriff meant. Of course, the Madame demanded service from everyone, and it was possible she might have made a few people angry with her. But, no, they couldn't think of anyone who would have been compelled to do the unthinkable.

LaFountain had kept his silence during the investigation, but now he leveled a direct gaze on Cole. "You think the scrim was deliberately cut, don't you, Sheriff?" he asked when a break had occurred in the questioning.

Cole turned his back and took his time examining the hemp lines over the pipe. "I wouldn't want to say," he said at last.

"They were deliberately cut, I know it." Nancy Springer managed a weak wail as she fanned her face with a discarded program. When she realized that the program was from Carew's final performance, she flung it away, and her wail turned to a shriek.

"You don't know any such thing," LaFountain snapped, a note of aggravation in his voice. "You breathe one word of that outside this theater, and we will never have a paying audience inside it. Now hush up."

"Mr. LaFountain is right," Jewel put in. "We should all listen to him. He is, after all, worldly, experienced, our voice of reason, our voice of sanity in an otherwise insane—"

"Hush up!" LaFountain boomed. "The Sheriff is attempting to ascertain just what happened here, and I'm certain he can not do his job with all this twaddle going on." He pinched the skin between his eyebrows. "I've got one of my sick headaches now, and there's not a cup of tea to be had in arm's reach."

Jewel shrunk back and perched upon the prompter's stool at stage right. Maudie watched her face. She believed Jewel was truly smitten with LaFountain, and could not for the life of her understand why. The man was surly, as big as an ox, his jaws drooped with hoglike jowls, and there didn't seem to be a civil tongue in his head, unless he was speaking to Cole Branch. Even his English accent seemed to come and go at will. Why did women pick the most unlikely of the male species to squander their love and spirit on?

On the spot, Maudie reaffirmed her vow to avoid love forever, or, barring that, at least be absolutely certain that, should she become unavoidably entangled in that hapless state, it be with an appropriate, honest man with a calm nature and serious approach to life. Definitely not any man in this theater. Including Cole Branch.

". . . and I'd like to ask you, Miss Dearden, if you have any ideas about what might have happened here?"

Cole's voice jolted Maudie out of her affirmations. "Excuse me?"

Cole turned his full attention on her. "I was just saying that since you are an experienced actress—the eastern theaters, I understand, is where you've spent your professional life, not unlike the unfortunate Madame Carew—perhaps you might wish to give us the benefit of your knowledge. Would you like to look over this equipment and offer a suggestion of what could possibly have happened to cause it to fall at quite this angle?"

Maudie cleared her throat and glanced nervously from Cole to the rigging. She stood in the same spot to which he had steered her; she had not ventured with the others up onto the stage. The others turned toward her, almost willing her not to answer. It was clear to Maudie that they expected the engaging Sheriff Branch to reach a brilliant conclusion. Pudding heads, that's what they were, pure custard pudding heads.

"Oh, Sheriff Branch, really, I wouldn't dream of second-guessing you in such a matter," she said a little too sweetly. "I'm certain you will arrive at the truth of what transpired here. I leave that in your . . . what's the word? Oh, yes, *capable,* your very capable hands. I'm certain you will get to the bottom of this mystery in no time."

"I pride myself in getting to the bottom of things," Cole said with a glint in his eyes.

Maudie grimaced. "I couldn't comment on that."

The four actresses let out a collective sigh. Relief, no doubt, Maudie thought. Their big, brave hero had gone unchallenged. In a tiny little way, Maudie was kind of glad of that.

"Thank you for that vote of confidence, Miss Dearden. In the meantime," Cole swept his gaze over the troupe gathered around him, "I think you can all rest assured that in this case, lightning will not strike twice. I assure you, you will be perfectly safe going about your rehearsals on this stage. I won't take up any more of your time now, but I will be back to . . ." He hesitated, seemingly searching for words. ". . . to search for more clues."

The women let out another sigh, this one even more insufferable to Maudie. They offered to be of further help to Sheriff Branch at any time day or night, should he need them.

"Thank you, Sheriff," LaFountain said.

"Yes, thank you, Sheriff, thank you very much," came a round of supporting female responses, and one haughty sounding one from Sterling Hale.

"All right, places everyone!" LaFountain boomed. "Act one, scene three."

Maudie stepped forward then, a question so swift on her lips, she didn't have time to consider whether or not she should ask it. "Did anyone here gather up Madame's personal effects after her . . . accident?"

LaFountain blanched and then glared at her. The others all shook their heads and murmured how they hadn't even thought to do such a thing. As their attention shifted to the director, LaFountain's shoulders jerked. Maudie noticed he suddenly appeared to become so moist in the face and around the collar that one might think he'd recently been rained on.

"I believe Lady Fan took care of that," he said tremulously. "Isn't that right, Fan?" He turned stage right.

Maudie's heart pounded. Was Lady Fan here? She hadn't seen her. Her eyes darted over the stage.

"Where is Lady Fan?" LaFountain waited.

Maudie waited. Her heart seemed to have stopped working.

Cole lingered as well. He gave Maudie a quick glance, then faced the director. "I thought you said everyone was here who was supposed to be here."

"She was called for this rehearsal, and I saw her just before the rest of you arrived," LaFountain said. Maudie noted he didn't seem all that irritated that his leading actress was missing.

"I did, too," Taryn put in. "She was here just before you sent me to fetch Sheriff Branch."

"It seems she's disappeared, doesn't it?" Cole's voice was heavy with suspicion.

"I hardly think so," Sterling sniffed. "She's hardly the sort to—"

Cole gave them each a last look, then started up the aisle. "That should be it for now. Let me know if you think of anything else regarding Carew's accident. I may be back later to have another look around."

Maudie watched him leave the theater.

"Well, then, we'll move back to act one, scene one and go directly into two," LaFountain announced. He turned to Maudie. "We won't be needing you for now. I'll expect you back in one hour." He turned back toward the stage where Taryn and Jewel were taking their places.

Confused, Maudie had the creeping suspicion that she'd been hurriedly dismissed. LaFountain was a pompous old goat, but up until that moment he'd treated her decently, almost grateful for her presence in the company.

Maudie started up the aisle toward the exit. She needed a breath of fresh air, if such could be found in Deadwood. The afternoon had been filled with enough events to make up a respectable variety show, and she felt exhausted from performing in each act.

Out on the street, she headed toward the Grand Central Hotel, intent on something cool to drink and a comfortable chair. She suddenly felt weary to the core. She suspected that was due in part to her earlier examination of the scrim rigging. Not to mention her puzzlement over Wild Bill's mention of the missing ruby jewelry and Cole Branch's reaction, or lack of reaction to that information.

Then, of course, there was the matter of the once again absent Lady Fan. Curious. Yes, it was very curious how the woman always managed to be just out of reach, and always out of sight. But it was even more curious why Maudie felt herself drawn to her, wanted to learn everything she could about the woman. She felt frustrated at never being able to connect with her. Almost as frustrated as she felt by her encounter with Cole Branch earlier. She *had* to get that whole scene out of her thoughts, the feel of him out of her senses, the taste of him off her tongue.

She took a chair at a small table at the back of the dining room and ordered a glass of lemonade. A few moments of relaxation alone and she'd be back to her usual self. The atmosphere of the dining room soothed her. She sipped the lemonade, too sweet for her tastes, but nevertheless refreshing and restorative. She held the glass against one temple, then rolled it over her forehead to the other. Blessed solitude. As she set her glass on the table, she felt a twinge in one shoulder. The aftermath of her acrobatic feats of the afternoon, most likely.

"Is there a seat available for this performance, or is it standing room only?"

Maudie blanched at the sound of Cole's voice. She raised her eyes wearily.

"You pay your money, you take your chances," she said evenly.

Cole dropped his hat on a nearby peg, pulled out the

chair opposite her, spun it around and straddled it, his forearms resting on its back. "Again will I be forced to pay?" There was a hint of amusement in his voice, and the suggestion of a smile played over his lips.

Then his expression grew serious.

"What did you think about the red thread?" He watched her carefully. "I know you saw it before you made your death-defying dive. You saw the frayed rigging lines, and the torn scrim eyelets. What do you make of it?"

Being an actress had taught Maudie well how to conceal one emotion while expressing another. She'd shortchanged Cole Branch in the discernment and intuition departments, but she didn't want him to know that now. It appeared he hadn't shortchanged her in those departments, and she didn't want to show her surprise at that either. Could she have misjudged him all along?

It was interesting that he'd asked her opinion. Had his perception of her changed since their . . . encounter? She leaned forward, propped on her elbows. She folded her hands over the top of the glass, and rested the point of her chin on her entwined fingers. No point in acting innocent, at least this time.

"I think the hemp lines weren't frayed from use. They are made of strong theatrical rigging, the kind used in established theaters, and they are too new to be weakened by use. I think they were cut, and I think they were resewn by someone who knew exactly how to do it." She raised her eyes and caught the concurring flash in his.

Cole leaned toward her and lowered his voice. "And

do you think the repair work was designed to conceal the cuts, and it simply didn't hold as well as the perpetrator thought it would?"

"Nothing simple about it, in my estimation," Maudie came back. "I think whoever did this wanted the scrim to fall again in exactly the same way it had before."

"For what reason?" Cole shook his head. "If Carew was already . . . out of the way permanently?"

Maudie sat up straight, feeling stronger, but impatient with him. It was as if he'd forgotten what had happened between them earlier. Now she was impatient with herself. Isn't that what she hoped he'd do? What she wanted herself to do?

"Well, how should I know that? You're supposed to be the sheriff here, aren't you? How about you doing a little figuring on your own? Don't you have an opinion yet?" she challenged in a firm voice.

Cole sat up straight. "Yes, I have an opinion, but . . . I'm just not willing to share it yet."

"Oh, for heaven's sake!" Maudie didn't try to hide her irritation. Just when she thought they might actually be working together, he went back to sounding as if he hadn't learned a thing. "Why don't you want to tell it to me? You've been pumping me for my opinion, my observation. By now I'd think your own well would be primed enough to spill out in a rush!"

A wave of heat passed between them.

"No need for you to get high and mighty about this!" Cole sputtered. "You're not exactly snow-white and spotless, lady. I have every reason to suspect you as much as anyone else, you know."

"Me?"

"Yes, you! Don't act so surprised."

"Maybe you can't tell time, *mister*, but if you used your head to think, instead of only as a Stetson hat rack, you'd remember I arrived in Deadwood *after* the incident involving Carew."

"Yes, but if you wouldn't let the color of your hair raise the temperature of your brain cells, you'd remember just exactly where I found you not too many hours ago, *lady!*"

Maudie stared at his face.

"What's the matter, one of Phatty Thompson's house cats run off with your rapier tongue?" Cole's mustache tilted provocatively. "You seemed to have no trouble using it earlier."

"I'll thank you to refrain from ever mentioning my tongue or . . . or any other parts of my body again!" Maudie instantly wished she could retract her words.

Cole squared his shoulders. "Sorry. A slip of my own tongue." He held her gaze for an uncomfortable moment. "But," he drew out the word, "for someone who only moments ago said she wanted to leave the investigation in my *capable* hands, how was it you suddenly came to ask everyone about Carew's personal effects?"

Maudie lowered her eyes. "It seemed like a logical question, and since you neglected to ask it . . . I did."

"I see. And what did you think of the answer?"

"Didn't think much of it at all," she lied.

"Really. From the looks of the way all the color left your face, I'd say you thought a lot about it. Makes me wonder quite a bit about this Lady Fan. Doesn't it you?"

174

Maudie sharpened then narrowed her gaze. Indeed she did wonder about Lady Fan, more than quite a bit. And she meant to deepen her own investigation and find Carew's personal things, what might be left of them, no matter who had them. And there was the matter of the missing rubies. . . .

"Mind telling me just why you didn't tell them you'd found me hanging by my fingernails up in the flyloft?"

Cole's mouth tilted in the corner with a smile. "I'm still trying to figure that out."

"What is there to figure?" she snapped. "I told you why I was up there. I just wanted to know why you concealed that bit of knowledge, that would have had them all wondering about me?"

He held her gaze for a long moment, then dropped his to watch his finger trace the wet circle her glass had left on the tablecloth. "I meant I'm still trying to figure out what exactly happened during our earlier appearance in the theater."

Stunned by his remark, Maudie gripped her glass with both hands.

He raised his eyes and leveled his gaze on her. His voice took on a firmer tone. "But that doesn't mean I won't tell the Pinkerton when he arrives. And he should know about the mysterious Lady Fan as well."

Maudie forced herself to hold his gaze. She ignored his last comment, even though she knew he'd purposely made a point of again mentioning Lady Fan. She noted how neither one of them mentioned the missing rubies.

"What alternative plans do you have in the event the Pinkerton agent doesn't arrive?" Maudie asked in earnest. The more she was in the company of Cole Branch the more she questioned the authenticity of his lawman status. And the more she questioned how long she could sustain her own role. She watched him fidget with the corner of the table, and anticipated his answer.

"He'll get here."

"Perhaps. But my experience has shown me nothing is certain, there are no guarantees of anything out here. There are too many variables, too many possible traps and pitfalls."

Cole appeared disturbed by her words. "The Pinkertons are known for fortitude and courage."

"So I've heard. I'm just saying, even *they* are human. It's quite possible the agent might be long delayed or never arrive at all." Maudie watched Cole's mustache twitch.

"I'm formulating an alternative plan. Why are you so concerned about what I will do, anyway? Unless, of course, you have something to hide."

It was a nice attempt to turn the tables on her, Maudie thought, but she was one step ahead of him. "Everyone has something to hide . . . *Sheriff* . . . don't they? That's what makes people so interesting, and other people so interested. Wouldn't you agree?"

"I'd agree you're very interested in me," he countered.

"As interested as you are in me, to be sure."

"What makes you think I'm so interested in you?" Cole squirmed a little in his chair.

"Aren't you?"

She didn't wait for his answer, didn't want to hear it,

didn't want to think one more moment about him. She rose then, gathered up her bag, and without another word walked out of the Grand Central. It wasn't until she'd picked her way through mud, rocks, and animal droppings and was almost halfway down the street that she remembered she hadn't paid for her lemonade. Once again Cole Branch would be forced to pay, another rescue of sorts. He'd even predicted it. She smiled.

Maudie thought about their unusual encounters as she headed back toward the theater, about how they held more high and low points, more entrances and exits, than any play script she'd ever read.

She thought about what she'd told Cole in reference to the Pinkerton agent. Usually Maudie prided herself on her ability to lie with a poker face. Only when necessary, of course. That was one of the devious little tricks she'd learned from her father and then honed to a fine art in the theater. But this time she felt a prick of regret. She'd kept her poker face, all right. But what surprised Maudie was how bothered she was by the fact that she had to withhold certain truths from Cole Branch.

Chapter 8

Lawrence LaFountain made some abrupt changes. The cast was stunned, but took his new direction with a minimum of open grumbling. LaFountain announced he wished to open his new company with a one-act play. Shock reverberated through the troupe. *His company?*

Maudie was stunned. She was relying on her role in *Scarlet Lady* to bring her into contact with the elusive Lady Fan, and now she'd had to accept a role in a play she didn't particularly like, and *Scarlet Lady* was being postponed for four weeks. Impatience was not a trait that Maudie suffered well, and she was mighty impatient to know the truth about Carew, and to get close to Lady Fan.

The last couple of days of dress rehearsals for *Burst Her Bubble*, the three-character play of LaFountain's own composition, arrived with Maudie more impatient than ever to get closer to the truth. The production was the most inane piece Maudie had ever had the misfortune of being associated with, but one good thing this new circumstance had offered her was time to snoop around. She only hoped she'd come out of it with her inquisitive nose intact. One day, she took the opportunity before Taryn and Sterling arrived for rehearsal to search the dressing room more thoroughly than she'd had an opportunity to do before.

Carefully she picked among each actor's belongings, from costume and prop bags to makeup and hair cases. She found nothing more out of the ordinary than an ash tray or two taken from hotels in the States. The discoveries amused her. She didn't know what she expected to find anyway, and even if she did find something she doubted very much it would jump out at her and scream "I'm suspicious! I'm suspicious!"

At the end of the long narrow dressing room with its dull mirrors and oil lights, was a set of doors. One led to the wardrobe where Lula Gale led a life of sewing and mending in dimly lit, stuffy quarters. Maudie imagined the room was what a monk's cell must look like. The other door had always been locked, and when she'd inquired about it she was told it was a storage cupboard for special props. She was determined that at the right moment she would pick that lock and gain entrance.

Maudie tried the wardrobe door. It was locked. Strange. It was never locked, if her memory served her correctly. Halfheartedly she tried the prop cupboard door expecting it to be locked as usual, and thinking of something she might use to pry it open. To her surprise, the handle turned. She pulled, and the door opened easily.

Maudie peered into the dingy room. It was much

bigger than she'd imagined. Not a cupboard at all but a small room. She pulled the door wide to let in light from the dressing room, and scanned the area with astonishment. Suspended from a hanger on a peg protruding from the far wall was a green suit and straw hat. Costume bags, fans, mirrors, and plumes were neatly propped against the wall. A makeup case, a tray of hair brushes and combs, hair dressings, and jars of powders and creams occupied a side shelf above which hung an oval mirror framed in brass, a silk-tufted low chair accompanying it.

Maudie stood stock-still. This had to have been Carew's private dressing room. Something told her Lady Fan occupied it now. Her heart pounded in her ears. She had to control that, she told herself, or she would be deaf to anyone coming into the theater. That admonishment faded away in the face of her thrumming pulse, shaking and perspiring palms, and queasy stomach. Maudie stepped farther into the room with a reverence she might have felt if she'd been entering a sacred chapel.

She touched the brush, the makeup case, the suit, the hat, as she turned slowly around the room. A bulging threadbare brocade knitting bag sat on the shelf between the mirror and the wall corner. Maudie pulled back the opening and peered inside. She placed her hand on some soft fabric. Carefully she picked up the bag and brought it to the outer dressing room to inspect it in the light. She lifted the fabric out of it, and unfolded it.

It was a quilt, a large quilt, double-sided; it appeared to be almost finished. The fabric pieces were very different in texture and sumptuousness. Some were quite plain and worn, and others were silk or intricately printed. Maudie lifted the quilt closer. The fabrics were pieced together with a fancy featherstitch effected with a fine hand. Exquisite work utilizing strong silk threads of many colors. *Like those in the little girl's clothing.*

Maudie ran her hands over the quilt. The artistic workmanship told some kind of story. She sensed that strongly. She turned the quilt over, then started to refold it and return it to the brocade bag when she caught her finger on a needle.

"Ouch," she whispered, and immediately thrust her finger against her lips.

She looked for the needle, hoping she wouldn't also find a blood-red stain from her finger. She found the needle, and her breath caught in her throat. Trailing from the needle's eye was a long spill of red. Thread, not blood. Strong red thread. Thread, she was almost positive, that would match what she'd found in the hemp rigging on the fallen scrim. Thread, she pondered, that might have come from Theo's hat shop!

Maudie stared at the quilt, still sucking her finger. She wasn't certain just exactly what she'd discovered. Carew's belongings? Lady Fan's belongings? A suspect's link to the actress's death?

Shaking, she edged back toward the door of the tiny room, half expecting to feel the cool mist of a ghost's presence. She set the bag back at the end of the shelf, and accidentally knocked something to the floor. Her heart pounding wildly now, she bent to retrieve the object, which turned out to be a theater program. It was tattered, the paper soft from much handling. She noticed that it was a playbill from a theater in Missouri. She set it down next to a small wooden case.

Her fear of being caught prompted her to withdraw, but as she started to turn around something caught her eye. She turned back. A chain spilled over the side of the wooden case and caught the flickering light. She peered closer, and her breath caught in her throat as she grasped the locket around her neck. She pulled her chain out from her neck and peered down. The chain on her locket and the one hanging out of the box were the same!

Her hands shaking wildly, Maudie reached out and touched the chain. She tried to open the box, but the top wouldn't budge. She tugged the chain. It was held fast by the box lid. Urged on by a sense that she was running out of time, Maudie frantically searched the little room for something rigid to use to pry open the box. Then she remembered her own bag. She'd left it by the dressing room door. Quickly she snatched it open and rummaged inside to find the long metal nail file she'd purloined from a nasty salesman she'd had to keep several steps ahead of in New York. She was grateful when her hand closed over it.

With the nail file she gently worked the little lock on the front of the wooden box until it opened. She prided herself on making a clean job of it. No marks, no telltale signs of entry. Not that she cared, but her old man would have been proud of her work. She lifted the lid slowly.

She traced the chain with her fingers and followed it to a small satin pouch. Being careful not to disturb the other trinkets around it, she lifted the pouch and looked inside. A heart-shaped locket lay at the end of the chain. Forgetting her earlier trepidation, Maudie withdrew the locket. She knew it matched her own. She lifted the tiny catch that held the locket closed, anxious to know, yet fearful of what she would find, and somehow knowing exactly what was inside. Her hands shook with the intensity of her racing pulse. She opened the locket. The likeness of the woman and baby inside matched exactly the one inside her own. *This was her mother's locket!* Her eyes stung with tears, her senses reeled.

Her heart pounding in her chest, Maudie slipped the locket back into its satin pouch, placing it as carefully back into the box as she might a newborn in a cradle. She was about to close the box lid when her eyes fell on something barely visible through a layer of tissue paper. Carefully she pulled the paper aside.

There lay a ruby necklace and eardrops, no doubt the very set of jewelry she'd been instructed to retrieve. She stared long and hard at the set until her tears dried. She ought to be excited, she told herself. Simply lifting them as she had so many other things, then beating a hasty retreat would in short order bring her the money she needed to get on with her journey to San Francisco. But did that even matter now?

Waves of astonishment and then disappointment washed over her. Her mind raced with the speed of her pulse. She fought to think through her discoveries, what move she should make next. She attempted to calm her thoughts, tried to add up what she'd found. *All right, this is what the evidence could show,* she thought. Lady Fan has to be the thief of the rubies. Carew could have been Maudie's mother, and Fan stole the locket before or after she killed her. Carew could have been the thief of the rubies, and Lady Fan knew it and took those, too. What was she planning to do with them? And what about the locket?

Maudie calmed her racing thoughts. As to what she should do with this knowledge, she could not be certain yet. Should she tell Cole Branch? How was it he hadn't found the rubies? Hadn't he made any kind of attempt to recover them? Or did he know about them and was covering up that knowledge? It wouldn't surprise her if he was in cahoots with whoever had done whatever had been done here. Wouldn't that be typical of a corrupt cop?

She set her jaw. Was this the end of her journey, the end of her life's quest? Not quite. If Carew had been her mother, Maudie wouldn't rest until she brought the murderer to justice. That was the only way to bring her life up to this point to a satisfying resolution.

Suddenly, the rubies and Cole Branch meant nothing to Maudie. She had to get to the elusive Lady Fan. Lady Fan knew a lot about Carew, and her mother, she was certain of that now. But she couldn't let on what she'd found. Reluctantly, Maudie closed the lid on the box, covering the stolen rubies, closing the light on the locket and its satin pouch.

She heard a noise beyond the dressing room. The others must be arriving for rehearsal. Quickly she shut the door to the tiny dressing room, then closed the lights and shut the door to the communal dressing room. She picked up her own bag and hurried down the back hall to the outside door.

* * *

Cole watched as Maudie slipped out of the dressing room and made a hasty exit. She looked guilty as hell, he opined. Guilty of what? And now what? Should he go after her and ask just what she had been doing in there? Knowing her, she'd tell him she was dressing. After all, it was a *dressing room*, wasn't it? And then he'd feel like a dolt, and his question would seem ridiculous. And justice would be thwarted. Justice. He hadn't thought much about the concept before he became sheriff. Anyway, why was he suspicious of Maudie? Maudie couldn't have killed Carew. The crime happened before she even got to Deadwood, didn't it? He had to stop thinking of it as a crime. It might not be one. It was probably just an accident. He hoped it was an accident.

But what if it wasn't? What if Maudie *did* have something to do with it? Maybe she paid someone to do in Carew. But with what? She appeared to be completely without funds when she arrived in Deadwood. Could she have stolen the rubies and used them to pay someone to kill Carew? If that were possible, then it was his duty to find out, prove it, and arrest her. *But, he didn't want to arrest her!* Why in hell didn't that Pinkerton agent arrive?

Cole slipped into the backstage area. He decided he'd remain in the theater through rehearsal. Listen for clues. What the hell did that mean? What did he know about listening for clues? He wouldn't know a clue if he fell over one. He stepped over a mound of fabric piled by the wardrobe closet and almost lost his balance as he hurried to his hiding spot behind the black curtains that masked the side stage. He could hear the others arriving by the theater's front entrance.

"I hate this play," Sterling Hale hissed to Taryn as they stepped up onto the stage where Maudie was just setting down her bag. "LaFountain is deranged if he thinks the public is going to buy tickets to this piece of pig meat."

"It's not that bad," Taryn countered. "I think the audience will laugh."

"At us, not *with* us," Sterling spat as he strode across the stage.

Maudie's pulse was still racing, and she worked at regaining her composure. "There you are," she said as the others drew near. "I was certain I was late for rehearsal."

"If you ask me, I think it would be better *never* than late," Sterling said, sniffing as he always did in his snits.

He wasn't much bigger than Theodore Bartles, Maudie noted, looking him over for perhaps the first time. But he didn't have Theo's commanding presence. She remembered how the milliner had said he loved the theater, and she wondered why he hadn't auditioned for a part in the plays. A well-placed foot against Sterling Hale's ankle could give Theo the opportunity for a stage career. Maudie laughed a silent wry laugh. She wasn't that devious. Was she?

"It's not so bad," Maudie said.

"Not for you, of course," Sterling snapped. "You have the best part."

"Shall we trade?" Maudie replied, sweeter than

honey. "I think you'd bring down the house in my costume."

Sterling gave her an insolent sweep from head to foot. "I daresay I might, given that I, at least, watch my figure."

"A lonely pursuit, I'd venture," Maudie shot back.

Sterling's jaw slackened. His eyes narrowed. "At least my audience respects me. Yours just ogles you."

Taryn stepped between them. "Perhaps we should go over our lines now. Mr. LaFountain will be here any minute."

"I think I'll go out for a breath of fresh air," Sterling snapped. "I'll be at Nuttall and Mann's should La-Fountain arrive during our lifetime." He stomped off the stage.

"Fresh air, if you like the smell of stale brew and ancient sweat," Maudie came back. What in the world was she doing snapping back at Sterling like this? She decided it was the frustration she felt over her discoveries in the dressing room.

"I think I'll go to wardrobe and see Lula," Taryn said. "Do you mind being alone?"

"No, no, go right ahead," Maudie told her. She was dying to be alone, even if for only a few moments.

Taryn had only been gone that long when Maudie thought about resuming her investigation. No, she couldn't do that. What if LaFountain returned and discovered her in Lady Fan's dressing room? She thought about Taryn and Lula Gale. Lula was the most unsociable of the group at the boardinghouse, when she was there, which was not on a regular basis. She had to have known Carew, and she certainly must know something about Lady Fan. Maudie thought it might be a good idea to visit Lula in her workroom, or at the very least listen in on her conversation with Taryn. She left her bag on the stage and headed for the wardrobe.

Cole stood a long time amidst the masking curtains. It appeared that snivelling little Hale had left the theater, and Taryn had announced she was going to wardrobe to talk to Lula Gale. He couldn't see or hear Maudie, and wondered if she was still on stage. Carefully he peered around a length of curtain. The stage was deserted except for Maudie's enormous canvas bag.

Satisfied Maudie had left the theater, Cole walked stealthily back along the hallway toward wardrobe. Maybe he could learn something listening to Lula and Taryn talk. Maybe not. In any case, he couldn't stand the ominous silence of the stage.

Cole found the door to the narrow wardrobe storage closet ajar, and slipped inside. He was instantly engulfed in the voluminous costumes hanging there, which seemed to have a life of their own and clutched him as he inched his way along the wall. Some of them smelled musty from disuse, and he wrinkled his nose and tried to hold his breath. From the end of the long closet he could hear muffled voices. He moved as quietly as he could in the dim light, aware that his nose was starting to twitch and his eyes had begun to water.

He was almost to the end of the closet when he felt the onset of a sneeze. He stopped and held himself rigid, squeezing his eyes as tight as he could, and holding his breath. Of all the stupid things to have happen!

Hiding in a stuffy, smelly closet, eavesdropping on the conversation of a pair of women he hardly knew and who probably talked about nothing but corsets and chest wrapping!

Cole clenched his fists, willing back the sneeze. His efforts were to no avail; the sneeze was building in momentum and even now threatened to burst his head wide open. He snorted and swallowed, and figured what the hell, he might just as well let it out and then offer some addle-brained excuse about what he was doing hiding in a closet full of women's dresses. He had no sooner reconciled himself to this course of action when something clamped onto his nose with a painful grip and the sneeze exploded into his forehead. Then the clamp came down and plastered itself to his mouth, and something pressed into his body and pinned him against the wall so fast he was stunned into momentary immobility. In the next moment, he lunged out with both arms and caught the offender in a grip that could have crushed a tree.

"Let go of me!" a choked whisper filled his ear.

He leaned back, loosening his grip only slightly. A shadowy shape took form. In an insane flash he thought one of the costumes had come alive with a legendary theater ghost. A few breathless seconds passed before Cole Branch realized he was chest to breasts with Maudie Boone Dearden.

"I said let go—"

He cut off her voice by crushing his lips down onto hers. He'd decide later if it was to keep her quiet or satisfy the escalating urge he'd been controlling since their encounter under the falling scrim. He kept his eyes plastered shut and heard the pounding of the hooves of a thousand head of cattle bearing down on him and waited for the moment when they would trample over him and pulverize him to the size of the dust particles that permeated the wardrobe closet. When they didn't arrive and he realized the pounding hooves had been his throbbing pulse, he relaxed, slowly lifted his lips from hers and replaced them with his fingertips. He opened his eyes and adjusted his vision to the semidarkness.

He tried to speak, but she in turn once again clamped her hand over his mouth. His chest seemed to be vibrating. Suddenly he realized the vibration came from the deep rising and falling of her full breasts against him. His lungs seemed to swell against the wall of his chest, straining to press themselves against that fullness. Lord, what in hell was going on?

Her eyes blazed with admonishment for him to keep quiet. He nodded impatiently until slowly she lowered her hand. He did the same, forcing his hand back over her shoulder instead of down to her breasts, where it wanted to go.

"What the hell are you doing here?" he whispered.

"Be quiet!" Maudie whispered in kind. "I might ask the same of you!"

"Investigating!" he shot back.

Maudie stared at him long and hard. "Now you're investigating a *wardrobe?*"

"Listen, Maudie . . ." Cole whispered.

"Call me *Miss Dearden,*" she hissed.

"Whatever. I have as much of a right to be in this . . . this . . ." he started to sneeze again and the clamp descended back upon his nose. He swatted at it and realized it was her thumb and forefinger. The lady possessed one hell of a grip.

The sneeze passed and Maudie lowered her hand.

". . . wardrobe as you have," Cole finished in a congested whisper.

"Oh really," Maudie whispered back.

"Yes, really," he concurred.

"For what reason?"

"To listen."

"Then, hush up and do it!" Maudie inched her way to the end of the closet.

Cole followed her and stayed well out of reach of her vise-like fingers.

"Oh, it was a glorious setting," they heard Lula say. "I was the only woman in the eastern theater who designed stage sets exclusively. Others pretended to if they owned the companies, but none were like me.

"Was this in the theater in St. Louis?" Taryn asked, obviously impressed.

Lula's voice took on an air of importance. "Yes. The setting was for *Scarlet Lady*. It was so much better than this abysmal thing that Carew designed."

"I didn't know you knew Madame Carew before you came to Deadwood."

"I knew her a long time," Lula said, "longer than I ever wanted to."

"I don't understand," Taryn said.

"No need to. Anyway, it was a beautiful stage set. I did most of the construction myself, the men were so inept. There was a very famous actor in the play. How he adored me! He told me he had never met anyone more talented in the theater."

"How wonderful," Taryn breathed. "And the leading lady? What was she like?"

"Stupid," Lula said cuttingly. "She didn't appreciate great art. She was all doe-eyed about the actor, couldn't see that he only had eyes for me. She was sick with unrequited love."

"What did she do?" Taryn's voice was hushed with anticipation.

Lula seemed to be throwing things around. "It isn't worth talking about," she muttered. "The last time I saw her she was hightailing it out of Missouri as if someone had struck a match to her behind."

"Why? Did you have an argument?"

"I think LaFountain must be looking for you by now," Lula told her. Maudie thought the comment sounded like a dismissal.

"All right," Taryn said with disappointment. "Will you tell me more sometime? I love your stories about the theaters you've worked in, all the wonderful actors and actresses."

"Yes, yes, now go along. We don't want LaFountain coming back here."

From their hiding place in the closet, Cole and Maudie heard Taryn leave. Satisfied that Lula had followed, Maudie turned to exit.

"Wait a minute." Cole stopped her.

"Why?" Maudie faced him.

"There's one more thing I want to investigate."

"What?"

"This."

He swept her into his arms, crushing her abundant breasts against his chest. Her eyes blazed with surprise, but before she could say a word his mouth was over hers, taking it fully, exploring it completely with his probing tongue. Her arms went under his and up over his back. Her nails scraped down the straining curve of his spine. He prolonged the kiss when he felt no resistance to her yielding softness against him.

When they broke apart they were both gasping for breath, chests pressing into one another. His arms were still wrapped around her, her hands rested on his waist.

"We . . . shouldn't be doing this," she whispered, taking in long breaths between words.

"Why not? It was incredible, makes me want more." Cole's lungs strained for breath.

"That's why."

"You enjoyed kissing me as much as I enjoyed kissing you, and you know it. So what's wrong with wanting more?" He bent his head, meaning to do just that.

She pushed him back. "Cole. I did enjoy kissing you, I admit that. But I just can't do it again."

"Why not?" He said, surprised that she could even think such a thing.

"You won't understand this, and I'm sorry for that. But, kissing you again . . . will only stop me . . . from what I have to do, what I must do. And I can not let that happen."

She pushed out of his grip and left him standing, stunned, in the middle of the cloying costumes.

Outside, Maudie breathed deeply. Her mind reeled. She had to think, had to erase the surging of desire she'd felt for Cole in the depth of that kiss. And in every moment of nearness they'd shared up to that moment. He had a powerful impact on her, disturbed her deeply. Her growing feelings for him were going to complicate everything.

She walked quickly down the street, forcing herself to think about the exchange she had overheard between Lula and Taryn. She hadn't missed Lula's reference to a theater in Missouri. She wondered if it could have been the one on the program she'd found among the things in Fan's dressing room. She hoped Cole hadn't suspected anything. She had to keep him from figuring out anything about Lady Fan. Maudie wanted all the information she could get out of Fan about her mother before Cole arrested her. Or before something worse happened to the actress. Anything was possible, Maudie decided. Anything.

A week later, on the opening night of *Burst Her Bubble*, Maudie was preoccupied with her thoughts. She'd be glad to get this play over with, as glad as the disaffected Sterling Hale would be. She desperately wanted to get into final rehearsals for *Scarlet Lady*. La-Fountain had to make that happen soon since the play would open in two more weeks. She'd have to see Lady Fan face-to-face then.

Taryn was as bubbly as the froth that stifled this play, Maudie thought as she watched the young actress apply her makeup. All this child wanted was to be on the stage, it mattered not what the play might be or in what insipid role she was cast. Maudie wondered if she'd ever in her life been that enthusiastic and hopeful and excited about anything. She couldn't remember. Yet, she wouldn't dampen Taryn's excitement for all the world. It must be wonderful, she thought, to feel that way.

Cole entered the theater that evening after the curtain had opened. With everyone in the place focused on what was happening on stage, he figured he'd have ample opportunity to snoop around. He tiptoed across the backstage area. He could hear Maudie speaking to Taryn. Maudie Boone Dearden's voice held for him a sensual attraction even when it was barely audible, a stage whisper. He'd been dreaming about Maudie's snapping eyes and full mouth the last couple of nights. That was, when he wasn't dreaming about the communion of her breasts and his chest. And other things, if he cared to admit it.

He came around to stage left and, if he hadn't caught himself in time, would have slammed his knee against a piece of stage property. He took a look at it. He'd seen something like it once in another theater he'd been in, but nothing as fancy as this. A metal footed horse trough had been fitted round with a wooden structure that resembled an elaborately carved bathtub. It had a high curved back and sloping sides and the bottom had been fitted with wheels for easy movement. It was filled with water and fragrant foaming bubbles.

Cole's attention was sharply diverted from the tub when Maudie strode across the stage and came into his view. He almost lost his balance when he saw her.

"Estellita, draw my bath immediately," she was saying to Taryn, who was playing a Spanish maid.

Cole heard her words as if he had his head in a full milk pail. He was stunned at her visage, couldn't take his eyes off her. She was long legged and looked even more so in the scanty scarlet costume she wore. What there was of it, he noted. From scarlet high boots over scarlet stockings up to scarlet garters attached to a scarlet lace form-fitting corselette that curved in at her waist and out over the full breasts he remembered so well. Her flaming hair was piled high on her head and adorned with gold feathers. She blazed in the middle of the stage under lights that illuminated her like a bonfire high in a dark sky.

"And remember to make the bath exactly the way I like it," she was saying to the maid. She sat down on a satin tufted stool and removed her boots, slowly and with precision, as if she were conducting a sacred ceremony.

"Si, señorita," Taryn said with an accent that sounded a bit like the Scandinavians he'd heard once in a theater in Minnesota.

Maudie rose, turned, and raised one long leg to rest it on the stool. Cole was hypnotized by the lovely round curve of her hip and thigh below the cut of the corselette. He watched her unfasten a garter. She slipped the stocking down her long leg, and the audience went wild. He saw her smile beguilingly. She lifted her other leg and repeated the tantalizing movement to escalating frenzy in the audience. He couldn't take his eyes off her.

A loud commotion at the back of the theater drew his attention away. He frowned. The stage manager, a burly, bearded man named Moe, had Sterling Hale around the middle and was trying to get his clothes off.

"Moe!" Cole whispered. "What in hell are you doing?"

"Undressing him, what does it look like?" Moe growled.

Sterling was draped over Moe's arm like a rag doll. He looked asleep.

"He's unconscious," Cole whispered. "Is he sick?"

"He's drunk! And I don't care if he gets sick in the middle of that stage, he ain't going to leave Miss Dearden out there alone."

"You can't shove him out on the stage in his condition!"

"Watch me."

Cole peered back onstage. Maudie was repeating the same lines and looking off into the wings. Taryn looked positively stricken.

"She's dying out there! What's she looking for?"

"Hale!" Moe hissed. "The idiot should have made his entrance five minutes ago."

Cole paced two quick steps to look out at Maudie, then turned back to Moe. He couldn't leave Maudie out there like that. The audience would be merciless, and think of the *Pioneer's* critic!

"I'll do it!" he whispered before he could change his mind. "What's he supposed to do?"

Moe dropped Sterling in a heap. "Get undressed."

It was Cole's turn to feel stricken. He stripped down to his underdrawers, leaving only his Stetson pulled down over his forehead. "Now what?"

"In there." Moe motioned toward the tub of bubbly water. Cole raised his eyes heavenward. "It'll be over 'fore you know it," Moe whispered. When Cole had eased himself down into the water, Moe said, "Enjoy yourself!" He gave a mighty shove on the tub and the thing rolled center stage to be stopped by a startled Maudie who burst into unrehearsed laughter at the sight of him.

Taryn ran toward the tub, a look of horror on her face. Maudie composed herself before she departed from the original script. "Why, Estellita, you've out-done yourself. This is the best bath you've ever drawn for me!"

Maudie stepped into the bubbles beside Cole. He smiled nervously, his hands gripping the sides of the tub. To thunderous applause, Maudie, still laughing, slithered down into the water and fitted her long legs around Deadwood's sheriff.

"Fancy meeting you here," she goaded with a lilt in her voice. "If I'd known how, uh, urgently you needed to see me, I would certainly have made myself available to you." The audience roared with laughter.

"I was going to ask you to join me in a cup of tea," Cole said, easing into his new role, "but I think the bathtub is a better fit, don't you?" Braddock's Bad Boy had just made a triumphant return to the stage!

Cole couldn't take his eyes off the stunning Maudie. He was mesmerized by her tantalizing lips, most supremely aware of her legs entwined around his hips in the slippery water. The audience was on its feet, applauding wildly, as the curtain came down with a loud thud.

"I'll . . . I'll get some towels," the abashed Taryn

said, and scampered offstage like a child who'd caught her parents in the act of lovemaking.

Maudie was still smiling when Cole came to his senses. He watched in rapt attention as the rapidly evaporating suds lapped against the underslope of her breasts. The thick suds were dissipating quickly.

Moe came over. "I'll get the pail and pull the plug in a minute. That all right with you, ma'am?"

Maudie nodded, still smiling. She had settled down comfortably in the bathwater. It was obvious she was enjoying herself.

Taryn came back with the towels. "You can get out now, Sheriff," she said, holding out a hand to assist him.

"Not yet."

"Why not?" Taryn asked, surprised.

"I'm not ready yet," he said through clamped teeth. What happened to his iron will when it came to women? Ever since he'd met Maudie, his body, usually very well controlled, behaved as if it was on its own.

Moe returned with a pail and placed it under the end of the wooden trough encasement. Cole felt a subtle vibration as he removed the plug.

Cole realized he was in a most inappropriate place to be exhibiting an unmistakable sign of lust for the woman with whom he shared the bathtub. In fact, it was practically paddling like a duck in heat to get close to her. If the water kept lowering at such a rapid pace, the thing might just as well be quacking for all the cover it was going to have.

Maudie laughed lightly. She felt an overwhelming urge to lean across the suds and kiss Cole. She acted on

199

her impulse. Realizing what she'd done, and with witnesses to boot, Maudie made a quick move to rise from the bathwater. The glittering necklace that was part of her costume broke and skittered into the tub. She reached down to catch it and her hand closed around something. It was not her necklace. Neither was it his leg. Or his arm. Suddenly she stopped laughing and just stared into Cole's face.

"One might think you were indeed ready," she whispered huskily, "for something." She laughed nervously.

"And you?" he whispered back, his dark eyes glinting.

There was a brief pause before Maudie released her hold. Bracing her arms against the side of the tub, she pushed up to her feet and grabbed a towel out of Taryn's hand, wrapping it around her as she moved. The water sloshed up to smack Cole in the face as she made her exit.

She strode offstage, pausing only once to look over her shoulder. In front of the audience it had been a great lark for her to tease him in a tub full of suds. Once it was down to the two of them staring at each other over dwindling soap bubbles, her amusement paled. She'd actually been audacious enough to kiss him! Kiss a policeman! Again! And worse, she'd just had the most intimate part of his maleness slipping around in her fingers. For a split second in that water, she'd wanted to stroke him. What was happening to her?

This whole scenario in the Deadwood Variety Theater was making her daft. She knew it. What else could it be? Her thinking was becoming clouded with scenes of her mother, Madame Carew and Lady Fan. She was obsessed, and she could be in danger of missing some crucial detail if she wasn't careful. And here she was sacrificing everything she'd worked for with a kiss, in a tubful of bubbles, with a lawman she couldn't even be certain was a real one. And considering doing even more with him.

It had finally happened. She'd stepped into a stage role and become the character, while her grasp on real life evaporated like theatrical bubble bath.

And Maudie Boone Dearden was scared.

Chapter 9

Rehearsals resumed at last for *Scarlet Lady*. The first one ran late into the evening, and by the time Maudie and the rest of the company left the theater, they were all suffering from exhaustion and short tempers. Moe announced that Lady Fan was feeling ill and had begged off the rehearsal, and LaFountain had allowed her to leave moments before Maudie came in. Lady Fan's face was still as much a mystery to Maudie as was Clara Carew's death.

Maudie entertained the idea of staying behind following rehearsal and resuming her investigation. She'd had no opportunity since that first search of Lady Fan's room. Someone was always around. Tonight was no exception. Lula Gale seemed to be at every rehearsal, constantly mending costumes. For the life of her, Maudie couldn't figure out why anything would need mending. Nothing had been used since Carew's tragedy, and her initial bit of snooping had shown what good condition the costumes seemed to be in.

Now Maudie stood in front of the theater, one of the

few boardwalks in Deadwood that had remained intact. Frustrated by the inaccessibility of the dressing room, and her continual inability to see Lady Fan face to face, she considered that a long walk back to the boardinghouse in the evening air would do her a world of good.

Maudie's body ached, and she looked forward to the walk. Her legs would benefit from the stretch, and her mind needed the time to ponder. Maybe another of Carolyn's special baths would ease her discomfort. Although even thinking about a bath brought to mind vividly the one she'd shared onstage with Cole. Her body ached even more.

The cacophony of sounds around her brought a smile to Maudie's lips. She hadn't been bothered by the clamor of a Deadwood night from the first moment she'd arrived. The music and laughter spilling out of the saloons and gambling houses, and the number of people on the streets at all hours reminded her of New York. While New York seemed a century behind her, she compared the cosmopolitan air of it with the primitive wildness of Deadwood. The two cities had a lot in common, she decided, although she knew New Yorkers would scoff at such a notion. And Maudie believed she had a lot in common with both places. She was as tough on the outside, yet just as raw and vulnerable on the inside.

The difference was that in Deadwood there were no welcome streetlamps and no friendly lamplighters to illuminate the way. There was only the light from oil lamps filtering through the heavily draped windows of whore houses, or illuminating the canvas sides of makeshift saloons. In Deadwood, crude wagons, mules, and saddled horses outnumbered New York's stylish carriages and horse-and-buggy rigs. In Deadwood there were no churches, no schools, no community meeting halls. New York had established districts for theaters, open markets, and even for houses of prostitution. In Deadwood each intermingled with the other.

Maudie strolled along the walk until it ended at a gash of mud over which some thoughtful person had placed a single board. Like a child teetering on a log suspended over a creek, she balanced herself with outflung arms and scaled its length. Where the boardwalk resumed she stepped up onto it, turned around and felt a childlike sense of pride in the accomplishment of making it to the other side without mishap, just as she had in a game of hopscotch a long time ago on the streets of New York.

She glanced overhead at the path of starry sky above Deadwood. It resembled a show curtain draped over scenery in the early stages of construction. The Black Hills towered even blacker on both sides of Deadwood Gulch, and Maudie thought about how on the one side they blocked her from returning to New York, and on the other they obscured the road to San Francisco.

The walk had a positive effect on her spirit. A feeling of expectation awakened in her. So many questions crowded her mind, and here in Deadwood there were so many places where answers might be found.

When she came upon the sheriff's office she knew it wasn't by accident. Maudie made friends easily, but she'd never had one strong friendship with anyone. She knew it had to do with her own battle over trusting people, men especially, policemen in particular. But more and more she was drawn to Cole Branch, sensed he might be the only other soul in Deadwood who understood how she felt about so many things. Perhaps for that very reason it bothered her that she hadn't been completely honest with him.

She peered into the office window and could see the glow of lamplight beyond it. Those were Cole's private rooms back there. She wondered if he was at home, or if he was out pounding the beat, or doing whatever it was western lawmen did. And she wondered what he might think about a lady making an evening call on the sheriff.

In the flickering lamplight of the waning evening, Cole hooked a pair of gold wire-rimmed spectacles over his ears, settled into the only comfortable chair in his living quarters, and scanned through the sheaf of wanted posters and crime notices from the States. What a way to spend an evening, he thought. Lately he'd been starting to feel older than he ever thought he could be. He didn't frequent the saloons or dance halls or gambling dens anymore, and he was beginning to think that the good times were things of the past. Perhaps that was best.

If he admitted the truth to himself, he knew he didn't miss that kind of life one bit. The idea of settling in one place was entering his mind more often, and it was a disturbing one. Why think that now, when he was stalled in a town aptly named Deadwood?

He tried to concentrate on the stack of papers spread

out on his lap and on the square pine table he used for dining, as a desk, and sometimes as an ironing board. The posters and messages warned lawmen to be on the lookout for certain people, gangs, renegade Indians, and even a couple of women. Women. His mother had always taught him that he must think about women differently than men, even if the same set of circumstances applied. She'd told him that women reacted differently from men to the same situations. Women felt things deeper, hurts as well as triumphs. When he thought of his mother, he missed her more than ever.

All right, admit it. You're studying all this, thinking about all this, to avoid thinking about Maudie Boone Dearden. About the vision she made in scarlet lace and garters. About a tub of bubbles. About her body, your body.

He had to stop this. Thinking about Maudie had him thinking about love and how much he wished he had it. He closed his eyes, and the image of Maudie formed sharp and clear. He envisioned their lips together again, their two bodies so close they became one. If she walked into his room right now, he wondered if he could keep from flinging himself over her.

"Cole?" An all too familiar voice coming from the office startled him out of his reverie. "Are you here?"

Cole cleared his voice and started to rise.

"There you are!" The door to his room swung wide open and his vision stepped in. "Don't get up. It's so warm this evening. You look very comfortable, and I'm certain you need your rest after the difficult few days you've passed."

She was here, in his room! And he didn't know if he was afoot or horseback! He swallowed hard. Given his most recent fantasy, thank fortune she hadn't shown up in that scarlet lace and those provocative garters!

"Difficult. Yes," he managed.

She watched him with her incredible blue eyes. "Don't worry, I'm not here to harangue you about investigating the murder at the Variety Theater. On the contrary, I'm here to applaud you for your auspicious debut on that stage. As I'm certain you are aware, the entire city is abuzz! I hope you didn't find it, shall we say, less than honorable for a man in your, ah, position?"

"I'd just as soon forget about that appearance, and I wish everyone else would, too."

"Nonsense. Under the circumstances, you performed admirably."

Cole watched her float into his room with a rustle of full-skirted azure blue taffeta and glide toward the table and the pile of dispatches. He set aside the stack in his lap and rose to get closer to her. He leaned down over her shoulder as she perused one dispatch, slid it under the others, and perused the next. A sweet aroma of flowers drifted up from her skin and floated just under his nose. He took in another breath to fill his lungs with it.

Maudie stopped reading and turned to look up over her shoulder at him. "Some of these are very interesting," she said almost as sweetly as her perfume smelled.

He leaned down closer. "Yes, they are," he managed to get out, even though something had taken hold of his throat and was making it difficult for him to breathe.

Maudie let out a long breath that steamed up his

spectacles. He leaned closer. Through the mist he could see her lips, full, soft, slightly parted, inviting. A fraction of an inch more and he'd capture them in his own.

She motioned toward a wooden chair that was slid under the table as if asking permission to be seated. He nodded, and was fascinated as she lowered her torso, perfectly encased in a fitted jacket of the same azure blue as her skirt. It was fastened with a row of tiny buttons covered in the same fabric that reached from her waist to her cleavage. Mentally he calculated how long it would take him to release each of those buttons.

Too long.

He imagined her tearing open the jacket in her heated desire for him. He even heard the buttons hit the floor like the sound of raindrops on a roof. Forcing himself to refocus, Cole was even more fascinated by the jacket's construction, the way the shoulders and high-backed neck curved around so that an expanse of pale flesh above her breasts was visible as an upside-down heart. He could not lift his eyes from that heart shape even though the lenses of his spectacles made things in the distance take on a rather fuzzy-edged appearance. With the lamplight illuminating her she looked to be sitting in a golden oval aura.

His sparse plain room had at once been transformed into a chamber befitting the likes of a queen.

"Are you all right? You seem distracted this evening."

Cole blinked at the sound of her voice. "Excuse me. Yes, I am distracted. I mean, it's this pile of dispatches from the federal marshal's office. I'm afraid I've ignored them. I've been so very busy with other priorities. You understand."

"Completely."

She sat facing him, calmly composed, with an enigmatic smile on her face, cool as a naked foot in a trout stream. How could she do that when he was certain he would melt from the heat in his own skin, and his insides were performing acrobatic feats? His mother was right. Women did react differently from men in the same situations.

Here she was, Maudie Boone Dearden, in his room, the place where he went to be alone and to be Cole Branch. Just Cole Branch. Not Sheriff Branch. She was sitting in a hard wooden chair in buttoned up blue taffeta looking more enticing, if that were possible, than she had in scarlet lace in a tub filled with bubbles and his body. And now she was sitting in his room alone with him, with no thought to propriety. And he admired that about her. She was her own person, owing nothing to no one.

His mind searched for a way to behave, a manner of conducting himself correctly. He removed his spectacles, facilitating a clearer picture of her. The golden aura had vanished, but the beauty remained.

"What . . ." he cleared his throat again, "what brings you out this evening? And to my office?"

"I couldn't relax after rehearsal. That always happens when I'm doing a play. The lines and scenes just whirl through my mind. I decided to walk a bit. Exercise is as good for the mind as it is for the body, you know. I saw your light on. I thought perhaps you might have discovered something regarding Madame, and I hoped we could discuss the case."

He watched her lips move as she talked. If he hadn't known her better, he'd have thought she was babbling like an embarrassed schoolgirl. He suddenly realized she'd made a statement to him that necessitated his response.

"Ah, no. No discoveries, not really. You?"

"Me? Oh no, not really." She fidgeted with her bag.

"I don't truly know what to look for," he admitted.

"Oh, nor do I," she returned quickly. As Cole gained control over his racing mind he had the feeling she'd just told him a small lie. He squared his shoulders and then squared the pile of dispatches, setting them on the floor next to the chair. "But I have a hunch we'll know it's important when we see it."

"Did . . . did you say, *we?*"

Maudie smoothed her skirt, keeping her sight fastened on the fabric. Then she raised her dark blue eyes and gave him a direct gaze that seemed to penetrate his skin and go directly to the part of his brain that controlled all sensible action.

Maudie took a deep breath and let it out slowly. "Given our enormously successful debut as a theatrical duo, don't you think we might just as well combine forces on this investigation? No use working against each other, now, is there? What one hasn't thought of, the other no doubt will. Isn't that right?"

How was Cole supposed to know what was right? Ever since this whole thing with Clara Carew's death had grown up like a toadstool in a pasture full of cow flops, he'd felt twisted around in his own boots. No, it wasn't just over Carew's death. He knew what it was, and he wondered if he should tell Maudie. He rose and paced the short length of the room.

Maudie looked down at her entwined fingers. "Cole, I think it's time I told you the real reason I'm so interested in Carew's death."

Cole faced her. She looked more serious, more troubled than he'd ever seen her. He took out the chair at the other end of the table and sat down, leaning toward her.

"I think it's possible she was my mother."

He straightened. "Your . . . mother?"

Maudie nodded. She told him the story of Gwen-Ada and Patrick Dearden, and the path her own life had taken since she'd left home.

"I can see why you don't think much of lawmen. I can assure you I'm nothing like—"

"I believe that now. Anyway, that's why I became an actress. And after a while I was pretty good at it. It's a profession that draws from emotions, after all. I could tap into my own with practically every role I was given. And other times it was a relief to put on the mask of a different person. While I was on stage I could forget my own misfortunes."

"You're a wonderful actress, Maudie. One would think you'd been one all your life."

"Thank you. In a way, I have been. I hadn't meant to be an actress. I was going to be a teacher. But I became consumed with finding Mama. I never believed she was dead. Until now."

Cole's chest tightened. "I don't think you are ready to believe it even now," he said softly. When she didn't respond he asked, "What brought you to Deadwood?"

Maudie lifted her chin. "The same thing that took me to a lot of other towns I'd like to forget, news of an actress who could have been my mother." She shifted her eyes to the pile of dispatches. "I half expected you to find a description of me among those."

Cole's eyebrows lifted. "You're not wanted for a crime are you?" He couldn't see himself arresting Maudie.

"Only breaking jail. I was caught stealing and was thrown in jail. There was another actress in with me. She told me about Deadwood and the death of the leading actress in the Variety company. Once again I thought it was possible that someone could be my mother. This time it was Clara Carew."

"But the name . . ."

"I know. My mother's stage name was Gwen-Ada Boone. Not wishing to be found, she probably changed it often."

Cole rose and came around to her end of the table. Impulsively he reached out and rubbed her back. "You've traveled a long, hard road, haven't you, Maudie? And now you're in Deadwood, and still don't have any answers."

"I won't give up."

He knew she wouldn't.

"That's why I've been so hard on you." She looked up at him with wide eyes. "I'm sorry for that now. It's just that it was your job to investigate, to solve the crime if there was one, and you didn't seem to be interested. I was angry and frustrated, and this time the possibility that the actress could be my mother seemed more real than ever, and I . . ."

"I understand," he stopped her. He wouldn't have withheld his own story now for anything. She deserved to know. He wanted her to know. "I didn't do my job because . . . because I'm not really a sheriff. I'm an actor, or was. And . . . I was afraid to go into a theater again."

Maudie didn't take her eyes off him. He moved to the armchair and sat down. Her inimitable scrutiny penetrated his already crumbling facade, but he felt no fear about telling her everything. He knew now how well she'd understand.

"I knew you weren't really a sheriff, or at least that you were new to the job."

Startled, he raised his gaze to meet hers. There was a softness in her eyes. "You're right. It's just another role in a play."

He told her the story of his life in the theater, and how eventually he'd cut himself off from his parents, Mary and Jared. He admitted, for the first time to someone other than himself, that his youthful escape from them had hurt him more than anything ever had.

"I was a lot like you. I took off on my own, taking odd jobs here and there, anything that kept me alive and out of theaters and acting. I wanted no more of that life, nothing to do with my father, nor with any other kind of involvement."

"There's been no . . . lady in your life?"

"Not any one lady for any length of time. I was too busy moving around. And, well, I was afraid to be hurt, or to hurt someone else. I suppose that sounds strange to you, but . . ."

"No, no it doesn't. I understand completely."

"Then, there's been no man in your life?"

Maudie gave a small laugh. "No."

"I can't imagine that," he breathed.

"Oh, I was social, and there were occasions . . . nothing serious. Like you, I was moving too quickly." She grew contemplative. "Did you ever see your father again?"

Cole emitted a hard sigh. Talking about all this with Maudie was difficult, yet he wanted to do it. He felt right about it, sensed he could tell her about his painful moments and she'd understand. "Yes. In a town in Missouri—I've forgotten the name—my father arrived with an acting troupe. But I kept out of sight, didn't want him to see me."

"Why not?"

"Stupid pride, I guess. Every now and then I'd catch a glimpse of him and an actress he spent a lot of time with. But I couldn't help myself, and I started going to the back of the theater once in a while. I watched them from afar and I could tell they truly cared about each other. My father looked sober, appeared to have straightened himself out. I began to have second thoughts about Jared, thought about forgiving him as an adult since I never could as a child." Absently he rubbed the arm of the chair.

"That's very courageous," Maudie said softly.

"If it was, then I should have been courageous sooner. I was too late." He hesitated, then drew in a deep breath. "I went to the theater one evening, determined to patch things up with my father and to meet the woman who had had such a good influence on him. He made a dramatic entrance, took command of the stage. God, he was better than ever! I felt an odd twinge of jealousy. Not for the actor I thought I could have been," he added quickly, "but in my heart I knew I should have been the one to take care of him, not some stranger."

He shuddered now, thinking back to that last night. It bore uncanny resemblance to the incident involving Clara Carew. Maudie was silent. He knew she was giving him time to gather his strength. In that moment he felt like running to her, dropping on his knees and burying his head in her lap.

He steeled himself. "I've never told anyone about this, not ever. During the final scene of the play, the scenery came down, bringing the roof of the theater with it. It fell on my father, crushing him beneath its weight. He . . . he was killed."

Maudie started out of her chair. He thought if she touched him now he'd crumble. He held up one hand to stop her, and she stayed where she was.

"I ran away. Can you believe that? I ran! According to the newspaper, the police discovered that the stage rigging had been deliberately cut. A woman backstage implicated an actress. She said the actress had been involved with my father and was jealous when she learned that she, too, had been having an affair with him. The actress disappeared. Everyone said it was murder, but there was no one to try for it."

Maudie shivered audibly. "Now I understand why

you didn't want to become involved in Clara Carew's death."

Cole nodded. "I've gone beyond that now. The similarities are too stark for me to stay out of it any longer. I didn't want to even think about it, but . . . I feel the way you do. I have to know. I don't have any proof, but I think the two deaths could be related. Listen to me, would you? Sounds like I know what I'm talking about, doesn't it? Just like an actor taking his role too realistically." He let out a small laugh.

"You're not acting anymore. And this is real." She tipped her head and clasped her hands together in her lap for a moment, then raised her eyes to meet his. "Thank you for telling me about your parents." She rose, a sad look on her face. "I shouldn't keep you from your reading any longer. I'll say goodnight now, Cole."

Cole left the chair and reached her side in two strides. Neither of them moved, both struggling with their separate resolves. He broke first, placed his hands gently on her shoulders, leaned down and softly kissed her lips. For a moment her hands came up and rested at his waist. When their lips parted, they stood with gazes locked, not moving for a long moment.

Maudie turned, dropped her hands, gave him a timid smile, then left his room.

Out on the street in front of the sheriff's office, Maudie paused and tried to regain her composure. For the entire time she'd spent in Cole Branch's room, she'd felt as if she'd been holding her breath, or been encased in a corset tied too tightly. She ambled slowly down the street, thinking thoughts that had nothing to do with play lines or theatrical scenes.

Strangely now, she felt that at least one of her burdens had been lifted. She was glad she'd told Cole about her family. It was as if his knowing had allowed some intimacy between them. And he'd been so honest with her about his reasons for avoiding the theater and Carew's death, she wished she could have been honest with him about the rest of her story—specifically, about the Pinkerton agent.

Why hadn't she been? The agent would never know. She hadn't heard one word from Golden since she'd arrived. Why hadn't he contacted her? What was she supposed to do about the rubies she'd discovered? What if the thief left town with them before Golden could get here? What if someone else stole them? Then what was she supposed to do?

She made a mental note to check Gaston's Freight Office in the morning to see if anyone had brought in a message for her. Or, she could try to get a message out to him. But how? And where? He'd never told her that.

Cole stood for a long time in his office after Maudie left, just thinking. His thoughts of her went deeper than the pure lust he'd been feeling up to now. The desire for her was still there, but now there was something more. He didn't know how long he had been lost in thought, when the office door opened once again.

"Sheriff?" Theo Bartles stepped inside and closed the door.

"Mr. Bartles, what brings you here?" Cole kept his spectacles off. There was no need to watch the little man through an aura.

"Call me Theo, Sheriff."

"If you will call me Cole, then."

Theo looked a bit taken aback. "Truly? Why, it would be an honor, Cole. It makes it sound as if we might be friends."

Cole grinned. "I think I'd like that very much," he said sincerely.

"As would I." Theo purely beamed.

"Is something wrong, Theo? I've been meaning to come by your shop but I've been very busy, and . . ."

"No, no. That's all right. I saw you the other evening in the one-act play at the Variety Theater. I had no idea you'd been cast. How extraordinary you are. A man of many talents."

Cole let out a long breath. "I was not cast in any role. I was merely acting as understudy when Sterling Hale was indisposed."

"Drunk, you mean. Everyone who saw the play has been talking of it ever since."

"That's what I'm afraid of."

"Don't be. You appeared very comfortable on stage, completely in control of the part. What a perfect foil you were for Miss Dearden! So unlike that Hale fellow. He is not her masculine equal. She shines. He pales in her light. But I think she's met her match in you!"

Cole stroked his chin. "Miss Dearden is an excellent actress. She would make anyone look good on stage."

"True, but you have an impressive stage presence of

your own. Something tells me that scene had nothing to do with acting."

Cole decided it was time to change the subject. "Is there something I can do for you this evening? Is anything wrong?"

"Yes. I mean—no. I mean, well, now that we're friends especially . . ."

Cole watched the slight man grope for words. He definitely had something on his mind, and Cole was thinking it had nothing to do with a theft. Of hat supplies at least. He turned slightly and gestured toward his private room.

"I have been known to partake of a little sherry before bedtime, Theo. Care to join me?"

Theo's face lit up with delight. "I'd like that very much . . . Cole." He gestured with his thumb and forefinger to indicate two inches. "Just a very little."

Cole motioned Theo toward his most comfortable chair. Theo dropped his hat over a peg near the door and sat down. Cole took two heavy glasses down from the single cupboard, then reached into a small pantry to retrieve a bottle three-quarters full of sherry. When he'd poured a half glass for each of them, he pulled out the chair Maudie'd been sitting in, turned it around, and straddled it, his arms draped over the back. He lifted his glass in a silent toast and sipped its contents.

"What's on your mind, Theo?"

Theo sipped, made a slight grimace, then swallowed. "I . . . I came to ask your advice."

"About what?"

"Women."

Cole coughed. "W-women?"

"Yes. I'm afraid I'm quite at a loss when it comes to them."

"You? I've seen you around plenty of women, all kinds of women. In your shop and on the streets. You seem to be doing mighty fine, if you ask me. And I'm no expert when it comes to women."

"Those are my customers. I am perfectly able to advise them when it comes to . . . to hats. It's just . . . well, they respond to you differently than they do to me."

"I don't know anything about hats."

"I know."

Cole smiled, remembering how every time he saw Theo on the streets, the little man would reach up and adjust his hat for him, muttering something about the correct way to wear a John B. Stetson. He took another sip of sherry and gave Theo a knowing sidelong glance.

"Are you perhaps concerned about one woman, in particular?"

Theo colored. "Well, if there ever comes a day when there might be one special woman, then, you know, I'd like to be ready. As I see it, that doesn't happen very often, the right woman coming along, I mean. And I think a man must take every precaution to be prepared so that he does not lose that one special woman. I mean, isn't that how it's done? Isn't that what you're doing?"

Cole felt the heat rise over his own throat. *"Doing?* I'm afraid I don't know what you mean."

Theo slid forward to the edge of his seat. "Just the way you walk, the way you speak to women, the way you are with Miss Dearden, for example. Most men turn into blathering idiots around her. But not you. You're preparing yourself, aren't you, for one special woman. You'll be ready when she is. Er, whoever that might be." Theo sipped rapidly and swallowed hard. He made a face as if the sherry burned his throat. "How do you do it? How do you manage to relax when you're around them? And how do you know what women want, anyway?"

Cole shifted uncomfortably, feeling as if he were straddled over a cook fire. He had an urge to act sure of himself, cock of the roost. The man's searching gray eyes were fixed upon him in anticipation. He was looking for instruction, advice. Should Cole play top cock and crow about his conquests in the hen house? Staring into those honest trusting eyes, Cole opted for the truth.

"Hell, I don't know, Theo. I never was very successful at the real thing."

Theo's jaw dropped in an astonished gape. "You mean . . . you're not relaxed?"

"Nope."

"Not confident?"

"Nope."

"Not preparing yourself for one special woman?"

"I wouldn't have any notion about how to go about preparing for something so monumental as that." Cole drained his glass. He poured another two fingers into it, then lifted the bottle toward Theo. "More?"

Theo drained his glass. He swallowed hard. "Yes."

Cole got up, refilled Theo's glass, then turned the chair around and sat down, tilting it so it teetered on its back legs and leaned against the wall. "You know women better than I do. What do you think they want? Besides a fancy hat."

"You're asking *me* that?" Theo said with astonishment.

"Well, yeah. Am I the one with a steady stream of women coming and going from my place?"

"Maybe not a stream," Theo said, looking down into his glass, "but I did notice one in particular coming out of here just a few moments ago."

Cole choked and pitched forward. The front legs of the chair hit the floor with a thud. "You mean Miss . . . M-Maudie?" he sputtered.

"Yes, Maudie," Theo said, smiling, and relaxing his rigid posture enough to slouch down more comfortably into the chair.

"Well, I don't know what you mean . . ." Cole tried unsuccessfully to settle back comfortably.

"You're going to sit there and tell me you haven't noticed Miss Maudie Boone Dearden is one of the two most beautiful women in this godforsaken place people call a city?" Theo's voice rose with each word. He slouched some more, drained his glass, then rested it on his stomach between both hands. "You're lying to one of us, Cole Branch, and I truly believe it's not me."

"Just what do you mean by that?" Cole stood up and filled Theo's glass as it rose and fell on his trim stomach. He filled his own and sat back down hard.

"You know exactly what I mean. You're not as dumb as you want some people to believe. Her most especially. You play up to Miss Brandy and Miss Candy and all their friends, and you've got that young Pettigrew wench fairly drooling all over your shiny black boots"—Theo took a big swallow of the sherry without the suggestion of a grimace—"and by the way, I've been meaning to ask you how you keep them so clean with all this damned shit ankle-deep all over everything—but when it comes to Miss Dearden, you act like a jackass one day, and a jackanapes the next, when what you should be doing is playing the jack of hearts." Theo laughed and slapped his thigh. "Say, that was quite good, wasn't it?"

"Just what was so dad-blamed good about it, buster?" Cole said with irritation.

"It was clever, of course, in its alliteration. I'm sure you see it. One day you're a jackass, the next you're a jackanapes, when you should one day be a jack of h—"

"I don't even know what that second one was that you're calling me, so I wouldn't know if you were making clever alliterations or not. If you ask me, you're being illiterate." Cole swallowed the last of the sherry in his glass, and laughed lightly. "Illiterations. Now that's dad-blamed clever!" He began to laugh heartily, then poured the last couple of drops from the bottle into his own glass.

Theo sat up straight. "Ouch." He rubbed his forehead. "Aha! Now I see where your problem with women lies."

"Where?" Cole jutted his chin forward. "I don't have a problem with women." Fascinated by the manner in which Theo was trying to focus his eyes, Cole decided the slight man was the fastest inebriate he'd ever been in the same room with.

"Yes you have. Your problem, as I see it, is your lack of seeing humor in a situation that involves you. A situation where you might be embarrassed for whatever might be wounding your pride at the moment. And you don't want to appear to be anything less than a big strong hero in the eyes of women, or at least in the eyes of one woman."

"What?" Cole shook his head in disbelief, then wished he hadn't. He never could drink more than one of these damned gentleman drinks. The stuff was potent enough to turn any rational man into a raving maniac, he could see that. That's the last time he'd buy anything from a two-bit snake-oil-selling thimblerigger.

Theo slumped back in his chair. "I still don't know how you manage to do it."

"Do what now?"

"At least look like you're relaxed with women. I mean, there you were on that stage in that tub of soap bubbles, and Miss Maudie standing there in that scarlet lace looking like a vision from paradise. When she got into that tub and slipped under those bubbles with you . . . well, I mean, I certainly do know what my reaction was!"

"Theo Bartles!" Cole said indignantly.

"What! I'm a living, breathing, red-blooded man, am I not? Even if I do make hats and things, and every other man in this town thinks I'm really a woman under these perfectly tailored suits. And if you were all contained under those bubbles, I mean . . . whew! That is truly control."

Cole said nothing. He tipped his head back, drained his glass, then with one forefinger wiped out the remaining residue and licked his finger. "Not so remarkable as you might think," he muttered over his finger.

Now you can get Heartfire Romances right at home and save!

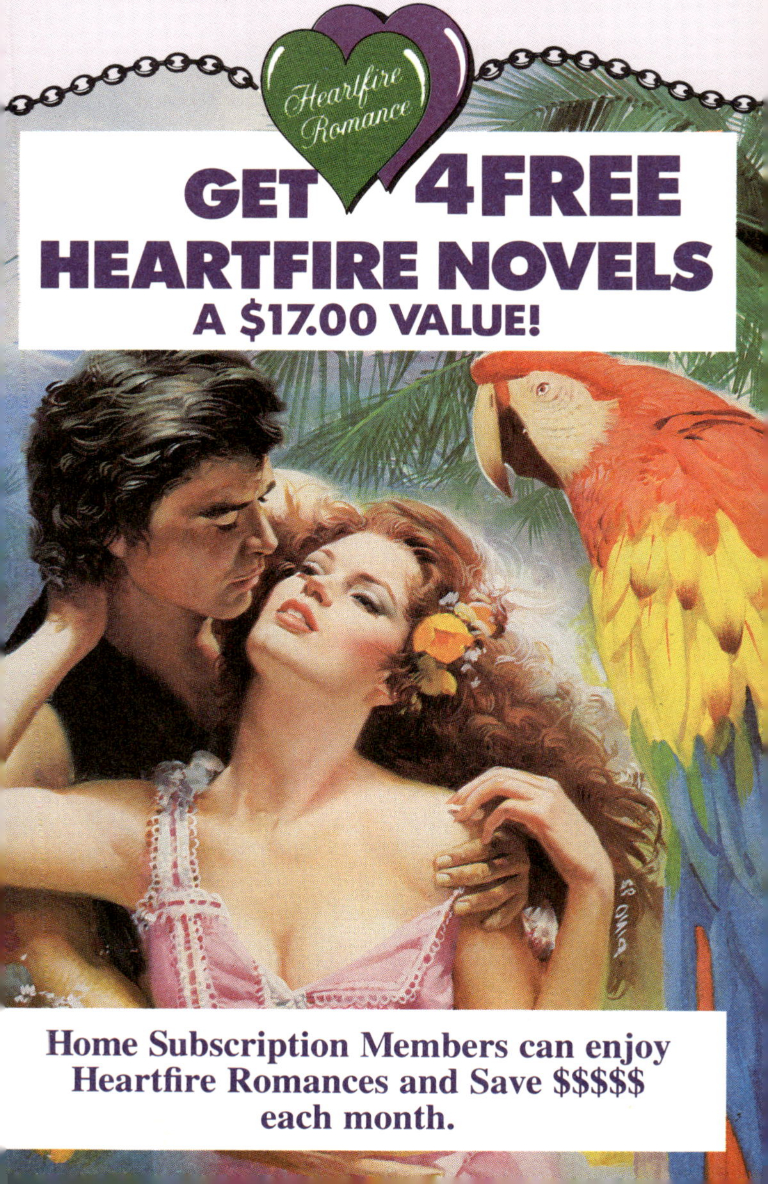

Heartfire Romance

GET 4 FREE HEARTFIRE NOVELS
A $17.00 VALUE!

TO GET YOUR
4 FREE BOOKS
MAIL THE COUPON BELOW.

FREE BOOK CERTIFICATE

GET 4 FREE BOOKS

Heartfire Romance

Yes! I want to subscribe to Zebra's HEARTFIRE HOME SUBSCRIPTION SERVICE. Please send me my 4 FREE books. Then each month I'll receive the four newest Heartfire Romances as soon as they are published to preview Free for ten days. If I decide to keep them I'll pay the special discounted price of just $3.50 each; a total of $14.00. This is a savings of $3.00 off the regular publishers price. There are no shipping, handling or other hidden charges. There is no minimum number of books to buy and I may cancel this subscription at any time. In any case the 4 FREE Books are mine to keep regardless.

NAME

ADDRESS

CITY _____ STATE _____ ZIP

TELEPHONE

SIGNATURE

(If under 18 parent or guardian must sign)
Terms and prices subject to change.
Orders subject to acceptance.

ZH1293

GET 4 FREE BOOKS

HEARTFIRE HOME SUBSCRIPTION
SERVICE
120 BRIGHTON ROAD
P.O. BOX 5214
CLIFTON, NEW JERSEY 07015

AFFIX
STAMP
HERE

ENJOY ALL THE PASSION AND ROMANCE OF...

Heartfire

ROMANCES from ZEBRA

After you have read HEART-FIRE ROMANCES, we're sure you'll agree that HEARTFIRE sets new standards of excellence for historical romantic fiction. Each Zebra HEARTFIRE novel is the ultimate blend of intimate romance and grand adventure and each takes place in the kinds of historical settings you want most...the American Revolution, the Old West, Civil War and more.

SUBSCRIBERS $AVE, $AVE, $AVE!!!

As a HEARTFIRE Home Subscriber, you'll save with your HEARTFIRE Subscription You'll receive 4 brand new Heartfire Romances to preview Free for 10 days each month. If you decide to keep them you'll pay only $3.50 each; a total of $14.00 and you'll save $3.00 each month off the cover price.

Plus, we'll send you these novels as soon as they are published each month. There is never any shipping, handling or other hidden charges; home delivery is always FREE! And there is no obligation to buy even a single book. You may return any of the books within 10 days for full credit and you can cancel your subscription at any time. No questions asked.

Zebra's **HEARTFIRE ROMANCES** Are The Ultimate
In Historical Romantic Fiction.
Start Enjoying Romance As You Have Never Enjoyed It Before...
With 4 FREE Books From HEARTFIRE

TO GET YOUR
4 FREE BOOKS
MAIL THE COUPON BELOW.

FREE BOOK CERTIFICATE

Heartfire Romance

GET 4 FREE BOOKS

Yes! I want to subscribe to Zebra's HEARTFIRE HOME SUBSCRIPTION SERVICE. Please send me my 4 FREE books. Then each month I'll receive the four newest Heartfire Romances as soon as they are published to preview Free for ten days. If I decide to keep them I'll pay the special discounted price of just $3.50 each; a total of $14.00. This is a savings of $3.00 off the regular publishers price. There are no shipping, handling or other hidden charges. There is no minimum number of books to buy and I may cancel this subscription at any time. In any case the 4 FREE Books are mine to keep regardless.

NAME

ADDRESS

CITY _____ STATE _____ ZIP

TELEPHONE

SIGNATURE

(If under 18 parent or guardian must sign)
Terms and prices subject to change.
Orders subject to acceptance.

ZH1293

GET 4 FREE BOOKS

HEARTFIRE HOME SUBSCRIPTION
SERVICE
120 BRIGHTON ROAD
P.O. BOX 5214
CLIFTON, NEW JERSEY 07015

Theo's eyes widened. "I think I'm drunk," he said very slowly. "I mean, I don't know truly if I truly am, you understand, because I've never been drunk. Don't truly know what it feels like. But if the way I feel right now is what being truly drunk is supposed to feel like, then I know for certain I am truly drunk. A-a-and . . ." he continued, "I heard what you just said. You just said you're just like all the rest of us stupid men. You don't know one damned thing about women!" He sat up and leaned forward. "A-a-and, you just said you had the same reaction to Miss Dearden under those bubbles that any other unconfident man would have had, too!"

"I didn't say any of that!" Cole protested.

"Did, too. I heard you."

"Well . . . even if I did, which I'm not saying I did, so what?"

"So, that makes you just as imperfect as I am."

Cole couldn't help himself. He smiled affectionately at the gentle man. "Even more," he said evenly.

Theo yawned. "We haven't solved one pressing problem."

"And what is that?"

Theo plunked his glass on the floor, and held up both hands, palms up as if holding two heavy trays, and sent an exasperating look to Cole. "What do women really want from men?"

Cole shook his head. "I don't know. How can we find out?"

"Well, we could ask one . . . or two . . . that we might know." Theo nodded as if to emphasize his brilliant deduction.

225

"Oh-h-h, no," Cole said laughing. "I do not have the confidence nor the courage to ever ask her—a woman—that kind of question!"

They both laughed quietly together then, and held brief moments of personal introspection. At last Theo stretched.

"You know?" He stood up gingerly, bracing himself on the chair arms. "I'm glad we had this talk. You've taught me a lot, my friend." He grabbed his hat and started to leave the room.

Cole stood up and clamped a warm hand on Theo's shoulder. "Me too, Theo," he said.

"I thank you for your hospitality," Theo drawled, "but I'll be taking my leave now. Wouldn't want to be sick to my stomach in my new friend's home."

"Can you get home all right?"

"Two doors down? I think I'll make it."

Cole watched Theo make his way down the street, carefully placing one foot in front of the other as if the earth might fall away beneath his shoes at any moment. Then he remembered something he'd said.

"Hey, Theo!" he called in a loud whisper.

The milliner turned at the door of his shop and leaned back to see Cole.

"About Miss Dearden being one of the two most beautiful women in Deadwood . . ."

"I knew you'd agree with me." Theo laughed and disappeared inside his shop.

Chapter 10

At the end of a particularly steamy day, just as the cooling breeze of dusk was rolling softly down Deadwood Gulch, Maudie took her customary walk around town. Several steps down the boardwalk she saw Lawrence LaFountain's rather ungainly walk. He appeared to peek into shop windows or peer down alleys, and she wondered about his behavior.

It was two days after *Burst Her Bubble* had closed. She let out a long breath, glad the ridiculous play was over. In spite of her opinion, the production had been well-attended due to its unique combination of assets—it was naughty enough to attract men with the money to spend, and nice enough for ladies to accompany them.

Maudie's fondest memory of that show was the night Cole Branch had appeared in her bubble-filled bathtub. Strolling along, she smiled even now, remembering it. Once Sterling Hale got over his snit and developed his part, things had gone along reasonably well with the play. But every night in the suds with Hale wasn't half so eventful as it had been the only night with Cole. She'd been thinking about it rather often ever since. He'd certainly shown outward signs that he found her desirable. When she'd felt that one specific sign against her leg under the water, it was as if a crystal ball of fortune had floated out of the bubbles to tell her just exactly what her feelings were, too. And they weren't honorable, not by a long shot! She found Cole Branch extremely desirable.

She knew her feelings went far beyond desire now. He'd told her about his life. And she'd told him everything about hers—well, almost everything. She'd withheld any information about love, not that there was much to tell about that. There'd never really been love. Physical involvement, yes—it seemed a long time ago. But she'd never fallen in love.

In respectable eastern social circles she'd been thought of as a woman of easy virtue. She hadn't let that bother her. Maudie thought of herself as a creature of the earth, flowing with the earth's natural rhythms. In other circles she'd be thought of as an old maid, a spinster, since the third decade of her life would be upon her in a mere two years. She'd never been bothered by that either. She'd been too busy, too dedicated to her quest to be worried about what people might think of her unmarried and childless state. She was without family, except for the sort of family she'd become part of with every new theatrical company she joined, or now at Mrs. Parrott's boardinghouse.

In any case, Maudie had stopped caring about the fuzzy-brained state of infatuation. She'd willed herself a celibate life. It wasn't difficult. Up until now. Now she was feeling that fuzziness again. But this time she knew it was more than that. And Maudie knew one thing about herself to be absolutely true—she was an all-or-nothing woman. Sensing she could be hopelessly lost in love, she wanted him to be hopelessly in love with her as well.

How was anyone ever certain of that? She'd have to control herself. There were times when she'd been with Cole that she wanted to flirt with him outrageously, make him succumb to her feminine wiles. But she knew that if she did that, she'd never truly know what his honest feelings were. She'd just have to concentrate on the reasons she was in Deadwood in the first place.

It would be weeks before the opening of *Scarlet Lady*. Maudie noticed Lawrence LaFountain cut rehearsals short almost every night. There would have to be a run-through soon, and she was anxious for it, anxious to come face to face with Lady Fan.

Her aimless strolling in the darkening evening air brought Maudie to the area of Deadwood known as the Badlands. Knowing this wasn't an appropriate place for her to be, she was about to turn around and go back into town when she saw Lawrence LaFountain enter Mrs. Mundy's House of Mystic Pleasures. For one crazy moment Maudie wondered if he were involved with Lady Fan—perhaps she was a lady of the evening when she wasn't on stage.

Her curiosity piqued, Maudie walked on to Madame Mundy's. Locating a back entrance, she stepped inside unnoticed. She could hear a clamor from what she presumed was a front parlor. Music from a tinny piano assaulted her ears, pounded by what she pictured was a player with clubs instead of fingers. Stale smoke and whiskey fumes filled her nostrils, mixed with the scent of enough cheap perfume to constitute a shop full of open bottles. Bawdy laughter drifted toward her.

She peered into the garish parlor from the cover of a draped doorway. Gold brocade draperies, red velvet settees and chairs, potted palms in garish urns, and sculptures of women and men in lewd poses cluttered the room. She recognized Brandy and Candy, and the one called Beauty, and a shudder went over her shoulders as she watched them draping themselves over unsavory characters whose dirty hands groped their bodies. Not one of those women with their painted faces and dyed hair could be Lady Fan, she was reasonably certain of that. Through the laughter she heard the phony British accent of Lawrence LaFountain.

"Is she ready?" LaFountain asked an imposing woman who lounged against a newel post at the foot of a curved stairway. Maudie surmised she must be Mrs. Mundy.

The woman launched her dark fleshy physique away from the post and sauntered toward LaFountain, cleavage spilling over a bright yellow corselette boned in black cording so stiff and unnatural it looked like two roasted chickens were being served on a platter. A cigar-smoking monkey sat perched on her shoulder, every now and then sticking the stogie into Mundy's thick red-painted lips.

"She's always ready for the distinguished English gentleman," the woman rasped in a voice heavy with mucus. "Down the hall, last door on the left."

LaFountain ascended the stairs to the upper rooms. She wondered if she was taking her role too seriously

as Cole had suggested he might be doing, because she
had visions of the director discussing Carew's death, or
a set of ruby jewelry with someone important in this
house. Maudie's eyes darted over her surroundings in
search of a way to follow him. She stepped back into
the shadows and found a rear stairway. On tiptoe she
ascended. Just as she rounded the top step into the
upper hallway, she heard LaFountain speaking, saw
him disappear behind a door. Quickly she stepped
down the hall to the next room. She knocked lightly,
her heart pounding, certain she would be caught.

No answer. Lifting the latch slowly and carefully, she
opened the door and peered in. The room was empty.
How long it would remain so was anyone's guess. By
the looks of the crowd downstairs, she'd wager it would
only be a few minutes. She shut the door and was
immediately enveloped by murky stale air. Thin curtains were drawn over the only window, filtering the
rising moonlight already streaked with cloud cover.
She moved toward the wall and felt her way along it
toward the corner. She heard LaFountain's voice on
the other side. A woman's vaguely familiar voice murmured low. He spoke again, she didn't resist him. Bedsprings squeaked.

Carefully Maudie moved onto the bed and knelt
near the wall. She felt kind of guilty but she kept telling
herself over and over LaFountain was suspicious and
this was simply one way she could do her job. He could
be hiding something.

The door latch jiggled.

Maudie's gaze darted toward the sound. Someone
was coming into the room! She dove under the thin

blankets on the bed, hoping whoever it was would think the room empty and just leave. She waited. The door latch moved again, then clinked against the upper bar. The door swung open accompanied by heavy boot steps. They came closer to the bed. They stopped. She held her breath.

Then the bed compressed on one side. Maudie froze and gripped the side of the thin mattress. It had to be a big person the way the bed creaked down like that. A man! It was definitely a man! And he was getting into the bed! She had to escape, but how?

Maudie summoned up her courage and calculated how she would make a bolt for the door. She was on the wall side of the bed. It would mean going around the end and passing him somehow. Well, she could be fast if she had to be, and she knew how to land a sharp knee, a poking finger, or a doubled fist with precise accuracy. She was about to throw herself from the bed and make a run for it when she heard voices outside the door.

The man in the bed stiffened, then yanked the blankets up and plastered himself right next to Maudie's form. He was down far enough on the bed so that if he moved his head the merest amount she knew he could bury it between her breasts.

The voices moved and continued down the hall. Maudie felt the man let out a breath, felt it against the naked skin above her breasts. His breath didn't smell like whiskey or stale tobacco. In fact, there was no distinct odor of sweat or animal emanating from the figure. Maybe this wasn't one of Mundy's regulars, and for that she hoped she could be grateful.

Maudie stayed very still, an increasingly difficult feat given the fact that she could feel the man's light breath whispering over her breasts. He stayed very still, except for that slight breathing. What was he waiting for? Why didn't he either make a move to grab her so she could make her move and get out of there, or else get out of there himself? She clamped her eyes shut. She wanted badly to breathe, wanted to calm her racing pulse. She couldn't. Didn't.

He moved slightly. His breath came even closer bringing a light mist with it. If she took in a deep breath her breasts would press against his face. *No breathing. Thinking, thinking, that's what you should be doing.* Too late. She had to breathe at least once or else she was going to expire.

She sucked in a quick breath. Just as she knew they would, her breasts came right up against his face. His mustache, to be exact.

Mustache! Oh my God, I'm in bed with Wild Bill Hickok! Maudie's eyes flew open. *No, wait. He's too tall to be Wild Bill. I think.*

The man breathed. His mustache tickled her. It was a long one with waxed ends that felt like little arrows penetrating her skin. Maudie stiffened. She knew immediately who it was in bed with her.

"Cole?" she whispered loudly.

"Sh-h-h."

"Is that you, Cole Branch?"

"Maudie?" he whispered hoarsely.

"Oh, for heaven's sake, what are you doing in here?" she whispered.

"I might ask the same of you," he rasped. "You were here first, you know."

As he talked his mustache moved up and down against her breast curves.

"What! Don't even think it!"

"Think what?"

"That I'm a . . . I'm a . . ."

"A Mundy girl? My dear Miss Dearden, given the fact that I find myself lying beside you in a place called the House of Mystic Pleasures . . . what do you expect me to think?"

"Oh-h!" Maudie lurched, attempting to push her way out of the sagging bed.

"Wait!" Cole's arm shot out over her waist and pinned her down.

"Just what do you think you're doing?" Maudie's eyes had grown accustomed to the darkness and she saw the outline of his profile, his mustache twitching as he talked.

"Investigating."

"Investigating what, me?"

"If you insist."

"I do not insist!" Maudie rasped.

"Sh-h-h! Someone's coming!" Cole put a finger over her lips, then grabbed the blankets and pulled them up over them.

The footsteps stopped at their door.

"I know I saw somebody who don't look right," a female voice said from the hallway.

"Honey, ain't none of 'em look right that comes in here," Mrs. Mundy replied. "Prob'ly one of the girls has got herself a new sucker."

"Maybe. How 'bout in there?"

"That's that English dude and his special friend," Mundy said.

"Then, here."

Maudie heard the latch click. Cole seemed to have stopped breathing. She thought that was a good idea herself. The door opened. Maudie kept her eyes clamped shut. Maybe if she didn't see them they wouldn't see her. Suddenly Cole was on top of her, and kissing her so deeply she couldn't breathe. She squirmed frantically, kicking her feet out from the blankets and trying to get a swipe at him. He had her arms pinned down atop her ribs.

The door seemed to remain open for a lifetime. Finally it closed.

"I was right," Mrs. Mundy gurgled. "One of them quirky kind likes to do it with 'em both wearin' their boots and him with his hat on."

The two women laughed, and their footsteps faded away.

Maudie squirmed hard and Cole released her lips. They were both breathing hard.

"You—!" Maudie whispered harshly.

"Yes ma'am."

She knew he was smirking. "What did you do that for?"

He arched his back, and his torso pressed her farther into the lumpy bed. "It seemed like a good idea at the time. Besides, I had to shut you up somehow."

"What? You thought I was going to give us away? That would be pretty stupid, now, wouldn't it?"

"Well, how was I to know you'd stay calm in such a situation?"

"Would you get off now?" Maudie's throat was beginning to ache from all the tense whispering. And everything below her stomach was aching from the pressure of his lean body. It was a warm ache, not wholly unpleasant.

Cole shifted his weight and pinned her even tighter. "Can I trust you to behave responsibly, like a lady?"

Why was he doing that with his hand, stroking the hair along her temple? His weight was squeezing the breath out of her, and she was starting to feel lightheaded. He slid his other hand up along her arm, over her shoulder, trailed it over her ear, then buried his fingers in her hair. He lightly massaged her scalp, lifting and entwining her hair in his hands.

"You, sir, are not behaving responsibly," she whispered hoarsely, and stared at him through the darkness. "And you're wearing your hat. Hardly gentlemanly."

"Oh, but I am acting responsibly," he whispered coolly. "I'm exercising supreme control." He lowered his head and kissed her once again.

Maudie resisted his enticing lips until she could resist them no more. She kissed him back with growing fervor. She knew she'd surprised him when she felt his length go rigid, his hands stop moving in her hair. Her boldness had taken him off-guard. It was easier than she might have supposed it would be to push herself up, drop her weight over him, and pin him flat on the bed. His hat dropped over his face. She grabbed it and flung it toward the door.

"Hey! Be careful! That's a John B. Stetson!" he protested.

"You won't be needing it," she gritted.

"A sheriff always needs his hat!"

"You're not a sheriff."

He jerked. She held him fast. "I am too a sheriff, right now anyway, and I need my hat!" he whispered thinly.

"And you don't need this either!"

Maudie grabbed one side of his mustache where it curved thickly away from his skin. She ripped it across his upper lip. It made a sickening sound like a petticoat tearing.

"Yeow!" Cole howled.

"Sh-h-h-h!" Maudie warned, flinging the hairy thing in the direction of the hat. She kissed him long and deeply.

He responded, enveloping her tightly in his arms. And giving her back as much and more. They kissed passionately, hungrily, until finally she withdrew her lips and hovered above him. They both breathed rapidly.

"What . . . what'd you do that for?" he whispered.

Maudie relaxed against him and let a out a long sigh. She could be sly, but she could never be coy. "I wanted to."

"Why did you want to?" he asked quietly. He was feeling mighty warm in the solid center of his body.

"Because you're not the usual kind of policeman."

He waited. Then, "That's it? That's all?" His whisper was almost childlike.

She stared down at him, her hair falling over her

face. "No, that's not all. Why'd you kiss me back like that?"

"I wanted to," he answered huskily. "And . . . I want to do it again . . . and again."

Maudie bit her bottom lip. She was about to lose herself. "So do I," she whispered.

He caught her in his arms and rolled her over, kissing her with heat and mounting desire. Then he pulled back and looked over her head at the rickety headboard and the shabby thin wall behind it.

"Not here," he said with conviction.

"Definitely not here," she agreed. She looked directly into his eyes. "And not until I tell you everything."

He tilted his head. "I thought you had."

She shook her head. "I will."

The escalation of voices in the adjoining room distracted them. Maudie moved to get off the bed. Cole dropped over onto his back. She struggled off him with a knee in his stomach.

He groaned. "By the way, I hope you're satisfied that you tore half my face away when you removed that mustache." He watched her lightly place her hands on the wall and lower one ear between them. "How'd you know it . . . wasn't real?"

"Sh-h. LaFountain's in the other room."

"Why would you want to eavesdrop on *that?*" Cole swung his legs, setting the creaking bedsprings in motion as he stood up.

"I just have a feeling he knows more about Carew's death than he's letting on."

"Maudie, you've got to be careful. You've got to stop doing that."

"Stop doing what?"

"I've admitted it, I'm new at being sheriff. And as long as I have the job I'll do my best at it. But you, there's no reason for you to act like some female lawman."

"Shush!" Maudie leaned closer to the wall. "That woman's voice sounds familiar. I wonder who she is."

"I think you should stop wondering. Why don't we wait for the Pinkerton man to get here?"

"You should give up waiting for him," Maudie whispered.

"Why? He'll be here any day now."

"He won't."

"You don't know that!" Cole's whisper escalated with exasperation.

"I do, too."

"How?"

"Because I'm him."

"What?!" Cole let that out loud.

"Sh!"

"What?!" he whispered back.

"There is no Pinkerton man coming. It's a Pinkerton woman. I'm him . . . her."

Cole tilted his head, doubting her. "Go on."

Maudie simply nodded her head sharply.

"How did you ever . . . ?"

"It's a long story."

"I'm in bed with a Pinkerton agent! If that ever gets out it will ruin my reputation!"

"Which reputation?" Maudie paused, listening.

"Quick! The door. LaFountain's leaving. See if the woman goes with him. Find out who she is."

The two quickly tiptoed toward the door. Cole bent to retrieve his hat, scooping up the mustache and letting it dangle over his index finger.

Maudie peeked out the door and saw LaFountain's retreating back. She waited. "Shoot, I didn't get a look at her." She backed into the room. "And here comes Mundy again."

Cole grabbed her around the waist and dove back into the creaking bed, snatching the blankets up over their heads. They barely breathed until after Mundy's heavy footfalls passed the door.

"We should talk about what just happened," Cole began under the blanket.

Maudie felt how close his face was to hers, close enough so that she felt him breathing. "What is there to talk about? LaFountain was in the next room, he didn't say anything important to anyone we could identify."

Cole sighed. "Listen, I've been spending my life staying two steps ahead of dangerous females, and the next thing I know I find myself in bed with one in Mrs. Mundy's House of Mystic Pleasures. I feel the need to talk about that."

Maudie tilted her head back. "Am I dangerous?"

"You most certainly are and you know it. *And* you kissed me!"

"You kissed me first!"

"So I did. What'd you come here for?"

"Just curious about LaFountain. What'd you come here for?"

Cole settled the side of his head into the pillow. "Making my rounds. Just doing my job. I've had to break up many a marital brawl down here when some of the good husbands of Deadwood didn't come home at the appropriate hour. Besides, I saw you come in here and I knew for certain there was going to be trouble."

"Well, thank you for the vote of confidence." Maudie rolled onto her back, then inched closer to Cole to keep from falling off the narrow bed. "How did we end up like this?"

"Working as officers of the law? Or in bed together?"

"Both."

Cole flipped onto his back and inched over as well. Their bodies touched from shoulder to ankle. "I couldn't explain this rationally if I wanted to."

"Nor could I."

"Are you angry?"

Maudie waited before answering. Then, "No, I don't think so. Are you?"

Cole waited. "No. Surprised, I guess."

"I'm that, too."

"I suppose we should forget this entire incident happened. I mean, that's what a gentleman would do."

"I suppose a lady would do that, too."

Cole turned his head toward her. "This is a violation of somebody's rules, isn't it?"

Maudie turned her head toward him. "It won't be as easy getting out of here without being seen as it was getting in. It sounds like the parties are breaking up downstairs."

Cole turned his head back and stared up into the same space. "No, I'm afraid it won't be."

"We'll be recognized. We'll be ruined."

"I'm not certain either one of us cares about that."

"I'm not ready to be found out yet. We have to think of a way to get out of here. We're actors, aren't we? We should be good at this." Maudie stared at him in the darkness.

Cole stared back. "You can use my mustache if you want."

Maudie nodded. "Thanks. You can use my petticoats."

Cole shut his eyes. "Something tells me I can forget about ever securing any leading man roles again," he whispered.

"I won't tell on you if you won't tell on me."

"Shake on it."

Maudie passed her right hand across her waist toward him. Cole took it and clasped it warmly. "I think we should kiss on it, too. Just to make certain we realize the importance of our pact."

"As long as we don't do anything else on it," Maudie said.

"I can't promise."

"This is against my instincts," she said, and leaned up and kissed him lightly. When she pulled back, she knew she wanted more. "So is this," she said thickly. And she kissed him thoroughly enough to provoke his arms wrapping around her tightly. At last she pushed him back. "I'm about to remove my clothes. Take yours off, too, and don't get any funny ideas."

"I don't know what you mean." Cole laughed into the blankets.

They edged out of the bed. Maudie took off her skirt and two petticoats, and stood in her cotton drawers. Cole took off his boots and then his trousers and stood in his long drawers. She flung the skirts across the bed toward him. He flung the trousers across the bed toward her. He heard her slipping her legs into them. She heard him stepping into the skirts and cursing softly.

"Give me your shirt," she whispered. "Here's mine." She flung her waistcoat over the bed.

"I'm not wearing that!" he whispered back.

"Well you're going to look mighty silly with those skirts on and your hairy chest sticking out for all the world to see, aren't you?" Maudie whispered loudly.

"I can't keep these skirts up. They don't fit around me."

"Use your belt."

"Whose idea was this, anyway?"

"It doesn't matter. All I want to do is get out of this place and back to Miss Parrott's before daylight. And I don't want to be recognized in the bargain. Now, please give me your shirt!"

Cole threw the shirt across the bed. She snatched it up and put it on. It carried his warmth through her camisole against her back and breasts. She had a problem with the trousers. Since he'd taken his belt back to hold up the skirts, she could not keep his pants around her. She rolled the legs of them up so they just covered her boots. Finding the mustache, she tapped it over her upper lip and put on his hat. He managed to get his arms into her waistcoat, but could not fasten it around him. He finally took a dresser scarf and draped it around his chest serape style.

"Ready to make your debut as a lady of the evening?" she whispered, laughing in his direction.

"I wouldn't be so quick to criticize. You look like a Mexican desperado in that getup. What am I going to do with my hair now that you've taken my hat?"

Maudie searched around the room. She found a feathered headdress and plopped it on Cole's head, pulling his collar length hair all around it. She stepped back to admire her handiwork.

"Fetching, very fetching. I'll have to hurry you through the place or I'll have difficulty holding on to you!"

"The way you look, I wouldn't be able to give you away!" he retorted. "Make no mistake about this, Miss high-falutin' actress, I will exact retribution. You can be certain of that!"

"How can you talk like that? I'm saving your overly inquisitive skin. If I told everybody you were only acting this sheriff part, think what they'd do to you. I'm doing you a favor."

"Some favor."

"Let's get out of here."

In the dim lamplight of the narrow hallway of Mrs. Mundy's House of Mystic Pleasures, the two crept along the wood boards to the back stairwell and started down. The tinny piano was silent. Voices murmured low from the parlor. The scent of whiskey and smoke and stale perfume hung heavy in the air.

Maudie could see the back door as they were almost

into the kitchen. The room sounded empty. A few more steps and they'd be outside and could make a run for it.

Behind her, Cole tripped on the skirt he wore and crashed into her back. She lurched and he righted himself. Hearts pounding, they waited. No one seemed to have been distracted by the disturbance.

Through the murky glass in the back door, Maudie could see the glow of moonlight. They were almost to the door. Not much time left. She had her hand on the latch.

"Aiyeee!"

Mrs. Mundy's monkey swooped down from the top of a cabinet where he'd been sleeping and landed on Cole's shoulder, gripping with his sharp nails. Cole let out a screech in tandem with Maudie's. She grabbed the door handle and pulled it open. Cole lost his skirts and stepped out of them. Once they were in the street he grabbed Maudie's hand. Behind them Mundy was yelling something about her monkey. Around her a chorus of male chortles and female laughter resounded.

They were rounding the corner of Gold Street when Buford the bank manager came staggering toward them, drunk as a lord.

"Evenin' Sheriff," he managed to slur, looking straight at Maudie.

Maudie just nodded her head under Cole's hat. Cole stepped back into the shadows avoiding the light from the moon. Buford grabbed her arm. Maudie stiffened.

"Always wondered about you, Sheriff," Buford gurgled. "Now I know."

"Know what?" Maudie answered in a gruff voice.

"If you liked women. I see you do. That's a relief. You like them big and ugly. Yes sir, big and extremely ugly."

"Don't think it's wise for the bank manager to be seen in your state," Maudie grunted.

Buford reeled. "I hope you won't tell on me, Sheriff."

"Get on home, Buford," Maudie retorted, "and I'll forget we ever had this conversation."

"Yes sir." Buford hurried away in a zigzag path down the street.

When he was out of earshot, Maudie started to laugh.

"And just what is so funny?" Cole whispered loudly.

Maudie pulled herself together. "He's right. You're the biggest, ugliest woman in all of Deadwood Gulch, including Spearfish!"

"Well, you're not the handsomest man I've ever been seen with either."

"I'm a better looking man than you are a woman, I'll wager."

"I'll take that bet!"

"All right, we'll ask the next person who ventures along what his opinion is. That will decide it."

Cole folded his lips in exasperation. "We're not asking anybody anything. I'm escorting you back to your boardinghouse, and then I and my petticoats will slink back to my room. And you'd jolly well better forget we ever had this conversation, as you said to Buford, and you'd better forget this entire evening happened to boot!"

246

Maudie walked several steps ahead of him. At the gate to Miss Parrot's house, she stopped.

Cole pulled the dresser scarf more tightly around his chest.

Maudie stepped through the gate, then turned back to face him. "Try as I might, I will never forget this evening, Cole. And I doubt you will either."

Cole knew she was right. "It doesn't have to end right now. Does it?" Where did that come from? His heart raced as he waited for her answer.

She turned and climbed the stairs to the boardinghouse, and he felt his hopes sinking fast. At the door, Maudie paused. She appeared to be pondering something. It seemed hours before she turned back toward him.

"You're right, it doesn't. If you'll wait while I change into something a bit more suitable . . ."

"I'll wait." When a cool breeze caught his dresser scarf serape, he reconsidered. "I mean, I'll go change, too, and be right back."

Her lips tilted in a most beguiling smile, and the moonlight caught the sparkle in her eyes before she disappeared inside the boardinghouse.

Chapter 11

Carrying a horse blanket he'd hastily grabbed as they'd hurried past the blacksmith's shop, Cole led Maudie up the stairs of a steep street, then along the terrace, and beyond that up a narrow path to the top of a hill overlooking Deadwood. Night had settled deeply, and the climbing moon, bright as a silver dollar, illuminated oddly shaped shadows around them. It wasn't until they stopped moving that Maudie realized he'd brought her to a cemetery. She shivered.

"I know," Cole said. "But it's quiet and private."

Maudie wrapped her shawl closer around her shoulders. She sat down on the blanket Cole spread out, her back against a fallen tree, her legs stretched out in front of her.

Cole dropped down next to her. He stretched out on the blanket and leaned his head on his elbow. "Maudie . . ."

She turned toward him, enjoying the sound of her name on his lips. Her hair was coming loose, unruly mane that it was, so she unpinned it and shook it out, letting it tumble down her back, and put the pins in the pocket of her skirt. The ritual gave her some time to think. Not that thinking had done her much good that night. She intertwined her fingers where they rested in her lap, and contemplated what the next span of time would mean to both of them.

Cole watched as the moonlight outlined the planes of her profile in a soft silvery glow. He thought about how beautiful she was, how spirited. How utterly without fear she seemed to be.

"I think . . ." He felt as nervous as an eight year old with a crush on his teacher! ". . . something has . . . developed between us." He watched for her response.

Maudie nodded, her gaze fixed on the ragged edges of Deadwood the moonlight revealed.

"I mean, well, you know what I mean," Cole managed. "We . . . all right, *I* have intense feelings about you. More than just lust," he added with haste, then wished he could have come up with a more palatable word for the physical attraction he felt for her. The trouble was, he didn't know the words for what he was feeling. He'd never felt these feelings before.

"I think," he ventured again, "you have those . . . or similar feelings for me." He watched her. She swallowed hard. Good God, couldn't he say anything right? "I didn't mean to imply you had . . . lustful feelings for me, I just meant that you had feelings, or I mean, I hope you have them, that is . . ."

Maudie didn't take her eyes off the restless town that was too busy to sleep. Now and then a drunken whoop of triumph echoed up the hillside from a faro table. She reached over and placed a hand over his where it rested along his hip. "I have them," she whispered. "Feelings for you, that is. And some of them are definitely lustful."

Cole wanted to sweep her into his arms, cover her face and throat and body with kisses. But he held himself back. They had more to say to each other. After that, his passion would know no boundaries. He would give her more pleasure than any man had ever given any woman since time began. She'd given him so much pleasure already.

He sat up straight and faced her. "When did you know I wasn't a real sheriff?"

"Since the first day I arrived."

"How?"

"Your mustache and my bustle." Cole let out a light laugh, and Maudie went on. "I could spot a theatrically built mustache a mile away, but when you knew that what I was carrying was a French wire bustle, then I knew you'd had a few intimate lady friends—and I don't mean of the Candy and Brandy variety. You could have been a women's clothing salesman, but I ruled that out. That left the theater."

"You can rule out the first idea as well."

"I find that hard to believe."

"There were a couple of ladies. Less than a few."

Maudie smiled. "I think I cinched the theater idea when we had supper together my first night in Deadwood. We talked about Mr. Hickok's less-than-stellar career as an actor, remember? You spoke so easily of the plays, the lighting, the scenery . . . well, it just didn't fit with the life of a frontier lawman."

Cole sighed. "And now that you know the truth?"

"Truly, it doesn't matter. I know you as Cole Branch, and that's what matters most."

"I don't want any more secrets between us. Including my name. It's Colton Braddock."

She didn't respond.

"When I first became sheriff, I admit I was acting the part. That's all I knew how to do. I was even enjoying it. I didn't think of it as the real thing, or as real as far as anything goes in Deadwood. And then you came into town."

Maudie nodded understanding.

"It wasn't long before I knew what was happening to me. I was . . . letting myself become involved with a woman, something I promised myself I'd never do. Not that I had any control over it. I thought about leaving town without the federal marshal finding out. I never did come up with a good plan. Much as I thought I wanted to escape, I allowed myself no exit."

Maudie turned to face him. She drew in a deep breath through her nostrils, then let it out slowly. "It's kind of like what happened to me. I had no choice but to take the Pinkertons' offer, or I should say, not to resist their demands. I needed them as much as they needed me."

"How did it happen?"

She related her encounter with the Pinkerton agent, Cutherbert T. Golden, telling him about the rubies she had been instructed to recover.

"So it looks as if we've been in this mess together right from the start."

"Looks like it." She shuddered.

"You're shivering," Cole observed. "Comes of staying up all night in the chill air. You ought not to make a practice of it." He grinned.

"I'll take that under advisement. The night air is probably only part of it." Maudie's voice sounded tired.

He pulled her shawl around her and helped her to her feet. "Let's go get you a hot cup of tea and something to eat."

Maudie let him take over, not something she was accustomed to doing. She didn't feel capable of making the most trivial kind of decision. Her mind was too full of questions.

His arm circled her shoulders protectively. She felt the intensely masculine warmth emanating from him, felt comforted in the strength of his arm, his hand rubbing the curve of her shoulder. She was grateful she had told him everything, that there was now a foundation of truth between them.

The truth had always been elusive to Maudie. One person's truth could be another's lie, and just the opposite. She'd been as focused on her goals as the glass lens spotlights used in eastern theaters, moving in a brilliant shaft of light that was always just a step ahead of her, showing her where to go next. Now, *now* it was as if the spotlight operator had thrown a blanket over the lens.

It was no surprise to Maudie when they arrived at the back door of Cole's living quarters behind the jail. She'd known where he was taking her, and she'd felt not one moment of trepidation at the prospect.

Cole lit a fire in the stove and put a kettle of water on to boil. Maudie sat at his wooden dining table, one end of which was still strewn with printed posters and other documents that were unmistakably government issue.

She looked around the rest of the room, something she hadn't truly taken notice of when last she was here. She caught a glimpse into the bedroom beyond a narrow door hung with a long, dark green curtain that was draped on a wooden peg. She was surprised to note that the bed was made and covered over neatly with a leaf-print coverlet. She could see a partial row of hooks upon which were lined trousers, shirts, and jackets *on hangers!* He was certainly tidy.

Cole retrieved a tin of tea from the one kitchen cupboard, and produced from a two-foot-long sideboard an interesting china teapot, and two matching cups and saucers. When he went back for spoons, Maudie picked up one of the cups and studied it. A pattern of dusty red roses on a background of ecru was set off by a gold rim. There was not a chip to be found. Its delicate beauty surprised her. What was Cole doing with a china tea set like this?

"This is quite lovely," she said at last.

Cole turned to look over his shoulder. "The cup?"

"Yes. The whole set."

"Thanks."

"And it's in remarkably good condition."

"It's very special." He turned back to pouring hot water into the teapot. "I bring it out only for special guests."

"Do you use it often?" Maudie wished she could have tied her tongue in a knot to prevent herself from asking such a personal question. It was none of her business how often or for whom Cole used his special tea set. She wished she didn't care so much.

Cole turned to face her. "This is the first time I've used it since it came into my possession."

Maudie shivered audibly.

Cole went around to the back entry and returned with a denim coat. "Here, put this on. You still look cold."

He helped her slip into the garment. He lifted her hair and fit the collar under. His fingers brushed the side of her neck, and a chill swept over her. But it had nothing to do with being cold.

He settled down at the table opposite her, and they sipped the tea thoughtfully.

"Mmm." Maudie savored the taste and fragrant heat of the brew. "You made it just the way I like it."

"It's exactly the way I like it, too. Strong. Not watered down like in some restaurants. You know what you're getting with this tea."

Their eyes lifted and lowered, catching and holding a brief gaze then letting it go. The gazes were repeated and mutual, full of unspoken questions, understood answers.

Maudie drained her teacup, rose and ambled toward the window that opened close to a hillside littered with the dark decaying trunks of ponderosa pines. "It's odd I should be standing in a room behind a jail talking to a sheriff. I promised myself I would never step foot in a jail again, let alone ever consider a cop as a friend. Yet, here I am."

"You think of me as a friend?" Cole spoke quietly.

"Yes. I'm amazed at that revelation, but yes, I think

of you as a friend. Perhaps the first real friend I've had since my mother . . ."

She heard Cole push his cup and saucer toward the middle of the table. The moon had risen high enough to shine a harsh light at the top of the hill and almost menacing shadows at the base of it. Cole rose and went to her. He settled his warm hands along the tense tendons from her neck to her shoulder. She leaned back into him.

"That's why you use the name Boone, hoping she, or someone, will come forward and tell you something you can believe." Cole's voice was low, almost caressing. "I hope you find out if Madame was your mother."

Maudie brought her arms up and hugged herself. "I think I wanted to accept that Carew was my mother, because then this endless traveling and searching would be over. I could put it all to rest. But, I think I'd know it in my heart if she was. I'm not certain I do, but I'm afraid to rule out the possibility."

"Are you planning to leave?" His voice gave his feelings away.

She turned to face him. "I've seen things that make me wonder still. Nothing is conclusive. And I have a role in *Scarlet Lady*. I can't walk out on that. And, Cutherbert T. Golden is going to materialize soon, I fear, in all his Pinkerton glory, and he'll want answers to his questions." Her eyes broke away from his after a protracted moment.

Cole swallowed over a thickening lump in his throat. "There is a lot to keep you here."

Maudie raised her eyes, and followed her hands as

they rose to rest on his chest. "That's not all," she whispered. She closed her eyes a moment, then opened them and gazed deeply into his. "You . . . were unexpected. And very complicating. I've been thinking about staying in Deadwood, living here."

Cole drew her into his arms and buried his face in her hair. His hand moved lazily up and down her spine. After a time, Maudie leaned back and looked into his face. "In a way we've both been searching for the links to our past to help us make peace with our present."

"I don't think I ever thought about it like that."

"I didn't either until recently. And you've hoped to meet the woman who took care of your father at a time when you couldn't."

"Yes. It seems that you and I have traveled a long and lonely road to get where we are now."

Maudie nodded. "Was it fate brought us to Deadwood, brought us together? Was this supposed to happen?"

He smiled wearily. "Spoken like a true child of the theater."

She left his arms and moved thoughtfully back to the table, picking up a teacup and running one finger round and round the rim. "What did you say your father's name was?"

"Jared Braddock. Why? Did you know him?"

Maudie ran her teeth over the corner of her bottom lip. The name had triggered a vague recollection in her mind, but she couldn't put her finger on it. "No, I didn't know him. The name sounded familiar is all." She pulled his denim jacket closer around her.

"Still cold?"

"Mm. And tired. And . . . I don't know. Not ready to sleep, not ready to face tomorrow." She lifted her eyes and held his gaze, finding a softening warmth in their dark depths.

Cole closed the distance between them. "A true friend would see to it that you were warm and comfortable."

Maudie nodded. "A trusting friend would gratefully accept such attention, and would repay it in kind."

With complete understanding between them, Cole and Maudie walked to the bedroom, arms around each other's waists, her head against his shoulder, his cheek nestled in her hair. It was with a natural concordance that they lowered their bodies onto the neatly made bed with its thick, inviting quilts.

"You're a wily woman, Maudie Boone Dearden." Cole's voice was husky with desire. His long, naked body pressed against her curvaceous tall one which he'd painstakingly uncovered from denim jacket to lacy underthings. He leaned above her now, his hands plunging through her hair. He lifted a thick lock of her dark flame tresses and buried his face in it, inhaling the fragrance of wildflowers she used in the rinse water.

"And you are a masterful man, Cole Braddock Branch." Maudie's voice was sultry, thick with sensuality. She trailed her fingers over his parted lips. "I think I miss your mustache, however."

"Any one in particular?"

With her forefinger she lightly traced the skin between his nose and upper lip. "I think the one with provocative ends that curved up."

He kissed her deeply. "Good choice. I thought I looked rather rakish in that one. Apparently some residents of Deadwood endowed with certain feminine pulchritude found it irresistible as well."

"Did they? Your modesty is almost overwhelming, but I'll venture you'll not remember one of those ladies when I'm through with you." She kissed him sensuously, her lips lingering lightly against him when she pulled away.

"I'll look forward to the process." His voice was thick, coming from deep in his throat.

"You will participate in the process." Her voice was provocative, enticing.

"You expect a lot, don't you?" He touched her full bottom lip with one finger.

"Indeed. Submission," Maudie said, and laughed huskily.

"What makes you think I will submit to such demands?"

"I know you will." Maudie nipped his finger.

Cole brought the finger to his own lips and sucked on it. "Why?"

"Because you want to submit as much as I want you to. The combination can't lose."

"You think you're quite clever, don't you?"

"I know I am."

"I see. I possess a bit of cleverness myself, you know?"

"Do you, now? I'm afraid I have not seen much evidence of it."

"You're about to see much more."

"How?"

"Like this."

He slipped along her body, his hot taut skin over her warm silky skin, settling his lips, quite cleverly she had to admit, in the places he knew would most attest to that cleverness.

Their lips engaged in a long, languid kiss as their hands explored each other's planes and curves and valleys. They were matched as perfectly as mated swans, their courting responses in sensual harmony. Where her body arched, his filled the curve. Where his body thrust, hers received. What her eyes and hands invited, his mind and body understood. What his eyes and hands demanded, her mind and body comprehended. Their loving was as wild and primal as the land upon which they'd come together. Every sensation a new impulse, a new experience in places where two could taste the exquisite sweetness that comes with complete oneness for the first time together.

Tenderly he turned her on her stomach and traced the curve of her spine with his lips, starting at the back of her neck and ending at the gentle slope of her hips. She turned back to face him, tracing the planes of his chest, commencing with the hollow at his throat and ceasing with a light nip below his flat abdomen, where the thatch of dark curls shadowed.

He sat up and leaned against the pillows on the headboard, spreading his long muscular legs. He lifted her body and nestled her soft round bottom against his thighs, then gently pulled her shoulders back to rest against his chest. Her head dropped back against him, and she let her eyes drift closed as his hands explored her, sliding sensuously over her skin, cupping her breasts, playing over her nipples with deft fingers as if playing a sonata on a finely tuned instrument. He slid both hands along her ribs, down her waist, and splayed them across her midriff until his fingers touched in the center pointing downward. Then he lowered them in a vee and slipped lower like an eagle knowing the warmth of its own nest was waiting, and headed directly to it.

She sucked in a small sharp breath and a moan escaped from the base of her throat as his fingers sought and found that special sensitive nub. He caressed it with such sensitivity that she thought she might lose consciousness from the sheer primal impact of it. With the fingers of both hands, he caressed her, exploring her secret inner caverns until she was hot and wet and eager for him.

She pushed against the insistent male heat behind her, straining toward his fingers for more of their stroking, their knowing touch. He licked the back of her neck, sending ripples of desire and rivulets of heat down her spine and along her nerves. As she moved against him, he emitted a feral groan and nipped her shoulder at the sensitive place where it began the curve of her neck.

She pushed away from him then and turned swiftly, until her knees straddled his thighs. Guiding his hard length with her hands, she leaned up and lowered herself upon him, settling over him. He groaned with pleasure, like a mountain lion revelling in the knowing ministrations of its mate. He cupped her buttocks with his eager hands and guided her snug wet heat around him, then pulled her forward. She rocked over him, bracing her hands against the hard muscles of his arms. He slipped his hands around her and up to cup her breasts. She dropped her head back, letting her hair spill down.

They gave themselves over to the primal communication of their bodies, the abandonment of their minds, and the deep sounds of wild mating felines in groans, hisses, and finally purrs. Then the deep satisfied breathing that followed total expenditure of energy.

There was not a thought of moving again until the next surge of primal desire fired them both to the mating fires. And then there was sleep, sweet, dreamless, welcome sleep.

Two mornings later Maudie emerged from the bank after a thoroughly disgusting encounter with manager Buford, who persisted in slavering over her like a boar in rut. Even the money he handed to her was momentarily distasteful to her, having been handled by the wretched man. The worst of it was, there was no one for her to complain to, no one higher up than Buford who might take him to task. She stalked down the intermittent boardwalk, fuming inside.

Maudie hated the feeling that she had no control over a situation, was forced to have business dealings with such a distasteful person. It frustrated her as much as the stone wall she'd come up against in the mystery surrounding Carew's demise. Maudie had to ascertain in her mind and heart whether or not Carew was her mother. That knowledge was crucial to what she would do next.

She stopped short and jumped back as a weather-beaten old man atop a rickety buckboard drawn by a swayback mule careened around the corner in front of her. As if she'd been abruptly reminded by a conscientious muse, Maudie remembered she had a job to do in Deadwood. She sighed. She'd best get on with that, too, or there'd be hell to pay without funds to do it.

It was a beastly hot late July day, as miserably overbearing as Miss Parrott had predicted it would be. Maudie's undergarments clung to her skin and seemed to encase her in a full-length cotton stocking. At least she'd left that straitjacket of a boned corset lying at the foot of the bed where Carolyn had carefully displayed it, and had forgone the use of a replacement bustle for the one that had been pitched onto the trash heap out back of the boardinghouse. She'd spied it only once when the little girl with the patched shirt had scooped it up to use as a carrier for her cat. That cat hadn't seemed to mind the rather elegant ride whatever, and Maudie felt the bustle had been put to much better use than its original intention.

She came upon Theodore Bartles' millinery shop and, on a whim, decided to go in and try on some of his creations. Maudie wasn't given to wearing hats very often. They always got in the way with her modes of transportation, or were a nuisance to care for. Yet, this morning she was feeling so buoyant, so feminine, she felt like trying them on and observing herself in a looking-glass to see what transformations they might effect. She needed to feel she had the power to change something in her life, feel she was in control again. Maybe her appearance was the only thing she had in her control at the moment.

"Good morning, Mr. Bartles," she called out as she opened and closed the door and set the little bell overhead to tinkling.

She entered his cool, fragrant shop and felt a soothing contrast to the hot, dusty street. A delicate aroma of roses filled the air around her. She scanned the shop and noted several open glass jars of potpourri. She smiled. Her senses welcomed the understated elegance, and she felt treated to something special.

"May I help you?" Theodore Bartles stepped from behind a damask rose drape that masked the opening to his workroom. "Oh, my dear Miss Dearden, forgive me if I kept you waiting. I was engrossed in a very special chapeau." He took her hand and lightly kissed the back of it. "I do hope you're passing a comfortable time in our fair city."

Maudie smiled at the gracious, impeccably groomed little man. "Thank you, Mr. Bartles. I do hope I'm not interrupting your work."

"Not at all, not at all. And, please, call me Theo."

"Theo, thank you. I hope you'll call me Maudie."

Theo looked down for a moment, and Maudie saw his pale complexion warm to a gentle pink. "Oh, no, miss, it wouldn't be proper to address a lady by her first name."

"Oh, but I'm not a lady." She swallowed at that ridiculous response. "I mean, I'm not just any lady." Now that was even more ludicrous. She shook her head. "What I mean, Theo, is that I hoped you might consider me your friend. I believe you are offering your friendship to me by allowing me to call you by your first name and by the warmth you have extended to me since the moment we met. I want you to know that I am offering the same to you."

Theo beamed up at her. "Well, when you put it that way, I suppose I could . . ."

Maudie waited a moment, inclined her head toward him and smiled broadly. "Let me hear you say it," she urged.

Theo swallowed, took a deep breath and whispered, "Maudie."

"There now!" Maudie exclaimed. "We're friends."

"Friends. Well then, is there something special I might help you with?"

"You might indulge me in a fantasy or two."

"Wh-what?"

Maudie laughed lightly. "Nothing untoward. I meant that I would just like to wander around your shop and try on some of your exquisite hats. I'd be very careful. Would that be all right with you?"

Theo relaxed. "Oh, of course, Miss . . . Maudie. Try on to your heart's content. And if your, uh, fantasy involves something that isn't in the shop, just describe what you're looking for and I shall do my utmost to create exactly what you desire."

Maudie felt a wistful mood sweep over her. "I wish it were that easy, friend Theo."

"Forgive my brash assumption, but you seem to be searching for something. Or perhaps, someone?"

Maudie smiled down at him. "You are a wise friend, Theo."

"It has been my experience—if indeed your search is for a person—that if someone wants to be found, he, or perhaps she, will come to the aid of the seeker." Theo rearranged some silk scarves on a small table, then set them back in their original design.

"If she is able to be found," Maudie said absently, her back to him as she lifted a straw hat bedecked with silk flowers from a faceless wooden head form.

"If . . . *she,* did you say? If she weren't able to be found, you would know that in your heart, and you would bring your search to a close yourself."

Maudie turned to face him. "Do you really think so?"

Theo nodded. "I really do."

"I've never thought of it quite like that. I've been going through life wondering . . . and wandering."

"Perhaps your journey to Deadwood will result in the end of your quest."

"Would that it were so," Maudie breathed.

Theo's serious visage softened. "You have a lyrical nature. Your life must always be a symphony of harmony."

Maudie held back a laugh. "I'm afraid I've hit more discordant notes than harmonic ones in my life."

"That is the way of it." Theo nodded. "It is your song alone. I'll leave you to your musings now. I will be in the back if you need me."

"Thank you." She watched Theo turn toward the damask rose curtain. He had an efficient, light gait. She admired that. "And thank you for your kind words, my friend."

Theo stopped and turned to look over his narrow shoulder. "I only wish to soothe the spirit of a new friend, Maudie." He disappeared behind the curtain.

Chapter 12

Maudie lifted the straw hat and set it lightly on her coiled hair. She moved toward a shelf upon which rested a round looking glass on an oak pedestal. Shifting her head this way and that, she analyzed herself. At first glance Maudie thought anyone stepping into the shop might think she was wearing a squirrel nest on her head. She adjusted it at a jauntier angle. Behind her stood a full-length oval mirror, and in the glass her gaze caught the back of her head and shoulders down to below her waist. She tilted her head, and sharpened her gaze at the sight. An image moved vaguely through her mind—she'd seen that back with a similar hat somewhere before. What did that mean? she wondered briefly. In a play no doubt, came the fleet answer.

She was about to remove the straw hat and replace it with a drapey blue silk one from another form, when Theo burst through the entrance to his workroom.

"This is an outrage!"

Startled, Maudie spun around. "I know, I know. I'm going to try the blue one."

"No, no, no, not you," Theo sputtered. "I am outraged that such a thing could happen when my back was turned not twenty feet away."

"What happened?"

"Yet another theft! I only recently received a new order of threads, and the one that is the most difficult to obtain, the one that is most important to my current work, was stolen." Theo's face was a furious rose red.

"Are you certain? Perhaps it just slipped to the floor."

"Of course I'm certain! I allow nothing to just slip to the floor. My materials are much too valuable to me. I know it was stolen."

"When? You mean, just now? When you were talking with me?"

"That's exactly when it must have happened. I was using the thread only moments before you stepped into my shop. The entire spool was in its specially crafted cherry holder. The holder is now empty, standing like a forlorn fence post in the middle of an abandoned meadow. I'm so upset I could just . . ."

Maudie knew he wanted to say *cry*, but he checked himself. She slipped her arms around his shoulders as he gently laid his head against her ample breasts, and patted his back. "I understand completely. I truly do, Theo. May I have a look back there?" She released him, and he stared up at her with wide, moist eyes.

"I allow no one in my workroom. Whatever for?"

"Perhaps I'll see something that will give me an idea of how the thread might have been removed."

"If Sheriff Branch hasn't been able to solve this mystery, I don't see how you think you can."

Maudie took Theo's hand, and drew him toward the opening. "Sometimes a woman has a better sense of these things than a sheriff."

Theo allowed her into his workroom. He was right. The cherry thread spool holder stood at attention, empty. Maudie looked around, under the work table, on the shelves, which contained boxes of fabric bolts, swatches, and large spools of colored thread. Nothing was out of place, she knew that instinctively.

"Is this the door to the alley?" she asked, starting toward the back wall.

"Yes, but I keep it locked."

"What's this?" She spied a square hinged door three feet off the floor in the far corner.

"That's a specially constructed delivery box. Sometimes Monsieur Gaston will leave off a package I've been waiting for if it comes in late at night or early in the morning when I'm not here. He knows how important my materials are to me."

"Is it kept locked? I mean, does he have a key?"

"No. There is no key to the delivery box. No one knows about it except Gaston and me. You're not suggesting that Monsieur Gaston would take . . ."

"Hardly," Maudie said, remembering well the beefy Gaston from the day she retrieved what was left of her belongings from the Weston freight wagons.

She opened the inside door of the delivery box, and pushed on the outside door. It gave slightly, but slammed back as if mounted with a spring. Which it was not. Maudie turned back to Theo and placed a silencing finger over her lips. He frowned. She dropped to her knees, braced both hands on the outside door and gave a mighty push. It flew open and the startled face of the little girl in the patched clothes stared back. Maudie shot out her hand and grabbed the girl by her dirty shirt.

"I wouldn't want to falsely accuse anyone of a crime here, but . . ." Maudie reached her other hand through and caught the child in a firm grip. "I think, Theo, that if you were to go around to the alley, you might round up a suspect."

Theo scurried out at her bidding, and rushed down the alley to where the child struggled in Maudie's grasp. He scooped her up in his arms. She put up a shrieking that Maudie could hear travel around toward the front door as Theo bore her along. Maudie slammed the delivery box doors and started to leave the workroom. Then something caught her eye. She looked down on Theo's table. A needle lay on a piece of white muslin, trailed by a long length of red thread.

Maudie leaned closer. *Red thread.* She picked it up and snapped the thread between her hands. It was strong, very strong.

Maudie remembered how she'd scoffed silently at Cole's vow to investigate Theo's losses. Now she suspected it might have been a good idea. She had an inkling the thread might match what they'd discovered in the scenery hemp lines at the theater.

"Maudie?" Theo called, interrupting her thoughts. Maudie quickly shoved the needle and thread into her bag, and came out through the door drape. "It appears we have our thief."

"I'm not a thief!" the child yelled, kicking back at Theo as he held her braced against his body.

"You are if you take things that don't belong to you," Maudie said calmly. "Why did you take the thread?"

"Thread?" The child kicked harder. "I didn't take no thread."

"Don't compound your predicament with lying," Theo admonished her.

"I didn't lie. Wild Bill told me never to lie less'n I had to for to save my life."

"Well, if you don't start telling the truth, I'm going to thrash you within an inch of it!" Theo shouted.

"Calm down, Theo," Maudie said. "Perhaps we should hear the child's explanation."

"Good idea." Cole pushed aside the drape to the workroom door and entered the shop.

Startled, Maudie whirled around. Her breath came rapidly, and she felt heat spread over her face. He looked wonderful, clean shaven, like he'd just stepped out of a bath. At the open neck of his shirt she could see a thatch of dark hair. Even though it was only two days before that they'd made love, it seemed weeks had passed since she'd entwined her fingers in that hair. Weeks since she'd . . .

"Good day, Maudie." Cole's voice was smooth as warm honey. He removed his Stetson, and ran a hand through his thick hair. His eyes spoke of private moments, shared moments.

Maudie was unnerved for a moment, then, realizing where she was, came to her senses. "Good day, Cole." Then, realizing where he'd come from, "How'd you get in there?"

"Through the back door, of course."

Maudie cocked her head toward Theo, who struggled with the wriggling child.

"I gave the sheriff a key some time ago. We thought it would make it easier for him to check the shop at night." Theo squinted at Cole, looking him over as if he were a floor lamp that might fit his decor.

"Interesting that a sheriff needs a key to a milliner's shop," Maudie said, and wondered at the twinge of suspicion she'd experienced.

"So, Patches, I think you should explain yourself to these people," Cole said to the child, ignoring Maudie's pointed remark.

The child eyed Cole with suspicion. "Wild Bill told me not to trust a lawman that looks like you do."

"Looks like I do? What does that mean?" It was Cole's turn to eye the child with suspicion. "Wild Bill is a lawman, at least most of the time. So he says."

"You *do* look different," Theo said.

Patches nodded. "Wild Bill said if a lawman looks like he has time to take a lot of baths, he ain't probably a real lawman. Don't trust 'em." The child stopped struggling, and Theo set her on her feet.

"I don't take *that* many baths." Cole looked down at his boots.

"In some of them you don't even bathe," Maudie needled him good-naturedly, regaining composure.

Theo's eyes widened. "Cole! Whatever made you decide to shave off that wonderful mustache? It was striking on you, you know. Not quite as stylish as Mr. Hickok's, but it gave you character."

Cole sent a cursory glance toward Maudie and thoughtfully rubbed the skin above his upper lip. "It was almost as if I had nothing to do with it, as if the hand of fate came out of the darkness and swept it away."

"Come again?"

Cole turned away, amused. "Let's say the moon must have been just right for howling, and the mustache came off practically of its own accord."

"I've heard of the moon affecting people strangely," Theo concurred, nodding. "Changes your whole face. You look a lot younger, almost . . ."

Cole spun around, holding up one hand. "Don't say it."

"What?"

"Baby-faced."

"I would never say that," Theo said quickly.

"Good."

"I will say I've seen better constructed ones than yours were most of the time."

"What?" Cole stared at Theo until he realized the milliner was telling him that all along he knew the mustache wasn't real.

Maudie worked hard at controlling her laughter. She fixed her attention on the child's shirt and pants. They were made of several patches of fabric stitched together. Some of the patches were of interesting printed fabrics, some heavier than others, almost like brocade, and the stitching was of a finely executed feather design.

"Is that your real name? Patches?" Maudie watched the child swipe her forearm across her moist nose.

"It's the one I got now."

"Who gave it to you?"

"The lady in the thee-ate-er."

"What lady?" Maudie asked.

"The prettiest one, with the angel hair."

"Lady Fan," Theo said, and his face turned rose red once again.

"Lady Fan," Maudie said. "How do you know her?"

"She made my shirt and my pants, too," Patches replied proudly, showing off her dirty garment.

Maudie felt a grip of jealousy contract her chest and stomach. It seemed everyone in Deadwood had had face-to-face contact with Lady Fan except for her. She was beginning to wonder if somehow this happenstance was effected by design. But whose?

"Do . . . do you see her often?" Maudie ventured.

"Just sometimes." Patches wrapped her dirty hands in the front of her shirt and twisted her slight body back and forth.

"Where?"

"At the thee-ate-er sometimes. Sometimes at her house."

Maudie brightened. "Her house? Can you tell me where that is?"

The little girl's lower lip quivered as if she might be about to cry. Maudie didn't mean to frighten her with her pressing questions, but the information the child held was of the utmost importance to her.

Just then a noise came from the workroom. Cole and Theo bolted toward the sound.

"I don't believe it," Theo breathed.

Maudie rushed through the opening to the room. Cole had already opened the back door and was searching the alley. Theo stood dumbstruck next to his work table. Maudie's eyes fell on the object upon which his attention was fixed. A large spool of red thread stood in its wooden holder. Its color matched the length of thread she'd placed in her bag earlier.

"Did you see anyone?" Theo asked Cole.

Cole closed the back door. "No one in the alley. There are so many people out on the street that anybody could get lost among them."

Maudie touched the thread spool. "Well, it looks as if Patches was telling the truth. She didn't steal the thread. Then . . . who did?"

"And felt compelled to return it," Cole added.

"Perhaps Patches knows." Maudie turned and went back into the millinery shop. The little girl was gone.

"Hold still," Lula commanded late that afternoon as she adjusted the bodice seams of Maudie's costume and pinned it along the tapering darts. Her huge sewing bag lay open on a cutting table in the theater's wardrobe room.

Maudie held her arms out. "What's this thing made of? Burlap? The lining is scratchy. Every tug you make digs into my skin."

Her skin. She remembered how Cole had loved every inch of it with his fingers and mouth. She still could feel his electrifying touch.

She had no real reason to think so, but Maudie wondered if Lula yanked harder on the garment than she had to, scratching her on purpose. Lula seemed moodier than usual today, even more sullen. But Maudie wasn't going to let Lula's sour mood dampen her

275

own soaring spirits. The memory of her night with Cole Branch buoyed her. She was in love! Truly in love!

"Muslin," Lula mumbled through a row of straight pins held between her narrow lips. "Seen better days." Maudie hadn't heard Lula speak in as animated a way as she had with Taryn the night she and Cole overheard her spinning a tale of life in the eastern theater.

"Really? When was this costume last used?" Maudie winced as Lula tugged again.

"Just one other run. Same play."

"Scarlet Lady? How wonderful. Who was the actress?" Maudie was excited to know that there was a history to her costume, as if she might be carrying on a legacy.

Lula breathed hard through her nose. "It was some time ago, back east."

"I might have heard of her. I'm from the east, you know."

"Yes, I know. Turn."

Maudie obeyed. "You're very clever with these costumes, the way you make them look brand new, as if they'd been sewn expressly for this play. Taryn's gown is exquisite." When Lula's expression softened slightly, Maudie pressed on. "Arletta was raving about your handiwork at breakfast just this morning."

"She's hard to fit. Turn. Thick in the waist." Lula tugged at the darts on the other side of Maudie's bodice.

"Well, you make her look positively svelte. Nancy and Jewel look divine, and Sterling is almost handsome in the tailed frock coat. The only costumes I haven't seen are those for Lady Fan."

Lula stood up and stuck the pins remaining in her mouth into a puffy felt cushion the size of a chamber pot. With both hands she yanked hard on Maudie's bodice and shifted it so roughly Maudie was certain her breasts would be raw from the friction.

"I don't work on her costumes," Lula muttered.

"You don't? Does she fit them herself?" Maudie remembered the excellent stitchery in the quilt she'd discovered in the tiny single dressing room.

"Thinks she's too good for me. Got someone else to do the work."

Maudie tilted her head at the costumer. "That must bother you."

"Lots of things bother me."

"What kinds of things? You mean in the theater?"

"Just in general. Nothing and no one can be trusted," Lula muttered, opening the back of Maudie's costume and lowering it to her feet.

Maudie stepped out of it and into her own skirt and shirt. Lula actually seemed willing to talk to her.

"I agree with you completely. Just when you think you know a person, you find out they're not who you thought they were. Is that what you mean?"

Lula eyed her suspiciously. "As if you'd know."

"I do know." Maudie busied herself adjusting the man's shirt she enjoyed wearing. "Men especially. I don't know why women never learn. We always seem to take up with the wrong ones. Why is that?"

"Let our hearts rule our heads, that's what." Lula hung up Maudie's costume, then set about picking up threads, needles, and fasteners, and stuffing them into her bag.

Maudie scanned the array. Not one length of the strong red thread she'd seen in the hemp lines and in the dressing room.

"Then you know what I'm talking about."

"It's better *you* know what *I'm* talking about, young woman."

"What do you mean?"

"That sheriff you've taken up with. You'd be wise to reconsider. He's not what he appears to be." Lula's gnarled hands folded and smoothed some squares of fabric, piling them next to her bag.

Maudie felt a twinge in her stomach. She thought no one in Deadwood had taken time out from prospecting, revelling, and whoring to question anything about Cole, especially not the costume mistress from the Deadwood Variety Theater. She felt the need to protect him. She told herself it was in both their interests that Cole continue to be believed as Deadwood's sheriff.

"I haven't taken up with him," Maudie said defensively, knowing she was lying through her teeth.

"Good thing."

"What makes you say he's not what he appears to be?"

"Nobody ever is." Lula stuffed some fabric pieces in her bag, filling it to the straining point.

It was clear to Maudie that was all Lula was going to say on the subject, so she tried another tack. "Have you always worked in theaters, Lula?" When Lula didn't answer, Maudie pressed on. "My mother was an actress, you know. Gwen-Ada Boone. She was around Madame Carew's age. In fact, they might even have known each other. Have you heard of her?"

Maudie saw Lula's back go rigid. "Can't say," she muttered. Maudie suspected it was a lie. Lula tried to close her sewing bag, but it resisted her attempts. Her hands shook.

"Here, let me help you with that."

Maudie gripped the sides of the bag. When Lula snatched it back, the bag fell out of both their hands upside down on the floor. Maudie grabbed the bottom of the bag and yanked it up, letting everything fall out all over.

"Now look what you've done!" Lula's voice was that of a croaking shrew. "Stupid and clumsy."

"I'm sorry. We'll have it all back together in short order. Don't worry." Maudie adjusted her movements to fit Lula's description of her, stupid and clumsy, to facilitate a thorough search. And suddenly, there it was. Her eyes lighted on a thick coil of the strong red thread from Theo's shop. Maudie dropped a swatch of brocade fabric over it and frowned. This was a significant find.

"Give me that!" On her knees, Lula snatched the brocade and the thread at the same time. "Let me do this myself." She gathered up her bits and pieces and stuffed them haphazardly into her bag. "Just like an actress. You wouldn't make much of a wife, that's certain."

Maudie stepped back and leaned against the cutting table. That was an odd statement, she considered.

"You're probably right, Lula. That's why I've never married. Have you ever married?"

"No," Lula snapped. Then her voice softened. "I could have once."

Maudie tilted her head in wonder. "I'm sorry. It sounds as if you gave your heart away to someone undeserving."

Lula kept her back to Maudie as she busied herself with her things. "He was deserving, more than someone like you could ever know. He'd have married me if it hadn't been for . . . her."

Maudie wondered at how women always seemed to blame themselves or another woman for a man's infidelity. "I believe that if a man and a woman truly love each other, nothing can part them."

Lula spun around, her eyes blazing with the intensity of Indian council fires in the Black Hills. "What would you know about it? She *did* keep us apart." Her voice was hard, guttural, possessed. "She seduced him, took advantage of his weakness, trapped him. She was a witch and she deserved to die."

Maudie felt shock grip her insides. Lula's face was contorted almost beyond recognition. Did she mean Carew?

"She . . . she died?"

"No!" Lula shrieked. "*He* died! He never should have been the one. It was a mistake! It was *she* who . . ." She spun around and gathered up her sewing kit. "A woman like her will get it, mark my words. It's better she didn't die quickly. There are other ways to feel living death. Permanent, painful, living death. I ought to know." Then she hurried out of the wardrobe workroom and slammed the door.

Shocked, Maudie stood surrounded by the lifeless costumes. She couldn't shake the feeling that Lula was more than simply a bitter woman. She was dangerous.

The second of August brought a new excitement to Maudie. Dress rehearsals for *Scarlet Lady* would begin that night and she knew she'd have, at last, significant contact with the elusive Lady Fan. This would be the crescendo toward the completion of her goals, first to learn once and for all if Carew was her mother, and then to solve the mystery of her death. Then there would be the recovery of the rubies, the reward, the Pinkertons, and . . . beyond that lay the unknown.

She was scheduled to have another costume fitting with Lula Gale that afternoon and was not looking forward to it. Maudie checked the time. It was almost four-thirty. She knew she was late. Lula would probably stick the pins into her flesh rather than the folds of her costume for keeping her waiting. Maudie hurried down the walk toward the theater.

As she neared the Number Ten Saloon she saw the rat man McCall coming toward her. *Oh no, Phatty Thompson must have sent him after me to collect his fare for transportation from Cheyenne.* The last thing Maudie wanted was to have any contact with McCall, but there wasn't even an alley to dart into to get out of his way. Maybe courtesy would win him over and win her more time.

"Good afternoon, Mr. McCall," she said sweetly. "I

trust things are well with you." He gave her the heebie-jeebies just looking at him perspiring in the summer heat and sun. He smelled as bad as he looked; it was clear a bath was still an alien notion to him.

"They will be," he muttered, pushing past her.

She stepped quickly down the walk. No use encouraging him if he wasn't of a mind to confront her. She was almost to the theater when a gunshot pierced the layers of usual noise on the street. She backed immediately into a store front, her heart pounding against the wall of her chest.

The batwing doors to the Number Ten Saloon cracked open and McCall tore out, a gun smoking in his hand. Maudie felt a terror she'd never known before. McCall was bearing down on her; as if trapped in a nightmare, she couldn't make her feet move, couldn't tear her body away from the building she'd backed into. He was almost upon her when the saloon doors banged open again and a stream of men, their guns drawn, spilled out into the street.

"Wild Bill's been killed!" someone yelled. "Stop that man!"

Maudie didn't move. McCall was almost abreast of her when a hand shot out of nowhere and dragged her backwards inside a shop. Bullets flew through the air where she'd been standing. Maudie's breath suddenly exploded out of her lungs and she doubled over in pain and dizziness.

"Are you hurt? Are you hurt?" she heard a male voice.

Strong arms wrapped around her and she was

pressed to a hard chest. She looked up into Cole's terror-stricken eyes.

"No," she managed in a shaky voice. She felt his arms relax then, grateful they did not break their circle.

He let out a long breath. "Thank fortune. What happened?"

"Sheriff!" a pudgy man in a striped shirt with arm garters around the sleeves pushed into the shop. "Somebody shot Wild Bill! Come quick!"

Cole's body went rigid. "Wh-what?"

"He's kilt! That coward got him in the back! Come on, Sheriff!"

Cole pulled himself together and eased Maudie gently aside. "I've got to go."

Lord, how he didn't want to leave her! At that moment, his arms wrapped around Maudie and hers clutching tightly to him, the town could have fallen into Whitewood Creek and floated away with the rest of the dead wood from the mountains, for all he cared.

"I'll go with you," Maudie said, stepping gently out of the protective circle of his arms.

"No. You could get hurt."

"No I won't. The one who did it won't get far. He's too stupid."

Cole looked at her. "You know who shot Wild Bill Hickok?"

"Yes, a man named McCall."

"Right!" the man in the striped shirt agreed. "Jack McCall, the no good, dirty—"

Cole stopped him. "How did he manage to get Hickok? He always sat with his back to a wall so he could watch the door."

As they started down the street toward the Number Ten, the man in the striped shirt talked a mile a minute, explaining how the card game had been set up. The saloon was a mass of confusion and shouting. Hickok lay on the floor where he fell, his hand of cards fanned out over the green cloth, two pair, aces over eights with a kicker queen. A man with his back to the wall sat cradling his arm where blood seeped through a makeshift bandage.

Cole stared at the scene. Not that he could say he and Wild Bill Hickok were real friends, but they knew each other, and spent a little time together. He'd genuinely liked the man. Seeing his lifeless body, the blood still spreading out beneath him on the floor, renewed the pain of loss inside him. Life had been so much easier when he just played a part wherever he went. He'd always been able to move on before any attachments were made. Now, standing over the body of the man he thought of as a genuine hero, he wished with all his heart that he himself was real.

Maudie stood nearby, her eyes wet with tears as she watched Doc Pierce and several other men lift the great Wild Bill Hickok and bear him out of the saloon. A pool of blood remained on the floor. Maudie noted with shock how death had come so swiftly.

Was that how it always was? People existing in an aftermath rather than seizing the life of the living? Had she been doing that all her life for nothing, because she couldn't accept death and truth?

Maudie left the saloon and started on a rambling walk toward the east end of town. She had to get away from it all. While not untouched by the death of her father, the passing of Wild Bill affected her immensely. Maybe Hickok had been a bit of the hero, the revered lawman she'd wanted her father to be.

Outside Bartles Millinery Shop Maudie came upon the little girl, Patches, standing by herself crying. Maudie went to her, hunched down and gathered her into her arms.

"I loved Wild Bill," the girl sobbed. "I never had nobody to love 'ceptin' him and the cat." Maudie held her close. "Somebody said he wasn't never any good." She leaned back in Maudie's arms. "That ain't true, is it?"

Maudie hugged her again. "No, honey. That's not true. Wild Bill Hickok was a hero. Your own special hero."

The girl nodded and clung to Maudie. Excitement over Wild Bill's death swirled around them. Maudie's heart ached for the little girl in her arms and the little girl she herself had once been.

Three days later Cole sat in the sheriff's office reading the latest edition of the *Black Hills Pioneer*. An article two inches wide and six inches long summed up the killing of Wild Bill Hickok and the subsequent trial and acquittal of the assassin. Ever since Bill's death, Cole had been feeling subdued and introspective.

"Am I interrupting?" Maudie stepped into the office.

Cole hadn't heard the door open, but he'd sensed her presence before she spoke. The realization stunned him. He gazed at her, thinking deeply, vaguely beginning to notice that she was staring at him with a quizzical expression.

"Cole? Are you all right?"

He pruned his lips, lowered the paper, and removed his spectacles. "Yes, of course. Are you?"

"Yes. I still feel shaken by Mr. Hickok's killing. And that poor little girl, Patches. She hasn't talked since the day he died." Maudie took a seat at the chair closest to Cole's desk. "What did you think of the trial?"

"If you could call it a trial. It was more like a circus sideshow. Very fitting that it was held in the theater, the day after the shooting, with a hastily appointed judge, a deputy, and twelve guards. Where are they today?" He rubbed the space between his eyes. "Did you know Bill was just thirty-nine?"

Maudie shook her head. "The whole town, it seems, gathered at the saloons before and after the funeral. They did a rip-roaring business. The way they tell it, every man in Deadwood claimed to have had a hand in rounding up McCall after the shooting."

"I'm sure."

"Theo told me it was you who found McCall cowering in a barn across from the Number Ten. You brought him in to jail."

"You'll notice he didn't stay long," Cole said dryly. He set his glass-hard midnight eyes on her. "Tell me something, do you think that death is always an accident of nature? Or is it that when a man's time is up, it's up, and fate just puts the job in the hands of someone who's willing?"

Maudie leaned forward. She sensed Cole's troubled spirit but wasn't certain how to comfort him. "I haven't actually thought much about that. What do *you* think?"

Cole stood up and walked to a window overlooking Main Street. "There were six bullets in McCall's gun. Five were defective. The only live one was the first, the one he fired into the back of Bill's skull." He turned back to face Maudie. "So, would you say it was just a stupid accident, or that it was Wild Bill Hickok's time to die?"

Maudie winced at his harsh words. "I can't answer that, any more than I can say it's anyone's turn to die at any given moment."

Cole strode angrily back to his desk. "I don't want to talk about Clara Carew's death right now."

"I didn't mean her—" Maudie was at his side in a moment. "We're both feeling terrible about Bill Hickok."

He turned toward her and gathered her into his arms, hard and swift. She held him tightly, holding back tears yet letting his greater grief mingle with hers. He stepped back and slipped his hands around to her upper arms. She saw the moistness in his eyes. He dropped his arms.

"I didn't do a damned thing to prevent his killing," he said angrily.

"You couldn't have. No one can be in every place at the right time, or the wrong time." She took both his hands in her own and searched his angry, hurt eyes. "Cole, Wild Bill lived the kind of life that placed him in constant jeopardy. Maybe he wanted it that way. You had no control over that."

"It's my job to protect the people of this town. He was one of those people. I let him down." He stepped away from her and turned back to his desk. He picked up a stack of papers and threw them back down. "I've been trying to make some sense of these dispatches from the federal marshal's office that I should have been reading for the past two months. I've never had to handle much of anything beyond the nightly saloon brawls. And even those I could ignore most of the time."

"Cole . . .?" Maudie inclined her head toward him, and frowned.

"Once in a while I get called in on the occasional marital dispute down in the badlands, Mrs. Mundy's usually. Not that Mundy and her friends aren't perfectly capable of taking care of things themselves in their own way. But have you noticed lately that domestic disputes are escalating? Why do you think that is? I'll tell you why. When my back was turned, more women of the nonpleasure variety have moved into Deadwood. Married people are beginning to number almost as much as the miners, the gamblers, and the whores. And with marriage comes dispute. People just can't live together anywhere in peace."

"Yes, I know." She watched him lower himself heavily into the chair behind his desk. "Cole, you've been doing a fine job. Everybody says so."

"Everybody doesn't know their hind quarters from a hole in the ground around here!" he shouted, then instantly his expression softened. "I'm sorry. It's just that people expect too much from other people."

Maudie rose. "Sometimes I think they don't expect enough. Is that what's bothering you, Cole? Not that people expect too much from you. Is it that you don't expect enough from yourself?"

Cole contemplated her in dead silence. "I don't know what you mean." There was a gruffness about him she hadn't witnessed before.

"I think you do." She walked to the door. "I have a rehearsal, and I don't want to be late."

"I know. The play goes on no matter what happens, doesn't it?" He let out a sharp breath.

"That's the way it's always been." She opened the door. "If you feel like talking, you know where to find me." She walked out onto the street and closed the door quietly behind her.

Cole watched her pass by his window. "Damn it, damn it, damn it!" He slammed his fist on the pile of dispatches.

Up to now, Cole had been thinking, the role of a western sheriff was primarily a study of appearance and demeanor. A man could simply dress the part and stroll around the town, commanding respect and acknowledgement for a job well done simply by making himself and his Colt companion visible.

And up to now he'd thought it wasn't bad being in a place like Deadwood, where no one really expected him to uphold law and order, so he'd never be letting anybody down. Hell, there wasn't even an official government yet. Nobody could agree on much of anything here except the value of gold. Up to now Cole thought he could go on for awhile like that and he'd be perfectly happy. He always got itchy feet anyway if he stayed in any one place for more than a year. As soon as this place got real civilized and a law man was expected to keep the law, Cole planned to turn in his badge and head out of Deadwood to another new stage, another new role.

Up to now.

Up to the moment Maudie Boone Dearden had come into his life.

Up to the moment of death of a hero.

Should he stay? Should he go? None of the places he'd lived in up to now had appealed to him. Except possibly St. Louis, Cole reflected. That city was made up of a rare combination of civilized metropolitan folks and westward-looking adventurers.

He wondered how long Maudie Boone Dearden planned to stay in Deadwood.

Chapter 13

"Places!" Moe's deep voice resonated throughout the theater.

Maudie waited offstage for her cue as the other actors took their places, ready for the first dress rehearsal to begin. Nothing could prevent her from seeing Lady Fan's face at last, she thought. The woman would have to be in the theater tonight. No director in his right mind would allow a rehearsal as important as this one to commence without all the actors being present.

The wait seemed longer than the first act itself. And then the mysterious Lady Fan stepped out from the opposite wings from where Maudie stood. She strode with long, smooth strides, her limp barely noticeable, and stopped center stage, her face in Maudie's full view. She began the opening scene soliloquy.

Maudie shivered. What was she seeing? She narrowed her eyes. There was so much makeup obscuring the woman's features, which were framed by the unnatural, almost blue-black wig coiled high on her head, that Maudie couldn't ascertain from her place in the wings what the real woman might actually look like. Even without that clarity, did she look like a thief? A murderer?

Senses and images flashed through Maudie's mind like a hundred burning lanterns. Girlish images. Womanly senses. Sad images. Hopeful senses. Angry senses. Frustrated senses. Lost images.

"From the top once again!" LaFountain's voice boomed. "Miss Dearden . . . Miss Dearden?"

Maudie shook herself and stepped out from behind the black masking curtains. "Yes?" she said tremulously.

"Do you think, Miss Dearden," LaFountain began with amplified sweetness, "that you could make your entrance on cue? Indeed," his voice escalated to its original boom, "make your initial entrance at all?!"

Maudie felt warmth rush up from her chest over her face. She'd missed her entrance! How utterly unprofessional of her!

"I . . . I apologize to you and to the rest of the cast, Mr. LaFountain. There is no excuse for my behavior. It won't happen again."

"See that it doesn't. Once more please, ladies and gentleman."

The others stepped back into the wings opposite Maudie. Again Lady Fan took center stage and began her soliloquy. Maudie watched as the others made their entrances. She searched her mind over and over for her cue, but something had happened to her memory. She couldn't remember her cue, couldn't remember her lines. Perspiration dampened her underarms and her midriff. Her stomach churned. Good Lord, did she have stage fright for the first time in her life?

Suddenly she felt her legs move her out onto the stage directly toward Lady Fan, who stood regally straight. Maudie heard her own voice saying lines she felt she'd never heard or read before. It was as if her body was performing without the presence of her mind and emotions. It was as if she was outside looking in.

Lady Fan's eyes seemed enveloped in an opaque, dark cloak. Maudie knew the older woman was seeing the scene before her, seeing Maudie, but Maudie's own gaze could not penetrate the cover. She was consumed by fiery sensations that engulfed her body and mind. She felt caught in a dream and couldn't wake up.

"Cut!" LaFountain's voice penetrated the fog in Maudie's mind. "If all of you don't put more emotion into your lines, the audience will stay away in droves." He stepped back, an arm plastered against his forehead, in one of the most unattractive, melodramatic poses Maudie had ever seen. "I am working on a sick headache, and I'm certain you all know how I got it. I trust you will perform more convincingly in the second act. Need I remind you that we have only a few days left until opening night?" He turned and stalked up the aisle muttering something to the gods.

"Fifteen minutes!" Moe called.

The cast broke and headed for the dressing room, chattering among themselves. Maudie heard notes of irritation in their voices, and she hoped she wasn't the cause of it. She was feeling an impending headache of her own.

Lady Fan was the first one off the stage and had

disappeared into her own small dressing area before Maudie could catch up with her. She wondered if Fan were trying to avoid her for some reason. How she wished she had someone to talk to. She felt a sharp sensation that even though she'd confided a great deal about her life to Cole, this was something she couldn't, shouldn't, talk to him about.

Nothing was making sense to Maudie, and she was growing more confused with each day. She'd anticipated her first meeting with Lady Fan. Now she'd had it, and she still didn't know what to think. There had been . . . nothing . . . nothing to it at all. Then why had her senses overwhelmed her so?

By the time Moe called *places* again, Maudie had touched up her makeup, adjusted her costume, and pulled herself together. Act Two ran more smoothly, and the emotion put forth by the cast had deepened. LaFountain seemed pleased, Sterling Hale was in less of a snit than usual, and the others were excited enough to explode.

All except Lady Fan. The animation in her voice, the countless expressions on her face all during the play, never reached her eyes. Those were still a cloudy dark blue, and gave away none of what she was thinking and feeling.

Dress rehearsal came to an end with Maudie feeling at odds with herself and less sure of anything than ever before.

"Tomorrow night we're dark. Use it for rest," LaFountain announced. "I shall expect all of you to be perfect in the last dress rehearsal, and unequivocally perfect on opening night. Our public demands it and we shall give them nothing less. Opening night must be a performance that will live in their minds ever after."

Maudie waited in the wardrobe closet until she was certain everyone had left the theater. Fan was the last to leave, and Maudie followed a discreet distance behind. Fan took a turn down an unnamed side street and turned in at a gate to a little house. *This must be where she lives!* Maudie's insides clutched. What was she going to do now? Stop her before she went inside? Go up and knock on the door?

Maudie delayed too long. Fan entered the house. She noted that a lamp was already lit inside before Fan opened the door.

Curiosity compelled Maudie to enter the tiny yard. Once inside the gate, she stood in the darkness, her eyes fixed on the front door. Her nerve to knock on the door dissolved. Instead she moved through the darkness to a stand of thick shrubbery. Safely hidden in the branches, Maudie watched the two windows on the side of the house. Lamps glowed through lace curtains. Maudie strained to see inside, afraid to move nearer. She saw Lady Fan's form pass in front of the window. Then the form of another person. A man. Who?

At the far side window, Maudie could see Fan enter a room and step behind a screen. When she emerged she was wearing a dressing gown of pale green. She seated herself in front of a dressing table and set a pouch upon it. She lit another lamp next to that. Filtered through the lace curtain, Maudie saw in the mirror the heavily made-up face of the actress, saw her lean her chin on her hand and stare at her own reflection for several moments.

Then she raised her arms and removed several pins from the wig, and lifted it off her head. Her own dark auburn hair was secured with more pins which she removed. She shook out her hair, then brushed it long and smooth. Maudie saw the lamplight pick up silvery threads through it. Her strokes were controlled, smooth and careful, as if the act of brushing were an act of love.

From a covered glass pot on the dressing table, Fan lifted a scoop of white cream and spread it over her face, her eyes and her mouth. Then she took a soft cloth and began to gently wipe the cream away, taking the heavy makeup with it. Maudie watched with rapt attention as the thick rouge, dark eye kohl, and bright lip paint disappeared from Fan's face. She stood then and went to a wash bowl and pitcher on the other side of the dressing table. Maudie watched as she poured water into the bowl and then took a cloth and some soap and washed her face. She took a white towel and dried her face, then returned to the dressing table. She brought the lamp closer so that it shone on her face.

Hypnotized by the methodical actions of the actress, Maudie moved slowly from her hiding place in the shrubs and inched her way closer. She stood near the window at an angle, wanting to see the mirror's reflection as clearly as the filtering lace curtains would allow.

Fan raised her head and let her hair fall back. She took something from the pouch and raised it to her throat. She lifted her hair. She was fastening a necklace, Maudie surmised. Fan lowered her hands and adjusted something at the end of the chain. She lifted it to her lips, then set it down over the low cut bodice of her dressing gown. Maudie strained to see what it was.

The locket! The one in the dressing room! Fan was wearing that locket. Maudie strained harder to see the mirror through the lace curtains. Fan turned her head and Maudie caught her face in full view. Lit softly by the flickering light, Fan's face materialized and floated in her gaze as if in a dream.

Maudie's nerves froze. Her heart thumped to a stop, then started again, pumping against her chest as fast as a rabbit's. She stepped back into the shrubbery. Slowly she lowered her body to the ground and sat in a trance.

Maudie awoke to the busy chatter of magpies as dawn broke over the eastern hills. She straightened with some effort, then gently shifted her stiff back and shoulders. Her skirts were damp, and her bones felt chilled to the marrow. Her head throbbed. She had spent the entire night outside, uncovered, in an emotional state such as she'd never known.

She squeezed her burning eyes tightly shut, and rubbed her temples. In the awakening darkness of her mind, she visualized what she'd observed through Lady Fan's bedroom window the night before. Had she imagined the face that had emerged from under the heavy theatrical makeup? Or was it real?

How she wished she had strength enough to get back to Miss Parrott's and curl up in bed and hug her knees to her chest as she had when she was a little girl.

Somehow curling her body inward had kept her emotions from storming out of her, taking valuable parts of her with them. She'd lost so much, and she remembered wanting to keep inside what was left, no matter how tormenting it might be, just so she didn't lose any more.

What had possessed her to fall asleep in the shrubs? Had she actually slept? Was all that she'd seen a dream from which she could not rouse?

The front door to the little house opened. Maudie jumped at the sound of the woman's voice. She'd forgotten about the man until she heard him murmur something low. She hunkered down in the shrubbery and waited until they stepped into the street. They passed her hiding place. Then she saw the man. Theo Bartles!

Maudie blanched. Theo Bartles had been waiting in Lady Fan's house for her to return from rehearsal? And had stayed the night? She was stunned.

"Can you beat that?" a voice said behind her.

Maudie's heart jumped at the sound of it. In her present state, she couldn't twist around as rapidly as her reflexes demanded. She turned slowly.

"Who's there? Come out of there right now!" she demanded.

Cole stepped around from behind the shrubs. "Knock me over with a horse tail. I can't believe that, can you? Our little Theo and the elusive Lady Fan on the morning following a late-night tryst. Now I know what he was talking about!"

In the warming morning light she watched a smile play at the corners of his mouth. Cole was treating the discovery of the mysterious woman with the milliner as a kind of fairy tale with a surprise plot twist. Besides that, he had scared the wits right out of her.

"What . . . tell me just what it is you're doing here!" she demanded of him after she was certain her voice would carry the appropriate note of outrage at finding him lurking about in the shrubbery in the day's first light.

Cole strode toward her in a slow ambling manner. "Same thing you are, ma'am," he drawled purposefully, "investigating. At least I'm assuming that's what you're doing here so very early in the morning."

"Investigating my Aunt—"

"Your aunt's rear anatomy, I know. Poor auntie. Perhaps I was hasty. *I* was investigating. *You* were downright spying."

"As if there's a difference in this case!"

"I believe there is," Cole returned with a calm tone that exasperated Maudie. He drew her into his arms and kissed her deeply. Her exasperation dissipated. When he released his lips, he did not let go of her. "Are you all right?"

"Of course I'm all right," she replied wearily. "Why?"

"You seemed shaken, that's all."

"Why wouldn't I be? You scared me to death." Maudie wasn't prepared to discuss with him what she thought she'd seen from outside the window. She had to be certain she wasn't dreaming, or wishing something so much her perception was distorted.

"Good. I mean, I'm sorry." He kissed her again. "I've certainly been missing these little duels of ours, haven't you?" He didn't allow her to answer. "Now, I suggest we both go about our business before the love-birds return to the nest. Shall we?" He crooked his arm in invitation.

"I don't know what you had in mind, Cole Branch, but I—"

"Had the same thing in mind," he finished for her. "Seeing what the mysterious Lady Fan is hiding. Who knows what we'll learn? What crime in particular we may be able to solve in the next few minutes?"

"You're not suggesting for one minute that Lady Fan killed Carew." Maudie heard the note of protest in her voice, but her own suspicions played in the back of her mind.

"I'm certainly wondering about it," Cole's eyes narrowed as he studied her face, "and so are you. People in Deadwood can't remain anonymous for long. If they try to, everyone suspects they have something to hide, something they're ashamed of, and somebody finds out about it. Why only last week the intrepid Cora Petti-grew, along with her inquisitive daughter Penelope, discovered a little secret Lawrence LaFountain hoped to keep hidden."

"I don't care one whit what gossip they spread about him."

"I think you should."

"Why?"

"They're saying they know he frequents Mrs. Mundy's House of Mystic Pleasures. That he has a special woman there who claims to be a great actress, but who's making her living now as a courtesan. Don't you find that curious?"

"Why would I be curious about that?" Maudie was lying and she knew it. She'd wondered about the woman herself. She'd even wondered if Lady Fan . . . "The woman is most likely a prostitute."

Cole nodded, thumbing his Stetson to the back of his head. "Most likely. But the Pettigrew noses have discovered her name, or at least the name she goes by these days."

Maudie turned away. "I am certainly not interested in knowing the name of . . . any person Lawrence LaFountain meets at Mrs. Mundy's . . . or anywhere else for that matter." She busied herself with brushing off her skirts, adjusting her shawl.

Cole strolled around to face her. "Maybe you know her."

"I rather doubt it." Maudie brushed her skirts all the harder.

"The world of the theater is small. Sooner or later everybody knows everybody. Didn't you ever notice that?"

"Actually, no. I've never paid much attention to such things." She looked up into Cole's eyes and knew immediately he didn't believe her.

"This friend of LaFountain's calls herself Melody Sweet. Claims she was once in jail with a woman who resembles a certain actress appearing on the Deadwood stage."

Maudie's nerves froze for the second time in fifteen minutes. *Melody Sweet!* The Pettigrews must have discovered she'd been in jail with Melody once. If they spread that all around, her reputation would suffer

301

greatly. She'd never cared about that until now. It could jeopardize her quest.

"My guess is they've discovered something about our shady Lady Fan," Cole said.

Maudie's nerves heated now. She took in a sharp breath. "I don't understand why you think the idle conjectures of a couple of bored nosey women would be of any interest to me." She certainly hoped that sounded casual enough to keep Cole Branch's suspicious nature in check.

"I'm surprised your usually quick mind hasn't leapt to the conclusion mine did immediately."

"What conclusion? They have no proof that . . . Lady Fan has done anything in the least bit suspicious." She held her voice steady, a most difficult feat given the state of her emotions. "Exactly what kind of leaping did your mind do?"

"Exactly that it's only a matter of time before they start talking about who was in the Mundy establishment on one of the evenings of LaFountain's assignation."

Assignation, my Aunt . . . If Cole got even a glimpse of Melody Sweet he wouldn't put such an intellectual tag on what she and the director were doing. What a minute. Did he mean . . . ?

"No!" she breathed. "You think they'll start talking about you? Me?"

"Us." Cole didn't even attempt to hide his amusement.

Maudie couldn't think straight. How did things get so ridiculously complicated?

"Now, as I was saying, it behooves us to get on with our snooping . . . ah, investigation, while we still can.

The back door is unlocked. I checked." Cole started around to the back of the house.

"You're going in there when she's not home?" Maudie whispered loudly.

"I hardly think she'd invite me in if she came back and found me waiting in her yard. And, as I'm sure you've noticed, she hasn't exactly been holding tea parties and inviting the town notables, including you and me, now has she? Time we invited ourselves." He disappeared.

"Cole? Don't go. It wouldn't be right," Maudie whispered again. She shivered. The day was warming, but she was still chilled to her core. She wanted desperately to be inside that house, see for herself, feel, know. And yet she was scared out of her wits to be even standing in the side yard any longer. She watched Cole's retreating back.

"Come on," he called.

Maudie lifted one foot and then the other, at last propelling herself to follow him. "Don't go in there without me." Somehow she felt an overwhelming sense of wanting to protect Lady Fan.

Inside the cozy little house, Maudie once again felt a sense of curiosity overwhelm her. It was more than that, but she didn't name it, was afraid to name it. She walked around the two small rooms as if compelled by a hypnotist, wanting to touch the personal artifacts that graced the dwelling, but not daring to actually do it. In the bedroom she noticed a gold-backed hairbrush with matching hand mirror. Lovely. Personal. Tears threatened to fill her eyes. She was trying so hard to be strong, to be unaffected by what she felt inside the

303

house, inside her heart, but keeping her feelings from being visible on the surface to Cole was an almost staggering task in the face of the depth of emotion she experienced.

"Check the bureau drawers," Cole told her.

"I will not," Maudie returned, startled by the firm resonance of her own voice.

"Well, I don't want to be going through her feminine possessions. I think it's your place to do it. You're the female Pinkerton agent here. You may find something, a letter, something of Carew's, something incriminating. I don't know. Don't women hide important or suspicious things in their underwear? No offense intended, of course."

"Of course," Maudie whispered sarcastically.

She didn't want to admit she'd been considering going into the bureau drawers herself. She was overwhelmed by guilt. These things were private. But now Cole reminded her that it was her duty to do so. Summoning her courage, she overrode her own conviction of what was wrong in favor of what she deemed her duty. She wouldn't find anything incriminating. She just knew it. She prayed it now. She'd hadn't accepted the idea of a greater spiritual being since she was a child when her mother taught Sunday school. Sunday school. She'd forgotten those times. What made her think of them now?

She opened the first bureau drawer. Stockings and underthings. Nothing terribly interesting from a crime investigation viewpoint. But, of course, she'd expected just that before she even opened the drawer.

The second drawer held gloves and scarves, nothing

suspicious. Of course not. The third drawer the same. Maudie was aware that her racing pulse had calmed considerably. She was about to close the bottom drawer when her sight fastened on something different. She lifted it out of the back of the drawer. It was soft, white, tiny. She unfolded it and held it up to the window light.

A baby dress.

Her pulse quickened again. *The dress I'm wearing in the locket picture!*

"Find anything?" Cole said, entering the bedroom.

Maudie turned around slowly, still holding the baby dress. She couldn't say anything, do anything except continue to stare at the dress. Questions tumbled about in her mind, laying strewn among its recesses like the falling timber along the mountainsides that gave the town its name. A revelation burned into her thoughts. Should she allow it expression? Should she even listen to it? Dare she even think it?

Could . . . this woman who calls herself Lady Fan . . . be a thief, a murderer? My mother? Was my father right about my mother all along? Has the whole of my life been a lie, a waste?

Cole watched Maudie, wondering what it was that had rendered her speechless. "Maudie? Is there something about that baby dress that upsets you?" She didn't move. He went to her side. "What's the matter? Please tell me. I'll help you."

When Cole put his arms around her shoulders, his touch was shattering. She dissolved into tears, clutching the dress to her bosom and sobbing from the depths of her soul.

"Tell me, sweetheart, tell me," Cole pleaded. "I'll

help you, I swear I will." He rubbed her back, her hair, kissed her temples, did all he could to soothe her.

As quickly as the storm in Maudie had come, it subsided. She pushed out of his arms. There was nothing he could do to help her now. In fact, she was beginning to think it was possible for him to hurt her more deeply than he could ever know.

"It . . . I just had a bad memory, that's all." With shaking hands she refolded the baby dress and put it back in its place in the bureau. When she closed the drawer she had the feeling she was closing the light on her infancy.

"Are you sure? You look terribly upset."

"I'm fine now," she said firmly. "It just reminded me of my childhood. I'm fine."

Cole touched her face. "I understand."

Maudie thought he wanted to understand, she believed he truly did. She wanted to trust him with her burgeoning knowledge, but old fears took over. She had to protect . . .

"Did *you* find anything interesting?" Maudie swallowed her emotions and tears.

"Not yet. I'm still looking."

Cole turned away from her, then looked over his shoulder and watched her carefully. She'd lied to him just then, he could feel it. He thought they'd progressed beyond distrust. *He* had. Now he knew she hadn't. That disturbed him greatly. Maybe she hadn't been completely honest with him about everything.

At the bottom of a bookcase, Cole discovered something that looked intriguing. A scrapbook. Pages of theatrical playbills, newspaper reviews, articles about certain actors, and one in particular about the death of the well-known leading man Jared Braddock. He swallowed hard and read further.

Lucille Galarzyk, a scenery designer, had named the leading actress in *Scarlet Lady* as a suspect in the death of Braddock. The name of that leading lady, the name that figured prominently in the articles, was Gwen-Ada Boone. Cole stood still, stunned by his own revelation.

"Did you find . . . anything interesting?" Maudie broke into the tense silence.

Cole ran his fingers over the edge of the scrapbook. "I'm not sure," he said distantly. "You mean anything interesting concerning Lady Fan, or Carew's death, or . . . something?"

Maudie swallowed. "I guess so." She moved close to him and studied his face. "Or to you . . . personally?"

He let out a long breath. "Quite possibly."

Maudie sensed a vulnerability in him, and set aside her own reeling emotions. "Can you tell me about it?" she asked gently.

Cole's lips tightened, and pleats formed between his eyebrows. "I'm not certain I can, yet. I have to think about it some more. Come on, let's get some breakfast."

Maudie followed Cole out, stopping once to look over her shoulder before closing the door.

Cole waited until the cast was assembled on stage for the evening's rehearsal before he made his move toward the dressing room. Once inside, he carefully went through the array of pouches, cases, and other belongings strewn along the shelves and under them. Nothing appeared out of the ordinary to him, but then he didn't have even an inkling of what he should be looking for or even if he'd know what it was if he found it. Sterling Hale's case was the only one containing anything interesting, a woman's lacy underdrawers, but that wasn't all that suspicious. He knew about men like Hale from his own theatrical past.

At the back of the dressing room he saw something he hadn't noticed before. A door to another room. It was ajar. He started to push it open when he heard a noise coming from inside. Stepping away quickly and pressing into a rack of hanging costumes, he peered around the door opening. A woman in a costume of opulent embellishment, black hair coiled high around her head, stood with her back to him. This must be Lady Fan, he surmised.

She was searching through a wooden case. Cole saw that she did it carefully, lifting things, setting them aside, lifting more. She turned slightly and he could no longer see her back, just part of her side and her hands. Her face was concealed by the door. In her hand she held a chain. At the end of it he guessed was a locket, for it looked as if she pried something open. She leaned forward and he saw her profile. She looked sad yet loving as she gazed into what he imagined was a picture in the locket.

"Places!" the stage manager's voice boomed. Cole jumped and clamped a hand over his heart.

He watched as the woman quickly placed everything back in the case. He knew she was about to come through that door. Cole pushed back into the costumes and let them drape around him. He stood perfectly still. The woman hurried out of the little room and pulled the door shut. Cole's hopes to gain entry sank. Soon she was out of the dressing room. He picked his way through the costumes and went to the door, conjecturing how he might pick the lock apart and gain entry. He was examining the latch when the door moved open against the pressure of his hand. He was surprised, but a little bit dissatisfied. He'd felt a twinge of the thrill of doing something sneaky against the pressures of time and the possibility of getting caught. This seemed just too easy.

Inside the room, Cole was impressed by the atmosphere. The space was small enough to envelope him with the pieces of a woman's life. Clothes, a large faded brocade bag with what looked like a quilt pushing out of the top. His gaze fell on the wooden box. Sensing escalating guilt at what he was about to do, Cole reached for the box. Even with the right to investigate he had difficulty bringing himself to the point of snooping through other people's private things. But, duty was duty. His hands shook a little as he opened the case.

The locket Lady Fan had been looking at lay on the top of a layer of cotton. He lifted and opened it. Inside was a tiny likeness of a young woman and an infant. He wondered briefly about it, but saw no significance in it. He was about to close it when something else caught his eye. The baby dress on the infant. The likeness was faded and tiny, but was the baby dress the same one Maudie had found in Fan's bureau? He closed the locket and returned it to its place.

He searched through some pieces of jewelry and came to a packet of tissue paper. He lifted it. It was heavy. Frowning, he opened the packet, willing the paper to be quiet. In the paper nest lay a necklace and eardrops of rubies. Rubies! These were undoubtedly the stolen stones. Madame Carew had been suspected of stealing them. Then how did Lady Fan get them? Had she stolen them from Carew? What in hell—?

At the bottom of the box where the rubies had lain Cole glimpsed a playbill. He lifted it out. It was from a small theater in Missouri, the very theater in which he'd last seen his father. Cole's hands shook even harder. He was afraid to look at the cast list, yet couldn't deny himself the opportunity. He opened the playbill and with great trepidation read the names. There was a name he should have remembered. Clara Carew. She was listed as author and producer. He scanned below looking for the name. There it was, Jared Braddock, his father in the leading role. Tears stung behind Cole's eyes as his gaze was riveted to the name.

He steeled himself to read the rest of the list, something he had never done when he last saw his father. He'd entered the theater after the play had started and never saw a program. He searched out the character who'd been the love interest to his father's character. There. Gwen-Ada Boone. Maudie's mother.

Too much was falling into place too fast. Gwen-Ada Boone had to be the woman who'd been involved with his father! It was Maudie's mother who'd saved Jared Braddock from his drinking binges. He'd never known her, but he knew he'd be forever grateful to her.

Why would Lady Fan have the program stashed away at the bottom of her jewel case? And why would she have these rubies? Was she the one who killed Carew?

He was about to close the playbill when another name caught his eye. Lucille Galarzyk. She was listed as scenic designer. He remembered the clipping he'd seen in Lady Fan's scrapbook, and something vague from when he was a child actor. She'd been talked of and seen around several theaters they'd been in. She must have been well-known in the scene shops, Cole thought now. Or something. His memory was no clearer than that.

He lowered the playbill to return it to its hiding place. A piece of paper fell out of it. He retrieved it from the floor. It was a clipping from a newspaper. He opened it. It was a story about the opening of the Missouri production of *Scarlet Lady*. His father's face stared up at him. Next to it, curiously, was a photograph of Lady Fan. He frowned, then lowered his gaze. Beneath the photographs was the caption, *Stars of Madame Clara Carew's Scarlet Lady, Jared Braddock and* . . . Cole read the names over and over, hardly believing what he read. *Jared Braddock and Gwen-Ada Boone!*

A chill coursed through his body.

Did Maudie know? Had she known the truth all along, had she tried to keep it from him? Or had she been as in the dark as he? What was he going to do now? Should he tell her what he had learned? That Lady Fan was actually her mother, Gwen-Ada Boone? And that she'd been accused of murdering his father?

The atmosphere in the tiny room was becoming

cloying. Cole had to get out of there for his own sanity as well as to prevent his being caught. He peered out into the dressing room and, seeing and hearing no one, slipped out.

The clipping lay on top of the Missouri playbill, where it had slipped out of his hand.

Chapter 14

Maudie stepped along the boardwalk toward the sheriff's office, her booted feet making a rhythmic drumming to her stride. She hadn't seen Cole since they'd been inside Lady Fan's house. After that he'd seemed withdrawn. In fact, while they'd shared breakfast that morning in the Grand Central dining room, he'd barely spoken to her.

She wanted to talk to him about what she'd learned, but she was afraid. He had his suspicions about Lady Fan, she knew that. What if he decided to tell the federal marshal Lady Fan was a thief, possibly a murderer?

She had much more important things to think about now, and she wanted to talk with Cole about them. She wanted to present herself to Lady Fan, tell her who she was and that she knew Fan was her mother. She was frightened of it. Here was what she'd been living her life for, here was her mother, within reach at last! God, how she wanted to talk to Cole!

Since Wild Bill Hickok's death he'd seemed subdued. She knew he missed him, and she thought she knew why. She missed Mr. Hickok, too. Even though they both knew he was as flawed a character as any schemed in the mind of a playwright, Wild Bill Hickok was a living legend, a hero to many. They'd been touched by him. In the same way. They were missing what his presence represented to them . . . someone to believe in.

But beyond that, Maudie believed the two of them, she and Cole, were in some sense as much alike as they were different. She missed sparring with Cole, the mutual challenge they offered one another. She wanted to regain the kind of high-spirited repartee that marked the beginning of their relationship. But not over *this*. Now was not the time. How had they lost that? What could she do to get it back? She had to think, to be clear, to know for absolutely certain that he still wanted them to be together as much as she did.

But she sensed that Cole was purposely avoiding her. She knew it, and she was certain she knew why. It saddened her, but there wasn't one thing she could do about it now. What was done was done, and done a long time ago. Desperately she wished they could talk about it. Desperately she longed for him to understand.

It was barely an hour past sunup and already the day was growing warm. Maudie's discomfort had more to do with her determination than it did with the weather, but she couldn't hold it inside any longer. She opened the door to the sheriff's office and stepped resolutely inside. The office was empty.

Her spirits dropped, but she would let them go only so far. She wasn't used to this feeling of waning grip on her courage. At least not when it came to men. She knew why, guessed she'd known it for weeks. Feeling in love took away all the bravado that was part of her. She headed down the narrow hall to the door of his private quarters. Without knocking she barged right in.

"I know why you've been avoiding me and I want to talk about it right now!"

"For God's sake!" Cole whirled around and dropped the black pants he'd just begun to step into. He was naked as the day he was born.

"I want to have this out right now!" Maudie strode right past him and plunked herself down on a wooden chair by the table.

Cole fought to regain his breath and his composure. His heart was slamming against his chest as much from the shock of having Maudie burst into his room so early in the morning, as it was seeing her fire, and feeling his own stark vulnerability.

"As it is apparent you have not noticed, everything *is* out right now. I think it's common courtesy to knock before entering someone's home, just in case they aren't prepared for visitors." He pulled on his pants and with shaking hands buttoned them.

"I couldn't take the time to stand on social amenities. Apparently you have changed your feelings about me because of something in my past. Your avoidance of me, discussing it with me if it bothers you, warrants my behaving in just this manner."

"I'm . . . not certain what you're talking about. Do you want some coffee?"

"You know exactly what I'm talking about. Yes."

315

"Maybe we should wait to discuss it." He set about preparing coffee in a battered old pot.

"After we . . . since we've moved our association beyond that of friendship, you have seen fit to avoid me. I know why that is, and I want you to know I have no feelings of guilt or recrimination."

Cole turned quickly and levelled his gaze on her. What he'd thought she was talking about, apparently she wasn't talking about. "I haven't avoided you since we . . . were together. Things with McCall's murder trial, and the fact that I've had word the federal marshal is on his way here and wants to ask questions about Carew's death, have kept me busier than I want to be, that's all. Other than that I don't know what you're talking about, so I'm glad you don't feel guilty about whatever it is you have no recriminations over." He turned back to the business of making coffee.

Maudie watched his back as he fussed with mugs and spoons. She could recognize avoidance when she saw it. "Busy. Hah! I know that a proper lady isn't supposed to make love with a man unless she's married to him. I don't happen to feel that way. In this case, I mean. I'm more honest than that. I wanted you, you wanted me, and I believed we trusted each other. I never tried to fool you, never tried to play a female trick of making you think I was something I'm not."

Cole turned with a puzzled look on his face. "I do wish I had even an inkling of what this conversation is about."

"Don't play dumb with me!"

"I'm not playing!" Cole ran his hand through his hair with exasperated intensity. "What is it that you

316

aren't that you didn't trick me into thinking you were?"

"A virgin!" she shouted. "I'm not a virgin, and I didn't try to hide that fact from you."

Cole stared at her with an intensity that almost, but not quite, unnerved her. *"That's* what you're ranting about?"

"Go ahead, berate me if you want to. But I never let you think anything different. I know my letting you do what you wanted to showed my lack of—"

"Letting me! Wait a minute, lady. We were in that together. I believe I even remember some talk about submission. You certainly seemed to enjoy it as much as I did." His voice lowered. "It was . . . shattering for me."

She stared back at him. "As it was for me. In fact, I've wanted to make love with you again. And again."

Cole's dark eyes bored into her. "So have I. More than you can ever imagine."

Maudie let his words, spoken with a husky voice, sink into her mind. She lowered her gaze and focused it on her lacing and unlacing fingers. "But that doesn't mean I'm even slightly like Mrs. Mundy's group of women." She sounded like a little girl who'd been accused of doing something naughty.

"I never thought that!" Cole yelled.

"Then what *did* you think?" she yelled back.

"If we don't stop shouting, all of Deadwood is not going to have much difficulty in reading both our minds when we walk out of here."

"As if that matters."

"It does to me. What we . . . shared together is

private, if you don't mind. And I want to keep it that way."

"All right." Her voice softened.

"As far as you're being a virgin, I never expected you to be."

"I knew it!" Maudie flared. "You had formed an opinion of me right from the start, and—"

"Will you stop exploding long enough for me to finish, please? What I meant was, we are more alike than you think. You are a very sensuous woman. And you're in the theater, the real theater, and isn't the essence of theater about feeling, emotion, senses, expression? I've had a few moments in my life like that, too. I'm not a man who has to frequent the row of houses in the badlands to take care of my physical needs. There's more to me than you know. I don't care that you're not a virgin. And I don't think you are in any way like Mrs. Mundy's girls. You are you, with all the fire and life that entails, and I won't pretend to know or understand all of it." He paused to take a long breath.

She waited, then took a breath herself. "Two. There have been two men. I was young and I thought I loved one of them. He died. The other one . . ."

"I don't need explanations."

Maudie stood up. Her pride was wounded, an uncustomary feeling for her, and she'd done the wounding herself. "You . . . you mattered to me more than I ever expected. And no one is more surprised than I am to know that it was important to me to know that I mattered to you. I believed it, up until these last few days. I am not the sort of female who throws herself at the feet of a man begging for his love." She turned and headed for the door.

Cole caught up with her in two steps, grabbed her elbow and spun her around. Roughly he caught her lips with his own and consumed them, grinding against her, twining her hair urgently around his fingers. When he released her lips he was heaving for breath.

"You do matter to me, dammit," he said gruffly. "And if you think you're surprised about your feelings, you haven't any idea how shocked I am about mine. I've spent my entire life avoiding entanglements, attachments. I didn't want to be dragged down in the quicksand of caring for someone, the suffocation of marriage. I've seen what that can do."

Maudie's eyes bore into his. "So have I! You don't know what I've seen, what I've felt about marriage."

"I didn't want this to happen."

"What? The fact that we made love? Or did you think it was just a mad scramble in the quilts?"

"No, you exasperating, incredible woman! That I . . . I love you. I'm in love with you, dammit! And I'm not terribly elated about that fact right now. I had no control over it. I've never been in this kind of mess before."

"Mess!" She stepped back. "You . . . you *love* me?"

"How is it that you are so smart and you hadn't even noticed that?"

"You did a great job of hiding it."

"Well, I didn't know it myself for a while."

"Well, neither did I."

"Well, good!" His hands gripped her upper arms.

His eyes bored into hers. Then he blinked. "Neither did you what?" he asked with a hoarse quietness.

Maudie bit her lower lip. This wasn't right, the timing. Everything was so confused, and she hadn't had time to figure out what she could do, what she had to do.

"Neither did you what?" Cole shouted. His fingers pressed into her arms.

"Why do you have to make me say it?"

"Because I want to hear it! You are the most exasperating female I've ever had the misfortune of being associated with! Now, say it!"

"All right, I will!" she shouted. "I love you! There! Are you satisfied now?"

"No, I'm not!"

"What more do you want?"

"I don't know! Freedom!" he shouted, releasing her arms and throwing his over his head.

"I knew it! You can't deny it now, can you? You have been avoiding me since we made love."

Cole sighed and dropped his hands. "All right, I have been avoiding you. But I can't tell you why."

"Why not?"

"I just can't right now. I haven't figured it out yet."

"What do you have to figure out?"

"More than I ever figured I'd have to." He looked sad. "I hope I can make things right."

Maudie watched him closely. Her heart felt heavy. "Can I help?" she asked gently.

"No, you can't. The best thing you can do is stay away."

"For how long?"

"I don't know."

Maudie lifted her chin and let out a breath. "I see." She turned and left Cole's room, closing the door securely behind her.

Cole's arms hung limply at his sides. He stared at the closed door a long time. "No, my beautiful Maudie, you don't see. And I wish you never had to."

It was a long time before he moved, before he finished dressing to go to work. Being the sheriff of Deadwood was work, work he wished to hell he'd never taken. Ever since Maudie had stripped him of his mustache, he'd been having great difficulty finding a place inside himself to settle down.

Without even knowing it, she'd been forcing him to think about his life, think about what he wanted to do with his future. He never even thought about a future before now, preferring to live day to day, however he felt like it, week to week, month to month, year to year. It never mattered before now how his time was spent.

Now he had his own work to do. Get out of this job of being sheriff no matter what it took and soon. He knew too much, and he didn't want to be forced to use what he knew and what he suspected. He had to get out of this before the federal marshal came back. He was desperate now. He had to recruit somebody to be sheriff, *anybody!*

Theo put the finishing touches on a chicken dinner he'd been preparing and left it simmering on the stove. The steam filled his rooms with an aroma of the special herbs he'd brought to Deadwood with him. He enjoyed cooking as much now as he had when he was a boy. His father had taught him well, Theo thought, and he might have been as great a chef as Angus Bartles if his life hadn't taken a drastic turn.

"Would you like a glass of wine, my dear?" Theo entered the living room that still smelled of new wood and varnish.

"Perhaps just a little. I am a bit nervous about tonight."

The woman standing in front of the settee that was covered in maroon flowered chintz smoothed her hands over a long pale green gown. Her reflection in the oval free-standing mirror made Theo think of a life size cameo. She was still utterly beautiful to him, and he was as much in love with her now as he was over twenty years ago when he'd first seen her.

"Are you having a problem with the fit?"

"Not really," she said quietly. "It feels just a bit loose at the waist. Nothing important. As always, you did perfect work. I marvel at your talent with costumes."

Theo walked up behind her and adjusted the back of the gown. "I think you've lost some weight. That's why it might feel loose. You have to take care of your health, my love."

The lovely face softened into a smile showing tiny lines near the eyes. "You do that for me, now, don't you? It's a wonder I'm not the size of an ox, the way you feed me." She leaned over and tenderly kissed his cheek.

If there was anything to be marvelled at in this world, Theo thought, his heart swelling, it was this wonderful, exquisite woman who'd sacrificed so much in her life, and had bestowed her love upon him. How he'd been so fortunate to have the gods shine upon him with such a glorious gift, he'd never know. He gave up long ago questioning such wealth. As always, he was just happy to be in her presence, overjoyed to have her in his life now, the way he'd always dreamed.

He went out to the kitchen and returned with a stemmed glass half filled with a light wine. "This should help your nervousness."

"I doubt anything will," she said sipping it. "I'm afraid I shall flop miserably this evening."

"You've been through countless opening nights with nary a thought to your performance, which has always been perfection, of course."

She set the glass on a nearby lamp stand, and turned around slowly. Her limp seemed more pronounced tonight. Perhaps it was because she was weary and faced the evening with a great deal of trepidation.

"Are you satisfied with your work, Theo?"

"The gown is perfect on you. You are perfect in it." He beamed upon her.

"Help me out of it, then, will you? I don't want to soil or wrinkle it before this evening."

He assisted her in removing the dress and brought an emerald-hued dressing gown. She slipped into it as he held it for her, then wrapped and tied it loosely around her. She picked up the wine glass and lowered her body wearily to the settee.

"Is it really so different tonight?" he asked, knowing full well this would be the most unusual opening night she would ever experience in her life.

"You know it's different. I never thought this night

would come, never thought I'd see her again, let alone tell her . . ." Tears formed in her eyes, and as always she held them in check.

Theo rushed to her side, and took her in his arms. "My beautiful sweet lady, she will adore you as much as I do, as much as she would have if she could have known you all these years."

"I'm afraid she'll never understand."

"You'll help her understand."

"How? I hardly understand it myself. All these years . . . all these wretched years without her. If not for you, dearest Theo, I would be dead now . . . or worse. You saved me, you gave me new life by devoting yours to me, and now you give me renewed life. Birth. You brought me, brought my daughter, brought us to each other. I only hope we don't let you down."

The actress known as Lady Fan dropped her head down to Theo's shoulder, nestled her dark auburn red hair sprinkled now in her forty-eighth year with a dusting of silver, and allowed herself to be comforted in his arms. Her height, a head taller than the milliner, and her stature in the theater, had never been means to drive them apart. It was during the years when she was locked away in a dreadful asylum had she lived the life of a mole.

Theo had first seen Gwen-Ada Boone Dearden in a play in New York. He was working in his father's restaurant then. But once he saw her, everything changed. He took up his mother's profession, seamstress and milliner, and gained some acting work and some costume work in theaters just to be near her. He had loved her from afar from the first moment he saw her.

Theo knew about her husband, about her little girl. When, some years later, he learned what her husband had done to her, Theo found her and helped her escape the asylum. In their process of escape she'd jumped from a high window and damaged her hip and leg. She'd considered it a small price to pay for freedom.

Theo had helped her get back into the theater. She never gave up her dream to see her daughter again, but after each attempt Gwen-Ada had seemed more disheartened than ever. Theo learned Maudie had left New York, had disappeared. He told Gwen-Ada, but that hadn't stopped her search. After a while he thought she'd given up hope of ever seeing her daughter again. But whenever they could be together, he always tried to keep her hopes alive. He dreamed along with her that someday they'd be reunited. He never let her know about his own dreams of her.

That's when she met Jared Braddock. Braddock fell in love with her, and then she'd helped him overcome some terrible tragedy and his battle with alcohol. Theo always wondered if the two of them would have married if Braddock hadn't been killed in a theater accident.

"She's the age I was when I last saw her, you know." Gwen-Ada's wistful voice broke into his sad memories.

"Yes, I know," Theo whispered. "And she looks just the way you did then."

"Maudie, my darling daughter." Gwen-Ada stifled a sob. "She has more grit and courage than I had."

"She's lived a different life," Theo responded.

"I can't believe it's finally happened." Gwen-Ada sat up and smiled at Theo, her dark blue eyes shining with tears. "Oh, she's so spirited, isn't she? How'd she get that way? She did it herself, I know she did. No matter how hard her father tried, he couldn't squash her, could he?"

"No, he couldn't. She has your spirit, your will, you know. That's why she's survived so well."

"I only hope she'll forgive me for what I'm certain she thinks is abandonment." Gwen-Ada sighed.

"She will embrace you with love. Once she knows what you sacrificed to keep her from harm, she'll understand everything."

"Oh, Theo, do you really think so? I can't imagine a little girl understanding a mother who ran away and left her with a horrible man who could never be the loving father you could have been."

"She's not a little girl, anymore, Gwen. She's a grown woman, and she's smart. She'll understand. You didn't just run away. You tried to take her with you. He threatened her life and then yours. Once you tell her that . . ."

"No child should know about a father who wishes her dead."

Theo rubbed her back. "Give her credit. You gave up a lot for her. I know she'll understand."

"My darling, you gave up so much, too, just to take care of me." She caressed his cheek lovingly. "You were a wonderful actor, with a great future. I know that."

"And I became a great costume designer, if I do say

so myself," he replied, touching the tip of her nose with the tip of his finger.

"Yes, you did. My costumes have always been the best in any of my productions. This one is no exception. I can hardly believe I'm doing *Scarlet Lady* again."

"I'll never forget your performance in the production in Missouri."

Gwen rubbed his hand. "If the accident hadn't happened . . ."

"I know. I'm sorry about Jared to this day. Poor man. He was just getting his life back together."

"I know. He was on the verge of greatness." She looked into his eyes. "I'm sorry. We shouldn't be talking about a past love."

"Nonsense. I am your present love."

"My only love forever. How was it I never knew how you felt until after Jared was gone?"

"You were busy taking care of him and staying out of harm's way. It was all right that I loved you from afar. You were a glittering star, and I a supporting player. I never dreamed that you would respond to me, never expected . . ."

"I'm glad we could surprise each other."

"True love is always a surprise."

"Yes. I hope a mother's love isn't a shock to Maudie."

"I believe she will welcome it. I know she's been searching for you, too."

"How do you know that?" Gwen sat up on the edge of the settee.

Theo eased her back. "I just know. Now stop worrying. Finish your wine while I dish up your supper. I'll get you to the theater in plenty of time for your nerves to calm. By the end of this evening you shall be reunited with your daughter, and we shall start life anew." Theo kissed her tenderly, then rose and went to the kitchen.

Gwen-Ada followed him. She set the table with dishes and silver, then sat down. "I'm not sure how it will feel to be known as Gwen-Ada Boone again."

"How about being called Mother?" Theo stirred his simmering stew, then sniffed the aromatic steam. "Just right."

"Mother. I've not allowed myself to think about it by day. But my dreams were relentless."

Theo filled their plates and seated himself across from her.

"I've often wondered whatever happened to Jared's little boy." Gwen-Ada stirred the stew to cool it. "From what Jared told me about him, he ran away when his mother left. I wonder if he knows about Jared, that he's gone, I mean." She lifted a piece of chicken and placed it in her mouth, chewed thoughtfully, then swallowed. "Mmm. Delicious, as always. I don't know how I got so lucky as to have you in my life."

"You aren't half as lucky as I am to have you." Theo smiled warmly. "I don't think I ever met Jared's boy. I remember the photograph Jared carried with him. The boy looked a lot like his mother. Same eyes and strong cheekbones. What was his name?"

"Colton Braddock. I believe that was his mother's maiden name. He'd be a man now. Somewhere around Maudie's age, I think. I never met him either. Jared talked about him often. I know he missed him.

He let his drinking get in the way, I fear, and then he thought his son never wanted to see him anyway. It's terrible what parents do to their children."

"Sometimes they have to do it, I think, to keep them from sinking in the same mud."

Gwen-Ada nodded. "You're very understanding, as always. You know, it was a long time after Jared's accident before I could feel safe in a theater again. I was always watching for Patrick to appear, even after I learned he was dead. Then after Jared was killed, I always found myself looking up at where the scrim was attached, or at how the scenery flats were constructed. This is the first time since then that I've appeared in *Scarlet Lady*."

"I know."

"If you hadn't heard about Clara's revival of it, and about her less than honest activities, I never would have considered doing what we're doing now."

"We needed the money. You needed to work more in the theater," Theo said as a matter of fact.

"I still don't understand Clara's behavior." Gwen-Ada shook her head. "And then to come to the same tragic end as Jared." She shuddered. "I hope we will be safe doing this. You know what they say about things happening in threes."

"Old actors' tale." Theo smiled at her. "When we get through this production, when you are reunited with Maudie, we will at last breathe easier. Together."

"I just hope the trick works, and nothing tragic comes of it. I hope the crime can be solved, the jewels returned. I hope . . ."

"I hope you'll be on time!" Theo chided. "Now get yourself ready and I'll escort you to the theater."

"You will stay for the performance, won't you? I have to know you're there."

"I will be there, my darling. But first I have to stop off and see a friend. Perhaps I'll be able to persuade him to join me this evening."

"I've brought something for you," Theo said to Cole, unwrapping a paper package and striding quickly over to the hat rack. "I hope you will accept it as a token of our friendship. I also hope it will pick up your dampened spirits. I've noticed you seem not to be your usual self these days."

"What is it?" Cole watched Theo take down the Stetson, choosing to ignore the remark about his spirits.

"A hat band. I fashioned it myself. I believe someone in your position should have an adornment befitting your stature." He lifted the circle from the paper, slipped it down over the hat crown, and fastened it at the side, then patted the Stetson like a favored pet. "There. What do you think?"

Cole got to him in two long strides and examined the hatband, turning the Stetson round and round in both hands. The narrow band was of leather, fashioned with gold thread worked into an intricate pattern all around, resembling some of the Sioux designs he'd seen since he'd arrived in the Black Hills.

"This must have taken you hours," Cole breathed with an air of wonder. "It's very handsome."

Theo looked down at his own new black high heeled boots, identical to the ones Cole wore, polished to a lustrous shine. "Thank you. I enjoyed the labor knowing it was a gift for a true friend."

"You mean you're not mad at me for that beast of a hangover you had several days ago?" Cole looked up rather sheepishly.

"I admit I used some words describing you that I don't use in every day polite conversation," Theo responded, the suggestion of a smile lighting his face. "but I've never engaged in such frank conversation with another man before in my life, and it, well, touched me deeply."

Cole ran his fingers over the gold stitching on the hatband. "I've never been given such a fine gift." He studied the hat crown, brushing it briskly, and didn't look up. "And I . . . am truly touched by your generosity." He was surprised at how comfortable he felt saying those words to a man.

"I'm glad you like it," Theo said after a long pause. "What's troubling you, my friend? Can I help?"

"Yes. Take this tin star and become the new sheriff of Deadwood," Cole said glumly.

Theo laughed heartily. Then he saw Cole was serious. "I thought you enjoyed this job. Except for the unfortunate killing of Mr. Hickok, of course."

Cole took the Stetson and sat down behind his desk. His fingers ran over Theo's hat band. "I did like it, in the beginning. I just didn't think it would last so long."

"Well, it won't much longer unless you really want it."

Cole's head snapped up. "What do you mean?"

331

"I hear that by mid-September we should have a real city government in place. That means an established law enforcement agency with a real law officer, unless you want to apply." Theo tilted his head to watch his friend's response.

"I don't want it. And September's too far away." Cole set the Stetson on his desk and leaned back in his chair. He opened the drawer and took out the Buntline special revolver. "And this thing is too handy."

"And big." Theo sat down in the chair opposite Cole's desk. "I take it you haven't always been a sheriff."

"Never. Here comes the confession. I used to be an actor."

Theo leaned back hard against his chair back. "No! When? Where? What roles did you play? Were you a leading man?"

"Hell no! I never stayed that long. I was a child actor."

"Oh, one of those incorrigible types."

"Right. I was known as . . . Well, that doesn't matter, does it?" Cole spun the cartridge chamber on the Buntline.

"Sure it does. I was an actor, too, once upon a very long time ago." Theo smiled enigmatically.

"No! Where? What plays? I wonder if I ever saw you in anything."

"I doubt it. I was never a leading man. I went by another name, too."

"Yeah? What was it?"

"I'll tell you mine if you tell me yours!"

Cole considered for a moment. "All right. It doesn't

matter anymore anyway. They called me Braddock's Bad Boy. Now you."

Theo's jaw dropped.

"Come on, Theo. Your name can't be as bad as all that," Cole urged.

Theo spoke in a monotone. "Wee Willie Waters. Did you say Braddock?"

Cole let loose with the heartiest laugh he'd felt in days. "Wee Willie—that's awful! Why'd you let them do that to you?"

"You know how things happen in the theater. Did you say Braddock?" Theo was still stunned.

Cole watched him more carefully now. "Yes, I did. Why?"

"Braddock. Any relation to Jared Braddock?"

"You . . . you knew . . . my father?"

Theo clamped his eyes shut, and sucked in a sharp breath. "I knew him," he said, letting out the labored air. "We had a mutual friend, a woman friend."

Cole's interest was more than highly piqued now. "Who?"

"A beautiful, wonderful lady. We both loved her."

Cole's senses picked up the truth of what Theo was saying. He remembered seeing Theo in Fan's house. Proof. The woman *had* to be Gwen-Ada Boone. Lady Fan. "Did . . . did she love him?"

Theo seemed suddenly pained. "Yes, she did. She picked him up out of the gutter . . . I'm sorry. You knew your father had become a drunk. He blamed it on your mother."

"He had no call to do that," Cole said bitterly. "It was he who pushed her away with all his other women, and . . . Theo, I know about Gwen-Ada Boone. I know about the accident that killed my father. So do you, don't you?"

Theo rose and went to the office window. "Cole, there's something I want to discuss with you. Something very important."

"Sounds serious, but if it's about women again, I'm out of the advice business." Cole watched Theo's shoulders slump.

"It's serious, all right." Theo turned to face Cole. "And it's about a woman, two women to be exact. And it's even about your father."

"What about my father?" Cole frowned, and felt his temples throb.

"I'll tell you. And then we have to go to the theater. It's important that we both be there tonight."

Cole rose. "Theo, I can't . . . I can't go to the theater anymore."

"Yes, you can. You have to. Tonight especially. And we have to trust each other to make things come out right."

"What things?"

"Sit down. I have a story to tell you." Theo went back to the chair near Cole's desk.

Cole eyed him warily. "Theo . . . I don't know if I can take any more real life stories. I've had my fill of them, and they don't seem to have happy endings."

"You want to stop running away, don't you?" Theo shot back at him. "You want to tie up all your loose ends, right? I know what that feels like. I've been running all my life. Or perhaps it's more to the point to say

I've been following. Well, I don't want to do that anymore. I plan to change things. Right here in Deadwood. Tonight. I think you'd better listen to me."

Cole sat still. And listened.

Chapter 15

As Maudie entered her room, her boot scuffed over something unfamiliar. An envelope had been slipped under the door. Wearily she bent to retrieve it. She extracted a piece of folded paper and opened it. *Arriving Deadwood five August. Know you have rubies. Good work. Will bring reward. Golden.* Maudie slumped down on the bed. Golden was arriving soon. She didn't have the rubies. Why in the world did he think she did? It was true she knew where they were hidden. She hadn't made up her mind if she planned to tell Cole about them, let alone the Pinkerton agent.

She huddled under the bed quilt hugging her drawn knees to her chest and resting her chin on the valley they made. She stared unseeing into the gathering gloom and listened while Taryn and Jewel scurried about in the next room getting ready to leave for the opening night of *Scarlet Lady*.

Cold gripped her senses. Not an external cold, for while the nights were cooling in Deadwood, the days were still warm with summer. This was an internal cold, an old chill contained in her marrow, controlled by the sheer force of her grit and determination. Now, faced by what, who, she believed to be the object of her lifelong quest, Maudie felt enervated, unable to summon the fire she needed to sustain her in the confrontation.

She struggled with the age-old question—fight or flight? Should she fly away like an alarmed little bird sensing the presence of a cat, or stay and risk the loss of a part of herself forever? Would it be less painful to wonder and wander for the rest of her days, or face the truth and possibly destroy any love that remained inside her?

The truth.

Lady Fan. Gwen-Ada Boone Dearden. One woman. Her mother.

Maudie knew it in her heart, no matter how much her mind rebelled at the thought. This was not a dream. Gwen-Ada Boone was alive, not dead, not locked away in an insane asylum wracked with guilt as her father had told her. Aside from her limp, something Maudie hadn't remembered, Gwen-Ada seemed healthy. She was beautiful, just perfect, as a matter of fact.

She'd seen the truth with her own eyes. Hadn't she? Her mother. The woman couldn't have been a dream. She was real. Maudie saw the mask of makeup come away by Lady Fan's own hands, revealing the face of Gwen-Ada Boone.

As she stared into the darkness collecting around her now, she recalled how she'd lived the next hours in a blur, a trance she'd walked through in some hypnotic state. The scent in the house. The feel of the air. The presence of the woman. Her mother. The baby dress. *Cole! He knows, too! What will he do with that knowledge?*

A rap at the door jarred her back to her senses.

"Maudie? You coming?" Taryn sounded insistent. "Maudie?" She rapped again. Maudie heard her voice fade. "She must have left already. We'd better hurry too. You know how Mr. LaFountain hates tardiness. He's especially nervous on opening nights."

"I wouldn't want to make him angry." Jewel's voice. Maudie heard their steps retreating.

Opening night! An audience would be there. What was she going to do about opening night? Her experience in the theater had taught her many things. The number one rule: the show must go on no matter what. Never let the company down, play your part with discipline and self-control. Be loyal.

To hell with loyalty!

Maudie slipped under the covers and pulled the quilt up over her head, squeezing herself into the tiniest ball possible, just as she'd done as a little girl hiding from her father. Back then, she could never make herself small enough. He'd always found her. And then the pain would come. Maudie clamped her eyes shut. The pain was upon her now, and she couldn't hide in her smallness now any more than she could then.

Slowly she uncoiled, easing her aching limbs up and out of the cocoon of quilts. Why should she care so much? If her mother had cared this much, wouldn't she have come back for her daughter, saved her from the desolation of abandonment, from the profound hurt she suffered at the hands of Patrick Dearden?

338

Maudie knew in her grown woman's heart that he'd been unfit as a husband and companion to Gwen-Ada. But when Gwen-Ada disappeared, he took his rage out on Maudie. She hadn't deserved that, had she?

Sometimes in her brave little girl's heart Maudie dreamed of finding Gwen-Ada, saving her from the trap she must have been caught in, a trap made more horrible because she was being kept from her daughter. And other times in her scared little girl's mind, Maudie saw herself kneeling on a grave in an abandoned cemetery on some isolated, cold piece of ground, placing flowers at a headstone, and weeping desperate, lonely tears.

The truth was nothing at all as she'd envisioned it all along. Why should she continue to care now? How *should* she feel?

Maudie felt the locket around her neck. For the first time it felt heavy as a millstone. She opened the clasp and let the chain fall loose. She released the tiny latch and opened the heart. Mother and baby were still there, still locked in time, just as the baby was locked in the mother's protective, loving arms.

Maudie's throat constricted. Her eyes burned. And then the suppressed emotions of her young life and her ripe womanhood flooded over her in a powerful wave of wracking sobs. She withheld the tears, having shed enough of those already to last another lifetime.

"Oh, Mama, how could you desert me? It wasn't my fault he was so awful. You could have come back. You *could* have come back, but you didn't. You left me. He was right. You left because you didn't love me."

Why did she feel so angry? Shouldn't she be happy,

ecstatic that her mother was alive and well? Maudie wailed inside her head. What did she want? Would it be better if her mother was dead and she could go on mourning? Is that what she wanted? Hadn't she been hoping for just this? Why did she feel anger, almost hatred for Gwen-Ada now?

Maudie clenched her fist over the locket until the metal bit into her palm and she felt the moistness of warm blood. And then she hurled the locket away from her. It hit the wall and fell to the floor with a force that surely had broken it. Like Maudie's heart was breaking now.

The show must go on.

In a numbed state, she lifted the quilt and got out of bed. She went to the wash stand, methodically poured water into the bowl and bathed her face. She peered into the mirror, hoping the refreshing cool water would reduce the puffiness around her eyes. With a cloth dipped in water, she pressed the chill against her temples, her throat, and tried to calm herself.

She brushed out her hair. Watching the long dark red strands sift through the bristles, she was once again reminded of innocent days when she and her mother had brushed one another's hair. She coiled it around and pinned it securely against her aching head. And took stock of the facts. Coldheartedly, without emotion. Jabbing a pin into her hair with each statement of fact.

"Lady Fan is Gwen-Ada Boone. My mother." Jab. "She lied to me, said she'd be back. She never came back." Jab. "She hasn't been locked away." Jab. "She's not hurt. Except the limp. She didn't have that a long time ago." Jab. "She's fine, just fine." Jab, jab. "Well, so am I! Just fine!" Jab, jab . . . "Ow!" Jab.

Maudie lowered her arms and spoke to her own reflection. "She's a thief, a . . . *possibly* a . . . a murderer. Golden will be here soon. I have to report this to him, and turn over the rubies." She picked up more pins and raised her arms to place them. "How could I do that? I couldn't do that. He'll arrest her. I can't let that happen. And I can't let anyone else do it either, can I?" Jab, jab. "But if she's not the murderer, then someone else is. My mother's life could be in danger!"

Maudie lowered her arms. Cole! Her hardening gaze clashed with the angry and hurt one in the mirror. She and Cole were a lot alike. Where they were different, their differences meshed and made a new whole. She'd never known that could happen between a man and a woman. When they'd exchanged life stories, the realization of what they were separately, as well as together, was staggering. While she never would have admitted this several weeks ago, she knew they thought very much the same way.

Cole! If she had figured it out about Lady Fan, then it was certain he had, too! And it would be only a matter of time before he did something about it.

An involuntary breath caused Maudie to shudder. Like mother, like daughter. She'd fallen in love with a policeman. In love! Knowing she was in it forever was a hot jab to her heart as much as the pins were to her head. She was in love with Cole Branch. Of all the ill-timed, ill-advised . . . He was paid to be sheriff, answerable to a federal marshal. And he had a job to do, a job with inherent expectations. If he didn't do that job he could suffer a harsh reprimand. If he did do it, and if he discovered Gwen-Ada was her mother, he'd be forced to do something he'd know would deliberately hurt her.

But maybe he hadn't quite figured out that part yet. Maybe there was still time.

The solution was clear to Maudie now. She had to keep her distance from Cole. And she couldn't reveal herself to her mother. The only thing she could do was protect her and Cole by making Gwen-Ada leave Deadwood as soon as possible. Before Cole arrested her, before the federal marshal arrived, before the Pinkerton agent showed up. She'd have to push both her mother and Cole Branch away from her. She knew there was no other choice. It was the only way she could protect them both.

"And I will keep my old promise to myself in the bargain. I will *never* love anyone again. Not ever." That was clear, too. If there was no one to save Maudie, she'd continue to do what she'd been doing all her life, protect herself.

Maudie scooped up her canvas bag and started for the door. She couldn't be late for opening curtain and for whatever else lay ahead. Then she turned back and dropped to her knees, frantically scraping her hands over the dark floor where she'd flung the locket. Tears burned at the back of her eyes. At last her fingers fell upon the chain. She scooped it up and saw that the clasp was broken and the opened heart bent. Folding her hand over it lovingly, she clutched the precious thing against her breast. She couldn't wear it tonight, make it visible to Gwen-Ada, let her know that her outward actions were not the expression of her heart. Perhaps, under the circumstances, it was just as well she couldn't wear it.

Saddened, she carefully placed the locket inside her clothing against her heart.

Cole paced the confines of his small room. His head ached. Everything was becoming clear. Too clear. He was in love with Maudie. Doomed to love. Love had toppled Cole Branch. That love had him thinking about staying in one town. Thinking about marriage. This was love with a completely inappropriate woman. At least inappropriate for him now. Now especially, when he was forced to do a duty he never would have dreamed he'd have to do. There had been so many questions. Maybe the answers that were coming to him were wrong.

He didn't know what to do, how to feel, how to act. Ever since Maudie had stripped him of his persona by stripping him of his mustache, he'd been having great difficulty getting a handle on who he was. Maybe that's why he didn't know how to act. He was supposed to be an officer of the law. But what about the man inside the role?

He mulled over the story Maudie had told him about her life, her mother and father. She'd been wondering if the late Clara Carew was her mother. The way he'd been figuring it up in his head, she couldn't have been. The lockets were the key to everything. He knew it now. The locket in the box in Fan's dressing room, the locket around Maudie's neck. They were the same. The baby dress in Fan's house. Unless Maudie was denying the truth to herself, she knew now what he'd discovered and what Theo had confirmed. Lady Fan was Gwen-Ada Boone, Maudie's mother.

He'd told Theo he'd meet him at the theater in time for curtain. But he needed time to mull over all that Theo had told him. He hadn't bargained for this. Theo's confirmation that Gwen-Ada was Maudie's mother, and his father's lover. Theo had been there to witness it all. How difficult it must have been for him.

Other images came to Cole's mine. How strange to realize that he'd seen Gwen-Ada Boone in a play with his father. The last play he'd seen him in, the night Jared Braddock had been killed, the night Gwen-Ada Boone had disappeared.

If he'd figured this out, Maudie would learn of it soon, if she hadn't already. Once the federal marshal arrived, he'd have to turn Gwen-Ada over to him along with the rubies. If the Pinkerton agent arrived sooner, Maudie would be forced to turn her own mother over to him. That would kill her.

How could he possibly take care of all this? He knew how desperately Maudie had fought all her life to find her mother, to have her questions answered. And now here she was, alive, seemingly unharmed. And all the evidence suggested she was a thief and a murderer twice over. How could he arrest Lady Fan and turn her over to the authorities? And for what? Nothing was worth the pain he would inflict on Maudie.

And what about Theo? Here was his first real friend, and he'd be forced to hurt him, too, if he dealt honestly within the law where Lady Fan was concerned. Theo had confessed Gwen-Ada was the love of his life. He'd suffered so much already watching the love he craved go to Jared. How could any man be that loving? Theo had sacrificed everything for her. Cole simply couldn't hurt the man further.

He'd forced himself to stay away from Maudie. Being near her only muddled his thinking. Gwen-Ada was the person he'd been looking for, the object of his search. He could admit that now. Gwen-Ada, so the papers had said, was a suspect in the accident that took his father's life. Yet, hadn't she also been the one who had saved him? Brought him out of his despair, helped him gain back his life as an actor? It didn't make sense that she would cause his death.

The solution was becoming clearer. He'd have Maudie turn the rubies over to the Pinkertons so she could claim the reward. He'd say the rubies were discovered in Carew's things and that Carew had indeed been the thief. He'd say her death had been ruled an accident. He wanted to spare Maudie any unnecessary pain.

He'd handle his own pain later. Much later, when he was out of Deadwood. And Maudie and Gwen-Ada were out of his life. There was a lonely echo to the sound of those words in his mind. But what else could he do? If Gwen-Ada was guilty of everything . . .

Cole stopped thinking.

Unless someone else was to blame . . .

Cole straightened. He'd told Theo he'd meet him at the theater, and that was exactly what he intended to do.

* * *

Maudie steeled herself in the stage-left wing. The final scene of Act One was about to commence. She watched as the actress known as Lady Fan entered from the right wing and commanded center stage. Applause swelled from the audience. Maudie marveled at the physical control she exerted over her limp. It was barely noticeable; her mother was a glittering presence on stage. A shiver went over her as Maudie thrilled at the sight of Gwen-Ada in the limelight, the consummate tragedienne.

Gwen-Ada's passionate delivery of her lines made Maudie's chest heave. As the actress turned, the lights glinted off something that hung around her neck. Maudie tore her gaze away from Gwen-Ada's face to lower it to the glitter in the limelight. The locket! She was wearing the locket!

Maudie's knees buckled. She clutched a black masking curtain to steady herself. For one blinding moment she wished her own locket could be visible to her mother.

She listened carefully for her cue, not certain she'd be physically able to walk out onto that stage and face Gwen-Ada, for the first time knowing she was her mother.

Beyond, Maudie could see into the stage-right wing where Taryn waited for her entrance, worshipful eyes pinned on Lady Fan. In back of her, seated on a low stool, was Lula, her trusty sewing kit at her side as she worked on a last-minute repair to the hem of Taryn's costume. Lately Lula had seemed in darker spirits than ever before, displaying even more erratic behavior than she had during the costume-fitting sessions. When she spoke about almost anything now it was with acrimony. Bitter was the only way to describe her demeanor. It seemed Lula had become obsessed with the memories of her former life, almost to the point that she no longer lived in the present.

". . . and if I could have my daughters around me once again . . ." Maudie heard Gwen-Ada begin the speech that would bring her, and then Taryn, onstage for their scene together. ". . . this life without passion would be no more. Oh, that the cruelty of fate that made me the fallen woman that I am could have been cleansed away with the tears of a mother's heart," Gwen-Ada sobbed. "Oh, that I might be reunited with the children of my womb."

Trembling, Maudie took her first step onto the lighted stage for her scene with Lady Fan. Gwen-Ada Boone. Her mother. Her voice cracked with heavy emotion as she uttered her opening line. "M-mother . . . you've come back. I . . . we thought you were dead."

Beneath the harsh makeup, Maudie saw Gwen-Ada's face contort with pain, her eyes fill with tears as mother and daughter, not actress and actress, knowingly stood before one another for the first time in two decades. Time stood still, locked between them. Gwen-Ada was visibly moved, rooted to her place. Her lower lip trembled. Maudie's shoulders shook, her pulse raced, her heart pounded so heavily in her ears that she barely heard Taryn's delayed entrance and the faltering delivery of her first line.

"Mother dear, it is I, the . . . the babe who was

sn-snatched from your arms when you sinned." Taryn walked stiffly toward Gwen-Ada.

Gwen-Ada's timing was off, Maudie noticed, but at last she lifted both arms to embrace her fictional children. It was clear the audience hadn't noticed the delay, for they burst into applause when the three women embraced. The curtain came down, signaling the end of Act One.

Maudie's face was buried in the thick costume fabric that covered Gwen-Ada's bosom, yet she could hear the erratic beating of her mother's heart. Gwen-Ada breathed hard against Maudie's ear, and Maudie felt something wet in her hair. Could it be tears? The two still clung together after the curtain had been lowered.

". . . and the audience loved the scene, too," Taryn was gushing breathlessly when Maudie lifted her head.

Gwen-Ada pulled into her full height and tore her gaze away from Maudie's face. "Yes, I think they did." Her voice was . . . soft and low like the one Maudie remembered in a bedtime story. "We should be very grateful." Hushed, as if exhorting prayers before sleep. "You . . . you *both* were wonderful." Uplifting, as if in praise of a little girl . . .

A voice deep in Maudie's consciousness, always remembered, always loved.

Taryn scampered off in search of Lula, saying she'd been so nervous she'd popped the fasteners in her bodice. The scenery crew was busy striking the first set and preparing to bring in the one for Act Two. Using the rope and pulley system, they hauled up the flat painted with the city walls, and then rolled down the scrim painted with the outdoor scene. Maudie shivered, remembering the hemp lines in the flyloft. A moment of fear gripped her.

She read the pain in Gwen-Ada's eyes. She wanted to fling herself back into her mother's arms, but her feet were heavy as lead and kept her rooted to the stage boards. She struggled for her voice. And then she saw him in the wings. Cole Branch stood still, watching them, a look on his face Maudie couldn't understand at first.

And then it came to her.

He knows! He's going to arrest her! No!

LaFountain pushed his way around Cole and came out onto the stage. "What are you doing out here?" he rasped in a stage whisper. "You have ten minutes until the opening of Act Two. Get into your costume changes immediately!" He stalked back off the stage, then turned around. "It was a good first act. Maudie, work on your voice projection. They can't hear you in the back. Lady Fan, well done." His voice softened with respect as he addressed Gwen-Ada. "A bit quicker on your timing would pick up the pace. Only if it feels comfortable, of course."

Gwen-Ada nodded silently.

Maudie forced herself to move off the stage. She pushed past Cole without speaking. When she reached the wardrobe closet, she buried herself in the hanging costumes and just trembled, her breath coming in sharp gasps. This was all too much, having to act a part that in real life was breaking her heart.

She was seeing her mother for the first time in so very long, and would have to push her away before they could even speak personally as mother and daughter. She was feeling love for a man for the first time ever, and was forced to run away from him. She had no time to be weak, yet no will to be strong. What must be done must be done quickly and cleanly, she thought, her face buried among the costumes.

Cole had a feeling. One of those feelings he used to get in the theater when he was very young. He hated that feeling. It was an old theatrical superstition, like remembering not to throw your hat on the bed so as not to bring bad luck down upon yourself. It was a portent of bad things to come. He walked around behind the scrim and peered up into the flyloft. It was dark, and the smell of the kerosene from the stage lights was thick.

The two-man scenery crew was preoccupied setting up the sound equipment to create the noise of an earthquake that was to shatter the closing scene of Act Two. They would effect the earthquake's rumble and destruction by banging rocks against overturned wooden crates and pounding wooden clubs on calfskin-covered kettle drums. Cole remembered how clever some of the people who worked behind the scenes were. Scenery and costume people were just about the cleverest . . . Now where was this line of thinking leading him?

He waited until the scenery crew moved away, then stealthily walked to the base of the rigging ladder. Certain no one saw him, he ascended.

The second act was about to begin as Cole reached

the rigging pipe. He waited motionless, feeling the hot pulse of his blood course through his body.

Here it was again. That play, *Scarlet Lady*, the one Carew was doing when she died. The play his father was doing in Missouri, the play in which Gwen-Ada Boone performed as his leading lady, the night . . .

He spotted Lula sitting on the other side of the stage, holding a costume she'd been hemming, staring up into the flyloft. The way her jaw flexed, the way the light sharpened her profile, she looked more familiar to him, like someone he used to know. Cole shook his head. Impossible. But why was Lula looking up into the flyloft?

Cole climbed the rigging ladder. The stage lights went down just as he started to climb to the narrow scenery bridge. He made it to the bridge as the stage went black. The bridge wobbled under his weight. He inched along it behind the upper masking curtains, feeling his way along the scrim pipe, testing each hemp line and eyelet. His findings told him the rigging at that end was secure.

The stage lights started up falteringly, slowly illuminating the setting for the opening scene of Act Two. Cole looked down onto the stage, then back up into the flyloft. When his eyes adjusted to the light differences, something at the other end of the bridge caught his vision. Cole crouched down farther still. What was it?

It moved. It turned. A man. Theo!

What was he doing up there?

Cole watched as Theo's hands ran quickly over the hemp lines and eyelets at the other end of the scrim

351

pipe. He looked up and saw Cole. He froze. Cole's narrowed gaze bore into him.

Listening intently for her cue, Maudie felt jumpy, wary. As soon as Gwen-Ada said the line, *my heart is broken,* that would be her cue to rush onstage and act the part of the daughter to Gwen-Ada's mother. Had the line been delivered yet? No, she didn't think so. She tried to concentrate, felt desperate to keep her mind on everything, to be ready for anything. This opening night of *Scarlet Lady* was building into the culmination of every one of her life's searches.

Across the stage in the opposite wing she could see Lula sitting on the low stool, a costume draped over her lap. Maudie had a flash of a scene from a novel she'd read in school. Lula resembled Madame DeFarge in *A Tale of Two Cities,* sitting calmly knitting while observing the latest death by guillotine in the public square.

"For if I'm to die without a daughter's life in my heart," Gwen-Ada delivered her lines to Sterling Hale as they entered from stage right passing Lula, "then let it be over quickly and cleanly. I cannot live another moment in my anguish."

"Your sins have long ago been assuaged," Hale emoted. "Why is it you cannot accept the will of the people now? Have you more to hide?" Hale leaned forward in an exaggerated pose of shock and curiosity.

Gwen-Ada moved a few steps left of center stage. "Only the shame I cannot purge from my soul. I begged for my children to be reunited with me. They have been, thank the gods of fortune. But oh, the pain of their rejection later! I told them the truth, for I wished no more lies to cloud our love. They could not

352

conceal the disgust in their eyes, the abandonment they had felt. My younger daughter has renounced me forever. My elder daughter has run from me, never to return."

Maudie stood entranced by her mother's performance.

"Hear the distant rumbling? That is God's alarm that I am to be punished, killed in the earthquake." Gwen-Ada clamped her hands over her ears to quell the terror that consumed her character.

"It is the way you choose. Then let it be so that you lived the life of a sinner. I shall not share your punishment. Throw yourself upon the mercy of the gods, or save yourself." Sterling uttered his exit line, and disappeared into the wings.

Maudie knew then what she had to do. At the close of their final scene when the fictional earthquake was to fall and crush her mother's character, Maudie would make her move. Amid the confusion that would surround the scenery's planned fall, the curtain would come down, affording Maudie the best opportunity to pull Gwen-Ada away with her and help her to escape quickly. She'd stay and distract Cole. When Gwen-Ada was safely away, she'd confess to the crimes herself and give herself up to the federal marshal. If she managed this before the Pinkerton agent arrived, the deed would be done, the rubies returned, the Carew murder case closed.

"I lived my own life. My heart is broken." Gwen-Ada dropped to her knees, burying her face in her hands and emitting bitter sobs.

Maudie's cue line.

Cole watched from his vantage point on the scenery bridge. Theo turned and, with lithe movement, got off the rigging bridge and scampered down the ladder. Cole looked down. Lady Fan was speaking, moving center stage. Maudie was in the stage's left wing waiting to go on. She didn't see Theo, Cole was certain of it.

Cole inched his way quickly over the bridge. It wobbled even more erratically under his weight. He'd seen two men from the scenery crew on it before the curtain opened, and it appeared strong enough to support them. Odd, that it seemed so rickety now. He moved to the place where he'd seen Theo, feeling hemp lines and eyelets as he moved. He was at the point where Theo had been when he felt the difference. The ropes had been cut down to one strand. They'd started to snap in places.

The lights came up hot, bleeding into the loft. Cole blinked his eyes to adjust them. The light illuminated something on the cut hemp lines. Red thread! Heavy red thread was woven neatly through the strands, holding them together. It could give at any moment! Theo? Could Theo have—?

Maudie heard her cue line. She pulled into the professional actress she was and took her first step out on stage. Out of the corner of her eye she glimpsed a sharp movement. Slightly distracted, she turned her head and saw Theo dropping down from the rigging ladder and running toward the back of the scrim. What was he doing there?

"My heart is broken!" Gwen-Ada sobbed again, louder this time.

Maudie knew the actress inside her mother repeated the line for her benefit, believing, most probably, that she'd missed her cue. She moved onto the stage.

Cole looked back down. Maudie was just starting to go onstage. His eyes darted back to the rigging. Then back to Maudie. Then back to the rigging. It started to slip even more. The scenery bridge was wobbling under him. He heard the hemp lines rip. The counter-weights started down.

Maudie stepped out onstage, more resolute than ever before. "Do not weep for your daughters' lost love, mother of my heart's own making. Your elder daughter has seen inside her heart and knows the truth." She delivered her lines with more truth than fiction behind them, and crossed to the point where Gwen-Ada knelt sobbing.

Gwen-Ada looked up. Real tears streamed down her cheeks, streaking her heavy makeup. "You are kind, daughter, but I fear it is too late to atone for all that has gone before. The wrath of the gods is about to descend. I hear the earth's shaking, feel it deep in my bones."

"Come, embrace me as I've longed for you to do, let me feel my mother's arms around me once again. Together we shall perish, knowing the depth of love that is between us." Maudie crossed to Gwen-Ada, knelt down and drew her to her feet.

Cole's heart raced. His palms were sweating. On his hands and knees he backed himself along the bridge to the stage-right wing. Almost there. Just a few inches more. He looked down as he reached the ladder. Lula was standing. He saw her starting to hurry around in back of the scrim. What was she—?

"Thank you, my dearest daughter. You give me life and light again before death and eternal darkness," Gwen-Ada's line rang through the theater.

"We bring life, one to the other. My childhood has been returned to me, my womanhood made worthwhile." Maudie's character embraced Gwen-Ada's, as mother and daughter stood locked in each other's arms.

Cole was almost to the floor. He kept his eyes on Lula. Her face was caught in a shaft of light. Cole blanched. Of course! How was it he'd never realized? Why in God's name hadn't he seen it before?

Lula! Lula Gale was Lucille Galarzyk! Lucille Galarzyk from the Missouri theater. The same woman who'd handled the scenery for *Scarlet Lady* the night his father was killed, the same woman who worked with Clara Carew.

Everything was coming together in Cole's mind with white hot brilliance. Of course! He understood everything now!

Cole started around behind the scrim, following Lula, expecting to find Theo with her. Theo was after revenge, Lucille was simply crazy. They both were trying to kill Gwen-Ada, and in the process . . .

He stopped, every nerve in his body alive with terror.

Oh, God! *Maudie!*

Chapter 16

Cole apprehended Lula behind the scrim. He grabbed her arm, wrenching her around to face him.

"Lucille!" he rasped.

"Let me go, Braddock!" she hissed.

Theo ran to them. "Forget her, Cole!" His eyes were wild.

"Get out of my way, Bartles!" Cole growled. "I know what you're up to, and so help me I'll kill you, you two-faced—!"

Cole grabbed Theo and threw him against the theater's back wall. Lula was gone in an instant. Cole whirled and went after her, his glance darting overhead. The scrim pipe was tearing loose. He felt locked in a nightmare, as if he were wading through neck-high black water to get to his love, save her life. He strained against the weight of it, pushed with all his strength against the barrier of space and pressure.

He reached Lula, grabbed her dress sleeve and yanked her around. When she stumbled, he shoved her forcefully, and she fell into the masking curtains. Then he was on the stage, his heart slamming against his chest wall, lungs straining for breath. A few more steps and he'd reach her.

"Get away from me, Maudie!" Gwen-Ada yelled. Her eyes strained toward the ceiling. She pushed Maudie out of her arms. Maudie crashed against Cole, knocking them both off balance.

The audience murmured in confusion.

"Get out now! I don't want you here, I don't want you near me!" Gwen-Ada's voice escalated to a high-pitched shriek that sounded as if it came from the throat of a shrew.

Stricken by her mother's words, Maudie froze in the hard grip of Cole's arms. Unbelieving, she tried to grasp what was happening. Gwen-Ada was forcing her out of her arms and out of her life! Maudie's spine crumbled to dust, no longer able to hold her upright. She slumped out of Cole's arms and dropped in a heap at his feet.

Gwen-Ada was staring into the flyloft.

Maudie's gaze was fastened on her, her mind a whirlpool of confused images.

Gwen-Ada backed up in her direction. Her limp made her falter, her full costume hampered her movement. Bracing his arms under hers, Cole lifted Maudie to her feet.

Somewhere offstage, the scenery crew deepened the earthquake's rumble, making it louder, even louder, deafening. The stage floor vibrated. The audience applauded at the effects. From the top of the theater the scrim pipe gave way. The backdrop ripped. The scenery bridge swayed.

Gwen-Ada twisted and faced Maudie. She strained to run toward her daughter, but couldn't manage the exertion. Frantically her eyes darted overhead, then back to Maudie.

And then Maudie saw stark terror in her mother's eyes. She raised her own toward the flyloft and in a flash of comprehension grasped what was happening.

And she understood now that Gwen-Ada was trying to protect her, trying to shield her from the scenery that threatened to crush them both with its weight.

"Mother! Wait! No!" Maudie kicked against Cole and broke his grasp, determined to push her mother out of harm's way.

Lula ran from stage right, screeching like a wild cat in pain, hands raised in a clawlike poise to strike and slash. She stumbled in rage toward Maudie and Gwen-Ada.

Suddenly Theo burst from stage right. He leaped, propelling himself toward Gwen-Ada, catching her around her waist. They fell to the floor with his body over hers in a protective embrace.

Maudie raised her eyes to the flyloft and saw it all coming down toward her. The scenery bridge toppled. The pipe started down, the backdrop followed, the bridge in line. She screamed.

Cole reacted in a violent convulsion, launching himself toward Maudie and crushing her to the floor under his weight and length.

The earthquake built to a grand crescendo, and the scenery fell in a sickening rip to the stage floor.

Someone yelled "Curtain!"

The audience thundered its approval.

The opening night performance of *Scarlet Lady* came to a dead stop.

Maudie's heart pounded erratically in her ears. With great effort she forced her eyelids open. The side of her face was pressed flat into the floor. She tasted blood. Her lungs felt too compressed to accept air. None circulated around her anyway. A wave of dizziness, followed by nausea, swept over her. She tried to move. Couldn't. Something very heavy was holding her down. *Am I dead?*

She clamped her eyes shut again. The scenery must have fallen in a matter of seconds, but she could still see it in her mind as if she were turning the pages of a picture book. Her mind flashed other pictures, each one encased in a heart-shaped locket.

"Mama?" a tiny voice whispered, startling her. Then she realized it was her own.

The heavy object over her moved. She heard a groan close to her ear.

Cole! The earthquake. The scenery—we're under it. Where's Mama? Mama!

"Maudie?" It was Cole's voice. He coughed. "Maudie?"

She tried to move, but couldn't feel her limbs. "Cole."

"Oh, God, Maudie!" He sounded relieved, weakly ecstatic. "Are you all right?"

Maudie moaned. "I . . . I don't know. I can't move."

"Maudie? Cole? Are you all right?" Theo's voice, muffled, far away. "Don't move! I'm coming, I'm coming. Just don't move."

Slowly Maudie sensed feeling prickling into her

360

hands and feet, and then up her back, between her shoulder blades, and into her neck, which burned with pain. Her head throbbed.

"I can't breathe," she managed to utter.

"Don't move," Cole said gruffly. "You may have some broken ribs."

"I don't think so." She squirmed under his body.

"Stop that. You'll make things worse," Cole commanded.

"No, actually I think you'll make things worse. You'll either flatten me to death, or suffocate me. Would you please move?"

Cole let out a long sigh. "I don't believe it."

"Believe it. Under the circumstances, and under you, I wouldn't lie."

Cole tried to brace himself on his hands and push above her. His back felt broken. A heavy load fit for a team of oxen pressed into him.

"At least you're alive," he said. "We both must be alive. You're arguing with me. I wouldn't dream that."

"What about Lady Fan . . . my mother?"

"I don't know. All I've heard is Theo's voice."

Maudie strained against him. "We've got to get out of here. She could be hurt."

Cole pressed his face into her hair. He could feel the pile of scenery over them being moved, heard voices ordering the lifting. The moment they were out from under this, he knew everything was going to change again for Maudie and him. He wished that didn't have to happen.

"Before . . ." He searched for the right words. Hell,

there was no time for the right words. Just the *only* words. "I love you, Maudie."

"What?"

She tried to raise her head, but he kept it pressed down. He knew what would happen once she was free. She'd be wilder than any hill coyote protecting her young. That was, if Gwen-Ada was all right. Even if she wasn't, he knew Maudie well enough now to figure what she'd do. This was his last chance, and he wouldn't go to his grave without taking it.

"I said I love you. And I know you love me. We've put distance between us, and I think we both know why. That is, hell, I don't know anything anymore, except that I love you. I want to marry you. I want to settle down with you in a house with a yard and children. I want to work at a real job, like a farmer or something. I don't care. Just so long as we can be together."

"How can you talk like this under the circumstances? And me a captive audience? We don't even know how hurt we might be. Your timing is way off. Unless you're using this as a ploy. Typical of a cop. Besides, I don't—"

"I know, I know. You don't want all that house and children thing. I know I can adapt. Whatever you want. But I also know everything is going to be different the moment they get us out from under this mess."

He was breathless now, straining to hold the heavy load up, trying to make it easier on Maudie. He couldn't any longer, and flattened his body over hers once more. He could hear Theo's voice, shouts from Moe and the stage crew.

"Cole, I—"

"Don't say anything. Just let me say it once more before it's all over. I love you, Maudie, my incredible sweetheart, I love you."

The weight fell away from Cole's back.

"Maudie? You all right, honey? Cole? Be careful, boys. Help them."

Theo hovered over them like an old lady, Cole thought. Nevertheless, as soon as he was able, he'd probably kill the slimy little bastard. The one time he'd accepted a real friendship with a man, he'd been betrayed.

He turned and rolled carefully off Maudie's back, flopping onto his own with a groan. Above him Theo's visage was that of a stricken father, his eyes reflecting fear and tears. His forehead was gashed, and blood ran down his cheek and neck into his shirt.

"Mama?" Maudie tried to get up, but fell back down to the floor, wincing in pain. "Mama?" She was crying now.

"She's all right, she's all right," Theo assured her. "Banged up, but she'll be fine."

"Where . . . ?" Maudie sat up with Cole's assistance, and Moe helped her to stand.

Cole was up beside her, ignoring the pain in his back. He saw the terror on her face, saw panic sweep over it, replaced by determination.

"Take it easy, Maudie," he cautioned, placing an arm around her shoulders and a hand at her elbow.

"Get away from me! Mama? Mama, where are you?" She twisted out of his hold, and stumbled around in a circle.

"I'm here, baby," Gwen-Ada's weak voice came from the edge of the stage. Taryn was beside her, wiping her face with a moist cloth.

The bedlam beyond the closed curtain was subsiding. Cole heard LaFountain's voice issuing orders to the audience to leave quickly and quietly, assuring them they would be admitted free of charge to the next posted performance.

Maudie tripped over the rigging. Cole was beside her as quickly as he could be, given the gash in his shin now visible through his torn pantleg. She righted herself. With a shaking hand she reached out and picked up a piece of the hemp rigging and stared at it. Cole followed her gaze. Red threads gleamed in the flickering stage light.

Maudie fingered the threads. Cole knew that she was corroborating his conclusion. The threads were just like the ones in the quilt in the dressing room that once belonged to Madame Clara Carew, the room most recently occupied by Lady Fan, Gwen-Ada Boone. And they matched the thread from the spool in Theo's hat shop.

Maudie couldn't make her mind grasp the details of what she was seeing. What was crystal clear was the vow she had made to herself before the scenery had fallen down.

She stared up at Cole for a moment, holding back tears that threatened to flow and dissolve what little strength she had left. She dropped the hemp and ran to her mother.

"Run away, Mama, now!" She grabbed Gwen-

Ada's arm and tried to pull her to her feet. "I'll take care of everything!"

"No, baby," Gwen-Ada said, her voice weary. "No more running for either one of us. It's time we stopped . . . together."

"But, they know! They'll arrest you. If you go, they can take me! Don't you see? They know."

Gwen-Ada stroked her daughter's hair, then brushed a lock of it off her dirty face. She touched the soft cheek she had been longing to touch for so long. Then she frowned. "Know what, baby?"

"They know what you did. But, don't worry, if you hurry now, I can fix everything. Please, Mama, please. Go!" Maudie was on her knees begging, pulling on her mother's arm.

"Maudie, come over here, now," Cole rasped his command.

"You go to hell!" Maudie screamed back.

"Maudie," Theo pleaded, "please. It's important you go to Cole right away."

"Who are you? How do you know my mother?" Maudie glared at the little man, resenting him for reasons she couldn't explain.

"I'll explain later. Please, for your mother's sake and your own, go to Cole immediately." Theo gripped her arm and yanked her to her feet. "Go!" He pushed her toward Cole.

Maudie's rage escalated. Insanity reigned over them all! As soon as she stopped this dizziness and throbbing in her temples, she would straighten it all out. Mostly for Gwen-Ada's sake. Stumbling blindly, she fell.

Taryn was immediately at her side, and helped her to get to Cole.

"What," she said to him dully.

Cole was crouched over Lula. The scrim pipe and scenery flat lay near her, where they'd been dragged after the crash. Lula's face and right arm were hideously gashed and bleeding. Cole was holding a bandanna to her mouth, where blood gushed. Maudie's stomach clutched. She dropped down to her knees.

"Lula? Oh, dear, Lula, I'm so sorry." Maudie lifted her left hand.

Lula's face contorted in pain. "Don't . . . be sorry," she rasped, fluid bubbling in the back of her throat. "Bad Boy will . . . tell you everything." She strained to look up at Cole, and a wan smile tilted her mouth grotesquely. "I'm the one. Me . . . I'll be with him . . . forever. Not her." She coughed, and then went limp.

"Lula?" Maudie stared down at her, then lifted her eyes to meet Cole's. "She's . . . dead?"

Cole nodded.

Maudie swung her gaze back to her mother. Panic swept over her. She tried to get up.

"Wait, Maudie. It's all over now. Don't worry. Your mother is safe. You're safe."

"But, how?" Maudie asked.

"I'll explain after we're all out of here." He helped her toward Theo and Gwen-Ada.

"You won't arrest her?" Maudie searched his face for a sign of betrayal.

Cole gazed at Maudie's streaked and worried face. Then he swung his gaze toward Theo and Gwen-Ada.

Both pairs of eyes watched them with profound concern and care. "No, I'm not going to arrest her. I'm not even going to kill Theo."

"Well, you're a sorry looking lot," Theo observed, as he surveyed the varying degrees of injury afflicting Gwen-Ada, Cole, and Maudie as they gathered in Gwen-Ada's living room.

Doc Pierce had left them only moments before, having bathed cuts and bruises with clean water and antiseptic, and patched gashes, checked bones for breaks, and heads for deeper wounds. All four of them were bandaged and trussed, wrapped up more convincingly than any costume designer could have managed.

"You're not exactly the picture of health, yourself, pal," Cole muttered.

"Thank you for reminding me, dear and trusted friend," Theo rejoined. "Although I daresay I questioned your loyalty a few hours ago when you threatened to kill me."

Cole was instantly contrite. "I thought you were about to do something that warranted it."

"I know. It's hard to believe, though, that you thought I was planning to kill Gwen-Ada and Maudie. That is the most preposterous conclusion you could ever have come to, especially after all I had explained to you before we went to the theater." Theo poured some tea he'd made into a cup.

"Haven't you got anything stronger than that?" Cole asked.

"Top shelf behind the pots," Gwen-Ada said wearily.

"What have you got hidden back there?" Theo said mischievously as he disappeared into the kitchen. He returned sporting a wide grin and a bottle of brandy.

"How now?!" Cole brightened. "Break it open, my friend!"

"*Now* I'm a friend," Theo joked.

"At least you're a live one. Remember that!" Cole laughed.

Maudie hadn't stirred in her chair near the window. She stared unseeing out into the noisy Deadwood street. She was numb. Not from her injuries, none of which would keep her down for very long. Her mind was numbed, unable to understand, let alone solve whatever remained to be solved.

Theo filled four small glasses with brandy and passed them all around. Maudie took hers without acknowledgement.

"Here's to a new beginning." Theo raised his glass.

"A brand new beginning. Here's to us." Cole reached up to clink his glass against Theo's.

Gwen-Ada joined them in a toast.

"Maudie?" Cole pushed himself out of his chair with great effort.

Maudie didn't look up. She held the glass of brandy untasted in her lap.

Cole's eyes lingered on her a long moment before he turned back to the others. "You must have known who Lula really was."

"Yes, I recognized her as Lucille right away," Gwen-Ada told him. "She recognized me as well."

"I knew her, too," Theo added. "But she never acknowledged my presence, let alone any past acquaintance. I certainly didn't go out of my way to renew that acquaintance. I'd always felt uneasy around her in the past."

"Well, I sure wish I'd recognized her sooner," Cole put in. "Perhaps I might have been able to prevent all this. I'm sorry she's dead, but I'm grateful none of you were hurt."

He glanced back over his shoulder at Maudie, who registered no emotion. Cole wished she'd enter into the conversation, give him some inkling of what she was thinking, feeling. And much as he cared for Theo and now Gwen-Ada, he wished he and Maudie were someplace alone where they could talk privately.

"I'm certain she looked a lot different than when you last saw her," Theo said.

"Yes, but I admit I suspected everybody except her, you two included. I apologize to you now for that, but I didn't have a script for this scene, so I didn't know who was who nor who was capable of what. Then, when everybody was starting to look guilty to me, I thought I was going daft, thought I might be carrying my sheriff role a little too far. That's when I felt trapped. It wasn't until the last minute before the scenery came down that I figured out who had caused death in the past and was out to cause it in the present."

"Good thing you figured it out when you did," Theo told him.

"Lucille was way ahead of me. She recognized me the day my mustache came off." Cole turned back again, hoping Maudie might be moved to speak. Nothing. He turned back to Gwen-Ada and Theo. "One good thing came out of it. Before she died, Lucille explained about my father and Gwen-Ada back in Missouri. If she hadn't, I might still be wondering if I'd pieced it together correctly. If you can fill me in on your side of the story, I'd sure appreciate it. I've been going on my discoveries in the theater dressing room, in this house, and my own memory of my childhood."

"This house?" Theo cocked his head.

Cole looked down, feeling a bit sheepish at the confession he still had to make. "Yes. I'm sorry to say I walked in here right after you two left one morning. Maudie was with me."

Gwen-Ada looked surprised. "You . . . you've been in here, Maudie?"

Maudie turned slowly. She looked up, her eyes heavy with pain. "Yes." her voice was low and even.

"Did you know who I was then?" Gwen-Ada's lower lip quivered as she spoke.

Maudie let out a breath through trembling lips. "Just barely. I'd been wondering if Madame Carew was my mother. I'd been searching for her . . . my mother . . . all my life. I gave up once in a while, but then something somebody said somewhere would get me up and on the move, searching again." Her eyes grew hard. She gulped the brandy.

"You didn't think I was . . . dead?" Gwen-Ada's voice held a note of incredulity.

Maudie shook her head woodenly. "Yes, sometimes. No, most of the time. But I thought if you were alive you would have come back for me." She drained the brandy glass. "You didn't."

"I can explain about that, Maudie."

"Can you?"

"Yes, if you really want to hear it."

"I don't think I do."

"I don't blame you." Gwen-Ada set her glass on the side table and turned her face into her hand.

Maudie rose then and walked toward her mother with accusing eyes. "Well, I blame *you!* He was right, wasn't he? I hated him, my father, hated him for what he did to you and for what he did to me. I hated him with everything in me. And that was as much as I loved you."

"Maudie . . ." Cole stood behind her. He placed a gentle hand on her shoulder. "Maybe you should let your mother explain what happened."

Maudie wrenched away from his grasp. She never took her eyes off Gwen-Ada. "I thought he drove you away."

"He . . . he *put* me away, Maudie."

Gwen-Ada's eyes scanned her face beseechingly. Cole's heart ached for her. He could see his own mother's eyes pleading with him for understanding of why she had left him, why she had turned to other men to get the nurturing and attention she had craved.

"He said you went insane because of your guilt over leaving him . . . and me. He said you never loved me anyway. He said you were no good. I never wanted to believe him."

"He lied to you, Maudie, over and over." Gwen-Ada's voice grew soft, reflecting the soul-weariness she'd sustained for so long. "You were a child. He was your father. It's not your fault you believed him."

Maudie's harsh laugh bordered on hysteria. "Oh, but I *didn't* believe him. Not me. I went on believing in *you*. I *knew* you'd come back for me, *knew* you wouldn't abandon me, *knew* you loved me. When you didn't come back, I thought it was because you couldn't. Not because you didn't want to, but because you'd been prevented in some way."

"You were right."

"So I went out looking for you. Fourteen years old and I've practically crossed the continent and started back. I've spent my whole life chasing after a dream! That's the really stupid part, isn't it? Because you weren't insane at all. You were out enjoying life with your lover!" She spat the last words with venom, flinging her arm out toward Theo.

Theo wrapped his arms around Gwen-Ada, who sat still as stone. "That's enough, Maudie. I won't have you speaking to your mother like that. She's suffered too much for too long."

"Who are you to tell me who has suffered here?" Maudie shouted at him.

"I know what your mother has suffered!" Theo shouted back. "Your father had her locked away in a wretched asylum. When I discovered where she was, I found a way to see her. She was locked in a dark hole, wearing nothing but a thin dress, rocking back and forth, just saying your name over and over and crying like a motherless baby herself."

Gwen-Ada placed quieting fingers over Theo's lips. "Theo risked his life helping me escape."

"But not without your getting hurt."

"It was a small price to pay for freedom and the chance to see my baby again."

Maudie's knees had locked, it seemed. She stood listening to what they told her, their words coming at her but not their meaning.

Cole clutched her arm and turned her around to face him. "It's true, Maudie. I believe them. And I know something else. Your mother and my father were in love, and she saved his life."

Maudie stared up at him, shock distorting her face. "What are you talking about? Are you saying you knew she was my mother and you never told me?"

Cole circled her shoulders with one arm, supporting her. "I didn't know who she was until the day you and I were in this house together. Come over here and I'll show you how."

He took her to the shelf where Gwen-Ada's scrapbook lay. Patiently he pointed out the clippings, the story about Gwen-Ada Boone and Jared Braddock. And Lucille Galarzyk, the scenery designer.

"That's why I stayed away from you after we . . . got so close. Don't you understand? The federal marshal is due any day now. I thought I was going to have to arrest your mother for Carew's murder and for the theft of the rubies. On top of that, you confessed to me you were working for the Pinkertons. I thought if that agent got here and you had to turn Gwen-Ada over to him, thinking she had murdered Carew, believing Carew to be your mother . . . well, I just knew that when you learned the truth it would kill you. I didn't know anything beyond that."

373

Maudie shook her head as if the whole story were beyond belief.

"Back in Missouri, Lucille was trying to kill your mother. My father was killed instead. She went crazy."

"She blamed his death on your mother," Theo added.

Gwen-Ada sighed. "She sent the authorities after me. How was I to come back to you then? A hunted woman, wanted for a crime I didn't commit. I loved Jared Braddock, yes. I was devastated when he was killed. If it hadn't been for Theo . . ."

Maudie's mind whirled. "But what . . . how did you . . . you had the rubies as well as the locket. How . . . ?"

"I hooked up with Carew's acting company. One night in the dressing room I saw her pick up my locket, *my* locket. I almost lost my mind. She tossed it aside like it was trash. I could have murdered her myself at that moment. That night . . . how similar our lives have been! . . . that night I was approached by a Pinkerton agent who suspected Carew in the theft of some rubies. I knew what he was talking about. I had seen those rubies among Carew's things."

Maudie stared incredulously at Gwen-Ada. "I . . . I want to believe you, but how can this be true? Did you know all along who I was when I came into Deadwood?"

"Maudie, honey, I can explain everything. No, I didn't know who you were at first. We hardly saw each other. I was told to put some money in the bank for a Pinkerton agent who would be arriving in Deadwood." Gwen-Ada's eyes pleaded for understanding. "Please, dear, please come over here and sit with me. I want to hold your hands. I'll tell you all you want to know." She held out her arms.

Slowly, taking what felt like her first toddling steps toward her mother's waiting arms, Maudie walked to the settee. She was trembling so hard she almost lost her balance. Gwen-Ada reached out to steady her, and Maudie fell against her.

Cole and Theo studied the scrapbook together, giving mother and daughter time alone. The hard years melted away, layer by layer, like snow under the first warm sun of spring as Gwen-Ada told the story of their separation.

"Your father was a jealous man," Gwen-Ada began, as Maudie looked deeply into her mother's eyes. "And he drank too much. In his jealous rages, he would threaten my life. He constantly accused me of being involved with one actor or another, none of it true. I knew I'd made a mistake marrying Patrick, but, you see, then there was you, and I would have done anything to keep you with me. You were and are the greatest treasure of my life. I would have died for you."

Maudie reached out and touched her mother's face. The skin was as smooth as her own. She was made of the same flesh and blood as this woman before her. Without Gwen-Ada she wouldn't be who she was now. An overwhelming gratefulness surged in Maudie's breast, and a love that was great and growing.

"She was devoted to her daughter and would never do anything that would jeopardize her presence in her life," Theo took up the story. "In his cruelty, Patrick threatened to get rid of you, Maudie. He found a crooked judge who had Gwen-Ada committed to an insane asylum. He took everything away from her when she was locked away, and sold what little good jewelry she had, including the precious locket she was never without, the identical one to yours, Maudie. He sold it to an actress in a traveling theatrical company. Madame Clara Carew."

Maudie's gaze locked with Cole's.

"Years passed, an eternity of tears," Gwen-Ada continued. "And then a miracle happened. Theo found me, and helped me to escape. When I finally got back to our house, Patrick was dead and you had disappeared."

"She worked so hard I thought she might kill herself," Theo said. "But I knew she was trying to ease the pain of having lost her daughter. She worked with Carew's company, not knowing how they were connected. Then there was Jared Braddock, the love they shared, and well, you know about his tragic death."

Gwen-Ada traced Maudie's fingers with her own. Maudie knew she was tired, but she also sensed the need for them both to hear this story through to the end and never speak of it again. Her own tears threatened to fall, but she held them back. Watching her mother tell this story, knowing how much it pained her to relive it and the years of their separation, Maudie knew from whom she'd inherited her own strength.

"Carew knew that Lucille was responsible for Jared Braddock's death," Gwen-Ada said. "Lucille had learned that Carew had been stealing jewelry from people in every town they'd played. They each blackmailed the other to cover their own guilt."

Theo broke in again. "Your mother was recruited by a Pinkerton agent to help recover some stolen rubies. Her plan was to retrieve the jewels and her locket, and turn in the two women. Lucille learned of Gwen-Ada's plan and told her that if she carried through with it Lucille would find you and see to it that you came to an unfortunate end.

"Once they were in Deadwood, Carew told Lucille, now calling herself Lula Gale, that she was sick of the blackmail. She threatened to tell the sheriff, Cole now, the whole story if Lula didn't get out of town. Soon after that, the accident happened, and Carew was killed. Lula hadn't reckoned for Gwen-Ada to arrive in Deadwood, and she felt trapped."

"Oh, baby, I missed you with all my heart." Gwen-Ada's voice cracked. "I made friends with the little orphan girl, and gave her the name Patches after I made some new clothes for her. She didn't have anything, and she reminded me so much of you, full of spunk and spirit."

"Hasn't changed much, has she?" Cole interjected.

"No, thank God." Gwen-Ada smiled into her daughter's eyes. "Anyway, Lula had seen the red thread Theo gave me, and I know she saw it in the quilt and in the clothes on Patches. I think she saw a way of putting the blame on me again by stealing the thread from Theo's shop."

"When did you recognize me?" Maudie asked.

"The first day I saw you. I made the bank deposit for the next Pinkerton, not knowing the agent was you! I panicked, thinking Lucille might try to hurt you or worse, if she knew you were my daughter. I tried to avoid you so you wouldn't recognize me."

"Do you have any idea how frustrated I was over that?" Maudie gave a little laugh that relaxed her and her mother.

"Do you know how frustrated I was at being unable to hold you in my arms? Wondering if you hated me, or had forgotten me?" Gwen-Ada's voice cracked.

Maudie took her in her arms, rested her mother's head on her shoulder, and stroked her back.

"But what about the jewels?" Cole asked.

"Gwen-Ada had taken the rubies from Carew's things in order to give them to you or the marshal," Theo answered. "But when she learned later about Maudie's Pinkerton arrangement, she planned for Maudie to find them and return them for the reward. But then, her heart ached so to know Maudie again. She was trying to find a way to let Maudie know who she was and make her own decision on how to handle the discovery, when everything started to go wrong with Lula."

"I have something to give you, Maudie, something I've prepared for you since the moment I was free and became well again." Gwen-Ada started to rise, but Theo was at her side in an instant.

"I'll get it for you, dear." He went around to the bedroom and returned with her large bag.

Gwen-Ada opened it and withdrew the quilt Maudie had discovered in the dressing room.

"I always believed in my heart I'd see you again someday. So I made this for you so you'd know every place I'd been and that I'd been thinking of you constantly." She opened it wide and spread the quilt across both their laps.

Maudie gazed in awe at the beautiful quilt, which commemorated the tragedies of her mother's life, their long separation, her mother's undying love for her.

Gwen-Ada pointed to a tricornered piece of softly hued silk in a soft peach color. "See this? Theo made a costume for me to wear in *The Streets of New York*. It opened in Missouri. After I'd been cast in *Scarlet Lady* . . . and after Jared's accident, Theo destroyed the costume so I wouldn't be reminded of the pain. But he gave me this piece as a reminder of the beginning of our life together. He wanted me to put it into the quilt so that someday you'd know what we came to mean to each other."

Maudie touched the quilt, running her fingers over the red featherstitching. A chill went over her. The red thread had meant accident and death only hours before, but now it represented love and yearning. Each square represented a place or a play. They were made of costume pieces or a swatch of fabric fit for a child, then lovingly joined with a careful hand to show the story Gwen-Ada believed she would tell to her daughter someday.

As Maudie touched each square, she believed her hands walked her closer to the mother and daughter they'd been so many painful years before. She looked up toward Cole and saw his eyes were wet.

Maudie and Gwen-Ada threw themselves into one another's arms, and forced the walls of their separate lives into a pile of dust. When the wave of overpowering emotion subsided between them, Maudie gazed upon her mother's face as if she'd just been born, and Gwen-Ada took in the sight of her daughter's tear-stained, smiling face as if she would never get enough of the sight.

The next wave of emotion brought laughter and touching, and a closing of the abyss between them forever.

Chapter 17

The Black Hills Pioneer, Monday, September 25. An unusual attraction was offered at the Theatre last night, the bills announcing a lady and gentleman of Deadwood would be united in matrimony at the end of the play. During the day numerous parties were mentioned as the happy couple,—curiosity was on tip-toe— and bets of various denominations were staked on naming the bride and groom. Many thought it was parties connected with members of the new provisional government, and some had to pay heavily for this gross mistake. A large and expectant audience assembled, including the well-known Pinkerton agent, Cutherbert T. Golden, and new city marshal, Con Stapleton, both joining in the betting. At the conclusion of the first play the curtain rose and revealed the principal members of the company standing on either side of the stage . . .

Cole folded the newspaper and dropped it down between his legs on the ground, then folded his arms and braced them on his drawn-up knees. He let his gaze fall lazily down the cemetery hill to the spreading city of Deadwood.

Already the arrival of the first coach of the Cheyenne and Black Hills Stage Line was discharging passengers in Deadwood, including the first female coach passenger over that road. The *Pioneer* had reported earlier that a huge welcoming crowd would be on hand to herald the auspicious arrival in an unheard-of six-and-one-half days. That very morning the first quartz mill brought to the Black Hills passed through on its way to Gayville, and a large portion of Deadwood's growing population lined Main Street for that event. No doubt they stayed around to witness the coming of the Cheyenne Stage, Cole figured.

It was only a matter of time, the *Pioneer* further reported, before telegraph lines between Cheyenne and Deadwood would be completed and the first message sent over the wires. He suspected the telegraph might not have the same social impact on the city as had the first billiard table, which arrived perched on the back of a brand-new freighter. And the new city government was assessing the first taxes on every business as a means of raising revenues.

Cole shifted his head and regarded Wild Bill Hickok's grave marker. "It's happening, Mr. Hickok, just like we talked about. Only it's faster than you or I ever dreamed. Deadwood is turning into a civilized city, just like the kind we both kept moving away from. It's not like the old days, sir. You'd have had to keep moving on. Civilization nips at the heels of the wild and free, and soon these hills will be tamed to a copy of the east. You wouldn't be happy, would you?" He waited a moment, contemplating. "No, sir, you wouldn't be happy."

He turned into the waning sunlight and caught the

wash of gold that tipped the rough edges of Deadwood.

"I wish I knew if I was happy or not. Hard to tell. Don't know if I got what I wanted, or if I wanted what I got. This should be the best time of my life, and it's turning out to be the worst. What do you think I should do now?"

Cole waited several moments before reaching down and retrieving the newspaper again. He went back to the article he'd been reading.

. . . principal members of the company standing on either side of the stage, while the center was occupied by Madame Gwen-Ada Boone, heretofore known to this city as stage personage Lady Fan, the bride, and Theodore Bartles, Milliner, the groom. Madame Boone was attired in an elegant evening costume of the groom's design. Mr. Bartles was jauntily dressed and seemed as though he was about to perform in a merry farce instead of entering on the more solemn performance of the first act in the play of matrimony. That most scintillating flame of the stage, Maudie Boone Dearden, recently revealed as the long-lost daughter of the bride, stood in beaming attendance, while Deadwood's own sheriff, Branch, acted as the groom's witness. Sheriff Branch appeared nervous at appearing on stage, although rumor has it he possesses some surprise information that may attest differently.

Cole shook the paper to loosen the crease, then folded it back to one page. *Surprise information.* It was no surprise anymore. By tomorrow morning everyone in Deadwood who gave a rat's hind quarters would know he'd once been an actor. They'd also know he'd turned in his badge and was no longer Sheriff of Deadwood. Now he wished he had some surprise information for himself, like what he should do with the rest of his life.

He knew what he wanted, or thought he did. But it couldn't be a solo act.

He bent to finish the article.

Judge Kuykendall performed the ceremony with such grace and dignity that all agreed he would bear the gown or cassock with as much solemnity as any priest or minister in the land. At the conclusion his face beamed with good nature, and omitting the paroxysmal kiss, he shook hands with the pair, and after wishing them all happiness the curtain fell on the first marriage in Deadwood. The couple left for an extended visit to Cheyenne.

Cole shivered. Autumn was in the air, rustling through the branches of the pines over the cemetery, making it feel colder and more desolate than usual. No matter what season of the year it happened to be, it always felt like winter in a cemetery to Cole. The real winter season would be upon them soon and, from what he'd heard from soldiers and settlers, a Black Hills winter could freeze a man to the marrow.

Cole knew he should be long gone from this place, but every day he'd made a new reason—excuse?—for not leaving. In his heart he knew there was only one reason.

Maudie.

After consuming a late afternoon lunch she hadn't had the appetite for, Maudie sat on the settee in her mother's house and picked up a new script Taryn had dropped off for her to read several days before the wedding. She simply hadn't had time for anything, what with the reopening of *Scarlet Lady* and her emotional reunion with her mother. Not to mention the excitement of the wedding.

Maudie leaned into the corner of the settee and tucked her feet up under her skirt. She let out a long sigh and looked around the room. Since Gwen-Ada and Theo had left for Cheyenne, she'd been in the house alone. It had been blissful. To have a home all to one's own, even if it were only temporary. She'd been wondering what to do with the reward money she'd received for returning the rubies to the Pinkerton agent. Perhaps she would build a house of her own. She was free to do what she pleased. This was freedom at its best.

Yet, strangely, Maudie wasn't feeling free in the least bit. She thought once the impact of reuniting with her mother had diminished she'd be eager to start a new life. But she didn't feel that way. In fact, she still felt burdened by unanswered questions.

She and Gwen-Ada had agreed that they'd stay in Deadwood. The city had been the place for their reunion, the place where Gwen-Ada and Theo had decided to marry. The thought of settling down appealed to all three of them.

And Maudie had her own reasons for wanting to stay in Deadwood.

Well, at least you can admit it, you haven't stopped thinking about Cole.

In the days and daze that followed the accident on the stage, she kept thinking of something Cole had asked her. Something very important. *Yes, like asking you to marry him!* But she couldn't be certain that it had really happened. She thought perhaps she had been a

385

bit delirious after the accident. And he hadn't said anything about it since. And why should it matter to her anyway? She never meant to marry in the first place. But she had to admit she'd certainly been thinking about it since she'd arrived in Deadwood. Why was the notion becoming more insistent now?

"Because you are in love with Cole, you ninny!" Hearing her own voice out loud made her jump.

She relaxed and let her mind drift again. She sensed that once again she and Cole were talking around the edges of things. And she felt shy. Unbelievable. Maudie Boone Dearden felt shy around a man! She should just come right out and say it, shouldn't she? *Cole Branch, did you or did you not propose marriage to me when we were lying beneath a pile of fallen scenery?*

"Right," she muttered, "you should just come right out and say it. Propriety be damned."

A light knock came to the door. Maudie's heart pounded anxiously. Maybe it was Cole, coming to her at last. She stood, smoothed her hair, took a deep breath, and glided slowly toward the door. Collected, that's what she was, collected. She wouldn't want to seem a woman anxious to extract a marriage proposal out of a man. With an air of nonchalance, Maudie squared her shoulders and opened the door.

"Hello, Maudie, I hope I'm not disturbing you." Taryn walked right by her and dropped down on the settee. Maudie didn't know whether she was disappointed or relieved. "You've simply got to help me, help all of us. That's all there is to it. We simply don't know what to do."

Maudie closed the door and sighed deeply. "You're

not alone. I'm very confused myself." She sat in the chair opposite the settee.

Taryn's eyes widened. "Oh, dear, Maudie, I'm so sorry for just barging in on you like this. I should have sent a note around first. Of course you're upset. You've only recently learned Lady Fan is your mother, and now she's up and gotten married." She took out a handkerchief and dabbed at the tears that had formed in the corners of her eyes. "But it was so romantic, wasn't it? I mean, Mr. Bartles loving her from afar for so many years. Just imagine. It's so heartbreakingly sad, isn't?"

"There's nothing at all sad about it," Maudie snapped. "They're together, aren't they? Somebody got up enough nerve to ask somebody to marry him, didn't he?"

Shock spread over Taryn's childlike face. "Well . . . of course . . . somebody asked. I mean, Mr. Bartles asked Lady Fan for her hand. A lady wouldn't, that is, most ladies wouldn't ask that of a man. It's so . . . so demeaning, isn't it? As if one couldn't secure a proposal of marriage of one's own so one had to ask the gentlemen and take the chance of being horribly humiliated."

"Stop babbling, Taryn. This is 1876. This country is a hundred years old. We didn't just have founding fathers, you know. There were plenty of founding mothers or there wouldn't have been any sons and daughters to follow." Maudie patted the back of her coiled hair with a more arduous touch than was necessary.

Taryn's face reddened. "I'm sorry Maudie. Did I say

something to upset you?" Quickly she lifted her hand to her blushing cheek. "Oh my, she did ask him, didn't she?"

Maudie tsked. "Of course she didn't ask him. Ladies aren't supposed to do that, are they? They're supposed to sit and wait and do needlework till the gentlemen decide whether they wish to be trapped in a lifetime of what they're certain is nothing but drudgery and unpleasantness."

Taryn fidgeted while Maudie burned. "Yes, of course. I mean, that's usual . . ."

"Ha! Have they ever had babies? Not a one of them. What do they know about drudgery? I daresay nary a thing. I'm right, aren't I? Of course I am."

Taryn nodded vigorously. She sat rigidly, hands in her lap, twisting her handkerchief round and round through her fingers.

"Makes a woman wonder why she wants to get married in the first place, doesn't it?" Maudie asked, then answered her own question without waiting for Taryn. "Well, she's supposed to, that's why. It's expected. A woman is considered a spinster by the time she's twenty if she doesn't have a marriage prospect on the horizon. That's what they say in polite society."

Taryn sniffed. "I'll be twenty in December."

"Well, don't fret it," Maudie said in clipped tones. "In case you haven't noticed, Deadwood could hardly be considered polite society."

"Oh, but a lot of ladies have been moving into town. I've seen them everywhere with their fine clothes and expensive hats. And some of them have marriageable daughters. I'll never get married!" Taryn sobbed loudly into her handkerchief.

Maudie rose quickly and went to the settee, putting her arms around the girl.

"There, there. You'll find a man to marry. Even Penelope Pettigrew isn't married yet, and she must be . . ."

"Eighteen, she's just eighteen!" Taryn snapped her head up and stared at Maudie with tear-reddened eyes. "Besides, she's set her cap for Sheriff Branch. Well, he's not sheriff anymore, but she doesn't care. He's the one she wants and she means to have him." Taryn cried loudly.

Maudie felt a stab of jealousy. *For heaven's sake, Maudie, how can you possibly be jealous of that little snip? Cole wouldn't even think of giving her so much as a glance. Would he?*

"Sh, sh. Stop crying now. Just because Penelope has set her cap, as you say, for Cole Branch, doesn't mean he'll fall into her trap. Sometimes people get married because they want to, you know."

"Maybe not a man, but a woman will marry anybody. You would, but now you're a spinster, so who'd marry you anyway?" Taryn instantly bit her lip, and her crying stopped abruptly as if the door of a dam had slammed shut on her tears.

Maudie straightened. "Who indeed?" She raised her chin at a haughty angle. "I'm sure you couldn't know this, Taryn, but many men, many *many* men have asked me to marry them. However, I've planned never to marry. I've wished to remain in my present happy state for the rest of my days. Now, suppose you tell me what it is you came here for."

"I . . . I'm so sorry, Maudie. I didn't mean . . ." When Maudie brushed her hand through the air dismissively, Taryn changed the subject. "Did you know that Mr. LaFountain and that unbearably homely Sweet woman have left town?"

"No! When?"

"Just this afternoon on the new Black Hills Stage. Oh, he was insufferable with his gesturing and waving from the coach window, raving on about how the great theaters of San Francisco were beckoning him and his lady love. Lady love, my foot!"

Maudie narrowed her eyes at Taryn. "Why are you so upset about LaFountain leaving? Don't tell me you fell for his phony charms as much as Jewel did?"

"Pooh!" Taryn spat. "Not I. I may be rapidly moving into spinsterhood, but I could not abide that man, not one whit." She softened. "Jewel is inconsolable right now, of course. But I think she'll get over it. A secret admirer has been sending her flowers."

"Good. Well, then, what has you so agitated?"

"Maudie, the theater is closed! What will we do?" she wailed.

Another knock sounded at the door, and Maudie started up in anticipation. Again, she adjusted her demeanor and struck a pose of nonchalance. *You picked a bad time to come over to propose to me now, Cole Branch. You'll simply have to make an appointment and come back later.*

She opened the door to Sterling, Jewel, Nancy, and Arletta. Again she wasn't certain if she was annoyed or relieved it wasn't Cole.

"Well, will you do it?" Sterling asked as he pushed by Maudie.

The others followed and took seats where they could find them. Sterling leaned back against the door. Maudie got the distinct impression he was trapping her.

"I don't think I heard the question."

"Taryn . . ." Nancy whined.

"I just didn't get the chance to ask her yet," Taryn retorted.

"Ask me what?" Maudie said impatiently.

"Leave it to me," Sterling said authoritatively, and Maudie noticed his ever-present snit seemed to have been tempered a bit. He turned toward her. "As I'm certain you are aware, our esteemed director has taken leave of Deadwood as well as his senses, it seems, and moved on to brighter lights with one whom he believes is a brighter star. I shan't comment on his choice of Miss Sweet. In any case, what with Carew gone and Lady Fan, beg pardon, Mrs. Bartles away——"

"She'll be back," Maudie interrupted.

"Yes, I'm certain she will. To continue, the Deadwood Variety Theater is dark, a most depressing circumstance. The Langrishe Theater has its own troupe, one which none of us is anxious to penetrate, even were that a possibility. Further, we don't wish to even show our faces at the Gem or Melodeon. Finally, we want to remain in Deadwood. We've grown accustomed to the place, surprising as that may sound, and there are growing indications to suggest that one day it will be a great and thriving city."

Maudie tilted her head expectantly.

"Therefore," Sterling histrionically resumed, "we took a vote and it was a unanimous decision. We have chosen you as our new producer, director, and when you wish, leading lady. We pledge our allegiance to you. You have a strong company to support you."

He stopped talking, presumably waiting for Maudie's response. She scanned the eager faces all turned upon hers, eagerly awaiting an answer. There seemed to be a collective holding of breath. Inside, her stomach fluttered, her pulse raced. This was the opportunity of a lifetime! This was a position offered only the truly great actresses, or at least those with a great deal of money.

She held back. What would this mean to the next phase of her life as she'd only a short time before been considering? What would Cole Branch think about the idea? Would it even matter to him? So, she loved him. They'd made love, wonderful love. He'd said the distance afterward had had to do with what he presumed was the guilt of her mother in the death of Madame Carew. In a more rational moment before the accident, he'd said he loved her. But he was yet to put in an appearance.

Would that mean the end of everything else in her world? Not on her Aunt Fanny's fanny!

"I have one statement," she said at last. The breaths held and five pairs of eyes were upon her. "Gwen-Ada Boone Bartles is a permanent member of·this company as long as she wishes to be. Agreed?"

They all chattered at once. "Agreed! She's wonderful. We love her. Whatever she wants. She's more than welcome."

Maudie took a deep breath and held it, then let it out with her answer before she could change her mind. "Then I accept your proposal. The Deadwood Variety reopens tomorrow morning at ten. Please be prompt. We have much work to accomplish."

The collective breaths were released in a whoosh, and smiles beamed light around the room. They were up on their feet and jumping around excitedly, even Sterling, so quickly that Maudie couldn't help but join in. With a round of hugging and a great chorus of thank-yous, the company of actors trooped out of the little house and chattered amiably as they walked back toward town.

Maudie sank down on the settee. No need to wonder further what she would do with the reward money for the return of the rubies. Her own theater company would absorb the greater portion, if not all of it.

A sense of satisfaction swept over her. Her own theater company. This was what she'd thought about over all the years when she was traveling. She'd watched other theatrical company owners, women with a strong idea of what they wished to accomplish. She marveled at their ability to produce a play and command the loyalty of a company. Some were better at it than others, and in her mind she'd always thought about how she'd do it better. Now she had the chance.

Yes, this was a most satisfying feeling. Then, why was there still a gnawing loneliness in the empty space around her heart? She knew the answer to that, and she knew what would fill it.

Cole.

"Cole? You back here?"

Maudie's rich voice sliced through the chill and

warmed the air around Cole. He turned and saw her striding up the hill toward him, her breath forming a light mist just outside her lips. She was strong, he knew that about her spirit, and he was seeing it again in the way she moved her body. No motion was wasted. She moved in harmony with the earth, with a soft, fluid grace. She was a soft, rhythmic poem with power in every line.

And Lord but she was beautiful. She was a woman through and through. He'd never known a woman who could match her in beauty and spirit and heart.

A shiver ran over Cole once again, and this time it had nothing to do with the rapidly chilling air.

"Something told me I'd find you up here." Maudie walked to his side. "May I join you?"

He took off his jacket and spread it out on the ground next to him. "Sorry, but the house seats seem to be taken."

She smiled and dropped down next to him, and the air around him seemed instantly warmed and fragrant. "On the contrary. I think these are the best seats in the house." She held his gaze a protracted moment before shifting it to the city below.

Cole found his voice with some difficulty. "Wild Bill's buried right over there. Sometimes I come here and talk things over with him."

"I'm sorry to say this is the first I've visited his grave." Maudie's voice lowered. "He doesn't advise you, does he?"

Cole sighed with a wistfulness he sought to control but couldn't. "I wish he could sometimes." He ran a thumb and index finger over the real mustache he'd been growing. He meant to grow it into stallions' tails like Mr. Hickok's. "This has been a difficult summer."

"I'll agree with that," Maudie breathed. "With all that's happened, I should be flat out in total exhaustion. But, I'm not. I've actually felt exhilarated!"

"I felt that way . . . at first. Everything seemed to happen at once. The Pinkerton arrived, the federal marshal, you produced the rubies and handed them over, the mysteries were explained. And then that woman with the yellow teeth, that friend of yours . . ."

"Melody Sweet? She'd been a cell mate, not a friend! And she almost got me arrested with her false testimony about the theft of the rubies. For heaven's sake, Cole!"

"All right, all right, don't get your wig in a twist! I must say I wasn't all that surprised to find out she was the one LaFountain had been visiting down at Mrs. Mundy's."

"How she ever imagined he would cast her in his next play was beyond me." Maudie shook her head.

"I hear he's going to do it, wherever they land."

"No! That's ludicrous. If he thinks he can make her into a leading lady . . ."

"That's the magic of the theater." Cole chuckled. "And it's going to take a lot of magic to turn her into a leading lady."

Maudie smiled in agreement. She sat quietly for a long time, just surveying the city, the trees, and then Wild Bill Hickok's grave. And then she leveled her gaze on Cole.

"Sometimes when I wake up in the morning I think

it's all been a dream, a blur of fantasy with reality, or the memory of a play I was once in."

"I know exactly what you mean," Cole said, then reached over and pulled her dark green shawl more closely around her shoulders, and raised the collar of her russet jacket up the back of her neck.

Maudie smiled at him, revelling in his touch. "But then I see my mother in the kitchen preparing breakfast for us, and I know it's all real. Even something as everyday as breakfast is a celebration of a new day, a new life."

Cole watched the excitement, the almost childlike joy in her face, the spark in her eyes, wishing he could have been the one who had kindled it. "You've enjoyed living with her in that little house, haven't you?"

"Very much. I knew it was temporary. I knew when *Scarlet Lady* closed, Mother and Theo would marry."

"Did that upset you?"

"Not now. At first I wanted her to spend her time only with me. I was jealous of the time she spent with Theo, or anyone else for that matter. But then I remembered how much she'd missed of love all her life, and here was a man who'd been giving love to her from afar, who'd stuck by her through the worst of times. They're very much in love, you know."

"Yes, I know. I thought Theo would be overcome with joy before the judge made the final pronouncement!" Cole smiled now at the memory of the wedding ceremony. Of how he had repeated the judge's words over in his own mind as he stood opposite Maudie. When Judge Kuykendall had asked, "Wilt thou take this woman?" Cole had fortunately caught himself in time before blurting out "I will!"

"It was a lovely wedding, didn't you think?"

Cole nodded. "Yes it was. Appropriate to have it in the theater, I thought. One of the best productions to have been staged on those boards."

"Judge Kuykendall had a good time," Maudie said, laughing.

"I think the judge has a good time whether it's a trial or a wedding."

"You had a good time, too."

"I know. So did you."

"I know."

They fell silent then, locking gazes over the waning daylight.

"Maudie—"

"Cole—"

Cole tilted his head toward her. "What were you going to say?"

Maudie inclined her head toward him. "Ah . . . it can wait. You spoke first." She shivered.

Cole sat still, studying her face. He knew what he wanted to say, but the words seemed locked away somewhere. "It's getting colder. We should be going back down the hill."

He waited expectantly, hoping she'd suggest they stay a while and talk. Hoping she'd answer the question he'd asked her a month ago when they were flattened under a pile of fallen scenery, and put an end to the quandary he'd been in since the accident. He'd asked her to marry him! He'd never asked that question of any woman ever. He never met a woman he wanted to be married to. Until Maudie.

Had he asked her that question in a dream, in some unconscious state? Why hadn't she given him an answer?

He guessed now he'd been waiting for her to give some kind of answer. If she said yes, he'd know what he was going to do. Marry her. If she said no, he'd know what he was going to do. Move on. It was all up to Maudie.

Her deep blue eyes were gazing into his.

"Yes, you're right. I guess we should be going."

Maudie moved to rise.

Cole's expectant spirits deflated. He didn't know in that moment if he felt relieved or disappointed. He rose quickly and extended his hand to assist her to her feet. She must have forgotten his question. Or perhaps she'd chosen to ignore it.

The heat radiating from her hand was his undoing. She came to her feet, one quick fluid motion, and he enveloped her in his arms. The feel of her against his skin electrified him. His arms crossed over her back, his hands cupped her upper arms. He rubbed them up and down, and buried his face in her hair. When she lifted her head from his shoulder, he trailed his lips across her ear and her cheek and finally her mouth. He tasted her lips and tongue, seeking more, much more, and was almost too lost in his own euphoria to notice that Maudie was giving and taking with as much fervor as he was.

Their lips parted once, and then sought one another again.

Maudie's mind whirled and her heart slammed against her chest. She was breathless with desire. He had such power over her, power she would never have given anyone else. She seemed unable to withstand that power, unwilling to resist it. Now with his chest pressed against hers, her nipples straining against him, his hard thighs molding to hers, and a primitive heat overtaking her, she knew she wanted more from him. Much more. Again and again and again.

She slid her arms under his and clutched his shoulders, arching fully against him, deepening their kiss. Her body compelled him to forget restraint, and his obeyed with a strength born of unbridled desire.

There was no need for words. They parted and slowly undressed each other in the rising moonlight, bestowing kisses as each piece of clothing fell away. Their eyes locked in a fiery gaze of resolution, as they dropped down to the soft bed their clothes had become.

It began with fury, raging heat, insatiable desire, then subsided to languid exploration, fingers slipping through dewiness in places no longer private, and lips testing with feathery caresses until just the right pulse was triggered. With the stars above them lighting one by one, they made love one to the other, the other to one, then two to two.

When it was over they lay locked in each other's arms while the evening breeze cooled their heated bodies.

"I think at this moment it's auspicious that I am no longer sheriff," he said with feigned seriousness.

"Are you saying that as an honorable lawman you

would never engage in so dishonorable, albeit over-whelmingly satisfying, an adventure?" Maudie teased.

He leaned up on one elbow, and gazed down at her face, bathed now as much in the glow of intensely perfect lovemaking as it was from the relentless mountain moon. "I'd never say that. I just mean I'm too exhausted to uphold the law." He lowered his voice to a lascivious growl. "Or, as you may have noticed, hold up anything else."

She laughed contentedly, and kissed his bent forearm. He felt over the ground around them until his hand caught her shawl. He spread it over her, feathering her breasts with a fringed corner.

She shuddered and laughed lightly. "Two can play that game, you know."

She reached down and caught the opposite fringed corner of the shawl, pulled away from him and trailed it up between their parting thighs where the skin still clung with heat and moisture. When she reached the apex of his thighs, she trailed the fringe as enticingly over him as he had over her, until the formerly exhausted member to which he had referred awoke with new fervor. And the moon made a spotlight over their private theater.

"This was rather wanton behavior for a spinster lady. I certainly hope Wild Bill was sleeping." Maudie began dressing one article at a time while Cole, stretched out naked, looked on in obvious enjoyment.

"I doubt spinster ladies would ever do such a thing."

"I just did. And if I'm to believe some of my acquaintances, I am a spinster." She stepped into her skirt.

"Spinsters are prune-like, all pinched up and dried up, like overcooked bacon." He leaned up and kissed the top of her thigh as the skirt closed over its brightness like a stage curtain going down. "Spinsters don't have skin like yours, or legs like yours, or . . . anything else like yours."

"Oh? And just how would you know that?"

"Wild Bill told me."

"Now that I believe!"

"You know," Cole started tentatively, then thought he should be dressed before he finished his speech. He'd feel braver. He was standing in his drawers buttoning his shirt when he decided that was dressed enough. "Your distasteful spinster status could be altered."

Maudie watched him step into his pants. She hugged herself against the cold and something more.

"In a rather auspicious moment," he continued, "I believe I asked a question of you that you have yet to answer." He watched her face, and seeing no change, pressed on. "Do you remember the question?"

Maudie looked up then. "I wasn't certain I had heard it . . . until now."

"And have you thought about it?" he asked tentatively.

"Yes."

"And?"

"That is something I'd like to discuss with you," she said, not looking at him. "That, and something more." She brushed the twigs and soil off the back of her skirts.

"I think you must know by now that I'll discuss anything with you, any time. What is it?"

"Something I'm thinking about doing. Something that would change my life."

Cole swallowed hard. "Are . . . are you afraid of it?"

Maudie raised her face and caught the corner of her bottom lip in her teeth. "Yes," she answered quietly, "extremely afraid. Up to now I've had one thing and one thing only on my mind, and that was to find my mother, whether I'd find her dead or alive. I had to know."

"And now you know."

"Yes. And I realize I've known no other way to live. Now I'm considering another way. But how can I know I'll do the right thing?" Maudie's voice grew tremulous. "How can I know whether I'll succeed or fail?"

Cole cupped her elbow. He stood close enough to her to feel the mist of her breath and be stirred by the lifting and lowering of her bosom as she breathed. "I guess I will be no help to you in making your decision, then, because I have no magic answers for you. But you have one for me, I hope."

Slowly Maudie linked her arm through his. "Come home with me now."

Chapter 18

As Maudie set about making coffee and slicing the last of a sweet cake she'd made for her mother's wedding celebration, she considered her options with Cole. All her life she'd been good at scheming and conniving. Those were necessary skills just to stay alive. This time was different. She knew what she wanted, but this time she wanted to get it without the scheming, wanted the object of her desire to want her as much as she did him.

Maudie took a deep breath and put her plan into motion, knowing she'd probably have to improvise a bit.

"Have you made any decisions about what you'll do now that you're no longer sheriff? I'm certain you've thought about how you'll want to use your talents next." She set a mug in front of him and the plate of cake slices.

"No decisions, but a lot of thinking. And waiting. For you." He took a slice of cake and bit into it with enthusiasm. "This is the best cake I've ever tasted, and to think you made it yourself."

"Yes, just think of it. Something as difficult as making a cake. How do I ever do it?" She knew she was goading him and she wanted to do just that.

"You do have astonishing gifts, lady, and cake making is the least of them."

The look he gave her over his coffee set the muscles at the vee of her thighs to fluttering. She could feel her face warming. The walk from the cemetery to the house had calmed her raging nerves after their love-making, but now even a suggestion of what had transpired between them started her blood racing again. He possessed a power over her that no other man had, and she knew she'd willingly given him that power. Now she longed to possess the same over him.

A smile played over her lips. "There should be a law against possessing as much talent as you have, sir."

"Let's leave the law to finer men than I," he replied. "So, what is it you're so afraid of? Answering yes to my question?"

Cole's fingers tightened around the coffee mug. Had he taken leave of his senses? Everything he would do from this moment forward depended upon her response to his proposal! When had he relinquished his own power and handed it over to her on a satin pillow? Or a pile of clothes in a cemetery? And if she kept looking at him like that, seductively over a coffee mug, he was going to leap over the table and take her right there, unceremoniously, on the floor.

Maudie set her mug down and licked her lips. "No. Yes. Well, partly. Have you truly thought of what it would be like, the two of us, married?"

"Yes, rather often, as a matter of fact."

"And?"

"It would be quite interesting, don't you think?"

"Interesting isn't the word for it! Neither one of us would survive the battles!" Maudie's eyes blazed.

"I prefer to think of them as skirmishes, some of which have had rather satisfying results."

She blushed becomingly. "We couldn't do that all the time."

"Why not?"

"There has to be time for work, for obtaining food, shelter . . ."

"Yes. You're right. If we were together all the time we could never manage things like work. How would we exist?" He took another slice of cake, and chewed thoughtfully. "Mmmm. Rather well, I think."

Maudie gave him an exasperated look. "But don't you want to work?"

"Let's see. I believe I mentioned farming, didn't I?"

"You'd never be good at that."

"You have no faith in me. I'm strong. I can hoe, and . . . whatever else it is farmers do."

"Slop pigs comes to mind."

"Un-hunh. The only part of pigs I want to have anything to do with is their feet, after they're pickled." Cole made a lip-smacking sound for Maudie's benefit.

She stood and walked to the front window and peered out into the dark street. "Have you ever thought of going back on the stage?"

Cole choked on a bite of cake. "You mean the one to Cheyenne?"

"Very funny. You're avoiding the question. Wouldn't you like to act again?"

405

"I gave that up long ago," he replied darkly. "It's a terrible life. The traveling, the unscrupulous theater managers, the broken-down theaters and broken-down actresses, the drunken actors. The theater ruins lives. I've had my fill of it."

"I know exactly what you mean. I've seen the worst of it, too. I thought I'd give it up one day, but I'm thinking differently now."

"What are you thinking?"

She turned back to him. "I think life in the theater doesn't have to be the way we've experienced it. It can be a good way to make a living, besides being very rewarding, knowing the value of what we do, what we bring to other people."

Cole made a production of scraping up cake crumbs from the embroidered tablecloth. "I've known many actors who talked like that, my parents included, but the truth of it is something else again. Besides, there's too much traveling involved. I think I want to find someplace and stay there for once. Let's talk about something else. Like what we were talking about . . . doing . . . earlier."

He rose and walked over to Maudie, sliding his hands up her arms to her shoulders. Maudie felt the heat of his fingers through her blouse. Time to take a different approach.

"Well, then, there's our answer."

"What do you mean?"

"I want to continue to work in the theater. You want to settle down and be a farmer. That will never do."

"I don't really want to be a farmer," he said quickly. "It was just a thought, and a bad one."

"Oh, well, then, what would you want to do? Let's see. You like to eat. How about being a cook, running a restaurant?"

"Never! Eating is one thing, cooking is quite another."

He was rubbing her shoulders and moving closer to her. Maudie fought to control herself.

"Hmm. Could you be a teacher?"

He ran a finger up the soft skin of her neck. "You know, I did think of that once or twice. I've never been in one place long enough to try it. And Deadwood doesn't even have a school yet."

"What about teaching adults? You'd be good at that, I think."

"You do? Have I taught you anything?" His voice was husky, and he leaned down and kissed her.

Had he ever! She had to steel herself before she let him get her off track. "That's not what I had in mind." Her own voice was husky. "Have you ever thought about teaching adults?"

He kissed her again. "No one other than you."

She stepped back out of his embrace. "I was under the impression we were having a serious discussion."

"I couldn't be more serious!"

She put two fingers to her temple. "You know? I've just had an idea. You could teach acting!" *God, what a terrible piece of acting that was!*

"Whoa. There's nothing serious about that. That's pretty impossible. I told you I want to settle down in one place."

"I know." *This is it!* "What about right here in Deadwood?"

Cole stared at her incredulously. "I can see the night air in the cemetery has done something to your mind. I can just see myself going up and down Main Street or down into the badlands hauling galoots and pleasure girls out of saloons and whorehouses and sitting them down to teach them how to act, at least differently than they act now."

"Of course not. How did you ever come up with such a preposterous idea?"

"From you! Have you been listening to this conversation?"

"More closely than you have."

"Speaking of closely . . ." He moved in toward her and started to run his hands up and down her arms and neck.

"Wait now, we haven't finished this conversation. You say you don't want to be an actor, yet everything else we've talked about doesn't appeal to you either."

"Right. End of conversation." He bent to kiss her.

"You know why that is? It's because you were born an actor to parents who were actors, and no matter how much you resist it, it has a hold on you. You performed brilliantly in the role of Sheriff of Deadwood. I think you'd perform brilliantly no matter what role you played."

Cole stepped back then, the light of comprehension starting to spread over his face. "All right. Aside from allowing you to avoid answering my original question, what is the point of all this conversation? And before you say anything, I think I'm getting the idea that you're suggesting we . . . I settle in Deadwood."

"That's a great idea!"

"It wasn't mine!"

"It just so happens that Lawrence LaFountain and Melody Sweet, if you can believe it, have left town together for greener pastures, or at least brighter lights. That leaves the Deadwood Variety with a troupe, but without a leader. Just recently I was talking with Taryn and Sterling and the others, and they want to stay in Deadwood, too."

"Wait just a minute, Maudie, that's not what I had in mind—"

"Theo and my mother plan to return and stay here as well. Can't you just see it? My mother on stage right here, with me, with you! We could lead the company, do wonderful plays. This town is growing. It needs more sophisticated diversions than faro tables, disreputable theaters, and Mrs. Mundy's. Society folk are moving into town, and soon there'll be streets lined with houses, and families and schools and churches and . . ."

Maudie's voice trailed off as Cole stepped away from her and walked to the door. He leaned against it, thinking.

"It would be wonderful, Cole. You, me, my mother, Theo, the others. I'd have a company of my own. What I've always wanted. If you were a part of that, it would make everything perfect."

"I think I see now."

"You do? Isn't it wonderful?"

"I don't think so. Your answer to my question is contingent on my answer to your question. Do I have that right?"

"No, Cole. It's not like that at all."

"Then what is it like? I thought I meant as much to you as you do to me."

She ran to him, placing her palms against his chest. "You do! Don't you see? This is what I've been so afraid of. I want to be with you. Permanently. I've never wanted that with any man ever before. And I want to do something else with my life besides being a wife. The theater is what brought us together. Why can't it keep us together?"

He couldn't help it. His arms went around her in a tight grip. He sighed into her hair. "You could be right. I don't know. I guess I just wanted to take care of you. Isn't that what a man is supposed to do? Take care of the woman he loves? Be her hero?"

"You are my hero. And I think taking care of me doesn't have to mean taking care of everything. Cole, I've always been a child of the wind, where it blew a possible word of my mother's whereabouts, I let it take me. I've taken care of myself all my life. I admit it sounds heavenly to think of being taken care of for once. But I wouldn't be happy for long. I'd be restless, and I'd make you feel restless too." She stepped away from him. "Maybe we were right the first time. Maybe we're too different. We can't possibly make something work between us."

"Dear God, Maudie, I love you!"

"And I love you, Cole, so very much."

"Don't you know you're my heroine?"

She leaned back. "No. I've never been anyone's personal heroine."

"Well, you're mine." He was bursting now. "I admire you, respect you, adore you, want to be with you!"

She threw her arms around his neck and kissed him deeply. When she drew back her heart was in her eyes. "But I don't want you to do something, stay here, if you won't be happy."

"Nor do I want that for you."

"Then what shall we do?"

"We should have children."

"What?!"

"In case you haven't noticed, we've just begun to plan a theatrical family dynasty. That takes children."

"I never thought about having children."

"Think about it."

"I can't yet. You've really thought about having children of your own?"

"Yes, I have. Even though I've avoided attachments, believed I'd never marry, I did think about wanting children now and then. I suppose that sounds funny."

"No, not really. But my mind's been reeling with all I want to do in the theater. Having children takes time, and I'd want to be the best mother I can be. Right now I'm too excited about being with you and having our own theater, and . . ." She kissed him again.

He turned her around and gently pushed her forward. "I believe the bedroom is this way."

Maudie whirled around. "I'm too excited to sleep."

"Who said anything about sleep? I'll make a deal with you."

"What kind of deal?"

"We'll get married, we'll have our theater, and we'll have our babies. You can still run your company, act in plays, and I'll stay home and take care of the children."

"Unheard of! That would scandalize the whole town!"

"Wouldn't it, though?" He turned her around and steered her toward the bed. Then he bent down and lifted her in his arms, kissed her thoroughly, then gently lowered her to the quilts.

As night slipped into early morning, Maudie lay in the arms of her real leading man. Together they dreamed of a brand new opening night of their own original play, slated to run for a lifetime.

About the Author

GARDA PARKER launched her career as a novelist with Zebra Books and the May 1992 release of *Arizona Temptation,* a Heartfire Historical, followed by *Out of the Blue,* a contemporary novel in Zebra's acclaimed *To Love Again* line. Zebra has published two of Garda's novellas in that line for Christmas 1992 *(Snow Angels),* and Mother's Day 1993 *(Bermuda Quadrangle);* a January 1993 Heartfire Historical *(Temptation's Flame);* and the May 1993 release in the *To Love Again* line, *Love at Last,* which received excellent reviews in *Publishers Weekly, Romantic Times,* and *Rendezvous.*

Garda lives in Central New York with her partner, Bob Milner, a public school teacher, and has worked at Colgate University for twenty-seven years. She is a runner for fitness and competition. Her daughter, Tamara, is a video and film producer in New York City.

Among many organizations, Garda is a member of Romance Writers of America, Western Writers of

America, Novelists, Inc., The Adirondack Railway Preservation Society, and The Antique Airplane Association. She is referenced in Marquis' *Who's Who in the East* and *Who's Who in Entertainment*.